An Invitation to Danger...

"Come in, Miss Martell."

Dallas watched her cool blue gaze crawl down the length of his body to the tips of his polished black shoes, then climb up again to grasp his eyes. His abilities didn't quite extend to the reading of specific thoughts, but what was on her mind was clear nonetheless. Her eyes had outlined his size, and the quirk that returned to one eyebrow asked why he didn't move that size to allow her more room. He stood his ground.

She smiled in return—a strong smile that told him she accepted his challenge. She carried a bulky camera case on one arm. Turning sideways to squeeze herself and the bag through the opening he had given her, she faced him, her eyes inches from his. She paused, adjusted the weight of the bag on her shoulder, tossed her head to extricate an errant tendril from her face, and sidestepped past him. Her gaze remained locked on his, her smile confidently in place.

His strategy backfired in his face.

Desire flared in him as her fragrance flooded his senses. Life itself had its own scent, but the chemistry of each individual seasoned it uniquely. This one was sweet and strong, the clean tang of her blood spoiled only slightly by the trace of artificial perfume. He could almost taste her heated skin on his tongue, honeyed and unspoiled. He inhaled her flavor, and it ran along his skin like the sweet sweat of arousal, insistent and undeniable.

One sleeve of her flowing silk blouse brushed his arm, and her heat freed her scent even more. Every breath filled him with the reminder of the covenant he had made with Death two hundred years ago. All the gentility and civilized living he could cocoon himself in couldn't change the primal need that animated him. That need raged inside him now more strongly than it had for a long, long time. It was the blood, but it was more than that...

To Chris and Rodney, this one's for you.

Other Books by
Jaye Roycraft

Rainscape
ISBN 1-893896-31-5

Afterimage
ISBN 1-893896-74-9
(Coming in February 2002)

Double Image

✻✻✻

Jaye Roycraft

ImaJinn
Books

DOUBLE IMAGE
Published by ImaJinn Books, a division of ImaJinn

ISBN: 1-893896-66-8

10 9 8 7 6 5 4 3 2 1

Books are available at quantity discounts when used to promote products or services. For information please write to: Marketing Division, ImaJinn Books, P.O. Box 162, Hickory Corners, MI 49060-0162, or call toll free 1-877-625-3592.

Cover design by Patricia Lazarus

ImaJinn Books, a division of ImaJinn
P.O. Box 162, Hickory Corners, MI 49060-0162
Toll Free: 1-877-625-3592
http://www.imajinnbooks.com

ONE

Natchez, Mississippi

"Sera, I'm so bored I could die!" Tia Martell cradled the receiver of the pay phone against her ear and sighed dramatically into the mouthpiece.

Her friend Serenity Adams sighed in return. "Hey, don't give me that. This is what you wanted, remember? If you want to see blood and death you could have stayed here."

"I know. I'm not really complaining, but I feel like a tourist. If I have to shoot one more pillared mansion surrounded by trees dripping Spanish moss, I'm going to be sick." Tia flipped a long strand of sweat-dampened hair away from her face. *God, why did she have to get this assignment in July?*

"Just say the word and I'll trade with you. Besides, didn't you say your shoot was over? So go ahead and have some fun. What about the night life there? Are you going to check it out?"

"Hmm. Yeah, the haunted mansion was a flop, but there's supposed to be a haunted inn, and get this, even a 'vampar' somewhere around here."

"A what?"

"'Vampar.' That's Southern for creatures who wander the night."

Laughter filled Tia's ear. "No more dead stuff! And you know I meant the kind of night life with real *men*, silly!"

"Don't worry, there's nothing scary about the dead down

here. It's all just hype to attract the tourists. And, yes, I did know what you meant. The last thing I need is another Bret Scorsone."

"Tia, Tia. Bret was two years ago. When are you going to move on?"

Tia normally had patience with Sera's scolding, but it had been a long, hot day. "Sera, I have moved on. I have a new job, I'm traveling..."

"And you're avoiding men."

"I am not. Hey, I have to go. The haunted inn beckons. I'll call you tomorrow."

Another dramatic sigh preceded Sera's reply. "Okay, I know when I'm getting the brush off, but be careful. I'm sure there are as many nuts running around down there as up here."

"I sure hope so. Bye, Sera." Tia stepped out into the late afternoon Mississippi sun, shaded her eyes, and glanced around. The quaint little town of Natchez was distressingly devoid of "nuts," running or otherwise.

The heat buzzed around her like a thing alive, and the ancient live oaks surrounding Stanton Hall reached crooked branches to each other like deformed fingers of giant hands, but there the mystery ended. She had just finished her tour and outdoor shoot of Stanton Hall, and the much-touted ghosts of Frederick Stanton, his children, and even his black cocker spaniel had all failed to appear. The mansion itself, though, lived up to all her expectations. Stately and elegant, it sat poised high above the surrounding streets like a *grande dame* taking her afternoon leisure in the sun. Black shutters lent an aristocratic accent to the all-white profile, and encircling pink azaleas added a strategic splash of color to the stark splendor.

Tia glanced at her watch. Six o'clock. Just in time to stop at her hotel for a quick shower and change before dinner with a ghost.

An hour later, as Tia steered her rental car to the center of town, turning the air conditioning all the way up in defense of the unaccustomed humidity, another twinge of guilt assailed her. *Tourist.* She rolled down the window and tried to shrug the feeling off. She was not a tourist, and she was not playing hooky. This was her job, and if she wasn't yet comfortable with it, that was her own fault. Sera was right. She needed to just relax and enjoy.

She pulled up in front of Bishop's Inn and idled the car, her attention drawn by the aura of the ancient stone building rooted high above the Mississippi River. Only one among many antebellum structures, and without the ornateness and grandeur of the nearby churches and mansions, still the inn sang to her. Finally, with a deep breath of appreciation, she turned the engine off and exited the car, pulling her camera case out with her. She squinted against the low early evening sun and decided there was still plenty of light left for a few photos. Tia walked across the street to get a better angle and snapped off several shots, taking her time with each. Then, her years of photographing details hard to shake, she approached the building, shooting the sign, the heavy wooden door, and the small window above the door that formed the shape of a bishop's miter. Nesting her camera back in its case, she entered, and the cool air flowed around her, beckoning her in. She requested a booth, but felt too silly to specifically ask for Veilina's booth. "Veilina" was the supposed resident ghost, the daughter of the inn's owner, who, after the death of her lover, committed suicide in one of the rooms on the inn's upper floor.

Tia took the booth shown her by the hostess and, as always, sat facing the door. She had resigned from the police department two years ago, but once a cop, always a cop. Old habits were hard to break. She always sat so she could view the comings and goings of those around her. Glancing across the aisle, she noticed a "Reserved" card perched on the table opposite hers. *Probably Veilina's sacred booth, and they don't want anyone sitting there.*

She ordered a steak, one of the specialties of the house, and while she waited for it her thoughts returned to her conversation with Sera. Her friend was absolutely right. Tia had acted like a petulant child who begs for a toy, then grows bored and abandons it soon after. After patrolling the worst areas of Milwaukee for four years, Tia had requested a transfer to the Identification Division. It was a way off the street and a way to utilize her photography skills on the job. But the three years of being an ID technician had grown increasingly difficult. With every crime scene she photographed, her nightmares had increased. Shooting homicide and suicide victims hadn't bothered her at first, but as time went on the death masks of children caught in crossfires, store and restaurant employees shot during robberies, and teenagers killed in traffic accidents haunted her during waking hours. But even worse were her nighttime dreams. They were personal. There were no victims other than herself, always the target, always on the defensive.

And Bret hadn't been able to help. She wanted to laugh. Bret had seen none of what she saw, yet was unable to cope with her job, much less lend support to her. He had left her in June, and in July, during the middle of a long, hot summer that promised to never end, she resigned her job.

Building a career as a free-lance photographer hadn't been easy, but it had been her way out—what she had wanted. She was just now starting to snag assignments and make sales on a regular basis. So why was she complaining?

Her steak arrived, and she took her time savoring it, in no hurry to leave. The excellent meal finally dispatched, she leaned back, mulling over the decision of whether or not to order dessert. She had already eaten far too many big meals this week, as if she were indeed on vacation and not working. She shouldn't indulge, and yet...

Movement down the aisle raised her downcast eyes, and she forgot about dessert.

A man approached, and he was no tourist. He moved with a slow, feline grace, and though his head didn't move from side to side, his eyes were everywhere. They caught and held hers, even as he slid onto the bench opposite, the booth with the "Reserved" card.

Maybe it was the cop still in her, but she was aware of everything about him. The shoulder-length brown hair, combed away from his face. The long-sleeved white linen shirt, open at the collar. The impeccable chrome-gray linen trousers. No, she amended, it was the photographer in her. He was impossible to look away from. Her detailed eye saw a man just under six feet with seemingly ordinary features, and she puzzled for a moment on what it was that held her.

When the answer came to her, she pulled her eyes away and felt the skin on her face go hot. It wasn't the cop or the photographer, but the woman in her that responded to him. It wasn't because he was classically handsome, or even that his stare had been that of a provocative come-on. Just the opposite—his gaze had been as cold as a raw, sunless dawn. No. What struck her was an air about him as tangible as that of the inn itself. It hummed through the currents of air and reverberated through the floorboards as he walked. *Sexuality. Strength. Masculinity.* And tied around that package was a warning all but the most foolish would be quick to heed. *Stay away.*

But more than all that was something harder to define. Tia had seen it numerous times on seasoned cops. It was the way you could tell a veteran from a rookie, and it had nothing to do with age. It was boredom, weariness, cynicism, but also confidence, skill, and, if not necessarily wisdom, surely a knowing—a knowing of people, places, and of all the horrible and sordid things that man is capable of doing to his fellow man. It was what enabled good cops to do their job. It was also what sank others into severe depression. It was the killer aura. *What doesn't kill you makes you stronger,* her partner once told her. Her mouth turned downward at the thought. In the end, she hadn't had it. This man shouldered it like a heavy cloak, yet looked to be no older than his mid-thirties.

Tia felt the flush extend downward from her neck, and her embarrassment grew into anger. She had stared at him, true, but his returning glare had definitely been rude in a place where hospitality was supposed to rule over all. She forced her eyes back to his, and saw they were focused on the camera bag beside her. Had he seen her earlier taking photos? Her 35mm camera, along with the extra lenses in the bag, were valued close to two thousand dollars. Was he thinking of robbing her? The town hardly looked the place for it, and he hardly looked the type, but her years of being a cop made her cynical.

"Good evening, Mr. Allgate. How are you tonight?" greeted a young waitress as she placed a glass of red wine in front of the man.

He looked up at the girl. "Doing well, Jaz. There'll be someone meeting me for dinner tonight. Let Angie know, would you?"

"Right away. If there's anything more you need, just let me know."

The girl turned to leave, and as soon as she did, Tia felt his eyes slide back to her, and by now her whole body felt on fire. As before, she couldn't look away. The face was rugged, yet his complexion was paler than the weathered tan she expected to accompany such features. It was his eyes, though, that held her captive. It was hard to see their color in the dim light of the inn, but the *killer aura* and every one of its facets radiated from their depths.

Why was she sitting here enduring this? She was finished with dinner. She would pay the hostess and leave.

A loud shout from outside the inn and the squealing of tires disrupted her plan. Inquisitive patrons near the door scurried outside to see what had happened, but none of them were quicker than the man in the reserved booth.

Tia grabbed her case, and by the time she reached the street, a small crowd had surrounded the crumpled form sprawled on the street. Allgate bent over the injured man and seemed to be talking to him. The ring of onlookers kept a measure of distance, and no one seemed eager to breach the space around the two men.

No one except Tia. She elbowed her way through to inside the circle, and kneeled on the opposite side of the injured man. Street lamps poured light onto the prone figure, whose left leg was twisted to the side in an unnatural way. Tia had seen enough hit and run victims to know the man had been struck by a car.

"Did you call for an ambulance?" she asked Allgate.

"Shut up!" Not even a cursory glance at her accompanied

the growl.

His words stoked the angry fire that had been lit inside the inn, but now was not the time for an argument. She turned to the curious crowd.

"Does anyone know if an ambulance was called? Or the police?"

"Yes, ma'am. A lady went back inside to call," replied a thin young man.

"Did anyone see what happened?" *What was she doing?* She was almost a thousand miles from home, and even if she were home, she wasn't a cop anymore. Most people ignored her, but a few stared at her as if they were wondering who she was to be asking. Strangely, Allgate was one of the few who turned, but she quickly realized from his sweep of the onlookers that he was more interested in hearing a response than in who she was.

The thin man who had answered her before eyed her camera case. "You a reporter?"

"No."

"Find the woman and make sure she doesn't leave."

The command came from Allgate, his low drawl somewhere between the resonance of a cello and the purr of a very big cat. She turned toward him, and their eyes met for the first time since they had been seated across from each other. The lamplight gleamed off his strange eyes, and this time they shone more like polished stone than living tissue. She resented being ordered around, but it was what she was going to do anyway, so she didn't argue. Besides, there wasn't time.

Tia hurried back inside Bishop's Inn, and the lady in question wasn't hard to find. She was at the bar, eagerly repeating her story to the bartender and waitresses. Tia listened for a moment before interrupting, taking the opportunity to size up the woman. Middle-aged, with a purse that could pass for a small suitcase, she sported the fresh splotches of sunburn that marked her as a tourist.

"...and then this big black car swung around the corner, swerved, and headed straight for this poor man. You know how you know something's going to happen but you can't do anything to stop it? I just knew the car was going to hit him. There was this terrible thud, and this poor man was thrown like a rag doll. I tell you..."

"Excuse me, ma'am. Did you call the police?"

The woman turned and stared at Tia. "What? Oh, yes..."

"They're going to want to talk to you."

The woman clutched a sweater to her chest and hitched the strap of her bag higher on her shoulder. "The police? I didn't do anything."

"You're a witness."

"I didn't see all that much. Really."

Flashes of blue strobed across the tavern's windows like the beat of a sad song. "They're here. Come on. I'll go with you." Tia beamed her best smile and cocked her head toward the door in encouragement. Maybe it was the smile, or maybe it was the shade of command presence, still evident after two years, but the tourist put on a brave face and went outside with Tia.

A silver squad car blocked traffic on the one-way street at the intersection to the east. Paramedics were working on the fallen man, one police officer was talking to Allgate, and a second officer was shouting at the crowd and moving everybody back. Tia called to the officer and waved to get his attention. After a moment he looked at her.

"Officer, this lady was a witness." Tia put a gentle hand on the woman's back, preventing her retreat back into the building. The lady reluctantly advanced and was moved even further from the crowd by the officer. Her duty done, Tia turned her mind to more selfish matters. She reached into her bag and pulled out her camera. If she was quick enough, she could snap a couple shots of the hit and run victim. She might even be able to sell a photo to *The Daily Democrat*. She knew the cops wouldn't like her taking photos at a crime scene, but she buttered her bread on the other side of the fence now, and there wouldn't be much they could do to stop her except to move her back out of range. Hopefully she could get what she wanted before that happened. She readied her camera, pulled the press card that hung around her neck from underneath her shirt, got as close as she could, and took three shots in rapid succession.

"Hey, what do you think you're doin'?" The cop doing crowd control strode towards her.

"Press!" she shouted.

"I don't care who you are. Don't you people have any respect? Move it back!"

Tia smiled. She knew the game from both sides. She had want she wanted. Almost.

She wanted to know what had happened, and she wanted to know about the man called Allgate. What had Sera said? *Blood and death.* It seemed she had found them after all in this land that time forgot.

Tia moved again, this time toward the witness who was still being interviewed by the other cop, but she was unable to catch any of the woman's statement to the officer. Undaunted, Tia slowly wove her way closer to Allgate, but couldn't hear any of his words either. For all the confidence the man seemed to radiate, he looked uncomfortable with the crowd's attention, the flashing emergency vehicle lights, and most of all, with the news media van that rolled up. Turning his back to the crowd and news van, Allgate slowly maneuvered his officer down the block to a spot where a stately magnolia shaded them from the glare of the street lights and the prying eyes of the crowd.

She followed, stood at a distance of one building away, and studied the man. Humidity dripped like honey, and Tia pulled on parts of her shirt that were sticking to her, but she would wait all evening if she had to. In spite of his discourtesy to her, he intrigued her. She very badly wanted to know who he was. *And what a shoot he would make.* Rudeness aside, if all females responded to him the way she had, she would have women drooling over photos of him. He stood now, relaxed but alert, like an animal that depends on its senses for survival. Though he spoke to the officer, she was aware that he knew she was watching. His restless eyes settled on her more than once, but there was no recognition in the look, no

accompanying smile, no gratitude for the assistance she had
rendered.

You are one cold bastard, Mr. Allgate. Suddenly she shook
her head. Of course! It was too easy.

Tia made her way back to Bishop's Inn and looked for the
young waitress named Jaz. She figured it would be easier to
pry information from a teenage girl than from the bartender,
who looked like he had seen his share of life.

"Excuse me, Jaz?"

The girl turned toward her. "Oh, were you ready for your
bill? I have it right here." She produced the slip.

"I'm finished. I can pay you right away." Tia paused before
handing over the bills. "The man who was sitting across from
me at the reserved booth—can you tell me who he is?"

"Mr. Allgate? Why, he's the owner."

"The owner?"

"He owns Bishop's Inn."

"What's his first name? I'd like to speak with him."

Jaz eyed the press card still visible around Tia's neck.
"About what? Are you a reporter?"

Tia nodded. It was a small enough lie. "I'd like to talk to
him about what happened outside just now."

The girl shook her head slowly, and her drawl became
even more unhurried. "Mr. Allgate doesn't care for publicity.
I doubt he'll talk to you. And he for sure won't let you take his
picture," she added, nodding toward Tia's case. Jaz was sharper
than she looked.

"Can you at least tell me his name?"

"No secret. Dallas Allgate." The sly hint of a smile that
curved a corner of the girl's mouth was full of secrets.

"Thanks. The meal was excellent."

"Tell your friends."

Tia smiled her prettiest smile, left the inn, and headed for
her car. She started the engine and turned the air conditioning
on high, not caring a whit if she felt like a tourist from up
North. Dallas. It was a strange name, conjuring pictures in
her mind of cowboys and oil wells. The owner of Bishop's
Inn might have money, and the man had an earthy, hardy

appearance, but cowboy was the last association she would have thought of. She sat up straighter as she saw him stride easily back toward the inn. Tia sucked in a deep breath, turned off the engine, and jumped out of the car.

Walking straight up to him, she fell into step beside him when it was obvious he wasn't going to stop for her.

"Mr. Allgate, I'd like to speak to you."

"No." He kept walking.

"You don't even know what I want to talk to you about."

His eyes flicked to her, and it was almost like a physical touch. A rather insulting touch.

"I know what you are. I don't do interviews."

Tia had to half run to keep up with his quickening gait. "I'm not a reporter. I'm a photographer."

He stopped dead so suddenly that she ran into him. Her face brushed his long hair, her breasts pressed against his back, and whether or not her legs actually tangled with his, she felt her sense of balance abandon her like a bird startled from its roost. She clutched his arm to steady herself and a swarm of new sensations filled the void. His body was solid and hard, and while he seemed unflustered by having a woman touch him in such a manner, still she swore she could feel the blood racing through his veins. She held him a second longer than she needed to regain her balance, then took two steps backwards, trying to slow her own heart rate.

A street lamp flooded his features. "If you want to know about the inn, talk to my assistant manager. Take all the photos you like of the building. No photos of me. Do you understand?" His eyes glittered with an inorganic hardness.

"Is that a request, an order, or a threat, Mr. Allgate?"

"Take it as you will. Have a nice evening, Miss Martell."

"How do you know my name?"

He fingered the cord around her neck and twisted it around his fingers. His hand was large, the fingers long and thick, and his nails were as pale as his skin.

She had always prided herself on not letting any man intimidate her, but Allgate's closeness robbed her of breath and thought. Finally, his gaze lowered to the press card dangling from his fingers, and with the hold of his eyes broken, she found her voice.

"Let go of me."

"Certainly. Syntia Marie Martell." He let the cord slip out of his fingers, and slowly raised his eyes to hers. Her name, whispered in the sonorous drawl, made her forget about his implied threat. His eyes made her forget everything else. *Green.* A clear, hard-as-glass green with flecks of gold, like green amber. She vaguely wondered what secrets were trapped in that amber.

"No secret."

"What?" The two words startled her to reality.

"Your name, of course. If you'll excuse me, I have pressing business. Do enjoy our town. Good night, Miss Martell."

***

Tia drove to her hotel on Devereaux Drive, trying to keep her mind solely on business. She needed to find the location of a quick photo, and she needed to find the phone number and office of *The Daily Democrat.* Newspapers, as a photo market, paid notoriously low. A local paper as small as this one was, well, she figured she'd be lucky to negotiate a sale for $50. And that was only if her photos came out as well as she hoped.

Addresses soon in hand, Tia drove the few blocks to a pharmacy that housed a one-hour photo, dropped her film off, and returned to her hotel room. As soon as she stepped inside and closed the door on Natchez and the night, her thoughts skidded from the images she had seen through her viewfinder to the images her eyes had burned into her mind of the man Allgate. *The man.*

Tia had met and worked with lots of men on her previous job, and, miraculously in the male-oriented field of law enforcement, had managed to get along well with most. In her heart, Tia had developed a real fondness for "the boys." Macho as they came, playing their computer combat games, buying and trading the latest off-duty weaponry, fishing in the summer and hunting in the winter, still they were boys to her compared to the man she had met today.

How could a stranger make such an impression on her, and in such a short span of time? Especially one who had been as unfriendly as Allgate had been? She had to know.

Her mind tried to return to business. How would he look through the camera's eye? She had an overpowering desire to shoot him from every possible angle, inside, outdoors, in every kind of light. But it was more than just business. Like an obsessive teenager, she wanted to tape photos all over her bedroom walls and commit every detail of every one to memory. Even as the fantasy formed in her imagination, she knew he'd never consent to the briefest of shoots. He had said "no photos" and had meant it.

She had to know what made him tick. Tia shook her head. Photos wouldn't do it anyway. She could stare at a hundred posed images and never see what was behind those eyes that were like one-way windows—staring out, but never revealing what lay behind the mirrored glass.

She would have to see him again. And she would. Her old job had taught her how to be aggressive, and her new job had taught her how to be persistent. Besides, it hadn't been just her eyes drilling holes in him. His eyes, with their cool facade of indifference, like the lady that doth protest too much, had indicated an interest every bit as strong as her own.

***

Dallas drove to the hospital, more upset than he had been in a very long time. The accident was aggravating only in that it jeopardized the receipt of information that could be important. Whether the man lived or died was immaterial to him. All Dallas was interested in was making sure he got everything Private Investigator Marty Macklin had come to Natchez to give him. Marty had been able to tell him little on the street, in spite of Dallas' insistent questioning. The man had been in too much pain, and the woman had persisted in interrupting him.

Miss Syntia Martell. He felt a muscle twitch in his cheek, a subtle reminder that while he employed the art of deception with others, he ought to be ever truthful with himself. His mouth twisted in acknowledgment. *Very well.* What happened to Macklin was an irritation. What happened with Miss Syntia Martell was a disturbance of major proportion.

He rarely gave women undue attention any more. Even the beautiful ones. It had been a long, long time since he had desired or been attracted to a woman in the way of the living. Even if such desire did arise, the object of affection could never be anything other than a victim of the serpent's art. The serpent played upon the lust of the wretched, tempting them beyond redemption, and just as easily lured the innocent into the quicksand of trust. But the end effect was always the same. His sustenance was the destruction of the contemptible and virtuous alike. It wasn't that he sought to destroy others out of malice. He was what he was—a creature existing outside the time frame that governed human actions, thoughts, and feelings.

Why, then, had he had such a strange reaction to this particular woman? Detached from the boundaries limiting the living, he perceived reality in a unique way, seeing all in her that a living man might—the beauty of her long black hair and the grace of her tall, lithe body. But he saw more. In eyes the color of the sky he rarely saw anymore, he saw a pain and sadness deeper than her years would suggest, and beyond that, an awareness of him that was even rarer than a glimpse of daylit heavens.

That awareness was a danger.

It made her the one creature the serpent feared. And he, with all his knowledge of survival, cunning, and art of manipulation, would be vulnerable. Regrettably, he had given up the beauty of the sunlight that debilitated him so much. Just as regrettably, he would avoid Miss Martell.

And if she couldn't be avoided, the serpent would strike back any way he could.

TWO

Dallas arrived at Natchez Community Hospital and waited in the emergency room waiting area until Macklin was out of surgery. A nurse, with only the slightest encouragement of Dallas' compelling stare, informed him that the man had sustained a broken pelvis and a fractured tibia, but internal injuries were minor, and he hadn't hit his head on the cement when he had been thrown. The man was extremely lucky. He would live, she said.

Luck. What a strange word humans used. He had experienced very little luck in life, or in his present Undead state, good or bad. "Good luck" was simply being smart, cautious, prepared, and, if need be, ruthless. "Bad luck" was the destiny of the foolish, the weak, and the uncaring.

Macklin had not been uncaring, but careless. Dallas thought about the little he had already learned from the man. One week ago, Macklin had phoned and introduced himself as a private investigator from Palm Beach Gardens, Florida. He'd stated he had been hired to find a man named Dalys Aldgate who may be using an alias of Dalys Alexander, Dallas Alexander, Dalton Allgate, Devon Aldgate, or a combination of any such first name and surname. Macklin said that when he found one Dallas Allgate in Natchez he thought he might have found his man. However, upon finding out that Dallas held a Mississippi P.I. license, Macklin had decided to afford Dallas the professional courtesy of a call before giving him over to his client. Still, Macklin had refused to disclose his client's name over the phone, even after a generous offer of money, but had agreed to come to Natchez to meet Dallas on the promise of reimbursed travel expenses.

When Macklin had been hit, Dallas had asked but one question—who had sent the P.I. to find him? All the injured man had been able to voice had been one word, "Flynne."

Dallas paced the waiting area like a lion in a cage, the room much too small for his present state of unrest. Having pushed Miss Syntia Martell out of his mind, Dallas was still bothered by several annoying questions. He needed more information from Macklin. The name Flynne meant nothing to him. He needed more to go on, and he needed it before dawn. Once the sun came up, Dallas would be forced to retreat to his mansion, Rose Hill. The rays of the sun weren't lethal, but sapped his strength to the point of almost total vulnerability. And one didn't survive by allowing oneself to become vulnerable.

The second question that plagued Dallas was the "accident" itself. There was the distinct possibility that the hit and run was no accident, but a deliberate criminal act. If that were the case, the driver of the car, suspecting he had not killed his victim, might come to the hospital to finish the job. Dallas would have to protect Macklin until he got the information he needed.

Lastly was the issue that had caused Dallas to take Macklin's initial phone call seriously and to offer to pay him to come to Natchez in person. Macklin had said that the man who hired him knew Dallas by several aliases—aliases that Dallas had used dating back to the early 1800's. The implication was clear. The person who wanted to find Dallas was a being who roamed the same realm of Midexistence that Dallas did.

The one who wanted Dallas was another of the Undead.

Dallas didn't necessarily fear his own kind. He had known from the beginning that others like him existed, had even learned relatively quickly of the formal vampire community, the Directorate and hierarchies of the local councils. In France, it was the *Coterie*, and in England it was the Circle. Here it was simply the Brotherhood. In every country he had been in, it had been the same, and there was nothing at all brotherly

about it. Organized, populated, and powered by the truly
ancient Undead, he had shunned the councils as much as
possible. Repelled by their squabbling and constant power
plays, Dallas had resigned himself long ago to co-existing
with his victims. Besides, Dallas was only two hundred thirty-
five years old, still considered a youngster by the Old Ones.

He was sure, though, that the Brotherhood knew of his
existence and present location. If they wanted him, they would
surely not hire a human to find him. Dallas could come to
only one conclusion. A vampire wanted him, but it wasn't one
of the Old Ones, and it was very personal.

Dallas had made the passing acquaintance of several of
his kind—other young vampires who chose to avoid the
machinations of the Brotherhood—but he hadn't parted on a
sour note with any that he could remember. He might have
actually believed that the desire to find him was nothing more
than a benign effort to renew an old friendship, if not for the
hit and run.

The "accident" made Dallas extremely wary of being
found.

It had been four hours since Macklin had come out of
surgery. Time was running short. No visitors were allowed at
this time of night, but that didn't worry Dallas. As long as the
man was not unconscious, Dallas would get the information.
He checked his watch. Three-fifteen in the morning. It was
time.

The hospital halls were quiet. No one else had come in
asking about Marty Macklin. The night shift nurse was the
only person Dallas could see. Two soft questions, accompanied
by the forceful stare he had mastered so long ago, told him
Macklin's room number and condition.

"It's imperative I see Mr. Macklin. Neither you nor the
doctor will have any objection."

She stared at him, her eyes like a doll's, round and
unblinking. "No, of course not."

Dallas eased down the hallway like a shifting shadow and
slipped into Macklin's room. There lay Marty Macklin, Gold
Coast Private Eye. Marty had been "lucky," though. No epitaph

yet. The Florida tan, dark and even, still glowed rosy with the warmth of life. The weathered skin and nearly all-white crown of hair may have added years to his appearance, but Dallas still put him in his fifties.

Dallas sat down next to him, slid the fingers of one hand to Macklin's temple and closed his own eyes, stretching his senses to read Macklin's condition. The warm skin burned hot beneath Dallas' fingertips, and he felt the blood racing through the man's veins like liquid fire. The pulse was sure and steady, and his heart pumped a strong rhythm of life. Vampire senses extended to the man's mind. There, Dallas could discern a determined will that churned bright through the darkness like a white wake through black water. Macklin would indeed be all right.

Dallas' pale hand lingered at the P.I.'s temple. He rarely got this close to people unless they were to become a victim of his need. The feel of hot blood pulsing under the sensitive pads of his fingers was a sharp reminder of his hunger, not yet sated this night. How different the heat generated by life was from that generated by fire or machine. There was a song to life's heat—a rhythm of sound and vibration and a melody of scents and aromas—that flooded his vampiric senses and triggered a need as elemental to him as water and bread to man.

Dallas' low voice vibrated through the air and demanded not only a reply, but compliance. "Macklin, this is Dallas Allgate. You will be able to hear me clearly, and you will answer all my questions. Who hired you to find me?"

The man stirred, and his eyes fluttered, but they failed to focus. Nevertheless, he answered, in a whisper so faint only Dallas could have heard it. "Conner Flynne."

Conner Flynne. Dallas tasted the name on his tongue, but found no association for it. "What does this Flynne look like?"

"Mid-twenties, tall, thin, dark hair. Strange eyes," breathed Macklin.

"Strange how?"

"Disturbing. Dark, opaque...restless."

"Did this Flynne leave an address or phone number for

you to contact him?"

"No, just an email address."

"Tell me."

"...don't remember..."

Dallas got up and went to where Macklin's things had been stored. He picked up the man's trousers, went through the pockets, and found a business card that listed the name Conner Flynne, an email address, and nothing else. Dallas slipped the card into his trouser pocket and returned to the sleeping man. "Tell me everything Flynne said to you about me."

"He said he was an old friend of yours but that you had trouble with an ex-wife and with the law, and that was why you had so many aliases."

A half-smile lifted a corner of Dallas' mouth. "Really."

"I didn't believe him..."

"Why not?"

"Most of my clients lie to me when they want to find someone."

The lip that had turned up now curled downward. *In this case the truth truly would shock you more than a lie would, my friend.* "You didn't email Flynne that you'd found me?"

"No..."

Dallas could feel that Macklin was tiring. Like a fish caught on the hook of Dallas' vampiric probe, the man had expended a good deal of energy in trying to free himself. Dallas would get little more. He released the P.I.'s mind.

Dallas heard a step down the hall, and his nostrils flared with the unmistakable stink of the Undead that only another vampire could recognize. Dallas rose and was at the doorway in an instant. At the far end of the corridor a young man with dark hair and eyes appeared to glide forward without the effort of taking individual steps. When the man saw Dallas, he snarled.

Dallas was not intimidated. On the contrary, the juvenile display told Dallas that the being not only had been transformed at a relatively early age, but that he was a novice vampire, only twenty or thirty years old by Dallas' guess. No vampire of even the tender age of one hundred snarled. By Macklin's description, this was the mysterious Conner Flynne. It was no one Dallas knew or remembered meeting. Most likely the novice was under the tutelage of an older vampire.

The creature, realizing its mistake, turned to flee, but Dallas was quicker, shifting his speed easily into the high gear of vampiric celerity, flying down the hall with a maximum of speed and a minimum of motion. Dallas, catching Flynne in the parking lot, gripped him by the throat and, in spite of Flynne being three inches taller, lifted him off the ground. Flynne's dark eyes widened, and his lips stretched wide across his face, baring long, extended eyeteeth. Vampires seldom grew such long fangs upon transformation. Most likely Flynne had had a dentist install extended artificial eyeteeth over his real ones, another juvenile affectation. Some young vampires, caught up in their own image more than in their survival, went all out to "play the part." They were usually quick to experience the True Death.

Dallas' disdain of the creature grew, and he couldn't resist jerking Flynne's body as if he were shaking dirt from a rug. Flynne's snarl-grimace only widened.

"You can't kill me, Aldgate." Flynne's voice was little more than a strangled growl, but Dallas didn't miss the message.

"I wouldn't waste my energy trying to kill a misbegotten monstrosity like you."

Dallas eased his vice-grip on Flynne's neck, not enough to allow the young vampire to escape, but enough that Flynne's voice could croak out words.

This time Flynne's answer was more understandable. "Ah, because I have what you want, don't I?"

"You have absolutely nothing I could possibly want. However, you do possess information that will be mine."

"You'll get nothing from me." Flynne paused before continuing, a glittering of light reflecting off his opaque eyes. "I'll kill the man Macklin. He was supposed to be working for me! You can't protect him all day and all night."

"I care naught for him, or any human, but you know what,

Flynne? I care even less about you." Dallas was willing to bet that a vampire as adolescent as Flynne would have limited skill fighting another of his kind, especially one with the benefit of two additional centuries of experience.

With one hand, Dallas grabbed a fistful of Flynne's long, slicked-back hair, and with his other hand pinched a nerve under Flynne's jawbone. It was a compliance hold that always worked on humans and usually worked equally well on novice vampires like this one. It would have considerably less effectiveness on a seasoned vampire.

Dallas fixed his hypnotic stare on Flynne, who still tried his best to muster a defiant gaze of his own. Flynne writhed in the physical and mental grasp that held him, but all that escaped was a line of spittle from his still open mouth.

"Who holds your leash, whelp? Who instructed you to hire Macklin to find me?"

In spite of being rendered incapacitated by Dallas' hold, Flynne's ability to resist was greater than Dallas had anticipated. *Someone has taught this pup well,* he thought.

One side of Flynne's upper lip curled inward, fully revealing one of his man-made "fangs." Dallas sharpened the focus of his terrible gaze on Flynne's eyes, and presented a mirror in which every perdition Flynne could imagine would be reflected.

"Tell me! Who do you work for?" Dallas' voice was as low as mercury signaling a frost.

Flynne managed a croak of a laugh. "It's no good, Aldgate. I'm no puny mortal to be frightened by the Other Side. I've already been damned, and I've already been to Hell and back."

"Hell is a playground, Flynne. If you think it's a dirty, deceitful, dangerous place, you'll never survive Midexistence. Go on, then. Slink back to your Master and tell him you found me. I look forward to the challenge of a real vampire."

Dallas released Flynne, flinging him the distance of two car lengths. Flynne was off the ground and out of sight in an eyeblink.

Dallas removed a starched white handkerchief from his breast pocket and wiped his hands, feeling as if he had just

touched something particularly nasty. Flynne was as much a
fool as most humans, mired in the muck of his creation, unable
to move forward.

He sighed. The evening had not gone well. First his
meeting with Macklin had been interrupted in an annoying
fashion. Then the woman Martell distracted him in an even
more disturbing manner. Conner Flynne had been a very
unpleasant surprise. And still he had not yet fed.

His hunger gnawed at his concentration. He couldn't think
about Flynne and his puppet master now. Dallas' thoughts
returned to Macklin. The private eye's life was now forfeit.
Flynne would kill him for sure and feast well in the process.
There would be nothing Dallas could do to stop it. He had
neither the ability nor the desire to be a twenty-four-hour-a-
day guardian angel.

Dallas made his decision quickly. Macklin would die, but
Dallas was going to make sure Flynne was not the one who
would get satisfaction from the killing. Dallas re-entered the
hospital and approached the same nurse he had spoken to
before.

He fixed his gaze on hers, and the whispered notes of his
bass voice vibrated across the counter. "You have not seen
me. I was never at the hospital tonight."

"I...have not seen you." The nurse said nothing more as
Dallas passed her station and proceeded back down the hallway
toward Macklin's room. No, Flynne would get nothing from
the private eye except disappointment in seeing his prey stolen
from him.

Dallas would not go home hungry. For the first time all
evening he allowed himself a smile.

THREE

Tia sat in her hotel room and flipped through the stack of photos quickly, looking for the hit and run shots. She could examine the rest later at her leisure. She stopped her shuffle. There they were. And they were great. The lighting was excellent, the detail sharp, and the composition good. Best of all was the compelling subject matter. She had managed an unobstructed view of the victim in two of her three shots, the paramedics leaning over his twisted body. Tia wasted no time. Her fingers danced over the phone's keypad as if it were a musical instrument.

Her good luck continued. *The Daily Democrat* was interested. Their set price for non-staff photographers was $40. It was low, but Tia wouldn't haggle over the price.

Nearly an hour later, after a trip to the newspaper office and a shorter trip down the hotel's hall to the ice machine, Tia was back in her room, relaxing for the first time all day. She poured herself a glass of ice water, settled back in the room's one comfortable chair, and carefully scrutinized the rest of the shots she had taken. The photographs of the antebellum mansions were breathtaking. Longwood, Rosalie, Stanton Hall, Dunleith...who could take a bad shot of such magnificent structures? Regal, elaborate, and with numbers of columns to rival ancient Athens, the photos had practically taken themselves without any effort or expertise on her part.

Next were the pictures she'd taken of Bishop's Inn. Tia examined them one by one, and with the scrutiny of each, felt her brows pull closer together and her lips compress more and more. They were good photos, every one of them. Why did she feel disappointed? Had she really expected to see some sort of ghostly aura, or a face in a window that didn't belong? She took a sip of cold water, then laughed. She hadn't really believed any of the stories she had heard, but even so, they had almost had her.

But they were just that—stories. Something had happened to someone once upon a time, and it had been exaggerated and embellished over time. Woven into the history, folklore and family chronicles of the area, the stories sounded not only plausible, but downright true as fact. Too easily believable, especially when fascinating characters like Mr. Dallas Allgate stepped right out of her fantasies and into life's everyday drama.

Her memory slipped his image effortlessly before her mind's eye, and she saw the details of his appearance as clearly as if she were gazing at one of her photos. She saw the rich, warm shades of brown in the long waves of hair and the green eyes that reminded her of an early morning lake reflecting dancing beads of sunlight. Darkness, yet light. Stillness, yet life.

She shuddered as the fan in her room kicked in and blew a wave of cold air at her. She squeezed her eyes shut, but his image burned bright in her mind. The straight nose, slightly wider than classical perfection, the long smile line creasing one side of his face and framing the too-perfect mouth that never smiled...

How can I persuade him to let me do a shoot on him? Money wouldn't do. She wouldn't be able to offer him much in the way of cash, and she had the feeling somehow that money wasn't the button to push with him anyway. She shook her head. She had nothing to bargain with. Besides, she didn't know the man, so she didn't know what would appeal to him. No, she would have to rely simply on her powers of persuasion. She returned to her photos of Bishop's Inn.

This time, not looking for ghostly images, her eyes saw other details. She noticed the red patio umbrellas, the splashes of color against the weathered brick of the building vying for dominance with the bright pink cones of the crape myrtles standing guard on either side of the front door. She saw how the low light of the deep afternoon sun turned the faded wooden fencing into stripes of amber and cinnamon. If only that black car hadn't been parked in front of the fence to spoil her view of the gate leading to the patio. It looked like the gate had been patterned to duplicate the bishop's miter design of the front door.

Tia put her glass down on the table with a slosh. She stared again at the photo, but not at the trees or patio. A black car. She brought the photo closer to her face and squinted. There was a license plate on the rear of the car, but the numbers were too small to read. She looked again at the car. A shadow darkened the car's interior. A man sitting behind the wheel? She quickly picked up the rest of her Bishop's Inn photos. In three of her six shots, she could see portions of the black car. One showed the entire length of the car, but not the rear plate. A man was indeed visible sitting behind the wheel, but he hadn't been facing her. The fact that she couldn't see his features or even the color of his shirt did nothing to diminish the tingle of excitement she felt building. The car looked like an 80's Oldsmobile, probably a "Ninety-Eight." It matched the description of the hit and run vehicle perfectly. *The police.* Her hand started to reach for the slim hotel phone directory, but her fingers did no more than brush the textured vinyl binder.

Contacting the police was the automatic response, but the image of Dallas Allgate froze her hand. The man had seemed to have a definite concern for the victim, and somehow she had gotten the impression that the interest had been more than that of a Good Samaritan. Had the victim been a friend of Allgate's? If so, Allgate might be curious about who had tried to kill his friend. The photos in her hands could very well be the bait she needed to land an interview with the mysterious owner of Bishop's Inn.

She needed more, though. She needed the license number on the black car. Undaunted, the thrill that coursed through her was the same feeling she used to have as a recruit fresh out of the Police Academy. Was it really eight years ago? She didn't want to think about what had changed her.

And she didn't. Truly excited now, her mind shifted to a higher gear, as it had so many times on the Job. She remembered seeing a self-serve booth in the pharmacy that made enlargements of photos using a scanner. She was familiar with the process, having done it using her own equipment numerous times. Two minutes later, Tia's glass of water sat abandoned on the table in its ring of condensation while the door to her hotel room clicked shut behind her.

***

The next morning Tia extended her room reservation, her car reservation, and canceled her flight out of Jackson. One thing was to be said for boring. It was easy on the pocketbook. Adventure wasn't. Tia grimaced as she thought about the additional hotel expense she'd have to eat. The photo she sold last night to the paper wouldn't come close to paying for the extra night's charge. If she was going to need more time in Natchez, she'd have to move to a cheaper inn. She didn't even want to think about the rental car or how much she'd now have to pay for her rescheduled flight home.

Tia's next phone call was to Milwaukee. At least she had a calling card for long distance.

A sleepy voice answered. "'Lo?"

"Val? Hi, it's Tia. Did I wake you?"

"Ummm. I guess you've forgotten what it's like to work early shift." A yawn served as an exclamation point to her friend's answer.

"I haven't forgotten, but I don't miss it. Listen, Val, I need a really big favor."

"Oh, sure, first you wake me up and then you want a favor!"

Tia smiled. She well knew Val's weakness. "I'll buy you dinner when I get home."

A sleepy sigh of surrender quickly followed. "Where are you?"

"Natchez."

"Where?"

"Mississippi."

"I hate you," said Val.

"No, you don't. It's ninety-seven degrees here, and it's not even noon yet."

"I still hate you. What do you need?"

"Do you work tonight?" Val was an office assistant in the Identification Bureau where Tia used to work.

"Yeah, which is why I'd like to get some sleep sometime soon. What's up?"

"Okay, dinner and drinks. Can you run a plate for me when you get in? It's important."

"Oh, Christ, Tia, you're not still playing cop, are you? Hold on, let me get a pen."

Tia didn't bother answering the rhetorical question. "Ready? It's a Mississippi plate." Tia gave her the numbers. "I'll call you at work around five, okay?"

"Dinner. Don't forget. And not someplace cheap."

"Me, cheap? Thanks, Val."

Tia's next call was to Bishop's Inn.

A woman's voice answered. "This is Bishop's Inn. How can I help you?

Tia assumed her cop voice. Polite, but no-nonsense. "Dallas Allgate, please."

"I'm sorry, he's not here right now."

"Can you tell me when you expect him?"

The drawl was unhurried, seemingly not intimidated by Tia's voice. "He's never here until late supper hours, eight o'clock or so, but he isn't here every night."

"Will he be in tonight?"

The drawl slowed to a crawl. "Ah, I'm not sure, but you can try calling back this evenin'."

Great. Tia checked the Natchez phone directory. There was no listing for Allgate. She called directory assistance. Nothing for Allgate in Natchez. On a hunch Tia tried Vidalia, a small town across the river, but there was no listing there, either. The man certainly did go out of his way to keep his privacy. Well, she wasn't out of options or perseverance yet, and she wasn't out of tricks.

She showered and went down to the hotel's lobby. The first order of business was finding a copy of *The Daily*

Democrat. She not only wanted to see her photo, but to read the story. Maybe there would be some information on Dallas Allgate she could use to her advantage.

The paper was easy to find. Her photo was even easier to find. It was on page one, below a large headline. "HIT AND RUN VICTIM DIES"

Tia hadn't expected this. From what she could discern at the scene last night, the man was going to be all right. She sat down in the lobby and read the complete article, no longer just interested in Mr. Allgate, but in the victim and the incident itself. The paper stated that the victim was one Marty Macklin, a licensed private investigator from Palm Beach Gardens, Florida, who had apparently been in Natchez on business. Police were still looking for a large, black vehicle with a single male occupant, but had little to go on. Macklin died early this morning at the hospital of injuries sustained in the accident. The article mentioned that the accident took place in front of the well-known Bishop's Inn, but there was no mention at all of Allgate.

She slapped the paper against her lap. The man with the killer aura became more frustrating by the moment, and someone else with a killer aura had just turned an accident into a homicide.

A homicide. I have important information regarding a homicide.

Tia now had what in her ex-cop's mind was a clear-cut duty. She would have to call the police right away and give them the information and photos she had of the black car. Of course, there was no proof that this was indeed the hit and run vehicle, but chances were good that it was. She was a little surprised the cops hadn't already come knocking on her hotel room door. A good detective, seeing the photo in the newspaper, might wonder if the photographer had seen more.

Tia went up to her room to call Natchez P.D. Moments later, she hung up the phone after receiving a promise that an officer would be out to talk to her directly. Her irksome conscience now clear, she wasted no time punching the number to Bishop's Inn again. There was nothing to prevent her from pursuing her own interests. One good thing about no longer being a cop was that she could freely share the information she had with whomever she pleased. She had extra prints of all her photos, and there had been no reason to tell the police she would soon know who the owner of the black car was.

"Bishop's Inn. How can I help you?"

"Yes, I'm trying to get in touch with Dallas Allgate. It's very important. It's about the man who was killed in the accident last night. Do you have a number where he can be reached?"

"Yes, but I can't give it out."

Tia was not surprised. In fact, she already had Plan "B" prepared. "Can you call him and relay the message? Then he can call me back."

"Hold on just a minute."

Tia heard the receiver thump to the counter, then heard voices in the background. Clearly, her Plan "B" request was being evaluated. Allgate had no doubt instructed his staff in the stringent safeguarding of his privacy.

A few minutes later the woman's voice came back on the line. "Ma'am? Okay, I'll take your message and pass it along to Mr. Allgate, but I can't promise he'll call you back."

"I understand. Please tell him it's Tia Martell. He knows who I am. Tell him I have vital information on Marty Macklin, the man who was killed last night in the hit and run accident. Ask him to please call me as soon as he can." Tia gave the woman her hotel name and phone number, and told her she'd be at the hotel the rest of the day and night.

Tia dropped the receiver into its cradle, leaned back in her chair, and checked her watch. Almost one in the afternoon. She drew a deep breath and closed her eyes. According to her original itinerary, she would just about be finishing her leisurely, picturesque drive on the Natchez Trace Parkway back to Jackson and her flight home to Milwaukee. Instead, she was waiting for a visit from the cops, a phone call from a man more intriguing than the ghost who inhabits his inn, and a call that could possibly lead to the identification of a killer.

Had she really told Sera less than twenty-four hours ago

that she was bored?

***

Dallas rose at seven in the evening, and, as usual, saw John Giltspur's familiar face before anything else. As blank as clean paper, Dallas nevertheless saw something in the man's face that signaled this was to be a day out of the ordinary. After last night, that was no surprise.

"Yes, Gillie? What is it?"

"A message from the inn, Sir. I didn't feel it quite urgent enough to wake you, but..."

For an inscrutable manservant, Gillie worried too much. "What's the message, Gillie?"

Gillie cleared his throat. "A woman's been calling the inn asking for you. A Tia Martell. This woman told Angie you know who she is and that you should call her as soon as possible. She claims to have important information regarding the death of the private investigator Macklin. Her phone number's on the table."

The woman. He had hoped to be done with her. "Anything else?"

"Macklin is dead, Sir."

Dallas nodded. "Thank you, Gillie."

Last night upon returning home to Rose Hill, Dallas had told Gillie about the accident, about Macklin and the information he had, and about Conner Flynne's visit. He had warned Gillie that more visits from Conner Flynne and the Master that pulled his strings were imminent, and that security and vigilance at Rose Hill should be the utmost priority. Dallas' secretary, valet, and confidant for twenty-five years, Gillie not only ran Rose Hill, he was the one human Dallas trusted. Gillie had traveled every bump and valley of Dallas' nature, knew his strengths, weaknesses, riches, and wants. However, Dallas kept most of his passions private, and saw no need to inform Gillie of each soul who became a victim of his need. Dallas had not mentioned the woman or the manner in which Marty Macklin had exited the world of the living.

As soon as Gillie's soft footsteps faded from the room, Dallas filled the void of silence. "Damn, bloody female!"

Dallas rarely cursed. He considered it a human frailty, something any being with even a meager command of himself should be able to avoid. The brief lack of control upset him even more.

He should have dispensed with her last night. She was a stranger to Natchez, a Yankee from her accent. No one here would have missed her or questioned her disappearance. But no...that was for the Conner Flynnes. In recent years he had tried to limit the number of humans he dispatched for the sake of his need, sustaining himself instead on animal blood. The change was not out of sentimentality, but safety and survival. In this high-tech age of computers and forensics, it was just too risky to leave a trail of bodies around, especially in a small community such as this one. Macklin had been an exception. Expediency, overwhelming need, and the desire to spoil Conner Flynne's plans had overruled caution. It had been a foolhardy thing to do.

It had also been foolish to believe that mere avoidance of one who possessed the rare perception this woman did would be enough. Her senses had seen something in him that humans seldom saw. Sometimes a human who had trespassed too close to the Gates of Death gained a kind of cognizance akin to that of the vampiric sense, but it was rare. Especially in one so young. *And beautiful.*

His mouth curled downward in disgust. As if beauty had anything at all to do with the knowledge of the Other Side. Most likely she had had a near-death experience. To think that such awareness was natural born...

He glided to the table and fingered the note with Tia's name and phone number. Gillie's precise handwriting made no room for error. Next to the note was today's copy of the newspaper. Dallas exhaled a long breath that was as close to a sigh as he ever let out. "HIT AND RUN VICTIM DIES"

It was to be expected, of course. Dallas scanned the article quickly, glad that no mention had been made of him. It was a standing request of all the *Democrat* reporters, reinforced as need dictated by a compelling glance.

The way Tia Martell had looked at him was one thing.

Her message was another problem altogether. She said she had important information regarding Macklin's death. Everyone knew Macklin was dead. What else did she know?

She had been following him. Had she shadowed him to the hospital? He was relatively certain she hadn't trailed him inside the hospital. He would have felt her presence. But perhaps she had been sitting in her car in the hospital parking lot and had witnessed his confrontation with Conner Flynne. Maybe she had even taken photographs. Either way, she would know neither he nor Flynne was human. And he wouldn't have known she was there. His senses in the parking lot had been totally focused on Flynne.

What was her intent? She was a reporter, and worse yet, a photographer. Exposure flashed first in his mind. *What else?* Blackmail. As owner of a popular tourist attraction, her supposition that he had a measure of wealth was reasonable.

Fortunately he had dealt with this problem before. Eliminating any kind of human threat was child's play. Unfortunately, this time he feared the solution would not be so easy. Once again, the thought of removing Tia Martell from the Side of Life somehow vexed him. A moment ago he had used logic to dismiss the option of destroying her. Now...

He ran his hand through his long hair and headed for his dressing room. He bathed, trying to summon an answer. What was it that really made him hesitant to dispense with her? *Sentimentality? God, I hope not.* He scrubbed on skin already clean, as if the action would help conjure a key to the enigma of Tia Martell. *If that's the case, my survival is doomed.* He couldn't afford sentimentality at any cost, even for a woman as young and full of life as Miss Martell was. *Was it her perception?* The life of the Undead was a lonely one. Did he crave the presence of another who could share even the tiniest burden of existence over two centuries of war and pain? Gillie was the closest thing he had to a friend, yet having the man by his side assuaged that burden not the least.

Dallas dressed in a silk shirt of pearl gray and lightweight black linen trousers. He took his time, as he always did, and yet the extra time did nothing to smooth a path for the revelation he sought. Perhaps it was those blue eyes that spoke a truth her prickly attitude tried to hide. *Truth.* It was a rare thing to find any human who bore the beginnings of wisdom. It was almost as though a truth were waiting to be awakened deep inside her—the truth of the human predicament.

Perhaps he was thinking too hard about this. Maybe it was just her dark hair, long and full of highlights, like a waterfall under a moonlit sky, that distracted him.

He combed his fingers through his damp hair. *God!* He didn't need this problem right now. Not with Conner Flynne and his cohort nearby, wanting nothing so mild as blackmail. Dallas pulled open the heavy drapes that lined the west side of the large room. The tinted windows took some of the brightness and flair out of the lowering sun, but made it possible for Dallas to safely view at least a portion of the sun's daily journey. He stood next to the window and soaked in the splendor of the reds and golds, ensanguined to burgundies and crimsons by the tinted glass. Rose Hill, appropriately built on a small hillock, afforded its residents an almost unobstructed view of the town's western edge as well as a strip of the Mississippi River and the bridge to Louisiana. The view was one of the reasons Dallas had bought the property so long ago.

He stood and gazed at the diminishing light, trying to calm his mind. Finally, as the midnight blue of the evening banished the daylight to a line of dying fire along the horizon, Dallas felt his mind clear. The power of the night was his power, and with its advent came the full force of Dallas' physical and mental strength. He stepped outside onto one of the verandas and took a deep breath of the sultry air.

Why had he even been worrying about the woman? She was nothing to him, and certainly no threat. He would call her and find out what information she had. If exposure or blackmail was indeed her intent, he would deal as swiftly with her as with any enemy.

FOUR

The harsh sound startled Tia from a nightmare-infested sleep. The room was draped in shadow when she opened her eyes, and for a moment she didn't know where she was. Fumbling, she groped in vain for a light switch. But the insistent trill demanded attention, so her fingers gave up on the light and grappled instead for the receiver.

"Hello?" Tia was vaguely aware that her sleepy greeting erupted as a very breathy whisper.

"Tia Martell."

The deep voice sounded her name more as a statement than a question, as if there was no doubt in the caller's mind he had reached the right party. Her senses started to come alive, or at least her hearing did. She knew instantly it was Dallas Allgate.

"Yes, Mr. Allgate. Thank you for returning my call." *Finally. What time was it, anyway?* She tilted the portable room clock towards her. Nine o'clock.

"What can I do for you, Miss Martell?"

Those suggestive words, like the soft rumbling of far-off thunder, promised danger to anyone daring enough to draw closer to the storm.

"I have information regarding the death of Marty Macklin. I thought you might be interested."

"So you told my staff. Exactly what information do you have?"

"Photographs."

"Not interested."

Damn the man! Why did he have to call when she was napping? Her mind was still trying to extricate itself from the web of disturbing dreams she'd been caught in. She hated feeling at a disadvantage with any man, but especially with this man. Of course photos alone wouldn't interest him.

"I have photos of Bishop's Inn before the accident happened. They show the hit and run vehicle and its license plate. I have the listing on the plate."

"And what makes you think I care about a license plate? Call the law."

"I've already talked to the police. From your interest in Mr. Macklin I thought you might want to know who killed him."

There was a pause on the other end of the line, but Tia could feel his energy nonetheless, like a Mac truck idling blocks away.

"What other knowledge do you have of the incident?" he asked, his tone seeming to suggest she knew more.

"Meet with me in person. Right now."

"What do you want in return for this font of information?"

The subtle suggestiveness laced the deep voice with a kind of electricity. *Thunder and lightning.* His voice was as good as his eyes. *Too good.* She was glad she was sitting. She didn't care for the challenge of seeing if the strength in her knees was equal to the power of his voice. "Let me photograph you. That's all."

Tia sensed more idling, faster this time, as if someone were giving gas to a powerful engine. A camcorder could record that incredible voice, but how to capture that energy? It was as tangible as the inflections that rippled through the phone lines.

"Come to the inn. Tell the hostess you have an appointment with me. She'll show you upstairs."

Yes! "Thank you, Mr. Allgate. I'll be there within the hour."

She rose from the bed, feeling hot and sticky in spite of the constant blowing of the air conditioner. *The nightmares, or Allgate's mesmerizing voice?* She wanted to take a shower and change. Her looks as well as her attitude had always served her well, and for this face to face, she wanted to make sure she had both arsenals at her disposal. No more giving this man any kind of advantage.

***

Dallas hung up the phone with care. So all she wanted was to show him some photos in return for taking some of him. He wasn't sure if he believed her or not. His vampiric senses, including even the narcotic effect of his voice, required a meeting of the eyes to function at their optimum power. But he would know soon enough if she was telling the truth. No human, even one with her rare awareness, would be able to lie if his eyes demanded honesty. Of course, either way, she would get no photos of him. The Undead feared few things in the realm of human ingenuity and technology, but the camera was one. He would deal with that problem at the appropriate time. Right now, Miss Tia Martell worried him more than her camera did.

Dallas waited for her in his private suite on the inn's third floor. The suite, in reality, was nothing more than a good-sized office, a bathroom, and a small storage room. In the inn's earliest days, the third floor had consisted of a series of small rooms, each no larger than a cell, with enough space only for a narrow bed or pallet and a single small chair. The rooms were meant for servants or those too poor to afford the larger rooms one floor down. Years ago, Dallas had knocked out most of the inner walls, leaving just the present three rooms. Angie had wanted him to turn the third floor into a bed and breakfast room, but Dallas had resisted the idea. He enjoyed a place other than Rose Hill that he could consider a sanctuary.

The office was dominated by an imposing wooden desk, behind which hunched a worn, leather chair. Two smaller chairs for visitors sat before the desk. A leather sofa and fireplace filled one wall, shuttered windows the second, and doors to the other rooms the third. Bookshelves, file cabinets, a buffet table, and the doorway to the stairs lined the fourth wall. All the furniture pieces were antiques, and the room as a whole was steeped with a feeling of age that Dallas found comfortable.

Still, he did not wait easily for Tia. So much of his life had been spent in the wait mode that he reminded himself he should be used to it by now. And he was. After all, the sphere of Midexistence he inhabited was nothing more than eternal waiting. Yet that didn't make it easy.

He leaned back in the leather chair and closed his eyes. The night made him strong, but the lingering made him tired. His mind, with the laxity that weariness brought, wandered far into the past.

London, 1786.

A deathly veil of silence cloaked the courtroom.

The magistrate paused in his rote recitation long enough to shift his eyes downward. Ostensibly to remind himself of the defendant's name, he sat scratching a spot somewhere high on his protruding belly.

Dalys Aldgate remained standing, silent as the rest, yet knowing that not another soul in the room, not even Viscount St. James, awaited the words to come with the anticipation that parched his throat with dread.

The magistrate raised his head and cleared his throat. "This Court, having accepted the verdict of the jury, finds the defendant, Dalys Aldgate of Knightsbridge, guilty of the first offense, conspiracy to commit robbery, and guilty of the second offense, conspiracy to commit murder, said offenses deemed to have been perpetrated against The Honourable Christian St. James on the second of May, Year of Our Lord 1786. This Court, having convicted Dalys Aldgate of two capital non-clergyable felonies, does hereby sentence said defendant to death by hanging."

Dallas' eyelids twitched at the memory, but they didn't open. *Would hanging have been preferable, after all?* Time, like sand from an ocean's depths, swirled and revealed more long-dead memories.

Young Dalys' stance did not waver, nor did he shrink his gaze from the small watery eyes that pooled above the magistrate's florid cheeks. It was no more than Dalys had expected. The charges were serious—hanging was the only punishment a judge could impose. Not a muscle twitched in Dalys' body, and when the magistrate's scrutiny took refuge in the papers before him, Dalys cast his eyes at St. James.

Bewigged and as seemingly bored as the sessions crowd, St. James met his stare, the affectation of slightly raised brows not changing, but a hint of a smile sending a message to the condemned man that the sentence would not be stayed.

Dalys held his breath, no hope for pardon and release.

It was known to happen, but not with a prosecutor and victim like Viscount St. James. No older than his own twenty years, St. James nevertheless had the advantage of position and wealth. The eldest son and heir of the Earl of Coventry, Christian wore the mantle of his power as easily as he did his dark embroidered suit. Dalys matched the challenge of arrogance with all that a common man could summon—strength that came not with titles or shillings, but honor and virtue.

The magistrate's throat rumbled again and the courtroom quieted. "The sentence of death is hereby pardoned on condition of transportation, said transportation to take place when and where practicable. Defendant is to be remanded to Newgate until such time. Sessions will continue with the next defendant at the hour..."

Dalys' chest expanded with his quick intake of breath, and the thick stew of courtroom air, laden with the aromas of sweat, dust, and smoke, filled him with a joy no pure meadow air could match. Transportation. Life.

The rattle of a windowpane snapped his mind to the present. His senses tested the room, but all was as it invariably was. The door to the stairs remained closed, and nothing but the soft glow from the rustic chandelier invaded the room's darkness. There was no wind to be heard whispering outside the casement, no raid of night sounds straining to pillage the utter stillness.

Ah, you relish torturing me, don't you, Veilina, my love? I can almost see that soldier's smile of conquest on your face. You tease me with Life knowing I am yours for eternity in damnation. And yet you will let no other harm me, will you?

The chandelier flickered on and off, and Dallas stared at it, the quirk of his mouth acknowledging the reply.

A rap on the door left Dallas alone with his bitter thoughts.

"Who is it?" The question was loud and abrupt, and Dallas immediately regretted his ill-mannered response to the soft knock.

"It's just Angie, Mr. Allgate. Miss Martell is here. You're expecting her?"

Regardless of how it had happened, Dallas had allowed his attention to be drawn from the present. Foolish, that. And while he felt safer at the inn than anywhere else, it was still dangerous to allow such a lapse in awareness. To be lulled to a dream state during the night, even in the sanctity of the inn, was inexcusable carelessness. However, it was no reason to take it out on his staff. He took a deep breath and ran the tips of his fingers through his hair, dislodging heavy locks that swung across his forehead. He rose and stepped to the stout door, pulling it open easily. Angie, used to the potholes in his temperament, stood with a bemused look on her face. Behind her, Tia Martell looked neither bemused nor amused. There was a slight upturn to one dark brow, but no hint of a smile.

His eyes stayed on Tia. "Thank you, Angie."

"Can I bring anything up right away?" Angie asked.

"Miss Martell? What can we get for you? On the house, of course." He watched Tia's eyes watching his.

"Just an iced tea, please."

His focus lowered to her mouth. Coral. Like her outfit. "Bring a menu, too, Angie. I'm sure Miss Martell will want something...in the way of a late supper."

"Right up." Angie turned and squeezed past Tia to descend the steep, narrow staircase.

Dallas opened the door wider, but took only one small step to the side. He had left room for her to enter, but just barely enough. Proximity to an opponent was a device of the Undead. Intimacy maximized the power of his senses and brought the mirror of his eyes directly before those who dared gaze upon it.

"Come in, Miss Martell."

He watched her cool blue gaze crawl down the length of his body to the tips of his polished black shoes, then climb up again to grasp his eyes. His abilities didn't quite extend to the reading of specific thoughts, but what was on her mind was clear nonetheless. Her eyes had outlined his size, and the quirk that returned to one eyebrow asked why he didn't move that size to allow her more room.

He stood his ground.

She smiled in return—a strong smile that told him she accepted his challenge.

She carried a bulky camera case on one arm. Turning sideways to squeeze herself and the bag through the opening he had given her, she faced him, her eyes inches from his. She paused, adjusted the weight of the bag on her shoulder, tossed her head to extricate an errant tendril from her face, and sidestepped past him. Her gaze remained locked on his, her smile confidently in place.

His strategy backfired in his face.

Desire flared in him as her fragrance flooded his senses. Life itself had its own scent, but the chemistry of each individual seasoned it uniquely. This one was sweet and strong, the clean tang of her blood spoiled only slightly by the trace of artificial perfume. He could almost taste her heated skin on his tongue, honeyed and unspoiled. He inhaled her flavor, and it ran along his skin like the sweet sweat of arousal, insistent and undeniable.

One sleeve of her flowing silk blouse brushed his arm, and her heat freed her scent even more. Every breath filled him with the reminder of the covenant he had made with Death two hundred years ago. All the gentility and civilized living he could cocoon himself in couldn't change the primal need that animated him. That need raged inside him now more strongly than it had for a long, long time. It was the blood, but it was more than that. It was the journey that led up to the blood.

She finally turned away from him, and the red-orange of her outfit vibrated before his eyes. He closed the door behind her, drew a deep breath, and followed her into the room to pull up one of the chairs for her. Light from the chandelier sparkled off rhinestones on the back of her blouse. Rhinestones arranged in a sunburst design.

His desire quickly cooled to anger. Did she indeed know what he was? Was this, so reminiscent of the sunset he had viewed just two hours ago, to mock him?

"Have a seat, Miss Martell." His eyes raked her and, both his appetite and ire still aroused, he allowed his gaze to linger on the sleek legs exposed by her short skirt longer than good manners dictated.

"Please, call me Tia. Miss Martell sounds so much like a schoolteacher."

"And you are certainly not that, are you?"

She dropped the smile. "No. And before we go any further, I'd like to say how sorry I am that Mr. Macklin didn't survive the accident. If he was a friend, I'm doubly sorry."

"Thank you. He was a business acquaintance. I, too, regret his death."

A knock sounded on the door.

"Come in, Angie."

The hostess entered and placed a drink and menu on the desk in front of Tia, who thanked her with a renewed smile.

"If Miss Martell would like anything more, I'll call down, Angie."

Angie nodded and left, pulling the door shut again. Tia filled the silence between them by taking a sip of her tea.

Her journey began.

When she raised her head again, his vampiric eyes snared hers—eyes that he knew would grow opaque and reveal nothing about him, but everything about her. She would see truth, not the absolute truth that philosophers debated about, but her own personal truth. She would see what she wanted to see—everything that was good, right, and necessary for her life, from this day on. Whether she consciously knew it or not, she would see before her the reality that was hers alone, not only the "is," but the "could be." The power of his eyes would reflect back to her everything she ever dreamed of, fantasized about, and lusted after, and she would see all as possible, attainable, and within reach.

The mirror never lied.

And Dallas would see it all. Not as a mind reader or

fortuneteller, but as simply the observer to whom she would bare all. Her journey would take her from appearance to reality, and when her reality was revealed, he would be ready for her.

Her eyes flickered with uneasiness and tore away from his, staring at the room around her as if for the first time. It was a manifestation of her resistance to him, and it vexed him.

"Is this Veilina's room?" she asked, her eyes still avoiding his. "Where she killed herself?"

"You're not squeamish about death, are you?" he asked softly.

"No. Especially not with something like this."

"Something like this?"

"A ghost story. For the tourists."

"A story, yes, but it did happen. Do you know the full legend of Bishop's Inn, Tia?"

"No, not the whole story."

"You know that the Old Natchez Trace was the nexus connecting the river with all points north to Nashville."

She nodded her head. "It was originally an Indian trail."

"Very good. You're right, it was. Well, if the Old Trace was the 'Devil's Backbone,' then Bishop's Inn in the late 1700's and early 1800's was the head of the beast. Generations of Kaintucks stayed here before starting their trek north, but it was more than just boatmen. Liam Bishop played host to preachers and politicians, traders and thieves. Liam employed a stable lad named Rowan Kiley, who was mute. He couldn't command the horses with his voice, but they responded to the touch of his hands. Liam's youngest daughter was a spoiled brat named Veilina who had hair the color of a red fox and a cunning personality to match. But Veilina loved only herself and other beautiful trinkets, including Devon Alexander, a rich planter."

Dallas paused, pleased to see that his eyes had her full attention once again.

"Rowan was nothing to her as he was only a servant. One day the vixen made up her mind to go out riding, insisting she take Liam's most spirited stallion, Forrest, a huge black beast.

They were barely away from the inn when Forrest reared, and Veilina was thrown and struck in the head by Forrest's flailing hooves. Rowan heard her cries and soothed the animal with a touch of his hand. He saved Veilina's life, but she was blinded by the blow she took. Rowan cared for her, and comforted her as he did the beasts, and soon she fell in love with Rowan, and he with her. She forgot all about Alexander, whose mask of beauty she could no longer gaze upon."

"Good riddance."

Dallas' brows twitched. "Why do you say that? He was wealthy and handsome."

"And arrogant, I'll bet."

"Perhaps. Well, Liam was furious at the prospect of losing a rich son-in-law, and he conspired with Alexander to murder Rowan. It was said that Alexander was maddened by Veilina's betrayal. In any case, Alexander did kill Rowan, and Veilina, upon hearing the news, took her own life in this room. But the legend is that Rowan rose from the dead and avenged himself on Alexander, for Devon was never seen again after that. For a long time people believed that Rowan and Veilina haunted the stables, but they burned down in 1852. Veilina still haunts the inn."

"And Rowan? What happened to his ghost?"

"After the stables burned, he was never sighted again."

"But Alexander's spirit was. I've heard the legend about him."

"Really. I'm impressed. There was never much written about Alexander. He was the villain in the story, after all."

"I was talking to an old caretaker at Longwood yesterday. He told me about the 'Vampar of Natchez,' the spirit of a spurned lover who still wanders the night, searching for revenge. The old man said that any time someone dies unexpectedly in Natchez the death is blamed on Devon Alexander."

He smiled. "That's the legend, yes."

"I guess he stays away from here. Veilina must hate him."

He smiled again, a sad smile. A thud sounded against the window, as if a bird had flown into it by mistake.

"No doubt," he said, feeling the smile slide from his face.

She rose from her chair and moved to the window. "You're not going to tell me that was her pounding on the window."

He was on his feet and beside her before she could do more than turn. "Belief can only come from within the eye of the beholder, Tia."

"Veilina's sight improved when she could no longer see. What do you suppose she ever saw in Alexander anyway? He was rich, but it doesn't sound like he had anything else going for him."

"Perhaps he knew how to please a woman." With that, he held her with his eyes long enough for his hand to cup her chin and lift her face to his. He did what he had wanted to do since the moment she blew into the room. He brought his mouth to within an inch of hers, and when she offered no opposition, he brushed his lips over hers. Unable to resist the taste of her any longer, his mouth worked gently on hers, savoring the life force that sweetened the warmth flooding his senses. He parted his lips, but when his teeth pressed against the softness of her lower lip, she jerked her head away from his. Her hand started to whip forward, but his was quicker. He gripped her forearm, pleased by the challenge of the strength he felt in her slender arm.

"Let go. If Devon was anything like you, I can see why Veilina left him."

Tia's empty chair fell backward to the floor with a dull thump. Dallas released Tia's arm and righted the chair with a sigh. "All right. I get the message."

He was afraid for a moment that she would storm out, but the moment passed. She hadn't yet gotten what she came for.

"Show me what information you have, Tia."

"First, do we have a deal?"

"Deal?"

"The information in exchange for a photo shoot."

"I don't make deals. And I don't allow photos. If you want to share your information, do so. If not, order whatever you like from the menu and enjoy a leisurely supper."

The first emotions of many to be revealed slipped past the

mask of her attitude. The quirk of compressed lips. The exhale that bordered on a sigh. The eyes that roamed the room for a decision on what to do next. She was a strong woman, to be sure, but she was human. And vulnerable after all to his power, as all the others before her had been.

Still, Dallas almost felt...something. An emotion that had touched him once, a long time ago, when he was human. His mind flew farther and farther into the past to snag the scrap of memory. Australia. When he was a convict, wrangling horses for MacArthur. The feeling he had when he broke a spirited animal. The memory and feeling dissolved, as quickly as they had formed.

This is what he did. *No, what he was.* There were no regrets. Could be no regrets.

"Well, Tia?"

"I'm not a mercenary, Mr. Allgate."

"Dallas." He surprised himself with that.

"Dallas." She paused, as if the name was foreign to her. "I came here to offer you help. That's what I'm going to do. I was hoping you'd consent to a few photos in return, but I'm not going to hold the information I have for ransom. Here." She opened her bag and slid out a photo mailer. Opening the envelope, she shook out several photos and a piece of paper. She arranged all of them on the table for him to see. "These are photos I took of the inn just before I went inside for dinner. The accident happened about an hour later. I had all of them enlarged. In this one you can read the license plate of the car, and in this one you can clearly see a man behind the wheel. Here's the listing on the plate. Unfortunately, it comes back stolen."

He glanced at the photos. It was no doubt the hit and run vehicle. And Conner Flynne, though only he would know that. The photo showed only the back of a man's dark head. *You were lucky, Conner. The camera caught the only good side a creature like you has.*

"How did you get this listing?"

"I have friends with the police."

"What else do you know about Marty Macklin or about

what happened to him?"

"Just what I read in the newspaper."

"What else do you know about me?"

The question seemed to surprise her. She sat back in her chair and stared at him, tucking a loose strand of hair behind her ear. "About you? Only that you have an unlisted phone number. That your staff won't give out any information about you. And that for a man who's too good looking for his own good, you shy away from having your picture taken. Or is that just part of the mystique you maintain for the sake of the tourists?"

He laughed, something he rarely did. Perhaps there was nothing to regret after all. Her candor was much more refreshing than the warrior armor she had arrived with. And she was telling him the truth. If she had known more about him or about Macklin's death, his eyes would have compelled her to reveal such knowledge.

"I don't photograph as well as you might think. Call it a phobia. I've had it for a long time."

"So what are you going to do now?"

"Do?"

She indicated the photos. "About what happened. Are you going to talk to the owner of the car?"

"I see no reason to. Macklin's dead."

"Exactly. I could tell you had an interest in saving him. Don't you want to find his killer?"

More than you know, Miss Martell. "That's for the law to take care of."

"I can help you. Talk to the owner of the car and let me come with you."

She surprised him again. *Just what was she after?* "Why? Why should you want to do that? And why should I let you?"

"I'm already involved with this. And I really can help." She glanced around the room and cocked her head. "I used to be a cop."

He laughed again, even harder this time. Who would have guessed that behind the irritating photographer was an ex-cop? But as quickly as his laughter exploded, he quelled it, shaking his head.

"No."

"I have experience with these things."

"No, Tia. Go back home to Minnesota or Iowa or..."

"Wisconsin."

"...wherever you came from. There's nothing but danger for you here."

"I'm used to dealing with danger."

"You've never dealt with this kind of danger, believe me. Did it ever occur to you that the killer has seen the photo you foolishly sold to the newspaper? He just might think you got a good look at him. That maybe you can identify him. It would be child's play for him to find out where you're staying."

She paused, her mouth open, but bereft of a swift reply. Perhaps the logic of what he was saying was finally getting through to her. He pressed his advantage.

"Come. It's getting late. I'll escort you to your car."

Her mouth closed, but he could see the wheels turning inside her head. He didn't like it.

"I wish you'd change your mind," she said, preceding him down the stairs.

"No."

"You're a very stubborn man, Mr. Allgate."

"Stubborn? Just because I know my own mind?"

"And arrogant."

He smiled, glad she couldn't see it. He was almost sorry he wouldn't be seeing her again.

The smile was forgotten as soon as he opened the front door of the inn to let her out. The warm breeze carried a fetid stench, and for the second time in two days the stagnant odor of another vampire filled his nostrils. He dared not go further outside with Tia. His own vampiric scent would be as telling to Flynne as Flynne's was to him. He couldn't afford to let Tia be seen with him. Her life was already in too much danger.

"Where's your car, Tia?"

"Across the street about half a block down."

"I'll watch you from here. Where are you staying?"

"At the Magnolia House on Devereaux, but it's my last

night there."

"Good. I'm glad you're finally listening to sense."

"No, I mean tomorrow I'm checking into a cheaper hotel."

He pulled her back inside the foyer and into a corner out of view of the main dining room. He gripped both her arms and gave her a little shake. "Look at me."

"Let go of me this instant!"

Dallas released one of her arms and held her head instead, the span of his hand easily reaching from below her chin to the top of her head. He tilted her head so that she looked him in the eye. He exerted his power on her and felt a subtle change in the tension in her limbs, as if a magnetic pole had been reversed. Instead of fighting him, she was fusing to him. It was the mirror, and she was immersed in what she saw. Once upon a time, he would have groaned at such a response to him, but playing by the rules of survival for so many years had bestowed a measure of discipline to his baser propensities.

"Your life is in danger. Go straight back to your hotel now and stay there the rest of the night. Tomorrow get on a flight back to Wisconsin and forget you ever met me, understand?"

Her eyes, iris-dark in the dim light, stared into his, but there was no affirming nod. Suddenly too conscious of the blood pulsing under his fingers and the heartbeat racing to outrun his, he stroked her silky black hair once, smoothing the strands he had mussed, then released her gently. "Go on, now."

She took a deep breath, adjusted the camera case strap on her shoulder, passed her gaze over his once last time, then turned and strode out of the inn. He held the door open and watched as she half-walked, half-ran to her car, the rhinestone sun winking under the street lamps.

"Excuse me, Mr. Allgate."

He didn't turn around. "Yes, Angie?"

"There are two men waiting for you on the patio."

"Ah, yes, I thought there might be."

"I told them you were occupied, but..."

"You didn't tell them who I was with, or even that I was with a young woman, did you?"

"No, just that you were unavailable, but they wanted to wait, so..."

"Thank you, Angie. I'll see them now." He had expected this, but not so soon. If Conner was with his Master, Dallas would be at a distinct disadvantage. He could handle Flynne, but not Flynne and a seasoned vampire. The meeting was inevitable, however, and it would be extremely difficult for even two vampires to kill him at night when his strength was at its peak. Besides, he didn't think a fight in the middle of town was what the Master had in mind.

Dallas walked back through the dining room and entered the patio from the rear entrance. The fenced-in area was empty except for two men seated at a center table. One was Conner Flynne, the other a vampire Dallas had never seen before. Transformed at a relatively young age, the man had tousled blond hair, long sideburns, and deep-set eyes, but sported none of the obvious affectations that Flynne did.

"Conner Flynne. And I don't think I've had the displeasure of meeting the creature who yanks your chain."

Flynne, with a lifting of his upper lip, started to rise from his seat, but at a gesture from his companion sank slowly back into his chair.

"Now, now. You see, Flynne? Even after two hundred years, his lack of breeding is evident." The blond vampire canted his head toward Flynne, but his dark eyes never left Dallas. "Aldgate. Do you remember the sixpenny whore who gave you life? No? No doubt you don't remember your father, either. I'm sure even your mother never knew which evening's coin begat you. Well, I am here to make you a gift of memories to make up for those you lack. Allow me to introduce myself. Jermyn St. James. I'm sure you remember *my* father."

St. James. Christian St. James. Indeed, how could he forget that name? "I should have known a spineless dandy like St. James would spawn an ill-bred perversion like you."

"No, Aldgate, there you're wrong. My father sired the man in me long gone. What you see before you was created by none other than yourself. Your vengeance gave me birth, and your hatred made me strong." St. James spread his arms wide.

"Aren't you proud of the work you authored?"

Vengeance. Hatred. They had indeed fueled his lust for survival. And they had made him, too, what he is.

A memory stirred, and like a demon startled from a deep sleep, it rose in his mind with an old, familiar anger. It was a madness that Dallas had thought, until tonight, to be dead and buried.

Sydney, Australia, 1788. Dalys Aldgate, convicted felon, had lost everything. Dalys thought of all the hard years of work at The Knights Chaise Company, all gone in a day. Hired as an apprentice blacksmith, the owner had soon seen that Dalys' quick mind and sober disposition were greater assets than even his robust physique. The company maintained chaises for hire out of Knightsbridge, and Dalys had perfected not only the skills of a farrier, but a coachman.

Christian St. James hired only the finest post-chaise for his travels out of London. On that day over two years ago, the regular coachman had taken sick and Dalys had taken his place. Unhappy with the weather, the loss of his regular coachman, and God knew what else, St. James had fixed Dalys with a baleful eye from the start. When two highwaymen stopped the coach on the common two hours later and bandied words with Dalys, the young Viscount took it that Dalys was an accomplice. St. James had pulled a weapon and was promptly shot and robbed by the highwaymen, who galloped off and were never apprehended. Christian's wounds healed, but he vowed someone would pay, and pay Dalys did.

Dalys had lost everything. All his money had gone for jailer charges and prisoner garnishes in Newgate. His friends, job, everything he had ever known, were halfway across the world. But St. James would yet pay. Revenge would keep Dalys Aldgate alive.

And it had, for a while. But even as life had ended, the bloodlust had gone on, and on, and on...

Jermyn St. James summoned Dallas from the past with a careless gesture. "Come, Aldgate. Sit down and join us. We have so much in common, the three of us. Lots and lots of memories to share. Conner here hasn't heard the best of them.

Or the worst."

"Of course. I'd be a poor host if I didn't join my guests, wouldn't I?" Dallas eased his frame into a sturdy wooden patio chair across the table from his visitors. It was still too close. The sultry air was almost suffocating with the musty odor that hung like a haze over the patio. *How can Flynne and St. James stand each other's company?* It was as if the stink withered the atmosphere itself, sucking the oxygen out.

Dallas searched St. James' eyes, subtly gauging the creature's power with his own. A slow smile spread on St. James' face, and Dallas felt an answering touch. Nothing overt, just a soft push to remind Dallas he wasn't a novice like Flynne to be trifled with. They understood each other.

Dallas matched his opponent's smile with one of his own. "Well, St. James, now that we are all well met, who shall recall the first story for the edification of the young brattie here?"

FIVE

Tia stood across the street and could just see portions of the three men through a crack provided by a broken fence plank. She had never had any intention of going straight back to her hotel, in spite of Allgate's dire warnings. She had driven around the block, parked her car on a nearby cross street, and prowled back to the inn. She intended to learn where he lived and, grateful now for her evening nap, would wait all night for him to leave if need be.

He had been playing some kind of game with her from the moment he invited her to step into the attic suite. She wasn't going to let it end with him telling her to forget she ever met him. Not with the way his eyes had tackled her. And certainly not with the way he had kissed her.

She had worn the dressiest outfit she had brought with her to Natchez, and if it also happened to be the sexiest, well, that couldn't hurt either, could it? She'd gone to the inn armed to the teeth with silk, rhinestones, and color that would attract the most nearsighted of bulls in the ring. If all that wasn't enough to ensure victory, she had had the tried and true weapon of the ages. A very short skirt.

When Dallas had opened the door to admit her and had thrown down the gauntlet, she had accepted and promptly lost the battle.

Dressed in dove gray and black, he had looked better than she had remembered. The monotone colors of his clothes only accentuated the richness of his hair, alive in the light with glints of auburn. His green eyes had a heavy, sleepy look to them, and like a raw recruit instead a veteran of the wars, all she could do was stare, wide-eyed, into their incredible depths.

Something strange had happened. The hostess had dropped off the menu, and Tia remembered thinking that the only thing she wanted to eat was already well done and sitting before her. The next thing she knew he started telling her the story, but it had been so much more than just the recitation of a legend. She had never believed in these things before, and yet it was as though she had been transported through time and was part of the story herself. Rowan, Veilina, and Devon had seemed so real that she felt she was with them, experiencing their passion, their anger, and their pain.

And then, while she was still caught up in the story, he had kissed her, as though he were Devon Alexander and she Veilina Bishop. And she had let him. It was a lover's kiss, as much of the spirit as the body, full of promise. But then a sensation of warning had arisen inside her and jerked her back to the present. Dallas Allgate was kissing her like he owned her, and that definitely wasn't on her menu.

Nevertheless, her will had been weakened. She allowed him to renege on their deal regarding the photo shoot, and she blabbed on about how she wanted to help him. She had even disclosed her experience as a cop, something she rarely did, but it got him to laugh. The sight and sound of mirthless Mr. Allgate actually enjoying himself, and her, had been well worth feeling like a teenager on a first date, overwhelmed by a single kiss.

After that, though, something had caused him to shut down. Before she knew what was happening, he was issuing her dire warnings and trying to get rid of her. She tried to remember what she had said to drive away the only real glimpse of the man she had seen in two days. Her memories were in disarray, though, and the only thing she could remember was the feel of him holding her close. His grasp had been almost painful in its severity, but when he held her head and forced her eyes to his, she had fervently wished his words had been something other than "go home." No man had ever looked at her like that, not even Bret during the stage of their relationship when he had done his utmost to be charming.

Go home. Well, she wasn't going home. Not yet.

She peered through the fence again. She had gotten the brush-off so he could have one with the boys. Funny, she would never have thought that the reclusive Dallas Allgate was the type. Yet there he was, sitting across from two men who certainly didn't look like tourists. They were both well dressed, but the one on the left reminded her of a ferret. He had sharp features, a longish nose, and a nervous quality about him, as though he found it hard to sit still for more than five minutes. The man next to him, however, could have been an actor or a rock star. He had spiky blond hair and features to die for. He and Dallas were smiling like old friends.

Tia sighed. *This could take a while.* She walked back to her car and drove it closer to the inn. She parked where she could see the entrance to the patio and settled in for a long night.

***

Ignoring Conner, Dallas acknowledged St. James with a slight nod of his head. "You're my guest, St. James. You begin. Besides, the pup here is salivating at the thought of hearing your wisdom dispensed."

Conner's eyes glimmered, but he said nothing.

"'Tis a pity, Aldgate, that you weren't as disciplined at Flynne's age as he is. If you had been, we wouldn't be here having this conversation."

"Say what you came here to say and be done with it."

St. James raised both brows and toyed with the narrow white scarf that looped casually around his neck. "'Came here to say?' Oh, you mistake my intention, Aldgate. I didn't come here to chat about old times, or even to instruct young Flynne here. These will be done, naturally, in the course of things, but I came here for a very different reason. Didn't I, Conner?"

"Yes, James."

"I came here for you, Aldgate, as you came for my father. This pleasant conversation is merely so that you fully understand who it is who will destroy you, and why."

Dallas laughed softly. *Did St. James take him for a total fool?* That intent had been clear from the first moment he had nearly choked on Conner Flynne's fusty fragrance at the hospital. "You're no match for me, St. James. Else you wouldn't have brought the pup with you as back up."

"I don't need his help to destroy you. But he is under my tutelage. I couldn't very well have left him behind on such an enlightening undertaking as this."

"Oh, naturally not. And, of course, the Brotherhood doesn't worry you."

"The Brotherhood has nothing to do with this."

"They might think otherwise. After all, I've done nothing at all to you since Mistress Death gave you renewed life. If you destroy me, an enforcer just may decide you need...an adjustment."

St. James made a dismissive gesture with one hand. "The Brotherhood worries me not the least. And the enforcers have more important matters to worry about, I'm sure, than the well being of the likes of you. Enough of this useless banter. I can see that Conner grows impatient. Very well." St. James adjusted the scarf and looked up at the moon. "I was first-born. I was to have been an earl, Conner, did you know that? An earl. A peer of the realm. A lord. My father, Christian, was the Earl of Coventry, like Edward, his father before him. Do you have any idea, Conner, what it's like to be a lord?"

"No, James."

"A pity. Well, neither does the bastard here."

"No, nor do I have any desire to know," Dallas responded.

"Ah, and yet you took that away from my father, didn't you? You stole his very life, and mine, without any conceivable notion of what you were doing."

Dallas twisted his mouth. "'Stole his life?' Isn't that a little melodramatic for one who lost nothing but a fortune he did nothing to earn? I was the one who had life stolen from me."

"Not by my father. My father was the victim of a crime. It was the court that convicted you, not my father."

"He brought the charges. He was the prosecutor. He cared not a whit for true justice or whether he had the right man or not. All he wanted was for some poor bastard to pay, and he chose me."

"Now, now. You keep interrupting me, Aldgate. You'll confuse young Flynne here. Your time to talk will come."

"I can see that you enjoy the sound of your own voice. Have at it, then."

"I first remember seeing you at Ashton Park in 1815. I remember the year because it was just after Waterloo. I was only fifteen, young enough to still be curious about strangers who had the exceedingly bad manners to call at the house without being invited. Always the commoner, weren't you, Aldgate? Fifteen was old enough, though, to remember everything that was said between you and my father."

His fingers finally still, St. James bore his gaze into Dallas with an unwavering precision that normally only the very old Undead are able to achieve. When he continued speaking, his voice echoed the stillness of his eyes.

"I wasn't allowed in the drawing room, but I had my listening posts, and I never forgot you. My father knew you, but he talked about how peculiar you looked. Of course, he had no idea you were the miscreant you are. You and he were born the same year, but while he was nearing fifty, he wondered how it was you looked no older than three and thirty. I remember your reply, word for word, for it was the most extraordinary thing the lad I was had ever heard. 'The Fountain of Youth,' you said. 'The Fountain of Youth isn't in Florida, it's in Australia.' He was an old man, Aldgate. Why didn't you just kill him and be done with it?"

"Oh, killing Christian would have been too easy. I wanted him to suffer the rest of his life. I wanted him to know what I'd known. Losing everything."

St. James was quiet for a moment and sat twirling the glass of water in front of him in its puddle of condensation. He looked up. "Conner."

"Yes, James?"

"What do you suppose Aldgate did to ruin my father?"

"I don't know."

"No, I guess you wouldn't. You weren't born until...when? Nineteen sixty?"

Flynne's voice lowered, and he spoke very slowly. "Nineteen forty-five."

"Same difference."

Conner stared at St. James. The older vampire smiled. "Aldgate, Conner grows bored with my voice. Why don't you tell the story of how you ruined my father...and me?"

***

The three men sat on the patio long after the restaurant closed for the evening. Finally, at two o'clock in the morning, Tia watched as the slim, dark-haired man and his blond companion left through the front gate and walked toward the river. They glided past her, and while the blond man swiveled his head in the direction of her car, she couldn't tell if he saw her or if his vision passed beyond her. At least four inches shorter than his partner, he still commanded her attention. He wore dark-colored dress trousers and a long-sleeved shirt with a standing collar that hung open to his waist. A white scarf banding his neck looked stark even against the pale skin and hair that burned with an ashen heat under the spotlight of the street lamps. She had never seen anyone in Milwaukee dressed like that. But even more riveting than his outfit was his face. A bored expression hung as easily on his countenance as an additional garment, and almost spoiled the finely chiseled aristocratic features. Another interesting subject for her lens.

She shivered. Dallas had strange friends.

Tia waited until the men were out of sight, then eased out of her car, leaving the door slightly ajar. She crept back to her spy post by the broken fence. Dallas sat alone with his elbows resting on the tabletop, his hands clasped in front of him. Slowly he leaned forward until his chin balanced on the back of one hand. A funny feeling washed through her— part rush, part guilt, as though she were a voyeur witnessing something very private. She slipped back to her car.

She remembered the endless nights of working until three in the morning all too well, but she wasn't used to keeping those hours anymore. Even with the nap, her eyes pleaded with her to close for just a minute.

She was in a squad car, all by herself, in the central city neighborhood she had once worked in, but nothing was recognizable. The houses were as dark and quiet as sleeping animals, and the tall lamp poles were like bars on a huge cage. The muggy heat of the day still loitered, but the coffin of night had snuffed out all other signs of life. Yet everything around her was alive. And waiting for her. She drove faster and faster, but none of the buildings looked familiar. Shots rang out, proof of life. Proof of death. She stopped the car and raced through the darkness, but the shots sang a knell all around her, fencing her in with fear, until her legs would move no more.

She woke with a start and eyed, with lingering fear, the street around her. Everything was as it should be for a slow southern town that prided itself on the grace and gentility of the past. Her silk shirt clung to her in sweaty folds. She was used to the dreams, and they were always the same. The shadows of the night were forever after her, seeking to steal her life. The nightmares had inhabited her sleep for years, and quitting her job as a cop hadn't been enough to evict them.

She started the car's engine, turned on the air conditioning, and looked at the clock. A little past three. Had Dallas left? She immediately chided herself for her stupid question. Of course he was gone. There were no lights coming from the upper floors of the inn. Unless he slept overnight in the third floor suite, she had missed him.

She leaned to the side over the passenger seat to pull down her skirt, which had hiked up during her doze. As she started to straighten, a movement caught her eye, and she froze. It was Dallas, and he was descending the outside staircase that joined the patio to the upper floors of the inn. A moment later he exited the patio gate and walked east, away from her. Unlike his friend, Dallas never glanced in her direction. Two buildings down he halted beside a large luxury car and vanished from sight. The car, black with tinted windows, started up and pulled away, still headed east. She quickly started her car and followed at a shy distance, afraid of being too conspicuous on the deserted streets. A dozen blocks and three turns later she stopped her car when Dallas pulled into a driveway at the opposite end of the block.

She killed her engine and waited for about five minutes, then got out and walked up the block. On the far corner a stately townhouse sat perched atop a hill. A lofty red brick wall shouldered the base of the hill, and a terraced slope of flowering shrubs she didn't recognize collared the wall with bursts of white, pink, and purple. White columns fronted the building, and pastel stuccoed walls rose above all. A broad staircase traversed the hill, but a wrought iron gate at the base of the steps gave the estate an air of aloofness. She tried the gate. Locked. No surprise there.

She looked at the black sign on the wall next to the gate. "Rose Hill, est. 1828." An appropriate enough name, she thought. She turned her attention to the driveway. There was no gate. Tia glanced around. Nothing moved. She hiked up the drive as best as her tight skirt and heeled shoes would allow, but didn't have far to go. The drive rounded the base of the hill to the back of the estate, where a large carriage house appeared to function as a garage. Another wall separated the driveway from the gardens and grounds to the rear of the dwelling. A walkway extended from the house, and gentle whitewashed steps, like a docile waterfall, wended down to the drive. A gate blocked the entrance to the walkway. It, too, was locked. Of course.

A motion detector triggered, and the drive was illuminated by a pool of light.

Tia swore, and with a backward glance at the walk, carefully picked her way back down the drive. No dogs barked, no one yelled, and no one came running after her. She reached the sidewalk, straightened her skirt, and headed back to her car, taking a deep breath.

The night hadn't been a total loss. She now knew where Dallas Allgate lived.

Tia wasted no time in driving back to the Magnolia House. It would be dawn soon. She wanted to make sure she got at least a few hours of sleep. Today would be a busy day.

***

An alarm buzzer chirred its warning.

Dallas looked at his servant. "St. James?"

Gillie checked a small monitor. "No, sir. A woman. A very beautiful woman, if I might add. In an orange dress."

Dallas swore. And swore again. He wasn't sure what upset him more, that the female had ignored his advice and warning, or that she had made him lose control again. Control. He could ill afford to lose it now. Not with St. James stalking him like the beast of prey he was.

"Might I hazard a guess that this woman is the persistent Miss Martell who was calling for you earlier?"

"Yes, Gillie, you might."

"I take it that she's involved with St. James as well?"

Dallas squeezed his eyes shut. The thought of Tia being "involved" with St. James bothered him more than it should have. She was just a human, and a troublesome one at that, but the fire in his blood red-zoned at the thought of St. James seducing her. What would Tia see reflected in Jermyn's eyes? What hope, what hunger would be revealed? Would her strength be undermined by the fatal desire to be with St. James, or would her extraordinary awareness allow her to see him as he was? Would she care? The thought of Tia seeing past the reflection and still craving St. James kept Dallas' pulse amping. Either way, St. James would bed her. And feast on her. Her pain would be his appetizer, the destruction of her beauty his main course, and her blood...his dessert.

Jealousy? No, jealousy was a human emotion. Dallas opened his eyes and shook his head, more to banish the disturbing image than to answer Gillie's question. "I don't know. If she is, she's in more danger than she knows. As soon as you can, send Raemon and some of the boys to the Magnolia House to keep an eye on her. If she changes hotels tomorrow, have them stay with her."

Gillie didn't often question his orders, but he stood now with both brows pressing wrinkles into his forehead. For Dallas to express such a level of concern for a human female was rare, and Gillie knew it. However, Dallas didn't feel like explaining something he wasn't sure he understood himself.

"Gillie, just do it."

While Gillie went to make phone calls, Dallas retired to the library. The men Gillie would be waking up were a select few that Dallas kept on retainer to do occasional odd jobs requiring discretion above all else. The men were young, but they had proven their trustworthiness over time. Along with Gillie, they were his daytime eyes.

Eyes. A vision of Tia's brilliant topaz eyes rose in his mind. The ice-cold eyes had melted and burned with a blue-hot fire when he had held her head and tried to compel her. It hadn't worked. Any other female would have "accepted" the suggestion of safety gladly, swiftly, and without question. But not Tia. The mirror had obviously shown Tia something else. She had seen something reflected in his eyes that was more important to her than the protection of life and limb. That she saw what others didn't vexed him no end.

And that lack of control bothered him. If not for Jermyn St. James, Tia might have proven an interesting sport. The danger would have been all hers, and he could have given her line or reeled her in as his interest and craving dictated. But with the arrival of St. James, Tia's danger was his danger. His inability to control and understand his reaction to Tia underlined a weakness that Dallas would have to eliminate if he was to prevent St. James from destroying him.

He would have to maintain total control. He would need an absolute mastery of all his vampiric senses and powers, but more than that, he would need a tight rein on his thoughts, his impulses, and most of all, his desires.

His hours spent with Conner and St. James had not been for the purpose of reliving old times, educating Flynne, or even for letting Dallas know the reason behind St. James' lust for revenge. It had been the age-old testing of opponents prior to battle. He, St. James, and to a lesser extent, Conner, had all prodded each other with their eyes and their minds, looking for any kind of weakness that could be exploited. They probed for a softness, the slightest recoil in the eyes, any pinhole or crack in the mask they donned to shield their intentions from the world.

Dallas knew he had been strong in life. As a lad of twenty,

he had met the stare, the accusations, and the victory of
Christian St. James without a flinch, but that had been human
to human.

During his first winter in New South Wales he had thrived
when most of his fellow convicts had fallen prey to depression,
drink, disease, and dwindling rations. Neither those nor the
strain of hard manual labor had weakened Dalys' mind or body
in the least. Dalys hadn't minded the hard work. Taller and
stronger than most, and with the skills of his trade, he had
quickly found a niche in which he could easily survive. But
again, impressive as his survival had been, it had been as a
human among humans.

His strength as one of the Undead was another matter. It
wasn't as though he lacked confidence or was unaware of the
skills he possessed. On the contrary, endurance was just as
important to him now as it had been two hundred years ago in
his fight for freedom. It was just that the daily play he now
directed was cast with beings far inferior. Humans recited their
lines and played their parts so well, so predictably, that
sometimes he took his powers for granted. His augmented
senses, the power of his eyes, his immunity from human
disease and debilitation, all these things were simply a natural
part of him, and he thought no more about them than an animal
would. Does a hawk meditate upon the extraordinary eyesight
that allows it to spot its quarry?

Only when a scene was acted out badly did he question
his mastery. Like tonight with Tia. She hadn't followed the
script he had laid out for her.

Would a similar weakness manifest itself with St. James?
Dallas had experienced limited contact with others of his kind.
He had wanted it that way, declining even to apprentice to an
older vampire such as Conner Flynne was now doing. Dallas
had preferred discovering and honing his abilities on his own.
It wasn't because he was weak or afraid. It was just his nature
to be independent. Even as a convict, he had kept his distance
from his mates. While the other lads had subsisted in a constant
state of drunkenness, he had kept his consumption of rum to a
minimum. And when the others complained, Dalys had kept

his mouth shut. *Life. He would embrace it like a lover.* The daily mantra of the man he had been once upon a time used to curve his mouth to a smile. Now he shuddered at the memory. And the irony.

He forced his mind back to the present. *The shadow of Life. The Other Side. His kind.* The other simple truth as to why he avoided his kind was the smell. Dallas just couldn't stand the suffocating effect of being near another vampire. The reek of decay was most unpleasant.

His opponent was obviously used to being in the company of his like. No doubt he was also used to the power plays for dominance that consumed so many of the Undead. Jermyn would have a distinct advantage over him. Dallas had sensed something else in their meeting as well, a kind of strength in St. James that had nothing to do with confidence, bravado, or experience. It was just there, a part of St. James, something he had been born with. Something that Dallas felt no answering chord for. Something Dallas lacked.

He sensed Gillie in the doorway behind him. "Yes, Gillie?"

"It's done, Sir."

Dallas gave no reply.

Gillie spoke again after a moment's silence. "You don't think it'll be enough." It was a statement, not a question.

Dallas presented a wan smile to the windowpane. The mental connection between John Giltspur and himself never ceased to astound him. "No, it won't be enough."

It was Gillie's turn to goad for more with silence.

Dallas responded. "What am I to do with her, Gillie? She won't listen to me, and St. James..."

Gillie cleared his throat, one of his subtle signals to his boss that Dallas wasn't making any sense. "What do you mean, 'she won't listen'? Can't you just, ah, use your 'influence' on her?"

Dallas sighed. It was no easier admitting his weakness to Gillie than to himself.

"No. She saw something else, something hers alone. God knows what." He paused. "St. James will have her." The flatness in his voice didn't fool Gillie.

"Ah, no, Sir, I don't think so. Not yet. If I understand your conflict with St. James correctly, he'll use her to get to you. If he thinks you have any interest in her..."

Damn the man. Gillie knew damn well he had an interest in the woman.

"What about the Brotherhood, Sir? Do you want me to contact them? Isn't this the kind of thing they get involved in?"

"The Brotherhood doesn't give a rat's ass what happens to humans. Any human."

A louder clearing of the throat rumbled from behind Dallas' chair. "I was thinking about you, not the girl. Doesn't the Brotherhood frown upon violence among your own?"

"You are not to contact them. Understand, Gillie? This is none of their damned business. They'd probably think I'm responsible for all this, not St. James. The last thing I need is sanctions imposed by a bunch of relics who have no notion anymore of what it is to live in the world."

Gillie sighed, his dissension thus voiced. "Very well. Is there anything else you wish me to do right now?"

"No. Just make sure the men stay vigilant and the alarms are all set."

"Not to worry, Sir."

Dallas stared out the window. He was worried. For the first time in two centuries, his survival was in jeopardy.

SIX

"You're WHAT?"

Sera's shocked response was something of a triumph. Over the years, Tia had relayed so many incredible stories to Sera, all stranger than fiction, that it took a lot now to make an impact on her friend. Tia, however, took no delight in the small victory.

"I'm not coming home. At least not yet."

"Oh, God, now what drama did you get involved in?"

Tia hesitated, chewing on her lower lip. How was she ever going to explain this to Sera? She took a deep breath. She decided on the four classic words certain to abolish Sera's censure. "I met a man."

"Really? In the past two days? Isn't that kind of sudden? Who is this guy?"

Great. Tia wasn't sure she liked this type of reproach any better. Worse, she didn't have an answer to reassure Sera that she hadn't lost her mind. Dallas Allgate was not exactly the kind of guy you brought home to show off to Daddy. What would Sera understand?

"He's to die for, Sera."

"Oh, God. Don't tell me some Southern gigolo got to you."

Another wrong set of four words. She tried again. "He's not a gigolo, Ser. He's the owner of the haunted inn I was telling you about. He's also got a mansion in town."

"Hmmm. Rich, and to die for. Okay, this guy is sounding better. So you really hit it off, huh?"

Tia sucked on her beleaguered lip. "Ah, well, not exactly. Not at first."

"Oh, I see the problem with Mr. Perfect. You've got a

crush on him and he doesn't know you're alive. Is that it?"

"Oh, he knows I'm alive." *He just doesn't want anything to do with me.*

"And, so? What are you going to do?"

"He'd make a fantastic shoot, Ser. You should see him. He's got long hair, the most fantastic green eyes you've ever seen, and sex appeal that goes off the scale."

"So he's going to let you shoot him?"

"Well, I'm still trying to arrange it. That's why I need a few more days."

"Oh, okay. So all you want is this photo shoot. For a minute there you had me worried. I thought you wanted a relationship with this guy or something."

Did she? What did it matter? He didn't want her. "I don't know. One thing at a time."

A smart rapping sounded on her room door. "Hold on, Sera. It must be the hotel people about something."

Tia looked through the peephole in the door. It was Dallas' blond friend from the inn. She grabbed the phone. "I'll have to call you back."

"Why? Is it him?"

"No, listen, I'll call you back. 'Bye, Sera."

She hung up and tried to organize her thoughts. What did this man want? And how did he know where she was staying? She had changed hotels this morning to the River Park Inn, and Dallas didn't even know where she was. She cracked the door, but left the safety chain attached.

"Yes?"

"Miss Martell? I'm a friend of Dallas Allgate. My name's James Mavrick. He told me you're a photographer. I wondered if we might talk some business?"

"How did you know I was here?"

"Dallas told me."

"He doesn't know I'm here."

The man shrugged. "This is the hotel he gave me."

Damn Allgate! He always seemed to have the advantage over her.

"You hungry? We can talk downstairs in the restaurant,"

he quickly added.

"Hold on a minute." She closed the door. He had mentioned business. Maybe he had a photo job for her. She could use the extra money. This hotel was cheaper than the Magnolia House, but the daily expenses of meals out, lodging, and the rental car were piling up. She supposed it wouldn't hurt to hear what he wanted. She checked her face in the bathroom mirror, grabbed her wallet and camera case, and opened the door to the hallway. For a moment, she was speechless. The man was magnificent.

In spite of the ninety-plus heat outside, he looked as cool as if he had just stepped out of an air-conditioned limo. He wore a long, black trench coat with ornate silver buttons, a black vest over a white shirt, and wide-leg black trousers. Around his neck dangled a silver pendant in the shape of a cross. Her eyebrows couldn't help doing an appreciative flip.

"Wow. I hope you didn't dress like that just for me."

A slow smile spread across the handsome face. "Actually, in a way, I did. I'll explain downstairs."

As they entered the restaurant, Tia was well aware that every female in the room turned to stare at the man at her side. Not one to show off, she suppressed a grin. Tia had to give credit to the hostess as well, who seated them without a crack in her professional demeanor. As soon as the hostess finished, however, Tia saw her waste no time in heading for the kitchen door, where the woman exchanged animated glances with two waitresses. James was sitting with his back toward the kitchen door, so he missed the show his admirers were giving. Even if he had seen it, Tia was sure he was used to it. No doubt he attracted similar attention wherever he went.

"I've eaten already. But go ahead and order whatever you like," he said to her with a renewed smile.

She looked at the menu, but couldn't help shifting her eyes between the list of entrees and his stunning features. He looked like a ghost.

He had pale skin, and his hair, half-shagged and half-spiked, looked like it had never seen sunlight. It was a dark blond, but a blond drained of all golden highlights, like brass tarnished by years of neglect. He had deep-set gray eyes immersed in shadow, and she couldn't tell whether he wore make-up applied for the effect, or it was just a natural consequence of his facial bone structure. His fair skin was clean-shaven and unwrinkled, and his nose was strong, with just a trace of a hook. The only failing she could see in his sensual face was a mouth that was a shade too thin.

James said nothing, and his features showed nothing overt, but she got the distinct feeling that he reveled in her appreciation of his appearance. His gray eyes never left her. She gave her order for grilled seafood to the waitress and smiled back at James.

"Okay. I have to admit it. I'm curious about all this," she gestured vaguely at his attire, "and what it is you wanted to see me about."

He propped his elbows on the table and linked his fingers in a steeple before his face. All she could see were the deep eyes, glinting like secrets from an abyss of shadow. "Simple enough, Tia. Do you mind if I call you that?"

She shook her head, her eyes glued to his.

"I want you..." He tilted his head forward in a nod. "...to take me."

She blinked her eyes. "Excuse me?"

"Take my picture, of course. For a CD cover. I sing in a band. You didn't guess, did you?"

"Well, actually, the thought did cross my mind. You don't exactly look like a stockbroker. Don't you have your own cover photographer?"

James shifted his eyes away from her for the first time. Tia followed the direction of his gaze, but only saw two men being seated across the dining room. His eyes returned to hers. "I fired him. I have the perfect concept for the cover. When my good friend Allgate mentioned you were a professional photographer, well, the idea came together."

"What's the name of your group?"

"St. Satan. My name's Saint James. It's a mouthful, so I go by James, but for band publicity I use Saint."

Somehow it seemed to fit him. The name was as bizarre

as the man. "So what's the concept for the CD? What's the title?"

"Well, we haven't decided one-hundred-percent on the title yet, but it'll be something like 'Trespassing the Gates.'"

"What 'Gates'?"

James lifted his shoulders in a graceful, unhurried movement that was almost sensual. "The gates to Hell, the Beyond, the Other Side. Whatever you want to call it."

She wasn't surprised. After everything that had happened in the last two days, the fantastic was becoming quite commonplace. Her food arrived, but she hesitated digging in. "Are you sure you don't want some of this?"

"Quite sure."

They were quiet for a few moments while she gave her attention to the meal, but her curiosity wouldn't allow her to remain silent very long. "And what's your idea for the cover?"

"There's a small chapel and cemetery just outside of town. Quite serene, actually. But with the right lighting, I think it could capture the mood I'm looking for."

This time Tia did laugh out loud. "Are you serious?"

"Quite. If we hurry, we can make it there with plenty of light to spare."

"You want to go out there now?"

"Of course. As you can see, I'm dressed for it."

Tia shook her head. "I have to admit I'm intrigued, Mr. Mavrick, but I don't have any experience with a shoot like this. The shadows will be very long and the lighting'll be tricky. It'll be new to me."

James leaned closer to her and beckoned her to do likewise with a crook of one finger. She moved her water goblet and plate to one side and inclined her upper body so that her face was inches from his. His gray eyes sparkled at her with the hardness of diamonds.

"Call me James. You want to do this, Tia, I know you do." His voice was no louder than a whisper.

His eyes were so beautiful, like gems winking from the depths of a velvet-lined jewelry box. And they were just as alluring. She saw the promise of everything she had ever wanted in their silver shine.

"Call me James," he breathed.

Yes. "James."

"It's done, then. I'll pay you five hundred dollars. Half now, the other half when I see the photos."

"And if you don't like any of them?"

"I'll find something I like, don't worry."

As they stood to leave, Tia saw that the pendant she'd thought was a cross was actually a dagger, the long blade pointing downward, the arms of the hilt reaching out on either side like an entreaty. *To Satan?*

She shuddered, but had no will to leave the side of the man before her.

***

The emergency alarm sounded in the cellar of Rose Hill. Dallas disliked being awakened during the day. It was usually left to Gillie's discretion to decide what was important enough to merit disturbing him and what wasn't, but occasionally Dallas left specific directions. He spoke into the intercom near his bed.

"What is it, Gillie?"

"St. James has Miss Martell, Sir."

Dallas swore. He had told Gillie to rouse him if this happened, yet that didn't make the untimely awakening any more pleasant.

"I'll be right up."

St. James must have followed her last night from Rose Hill. Dallas got up from the bed and exited the special room he used for sleeping. Fireproof, fortified, and fit with a series of locks even Gillie didn't have keys for, the cellar room was as impregnable as a bomb shelter. He ascended by one of several secret staircases to the drawing room where Gillie waited. The drapes were all closed, steeping the room in comfortable gloom, and air conditioning cooled the closeted room, yet even thusly shielded from the light Dallas felt debilitated and light-headed.

"What happened?"

"Miss Tia changed hotels, as you thought she might. She's

now staying at the River Park. Just before four, St. James called at her room. They sat in the hotel dining room while she ate supper, then they left. They're in separate cars, but she's following him."

Dallas looked at the time. It was half past five. "They met at four? Is Rae sure it was St. James?" Raemon Sovatri was the man in charge of those Gillie had sent to keep an eye on Tia. Ten years ago, when Dallas had played at being a private investigator, Rae had been his assistant.

"Positive. St. James was, ah, hard to miss. Or mistake."

When Dallas lifted his brows, Gillie explained St. James' attire.

So, the good news was that St. James, like Flynne, liked to play his part for the humans after all. That could indicate a weakness—overconfidence or recklessness. "By the way, what of Conner Flynne?"

"No sign of him."

Good. The bad news was that St. James obviously had a markedly greater tolerance for daylight than Dallas had. He had heard of day vampires, though they were uncommon. Different strains of vampirism produced Undead with differing strengths and abilities. It was probably the strength in St. James that Dallas had sensed during their meeting.

"I can't go after them, Gillie. It would be suicide."

Gillie nodded in understanding. "Of course."

"Is Rae following?"

Gillie dipped his head again. "He's been calling about every five minutes."

"All right. I'm going to dress. Give me the next call."

Dallas went into his dressing room, also similarly veiled from the light, and pulled on black jeans and a long-sleeved, V-necked knit shirt.

He knew exactly what his limitations in daylight were, having experimented with direct exposure to sunlight on a number of occasions. Full sunlight not only blinded him, but produced a loss of equilibrium that made even walking almost impossible. In the low light of an afternoon sun, such as was the present case, he would be able to function with the aid of sunglasses, but would have none of the hypnotic power of his eyes. *No hypnotic power.* He laughed. He would be lucky to have the puny mental and physical strength of a healthy human. It was a sobering thought.

He would have to wait until at least twilight. Even then he would be taking a risk, but at least he would have some command of his abilities. *Risk.* It had been many years since he had put himself at substantial risk for the sake of a human. He still didn't understand what it was about Tia that made him willing to even consider gambling with his life. Introspection was just not something a vampire spent time on. Especially during the day when his mind was like a bog and every thought slogged through the muck with an effort. All he knew was that he didn't want St. James to have her.

It was exactly the response St. James was hoping for, and Dallas was aware of that if little else.

The jangle of the phone suspended the agony of reverie. Seconds later, Gillie called out that it was Rae. Dallas leaned over to pick up the extension, trying to economize on his physical as well as mental expenditures of energy.

"Go ahead, Rae. Where are they?"

"They just pulled in to the Chapel of Light cemetery."

Chapel of Light. St. James' humor was not lost on Dallas.

Rae continued. "The woman brought a large case with her from her car."

"Large case? Her camera?"

"Could be. Right now they're just milling around, looking at the chapel."

"All right. Stay close enough to see what they're doing, but not so close you provoke St. James. He knows you're there, so don't bother going to too many pains to conceal yourselves."

"Got it. I'll call you back in a couple minutes."

Before Dallas could hang up the phone, Gillie was at his side. "It's quite clear, Sir."

"Nothing's clear to me right now, Gillie."

"It's just the early hour that makes you swimmy-headed. She's got her camera. She means to photograph him."

Dallas shook his head, even that small movement an effort.

"He'd never allow that. He may be a day vampire, but he won't photograph any better than I would."

Gillie's refined drawl slowed to that of a parent instructing a youngster. "No. You and I know that, and St. James knows that, but Miss Tia doesn't. She won't know until she develops the film. St. James has no intention of letting her go that far with it."

"You mean he won't let her live that long."

"He won't kill her until she's served her purpose. It's not her he wants. It's you. She's just the bait to lure you into the light."

Dallas' head swayed slowly to the side once more. "You're wrong about him not wanting her. Maybe age has diluted your desires, old man, but time does nothing to slack our lust. If St. James wants her even half as much as I do, he'll have her— and destroy her in the process."

Gillie visibly bristled at the reference to being an "old man." "If my love life suffers, it's because all my time is spent nursemaiding the Dead, not because I'm too old," he stated, stiffening like a beleaguered hedgehog.

"Undead, Gillie, Undead. There's a big difference," said Dallas, softening his words with a smile.

"Is there? Well, if you don't start exhibiting some sense about all this, you're going to be among the true Dead, because St. James will have won."

Dallas closed his eyes. Gillie was right. He would just have to wait. After all, he should be good at waiting. He had two hundred years of practice. The phone stirred the silence again, and Dallas reached for the receiver without even looking at it. "Allgate."

"It's me. No change. They're still wandering around the cemetery, looking at tombstones. She's got her camera out. It looks like he's posing for her," came Sovatri's voice.

"Okay. Call when there's a change, Rae."

Dallas hung up and looked up at Gillie. "I'm going back downstairs. Take the calls. Buzz me if there's a major turn or if he starts to...do her harm. Understand?"

Gillie sighed. "All too well, Sir."

Dallas rose and slapped Gillie softly on the back as he passed the man.

The cellar bed felt good beneath him. It was an elemental good, like a mother's embracing arms, holding him close, offering him quiet strength. The total darkness of the room, while not quite the true Anti-Light of night, still nurtured him as well, and he felt his mind clear a little with the power of the blackness.

All vampires had the ability to influence humans. Some had more compelling powers than others, but it was a basic endowment. So why was he so disturbed by Tia's trailing after St. James like a lovesick puppy? Obviously St. James had set the looking glass before her. Reflected in St. James, she saw something she wanted badly enough to follow him around town the same way she had followed Dallas around.

Dallas' laughter rent the darkness, mocking his delusions. Tia was no different from any other human female, and Dallas was no different from any other vampire, no different from St. James. Women saw but one thing in the reflecting pool that was the vampire—their fantasies, and the image of the vampire itself mattered not at all. Even creatures like Conner Flynne who, in life, had been unlucky enough to be graced with unflattering features, had no trouble "inspiring" fantasies.

Everything was in the eye of the beholder.

It was an answer, but not one that pleased him.

***

The cellar intercom buzzer broke the trance Dallas floated in.

"Yes, Gillie."

"Raemon's on the phone. I think this is what you were waiting for."

"All right. What time is it?"

"A quarter past seven."

Not late enough. "Is the car out front and ready to go?"

A sigh was amplified by the intercom. "Of course, Sir."

Dallas picked up the cellar extension. "Allgate."

"Hey, Dallas, I just thought you should hear this yourself. Miss Martell has been taking St. James' picture for a good two hours. He's been posing like a Playboy centerfold, leaning on mausoleums, lying on graves, embracing headstones, you name it. She started putting her equipment away a little while ago like she was going to pack everything up to leave when he started pulling her back into the cemetery. Looks like photos isn't all he wants."

Dallas tried to curb his impatience. "Rae, what's he doing to her?"

"Well, he's just kissing her now, but..."

"I'm on my way. Stay put, and don't interfere. Whatever happens, don't call the police, understand?"

"Sure, I've heard all this before, but..."

Dallas hung up the phone and left the safety of his chamber. He quickly gathered up keys, sunglasses, and a long, black leather coat.

"Gillie, I'm leaving."

"You can't go. There's still a good hour of daylight left. This is exactly what he wants you to do."

"He's not going to have her."

"If you insist on this insanity, then I'm going with you."

"No you're not. I don't want you anywhere near St. James. He would destroy you in a minute to spite me." Dallas headed toward the door, hoping to be out before Gillie could present an argument, but then halted just short of the townhouse entrance.

"Gillie. If...if St. James should prevail, you know what to do."

A long sigh floated forth. Long, even for Gillie. "Yes, of course. Your instructions are very specific."

"And call the Brotherhood. That'll be my retribution."

Gillie looked more unhappy than Dallas could ever remember seeing the man.

***

Fifteen minutes later Dallas pulled his Lincoln into the Chapel of Light. He spotted Sovatri soon after. He had told Rae not to bother with concealment, and the man had taken him at his word. Leaning against a magnolia, umbrellaed by Spanish moss, Sovatri stood smoking a cigarette. Long overdue for a haircut and a shave, Dallas could see from the man's muscled arms that one habit not being neglected was his daily forays to the gym. For a human, Rae was more than capable, but his services this day were at an end. From here on in, he and the others would only be a liability. Besides, the word "vampire" was not yet part of Rae's everyday vocabulary, and Dallas wanted to keep it that way.

"Tell me what he's done with her, then your part here is done."

Rae drew on the cigarette and let the exhaled smoke drift up into the moss. "He's like a kid behind the barn. A lot of kissing and groping. Sometimes it looks like she's enjoying it, other times it looks like she's had enough. Typical woman. In any case, you said not to interfere."

Dallas had to force himself to remember that Rae had no understanding of the power a creature like St. James had over even a very atypical woman like Tia. Concession to his ignorance, though, didn't lessen the irritation Dallas felt. Raemon would outlive his usefulness someday very soon.

"Go on, Sovatri. Take your men and get out of here."

Rae laughed, but it was not a happy sound. "You're crazier than I thought you were, Allgate. In case you can't count, if I leave, you lose the advantage of numbers."

"Good. I like the odds in my favor. Now go back to Rose Hill and make sure the old man stays put."

Rae shook his head. "No, Dallas. Gillie'd kill me if I left you alone."

Dallas caught Sovatri's eyes and extended a subtle compelling reinforcement to his command. His human minions needed such bolstering now and again. Especially Sovatri. "Since when do you answer to Gillie? Get going, or I'll kill you myself."

Rae stared at him, brows visible above the frames of the narrow sunglasses he wore, then wagged his head again. "If I didn't know you better, I'd think you were joking."

"But you know I'm not. If anything happens to Gillie, I hold you responsible."

"Okay, Boss. You win. Good luck." Sovatri flicked his

cigarette to the ground and left.

Luck. There was that useless human term again. *Lucky. Unlucky.* What had been his thought the night Macklin had died? *Oh yes...that "bad luck" was merely the destiny of the weak and foolish.* He feared the definition fit him all too perfectly at the present moment. The glasses and dark clothing helped, but he still felt the rays of the low sun licking his face with hot tongues of fire. Each unwanted caress blistered his resolve, and he wondered again what he was doing here. Did he want Tia so badly, or was it just that he couldn't stomach St. James having her? Was confronting St. James for her worth knocking on Mistress Death's door? It especially pained him to think that it could solely be the passionate lure of revenge that beckoned him on.

Revenge. It had betrayed him once already. The vengeance he had sought so long ago in the ruin of Christian St. James had never ceased haunting him. He had held that rancor for years, and anticipation of the deed had aroused and sustained his craving for everything that would bring him a step closer to fulfillment. The reality of the deed, though, had been as cold and spoiled as a feast laid out and waited upon too long, the climax as illusory as everything else in his life. It had taken decades for him to rule the beast of vampirism that was then so young and out of control. Divorcing himself from the cares of humankind had helped, but now, with Tia, human concerns were becoming all too important again. It meant the loss of hard-won control, and nothing frightened him more than that.

Dallas stepped into the shadow of the magnolia, closed his eyes, and pushed the memories back to the farthest recess of his mind. He hadn't accepted this invitation for revenge. He had come for the woman's survival, and his...what? Existence? Redemption? In any case, he would not let an ill-bred creature like Jermyn St. James dictate her fate, or his own.

He cooled his mind of his passions and started to think about his opponent as a hunter would evaluate his target. St. James had a tolerance for light. Even so, he had been exposed to the sun for several hours. Tolerance aside, St. James had to be feeling drained of energy. And Dallas would soon feel stronger with every minute that brought the dawn of night closer.

Dallas went to work with the cold calculation of his kind. He heightened his senses to those of a predatory animal, and the silence of the cemetery fled with the honing of his awareness. A requiem of animal sounds sang to him, almost drowned out by the underlying chorus of insect noises, strident and harsh. The hot breeze stirred the hair framing his face, and the invisible souls of the dead, like taciturn spectators at an arena, rose to regard him. Appropriately throned on a massive headstone before him, he even fancied he saw the specter of Mistress Death presiding over all. His Mistress, who ruled over all he was and all he did. With a nod to her image, he turned his senses to those not yet dead. Two distinct scents reached his nostrils, the sour smell of the Undead, and the sweet lifeblood of a human. Tia was still alive.

With movement so swift as to be out of time to human perception, he slid among the gravestones like the shadow of an overhead plane, stopping in the shade of a small mausoleum thirty feet from his quarry. He knew not to approach any closer until he knew what game piece St. James would move next. Dallas didn't fear firearms, but there were other weapons to fear, and he knew that an opponent with such an implement could strike from within twenty feet before Dallas could properly react.

He watched as St. James stepped into view, gripping Tia as a child might hold a disobedient pet, the hand clutching her by the back of the neck having also snagged a tangle of black hair, the other arm squeezing her waist. For all the distance between them, Dallas' inhuman vision could see that her swollen eyes were as liquid as drowning pools, and smudged eye makeup tracked their banks. Dallas swore silently. Even a cretin such as Sovatri should have seen that Tia was hardly a willing participant in St. James' little game. Her eyes reached out to his own, and her thoughts, as liquid as the blue depths, flowed into his mind. There was recognition at his appearance, but it was so colored by fear and confusion that he couldn't quite tell if the sight of him was a relief or new cause for dread.

Knowing Tia was unharmed, Dallas turned his full attention to St. James and would have laughed out loud had the situation not been so grim. Jermyn St. James stood in a full-length opera coat complete with vest and dress trousers. The only thing missing from the ludicrous outfit was a froth of ruffles at the neckline.

Dallas quickly sobered. Though not comfortable with introspection, Dallas had nevertheless learned a great deal in two hundred years about the ways and nature of both man and his own kind. The outfit could be more than just St. James' desire to act his role for the humans. It could be an indicator of the creature's personality. If so, it might be something else Dallas could exploit.

"What's the matter, Aldgate? Too scared to show yourself? Or does the sun hurt your eyes?" The echoes of the shout bounced off the monuments to the dead like a ball in a pinball machine.

"You don't scare me, St. James, any more than your father did."

Jermyn's laugh careened off the headpieces. "Bold boasts come easily to one who does nothing more than hide. Show yourself, Aldgate, then see how boastful you feel."

Dallas stretched his mouth in a slow cat-grin that did nothing to interrupt his concentration. He shrugged out of the long coat and let it slide to the ground like an oily stain, then unhooked his sunglasses and tossed them on top of the coat. Focusing all the power of his eyes and mind on St. James, he stepped out of the shade. The light assaulted his senses, sending fingers of dizziness through him, but he shrugged the distraction aside.

"Let the girl go. You have me."

St. James stroked one hand up and down Tia's side. His fingers circled her hip lazily, then roamed across the flat of her belly. "Hmmm. This female interests you, doesn't she? Else you wouldn't be here, would you?" He removed his other hand from the base of her skull and bent her head to the side, exposing the slender column of her neck. "I can't say I blame you, Aldgate. Have you tasted her yet? As sweet...rich...and fresh...as...nectar." The final sentence was punctuated by idle kisses to Tia's carotid. She squeezed her eyes shut, and her features froze in a mask of disgust.

Dallas' anger and desire both flamed, and he fought to cool the heat searing his control. This was what St. James wanted, to provoke a rash, unthinking attack. It wouldn't happen. As fast as Dallas could move, if he wasn't careful, St. James would still have plenty of time to kill Tia. He had to divert Jermyn's attention away from her, and right away.

Dallas spread his arms wide to each side. "She doesn't tempt me the way she apparently does you. Leave her for later. Why waste time being distracted by a toy when you have before you what you've waited one hundred eighty years for?"

St. James seemed to consider Dallas' words. His hold on Tia didn't slacken, but his shift of concentration was apparent in his gray eyes. "You would have me believe this tidbit doesn't appeal to you? I find that exceedingly hard to swallow." St. James grazed his mouth down the length of Tia's neck, his leaden eyes never ceasing their press on Dallas. "Because this is all too easy to swallow. Robust, full-bodied wine of life, offering itself up with gladness."

"Blood is blood, St. James, but it's not as sweet as vengeance." The sarcasm was there, too hard to stem, but perhaps Jermyn's lust would deafen him to it.

"Ah, yes. You've always preferred that to pleasure, haven't you? Perhaps she doesn't appeal to you. You haven't marked her. You are too blasé, Aldgate. Or perhaps you've just gone soft on humans, as so many of our kind have. You must really learn to take what's at hand." With that, his mouth returned to Tia's neck, and her strangled cry of terror and anguish erupted over the lament of insect chatter. When St. James flung Tia aside, a dark splatter was visible on her throat. "There. Now it's too late. She's mine. You really should have taken her while you had the chance."

"Is that what you came here to prove? That you can put

your mark on a female? I'll wager even the pup Flynne was able to do that within a week of being purged of humanity. Didn't you come here for me? Isn't that what your pretty speech was about last night? But beware, St. James. It's the dish served cold, not hot. Or have you never tasted it?"

Dallas' peripheral vision caught Tia regaining her balance and running back toward the parking lot. *Good.* The female had some sense, after all. With her gone, he had one less thing to worry about.

"Revenge. Yes, your favorite dish. I think I will save her for later. She'll make a fine dessert plate to a victory feast laden with the stupid mortals foolish enough to be willing servants of the likes of you."

"If you're referring to my men, they're superior minions to dogs like Flynne who are but one step away from becoming rabid beasts that'll serve neither humankind nor the Undead to any good."

St. James laughed, an animalistic sound. "'Good?' That's a word I've not heard a vampire voice in decades. Since when do we concern ourselves with 'good'?"

"Oh, but there you're wrong. You delude yourself if you think you're not concerned with 'the Good.' It's all you truly seek, isn't it? Not the blood. You take 'the Good' from every victim you prey on. You take their life, energy, and emotion, and try endlessly to fill your emptiness. But you know what, St. James? 'The Good' of a thousand females like that one couldn't repair the disintegration of Jermyn St. James that began in 1820."

A sound like water hitting oil in a hot skillet escaped from St. James' mouth. "And what makes you any different from me? The exact same things that feed me feed you. Don't tell me you wouldn't take her, and a hundred like her, without a second thought."

"Perhaps. But I see the reality of it. You live in a grandiose fantasy that rules everything you do."

"You almost disappoint me, Aldgate. I took you to be a more worthy rival than this."

"Oh, I think I'll provide sufficient sport for you."

"Then look at me. Gaze upon your self-righteous reality and see how prettily it sits." St. James' eyes silvered, and the diminishing light bounced sparks of white fire at Dallas.

It had been a long time since Dallas had forcefully opposed one of the Undead. In the skirmish with Flynne, it had taken all of Conner's strength to resist Dallas' eyes—the novice had had no power to return a compelling stare of his own. St. James, however, was no apprentice. Dallas' vision started to fade, replaced by shimmering shards of silver and iridescence, and a reflection of horror screamed at him. *Predator. Parasite.* Images from his past started to form against the glimmering background. Humans taken to satisfy his need were reborn in the reflections. *Restless. Bored.* More victims rose from their rest to torment him. *Needy. Dependent. Empty...*

Dallas, blinded by the vision, could no longer see St. James. He fought the debilitation of the twilight, focusing all his strength on shattering the mirror. The images burst with an explosion of will, and Dallas' sight cleared enough for him to see St. James soaring toward him, his coat billowing to either side like outstretched black wings. Dallas, with a speed to match, circled to his left, putting any remaining sunlight into St. James' face.

Jermyn's response was a cackle. "An old trick, Aldgate, but one that won't work on me. Mistress Light and I are old friends. She doesn't frighten me into seeking the isolation of the darkness like she does you. I don't have to hide from anything I've done."

"If you think the light is your friend, St. James, you're even more deluded than I thought. Take care that your Mistress isn't your undoing."

"She won't be, and neither will you. You're weak, Aldgate. You haven't the power to resist my will, do you?"

"You're wrong, St. James. The sky darkens. I grow stronger with each moment."

"As I do."

"Do you? I think not. You're but a pallid, narcissistic day-monster, basking in the light of your self-admiration."

St. James snarled. "You shadow-born perversion. Is hiding

nobler? Then hide, if you can, from this!" The leaden eyes
liquefied to mercury, and the power compelling Dallas to gaze
upon them once more flowed over him. The mirror formed,
and for a brief moment souls residing at the Chapel of Light
rose before him. Local victims of his need, they mouthed silent
obscenities at him. *Blood monster. Unclean one.* Dallas
smashed the image with a roar, and his vision unclouded
immediately, but it was too late.

St. James was racing toward him, his hand slipping beneath
the concealment of the long opera coat. Dallas backpedaled,
doing nothing more than giving St. James room to unsheathe
a short lance. Made of wood, tipped with a silver point, and
mounted on an elaborate silver hilt, Dallas knew immediately
what it was. It was cold fear that he hadn't felt in years. It was
panic fear that upset his natural grace and sent him staggering
backward over tree roots. It was mortal fear.

It was the Vampire Hunter. The Death's-head. It was the
surest way short of burning or decapitation to send a vampire
to the natural death. The True Death.

Dallas regained his balance in time to sidestep a lunge
and thrust from St. James, and the silver head, like the fangs
of a striking serpent, flashed inches from Dallas' heart.
Jermyn's momentum carried him past Dallas, giving Dallas a
chance to plant his feet and position himself. When St. James
turned, Dallas kicked at Jermyn's hand. The blow of the heeled
boot landed hard, and Jermyn loosened his grip. It was enough
to send the Vampire Hunter into flight, but the heavy hilt
quickly carried it to the ground. Both men fell to their knees
and tried to grab the handle, but Jermyn was quicker, closing
his fist around the silver grip first. Dallas pinned the hand and
weapon to the ground with his own large hand, and elbowed
St. James in the face with his other arm.

St. James swore, both men lost their balance, and they
toppled over, still fighting for control of the Hunter. Dallas'
strength was greater, and he rolled on top of St. James, pinning
him to the ground. But St. James was not about to submit so
easily. Raking a fistful of dirt into his free hand, he flung the
earth and stones into Dallas' eyes. Dallas let go of St. James

with a cry and fell backward, stumbling to regain his feet. Until he could clear his vision, he had to put as much distance between himself and the Vampire Hunter as possible.

Suddenly he felt something cool, long, and metal being shoved into his hand. Sensitive fingers probed the tool while flashes of light, one after another, exploded behind Dallas' eyelids. He heard St. James swear just as his own thumb pressed against a button on the metal object, sliding a blade free. Dallas blinked and saw enough. St. James was still on the ground, one arm flung like a shield over his eyes, the other arm, the one gripping the Hunter, supporting his weight. Dallas wasted no time. In a movement so swift as to be nothing more than a shimmer to the human eye, he circled behind St. James, seized him in a chin lock with his left arm, and thrust the blade into St. James' heart with his right hand.

He felt a tug on his sleeve and a voice only inches from his ear, clearer than the shriek pouring from St. James.

"Dallas, let's go! Now!"

His eyes, half blinded by the dirt and spots of color he saw dancing in front of him, still managed to register Tia beside him. Her hand, warm on his arm, pulled at him.

"Come on!

He complied, running with her back toward the parking lot. His fluid strides quickly overtook hers, and soon he was the one pulling her in tow. A touch of the Lincoln's remote unlocked the doors and turned on the interior lights.

"Get in," he commanded, indicating she get in on the passenger side.

"Can you see to drive?"

"Well enough." He slid into the driver's seat, started the engine, and put the car into gear with his foot already on the gas. The tires screeched and spit a cloud of gravel as the car lurched forward.

"God, Dallas, we have to call the cops. Where's your phone?" She expelled the words between great gulps of air. He could feel the heat and adrenaline in her body as intensely as if she were pressed up against him. It was a pleasant distraction in an evening overflowing with unpleasant diversions, but it was not the time to think or act on it.

"No cops."

She persisted in a nervous searching of the car's storage compartments that were within her reach. "Listen, I don't understand half of what I just saw, but you just killed a man. That much I know."

He reached his right arm across her and slammed the glove box shut, then, using a dexterity and speed bordering on celerity, snagged both busy hands in his. Clutching her hands tightly, he pressed them to her lap. "No cops, and that's final. It's over. Understand?"

He glanced quickly at her face. Her eyes were wide and her open mouth almost as much so, but the frozen expression seemed to indicate more lingering shock and fear than determination to oppose him. He released her hands. They stayed in her lap, but she gave no response to his question.

He shifted his eyes between the road and Tia. "Are you all right? Answer me."

She finally nodded.

"Good. Now stay quiet and let me think."

He had accomplished his goals. He had prevented St. James from having Tia, and he himself had survived the encounter. But in the process he had created a larger problem. Tia now knew too much, and with her resistance to him, he doubted he could successfully compel her to forget everything she had witnessed. It would be far too dangerous now for both of them to send her packing.

Much too dangerous. Because he had lied to her. It wasn't over.

SEVEN

He had to tell her the truth. It would awaken her suspicions about him even more, but if he didn't tell her the truth, he had no doubt she would persist in her quest to involve the police in this, regardless of how strong his admonishments were. He took a deep breath. "He's not dead."

She turned to him. "What?"

"St. James. He's not dead."

"That was nearly a five-inch blade on my tactical knife."

His eyes scanned the road ahead. "Thank you. You saved my life. What was the light I saw?"

"Don't change the subject. What do you mean he's not dead? A five-inch blade isn't the biggest knife in the world, but in the right spot kills a man. I know about these things."

He glanced at her. "The light?"

She sighed. "The flash from my camera. I figured if I got close enough, I could blind him long enough for you to do something."

"You shouldn't have gotten that close. He would have killed you had he realized what you were doing."

Another exasperated sigh. "You're welcome."

They rode the rest of the way to Rose Hill in blessed silence.

***

Tia was exhausted. Not from the ordeal, but from talking her head off to no avail. Since arriving at Rose Hill, she had lost every argument with Dallas Allgate. After having been introduced to John Giltspur and Rae Sovatri, she had appealed to them as well, but it hadn't done her a bit of good.

He wouldn't let her call the police. He wouldn't let her

return to her hotel. And he wouldn't let her leave Rose Hill. She indulged herself with a small smile, the first of the evening. A night at Rose Hill with Dallas Allgate was what she had wanted it, wasn't it?

Sure, just not while embroiled in the middle of another murder.

The minute they had pulled into the drive at the townhouse, Dallas had started issuing orders. Sovatri was to go the River Park Inn and retrieve Tia's luggage. The man they called "Gillie" helped Dallas clean and bandage the wound on her neck. It was small, the skin just having been torn, and it hadn't bled profusely, so she hadn't insisted on going to the hospital. After Sovatri returned with her things, which were put into the most spacious bedroom she had ever seen, Dallas himself went with Rae to pick up her car. She argued again to come along, but Dallas would have none of it.

"The police are probably there, and they'll see my car and want to know what *I* was doing there, and the next thing you know..." she said.

"The police won't be there, and neither will St. James. We'll be back in twenty minutes. Now be a good girl and don't give Gillie a hard time. He's already had two heart attacks. Wouldn't want him to have a third," Dallas said.

"*What?* Well, living with you I can understand it, but don't you think..." But the door slammed before she could finish her question.

She stood for a moment, then looked sideways at Gillie. "Is it true about the heart attacks? How can you stand working for that man?"

"He exaggerates. I've only had one. And, yes, it's not always easy. Mr. Allgate is rather, ah, set in his ways. Why don't you take the opportunity to have a shower and change, and I'll fix you something to eat. Might do to be fueled up for the next skirmish, eh?" With that the old man gave her a sly wink and walked her upstairs to the bedroom. She stuck on a smile, nodded her thanks, and closed the door behind her. The old man was a match for his boss when it came to eccentricity.

He was right about one thing, though. She desperately

wanted a shower. She was hot, sticky, and grimy. Catching her reflection in the bedroom mirror, she groaned. "Grimy" wasn't the word. Her white jeans were streaked with dirt, and her white and blue floral camisole top was spotted with blood.

Remind me never to wear white to a cemetery again.

Her reflection stared silently back at her, and she winced. Her eyes were as puffy and red-rimmed as if she'd been on an all-day crying jag, and her black eye makeup was in evidence everywhere but where she had applied it. Her tangled hair provided an appropriate frame to the nightmarish portrait.

Just what have I gotten myself into this time?

She stripped her dirty clothes off as fast as she could in a frenzied attempt to avoid answering the question. She pulled clean underwear, shampoo and conditioner from her suitcase and stepped into the spacious bathroom. The fixtures were old, but the room was fastidiously clean, and a modern shower had been added to the tub. Thick, fluffy towels hung neatly from a towel rack.

The pelting of the warm water soothed her, and she addressed the plaguing questions she had ignored thus far. The whole evening had been frightening and strange, to say the least, but the murder was all she could think about. It wasn't as if she was sorry James was dead. She had perhaps been foolish to go alone with him to the graveyard, even thinking he was a friend of Dallas', but what he had done to her had been inexcusable. She had been briefly charmed by his intriguing looks and outrageous persona. A nice change, she had thought, from Dallas' brooding, reticent ways. But after the first kiss James gave her behind a mausoleum—a hard, cruel kiss—the charisma had fallen away like a mask. What she thought was a charming, self-deprecating arrogance was a manipulative disregard for others. When she had told him "no" in no uncertain terms, he had continued his assault, invading her mouth with his tongue and fondling every inch of her body. She had tried the defense and arrest tactics she had learned years before as an officer, kneeing him in the midsection, kicking him, and using elbow thrusts, but his strength had been extraordinary. She hadn't even been able to throw him off balance. She had resorted to dirtier tactics not taught by DAAT instructors, but those, too, had been ineffectual. Most likely James was high on something. Drugs could give a person superhuman strength. She had witnessed the phenomena more than once on The Job.

When she had seen Dallas arrive, she couldn't have been gladder than if he were the proverbial cavalry. When James finally let her go, her first thought had been flight, but upon reaching her car, she hadn't been able to force herself to leave Dallas behind. She had grabbed her camera and the large folding knife she still carried in her car when she traveled. It was the extra weapon she used to carry while working the street as a cop. Not exactly legal, but if it saved her life in a fight, who cared?

She had crept back to watch Dallas and James, but had had trouble seeing them. Maybe it was the shadows of the dying sun, or maybe the ordeal had made her dizzy, but the men seemed to move so fast she couldn't follow their actions. Dallas appeared to be on the losing end, however, and when Tia had seen the strange dagger that James drew, she knew she had to act.

No, she wasn't sorry James was dead. She hadn't killed him, and it was no more than self-defense anyway. But she was definitely party to the crime, and she didn't relish the idea of spending hours before cops, detectives, and district attorneys explaining her actions. How could she articulate what she had seen and heard? Her eyes had registered little more than shadows and shimmers of black and white, and all she could remember hearing was strange talk about blood, feeding, and revenge. She shivered even in the stream of warm water. Maybe they were part of some weird cult, though she never would have thought Dallas the type.

Exiting the shower at last, she dressed carefully in a white, cable-knit top that showed off her tanned arms and a long, slim black skirt. If the cops were going to be questioning her, she wanted to at least look decent.

Tia heard engines on the driveway below and car doors slam. *Dallas, the police, or both?* She opened the bedroom door and padded on bare feet to the end of the upstairs hallway. The low, steel wool voice that could only belong to Dallas floated up to her, followed by the higher voice she recognized as Gillie's. No others. *Good.*

Curious now, she scampered back to the room and quickly donned a little jewelry and makeup. Dashing down the stairs as quickly as the tight skirt would allow, her hair still damp, she was disappointed to see no one but Gillie in the dining room. Only one table setting was laid out on the large table.

"Where's Dallas?"

"Like you, cleaning up. Have a seat, Miss Martell."

"Oh, Tia, please." She flicked her eyes at the table setting. "Surely I'm not the only one eating?"

"Mr. Allgate indicated he wasn't hungry just now, but he'll join you as soon as he's changed."

Tia sat, and Gillie disappeared before she could ask more questions. She glanced around the room. The pieces were all massive and looked to be authentic antiques. Dark, heavy drapes covered the windows, and though a large, ornate chandelier hung over the table, candlelight at her place setting provided the only light. She wondered where Dallas' bedroom was. He hadn't passed her on the stairs. She stared at the wall nearest to her, and somehow knew that his room was the adjacent one. The thought of him changing clothes on the other side of that wall brought a flush to her face. All the strange things that had happened to her, and all she could wonder about was how Dallas looked without his clothes on.

Gillie brought in cold chicken and ham, bread, fresh salad, fruit, and a bottle of wine, and arranged the platters on the sideboard across from her. Tia fervently hoped that Gillie's eccentric nature didn't extend to the reading of minds, but the artful smile he gave her made her believe he could. He left without a word.

She stood to step to the sideboard when Dallas stole into the room with the stealth of a large cat. She turned and ran into him, raising her hand before her like a stop sign to prevent a collision. It didn't work. Two hundred pounds of raw sex appeal dressed in chocolate brown snatched both her breath and desire for food away. In her heels she was almost as tall as he was, and with the warmth of his chest under her palm and his green-glass eyes just inches from hers, she forgot the two dozen or so questions she had wanted to ask him.

"Have your trials and tribulations rendered you speechless, Tia? This is serious, indeed. Perhaps you need medical attention after all."

He was making fun of her again. How could he look at her like that and make jokes? If she didn't owe him her life, she would...she would... Which reminded her, ignorant bastard though he was, she hadn't thanked him for what he had done.

"You saved my life," she whispered. "Thank you."

His eyes were an elixir, sweet and potent, and they told her that he saw her only too well. Suddenly she felt strangely vulnerable and forced her own gaze downward. She stared at her hand, still flat against his chest, and she vaguely wondered if the pounding she heard was his heart or hers.

Dallas reached for her hand and drew it slowly to his mouth. He pressed the heel of her palm to his lips and kissed it as if he had all night to enjoy the sensation. She closed her eyes, and the feel of his warm lips against her skin sent rivulets of tiny shivers down her body like a waterfall. *God, did he know what he was doing to her? Did she know what she was doing?* She didn't care.

He lowered her hand, and she opened her eyes just in time to see him lean into her. His mouth closed on hers, and the heat she had felt on her palm was nothing to the fire she felt now. His mouth was hot and soft and played with hers in a gentle tug of war that stirred more than her competitive spirit. She snaked her arms up to his neck and, holding him closer to her, ran a hand through his thick hair. It was heavy and still damp, and he smelled of pine soap.

He dragged his lips from her mouth downward along her neck, and when she flinched, he released her abruptly.

She looked into his eyes, and they were as ancient and hard as amber.

"My apologies. After what happened to you tonight, that was...unforgivable." The low voice, as elemental as his eyes, continued the effect on her his lips had begun. She stood stupidly while he glided to the far side of the table and shaped himself to the chair.

"Have something to eat. It'll be good for you, and Gillie'll be offended if you don't at least have some of his homemade bread."

The flinch had been automatic. What Dallas just did to her was not even comparable to what James had done. Could she explain that? Would he understand her if she could? She put some of the food on her plate, but when she sat down, she didn't touch any of it. He rose, opened the bottle of wine, poured a little into a crystal goblet, and swirled it. He held it to his nose, closed his eyes, and took a deep whiff of the golden liquid. Then, filling the glass, he set it before her.

"Aren't you going to have any?" she asked, watching his eyes as he seemed to pour himself back into his seat.

He looked at her for a long moment, and just when she wondered what was wrong now, he spoke.

"No."

She took a small sip of the wine and broke off a corner of the thick slice of bread she had taken. "Is my car okay?"

He nodded. "It's in the carriage house."

"And James?" She chewed the bread slowly, feeling self conscious that she ate while he didn't.

"His name is Jermyn St. James. He wasn't there. I told you, he's not dead."

"He told me his name was James Mavrick."

Dallas gave a small shrug. "An alias."

"Tell me why he isn't dead." *And don't shrug this one away.*

"It wasn't a clean blow. I felt the blade hit the sternum and slide sideways. A lot of damage to his pretty outfit, I'm afraid, but I missed his heart and lungs."

"I thought he was a friend of yours. I saw you talking together last night at the inn. I wondered how James knew to find me at the hotel, but he said you told him where I was."

"He was never a friend. And I never told him where you were. Do you believe that?"

She answered with no hesitation, just a heartbeat to gauge his eyes. "Yes."

They both sat quietly for a few minutes while she busied herself with her food. A bit of chicken, a little bread, and a few grapes found their way to her mouth, but the rest of her food found itself merely arranged in a new pattern on her plate.

"Dallas? Did you come to the cemetery for me or for St. James?" The sudden pounding of her heart was an unnecessary reminder of how important his answer was to her. She blinked, and when she opened her eyes, he was standing before the draped windows. He drew the drapes back and opened a French door that led to a veranda. Warm air blew through, flickering the flames on the tapers.

"I came for you."

He continued staring out at the night, and she wondered if not meeting her eyes was an indication of the sincerity, or lack thereof, of his words. She waited for more.

He let the drapes slide from his fingers. "I wasn't sure why you went with St. James. I came as soon as I could. I wish it could have been sooner."

"What are you saying?" Had he just been jealous, or did he know she was in trouble? She hated to put words in his mouth, but it was suddenly important that she know.

Dallas turned, picked up a cloth napkin from the table, and balled it in one large hand. "I know what St. James is like. I knew he'd hurt you." He whirled and threw the napkin down on the table. "Dammit, Tia, I'm no better than St. James, no more real than St. James."

"Don't say that. You're not like him. I know."

"You don't know me. You see what you want to see."

"No, you're right. I don't know a lot about you, but give me credit for knowing you're not like St. James."

"You went with him."

That hurt her. "It wasn't a date. I thought he was a friend of yours, and I thought it was going to be business, nothing more."

"Nothing more? Somehow I doubt that. What did he have you seeing that you wanted so badly?"

"What?" *Damn him. What kind of a question was that?* Suddenly she was very tired. It had been a hell of a day. "Believe what you want to believe. If you don't mind, I'd like to get some sleep. Thank Gillie for the dinner for me, would you?"

He voiced no response, but his eyes were cold and dark in the candlelight. It was enough of a reply.

***

Sleep was very long in coming. The room itself was decorated in soft greens and beiges, but instead of being soothing, the colors reminded her of Dallas' eyes. Men. If she had a hundred years she'd never be able to figure them out. Was Dallas really jealous because he thought she wanted more from St. James than a business deal? How could any man possibly be jealous after the way she had kissed him just minutes before? Did he think she kissed every man like that? Did he think she had kissed James that way? She had played too many games with Bret and the other men she had dated the past few years. Somehow she had thought that Dallas would be beyond all that. More mature.

Well, she had gotten what she wanted. A night with Dallas Allgate. At least in getting her wish, she could now move on. She wasn't a prisoner at Rose Hill. Tomorrow she would drive back to Jackson and arrange for a flight back home to Milwaukee. There was nothing to stop her plans now. Nothing...

***

Her assignment was to patrol the City of the Dead. Alone. She cruised her squad slowly up and down the unrecognizable streets, each building a gray animal against night's black cage. Lost souls stood in the street or crouched on porches, watching her. Sullen, hostile, waiting. Watching. She heard the sound of shots, dispassionate as far-off thunder, and she drove faster, not knowing where she was going. Shadows taunted her with movement, and the reflection of every eye caught in the headlamps burned with blind accusation.

She got out of the car and ran, not seeing where she was going, as blind as the others in the night. The eyes around her became flashes of gunfire, and she fired back at the light. Light was life, and life was death, and death was all around her. She looked at the gravestones surrounding her, and the names screamed at her. She knew she should know the names, but she didn't. She screamed back, unable to breathe, and a figure grabbed her so tight she knew it was Death come for her, too...

"No! No, let go of me!" She got the words out, but couldn't get enough air in. She was suffocating.

"Tia, listen to me! Wake up! Do you hear me? It's only a dream."

Strong arms seized her, and she tried to fight back, but the force that pinned her was overpowering. She fought harder to breathe. She didn't want to die.

The iron grip released her, and the room flooded with light. The brightness hurt, and for a moment she didn't know where she was.

Then a familiar, low voice rumbled in her ears, and a hand held her face. "Tia, it's Dallas. You're all right now. It was just a dream. Look at me, Tia, and slow your breathing."

Dallas? She blinked and found herself falling into a dark green well. So deep, so impenetrable. So beautiful.

"Tia. Say my name."

"Dallas..."

"Good. It's over now, understand? I'm not going to let anything happen to you. You're hyperventilating. You need to relax and slow down your breathing. Do you understand me?"

She nodded.

"Say the words. Tell me you understand."

"I understand," she breathed, but it was hard to do as he commanded. It was but a differing scenario of the same dream she had had almost nightly for years now. This one was more frightening than most, but she was used to the dreams.

She wasn't used to having a half-naked man in her bed holding her the way he was. The skin of his face and smooth chest was pale in the lamplight, relieved only by the day-old stubble shadowing the planes of his face. Long, thick twists of hair tangled around his ears and looped over one eye. One large hand still cradled her face while his other held her by the shoulder. Heavy biceps and triceps weighted each arm. What she saw in his eyes was too beautiful to bear.

The dreams were her reality. Why couldn't her dreams ever look like this?

"Are you all right now?"

She shook her head. "No." It was the truth. She fought to hold back sudden tears. She hated crying in front of a man. He slid into the bed and gently drew her head to his chest. She let him. The heat of his body put the Mississippi summer night to shame, and the steadiness of his heartbeat soothed her.

"Was it St. James?"

"No, it was the cop dream."

"The 'cop dream'?"

"Ummm. I started getting them when I worked the street. I thought when I became an ID tech they'd go away, but they didn't. They just got worse. Even after I quit the Job...it's been two years and I still have them."

"What happens in the dream?" His soft voice was corrosive and ate away at all the defenses she had erected since Bret.

"It's always the same. I'm alone, I'm on patrol, and then I'm running and firing my gun. It's never resolved. I never shoot anyone, and they don't shoot me, but..." She had never told anyone about her dreams, not even Bret. He hadn't wanted to hear them.

"Mistress Death is always there."

How did this man know? "Yeah. I think that's it."

"Are you afraid to die, Tia?"

"Of course. Isn't everyone?"

"Not quite everyone. To some it's a release."

She shivered in the warmth of his arms. To have found someone after all this time who understood how she felt... Someone who was strong and who was willing to talk about life and death, not just computer games, football, and deer hunting. And someone so sexy that just a glance from his eyes could make her body melt the same way his voice was dissolving her mental defenses. He was her fantasy come true.

She turned in his embrace until her mouth was just inches from his, and twined her legs with his. He had on black sweatpants, but her bare limbs could feel his heat and hard muscles with incredible ease.

"Are you afraid of death, Dallas?" she whispered.

His eyes opened to hers for a long moment before he answered, and she thought that for a moment pain floated in the green eyes, pain greater than any she had ever known. He blinked, and the soft look was gone, replaced by the glittering hardness she was better acquainted with.

"No. Not tonight. Tonight both of us will see only what we want to see, yes?"

She furrowed her brow just a little at the strange words, and her lips parted with a question, not a reply. He laid a finger on her mouth to still her question and drew the pad of his fingertip across her lower lip.

"Don't fear the night, Tia," he whispered, lowering his mouth to within an inch of hers. "Don't let your mind trap you in this realm of terror. There is an escape, if you will but allow your mind to see it."

She saw the escape in the spell of his eyes, but hesitated before their depths of darkness.

"Hanging on to your fear is not the same as being in control of your life. Free yourself, Tia, and take what you want. Trust in your wish, and the fear will disappear."

No one had ever spoken to her like that, and it scared her. How could he know her so well? She closed her eyes against hot tears she could feel building again, and when they threatened to spill, she fought in vain to hold them back. His lips touched her eyelids like a hot-press, smoothing the conflict that tore at her. She wrapped her arms around his neck, clutching his thick hair as if it were a life-saving handhold.

"Don't fight it. Just let it go." The sound of his voice was a throaty purr against her skin, yet she heard the words. They willed her to surrender, not just to him, but to the promise of freedom—freedom from all the facets of her nightmare. His lips slid down her cheek, and when he kissed her, she tasted her own tears on his mouth. Each deep kiss was a summons, commanding her to let go, and she couldn't resist any longer.

A shudder wracked her body, and she moaned with the

release he mandated with his mouth. Her fear fled, and into the void crashed waves of physical pleasure that swelled until she felt she could stand no more.

His mouth freed hers at last, and she heard his heavy breathing in her ear. For long moments he simply held her close, easing his hold at last just enough to smudge away the remnants of her tears with the pad of his thumb. He turned his wrist and brushed the back of his hand down her face, sweeping her long hair away from her neck. He examined the small bandage still in place. "Does it hurt?"

She shook her head, and her hair fell back in place. She felt him dust the other side of her throat with his finger, his hands asking the question, his eyes, shifting between her neck and her own eyes, waiting for her answer. She concentrated on accepting his touch and found herself reveling in it. This wasn't St. James. She reached behind his head and pulled him down to her, giving him his answer. She wanted more than a kiss, more than a haven from her nightmares. He hesitated briefly, and she felt his hot breath tease her neck before he finally burrowed his mouth into the heat of her skin.

Somewhere in the back of her mind, questions rose. Did she know what she was doing? Is this what she truly wanted? Sex with a beautiful stranger? No answer came forth, only the response that ignited in parts of her body she had little control over.

He groaned, and his lips drew on her skin, moving from just below her ear to the hollow at her throat, searching, until he groaned even deeper. She felt his teeth against her skin, smooth and hard.

"Your wish is granted, love." The words vibrated against her throat, so low she felt her body tighten.

She felt his teeth rake the length of her neck to her collarbone, and it was as though her past were being swept away, like dead leaves before a strong wind. A tremor shook her body, and she wondered if she had orgasmed. His response was a moan more animalistic than human, and he tore his mouth from her neck, only to bury it in her hair. Twisting her body beneath him, she twined her legs around his waist, not caring that the hem of her satin nightdress rode up her hips.

He spoke no more with words, but she felt a wave of energy, his energy, immerse her. More than just the physical electricity of arousal, it was a swell of thoughts and images that washed over her and engulfed her. She felt it on the tiny hairs on her arms, felt it on the sweetness she tasted on her tongue, felt it in the rising temperature of her blood. Memories flowed to her of people and places unrecognizable, but they comforted her, and she tried to share her own with him, like a young lover eager to return hungry kisses.

Unlike a young lover, though, she felt no guilt. In relinquishing her fears to him, she felt a freedom and passion she had never felt with any other man. This was no stranger. He understood too well what she needed.

Ravenous for more, she relaxed her legs and released his waist, trying to give him the mobility to access the rest of her body. He responded, dipping his hands to her sides. There was a rustle of fabric, and she saw him pass his hands over her, as if he were a magician and she an illusion to be performed. She suddenly knew she was naked, and yet he was motionless above her, only the rapid expansion and contraction of his chest evidence of his desire. She looked up at him, and he was beautiful in his masculine sensuality. His long hair, glinting with chestnut highlights, tumbled over his face to his shoulders, and only a gleam of reflected light off his eyes told her he was looking at her as well. A sheen of sweat made his skin glow like ivory silk, and shadows from the lamplight defined muscles that were both modest in the perfection of their sinuous curves and overt in the rawness of latent power. He divested himself of his sweatpants in the blink of an eye, and there was nothing modest in what she now beheld.

But before she could admire him further he bent low over her, and the curtain of his dark hair was all she could see. She felt his hands fan over her ribcage and his tongue touch one nipple like a wand. If she had been on the ground instead of on a very solid bed, she would have melted into the sodden earth. Instead, she bowed against him, her head thrown back and her hands roaming over his shoulders and arms, as if to remind herself he was real, and not a mirage.

His mouth suckled her, drawing desire from deep within her, just as his kisses had previously called forth her fears. Unlike her vanishing fear, however, the desire brought to the surface blossomed and grew, pushing her to both take more from him and give more to him. His lips and tongue petitioned her with silent invocations, and she answered with a demanding arch of her back and thrust of her breast against his mouth. His hands slid to the small of her back, then lowered to cup her bottom from behind. He pulled her flush to him, and she gasped at the feel of his hardness pressed to her bare skin.

Her hands streamed down his body from his shoulders to his waist and lower still to either side of his hips, and she felt the hard muscles contract and stretch under her fingers. She lifted her legs and wrapped them around his hips again, opening herself to him. Her desire pooled low in her body and transformed itself into an ache that was almost painful in its yearning for more. She squirmed against him, trying to maximize the contact of her body with his.

"Dallas..."

"Shhh. Not yet, love." He loosened the grip of her legs and pushed her higher up on the bed, still holding her thighs apart. She saw his head lower and felt his tongue on her inner thigh. The jolt of pleasure invoked an involuntary spasm, but his hands on her held her still. He licked the sensitive skin, his mouth unhurried in its journey upward to the juncture of her thighs. Her craving clawed at her with every touch of his lips and tongue, and she writhed with the want, but he held her fast and tarried even more in his voyage. When his mouth reached its destination at last and greeted its host with long strokes of his tongue, she could stand no more. The wet fire lapping at her most sensitive spot set off more convulsions, and her hands tugged at his hair.

"Dallas, please..."

He lifted his head and pulled her back down to him. Holding her top leg, he readied himself, pausing long enough to torment her one last time with waiting. Then, just as she thought she would go mad, he was one with her, a completion, but also the beginning of another journey. He started slowly and deliberately, so that she felt every inch of him stroke every part of her, filling her with a wonder that two beings so completely different could be in such harmony with each other. His speed gradually quickened, though, and every deep thrust tightened the coil of desire inside her until individual sensations melted together in a plea for release. Her fingers dug into him, she heard the sound of his name and felt his response in the increasing speed and hardness of his thrusts. They assailed her body, destroying the last vestiges of her control. She let go, and he slowed his rhythm, only to begin the journey anew after a moment.

Images unlike any she had ever seen before flashed before her mind's eye. The silver of day and the black of night strobed around her, faster and faster until, like a pinwheel, the contrast blurred together into a single shade of gray. Night held no darkness, day held no blinding light, and strangely, she was at peace. He drove her to the ragged edge of control again, and this time when her release came, she felt his as well, a final deep plunge followed by a shudder that shook his entire body.

It was over. He was very still, except for his hard breathing, which didn't seem to ease. He had climaxed, there was no doubt about that, and yet his breath came in labored gasps, as though he were still aroused. Either that, or he was going to have a heart attack. *Great. The best sex of my life, and he up and dies on me.*

He continued to hold her, but the dark web of his tangled hair hid his features. She would give anything to know what he was feeling. Maybe he wasn't real. It had certainly been too good to be true. She continued to stroke the hard muscles of his back, just to remind herself that he was not a dream.

"Who are you? What are you?" She breathed the words, softer than a whisper, not really intending them for him.

But he heard. He raised his head, and when she brushed the long hair out of his face, his eyes were hooded. His parted lips were drawn back, neither in a smile nor a grimace, but in a pained satisfaction, almost like a runner who had won a race, but had totally spent himself in the effort. For the first time she noticed his teeth. They were very even and very white, and the eyeteeth seemed to be abnormally long and sharp.

"I'm your fantasy," he hissed, his low voice making the words sizzle like lava sliding over rocks.

She laughed. He had been that, no doubt.

He swept her hair away from her until it fanned the pillow beside her, and he stroked her face with the back of his hand, his touch still as soft and hot as wind-blown ash from a stoked fire. His eyes dropped from her face and focused lower, and he gently pressed his mouth to the hollow at the base of her neck.

"Your final fantasy." His lips pressed a line of soft kisses all along her collarbone. "I'm every storm you've ever seen on the horizon."

She laughed again, but it was a smaller sound. She felt his teeth strafe the length of her neck, and her heart seemed to pound from within her throat.

"I'm every moonless night you've ever lost your way in. I'm every fever you've ever burned with."

She was silent now, mesmerized by the words and the feel of his tongue over her pulse point.

Suddenly he was off the bed with a hoarse sound like the flame on a candle guttering. "I'm every evil your father ever preached. Now sleep."

Tia tried to rise from the bed as well, but fell back as if she had been totally consumed, too depleted to wonder about any of the strange words, save his first. *I'm your fantasy,* he had said, and she had laughed at the tease.

Her final thought before she fell into a deep sleep was that Dallas Allgate never teased.

EIGHT

Tia snuggled down into the nest of satin petals, then, a moment later, stretched languidly like a cat, arching her back, pointing her toes, and rubbing her cheek against the scented velvet blooms beneath it. Floating just below the surface of consciousness, she had never felt better in her life. She was warm, safe, and swimming in the biggest bed of roses in the universe. She wanted to stay there forever, drifting with the suspended flowers, caressing the soft current, sealed away from all of reality's noise, violence, and cold. But her stomach rumbled, a shaft of red light touched her face, and she bobbed into wakefulness.

In point of fact the antique bed was overly soft, the kind that produced morning backaches without fail, but even so, Tia was loathe to leave it. Even without Dallas' solid length beside her, she thought that there was no sweeter sensation than burying herself in the twisted sheets and inhaling their warm, musky scent.

But as the sunlight probed the quiet room with greater force, the harsh realities of her situation prodded her one by one, and reluctantly she sat up and looked around. There was no sign of Dallas. Why was she not surprised?

She dressed and padded softly to the kitchen area, following the aroma of scents too numerous to ignore. She found Gillie, who informed her that Dallas had left early in the morning, before the sun had come up. He hadn't wanted to wake her, Gillie said, and left the message that business would tie him up for most of the day. Gillie also passed along an entreaty from Dallas for her to wait at Rose Hill for his return, with an emphasis on the danger that existed outside the townhouse walls. Tia had no need or desire to debate with Gillie on that point. She had enough unfinished business to discuss with Dallas to ensure her adherence to his request. In the meantime she would take full advantage of Gillie's wonderful cooking.

The basement intercom buzzed as insistently as an alarm clock. Dallas was slow to wake, and even slower to answer. Yesterday's interrupted sleep and voyage into the light had depleted him to the point where a second day of only partial sleep was not nearly enough to regenerate his strength. Only the thought that something had happened to Tia or that St. James was getting into some new bother prompted Dallas to answer.

"Yes, Gillie? Is it Tia?" Perhaps it had sunk into her exactly what she had done last night. He wouldn't be surprised if Gillie told him she was winging her way northward even as they spoke.

"No, Sir, she's fine. She's upstairs, resting I believe."

"St. James, then."

"No, you have another visitor. Someone I think you should see."

Dallas' enervation shredded his patience. "I'm not a mind reader, Gillie. Who is it?"

"Alek Dragovich."

He had to have heard wrong. The lack of sleep was playing havoc with his senses.

"Who, Gillie?"

Gillie's patience didn't seem to be in abundance, either. "Al-ek Dra-go-vich. He's from the Brotherhood." The emphasis Gillie placed on the word "Brotherhood" was unnecessary. Dallas knew exactly whom Gillie meant.

Drago. But it was impossible. "Gillie, so help me, if this is a game, you won't live to see another sunrise."

"Believe me, Sir, this is no game. Shall I put the, ah, gentleman himself on the line?"

Dallas sighed. "No. Tell him I'll be right up. Oh, and Gillie..."

"Yes, Sir?"

"Make sure Tia stays put. It wouldn't do for her to see our visitor."

"No, I suppose not." The dryness in Gillie's voice blew through the intercom.

Drago. Every Undead creation in the world knew Drago. The unlucky ones had met him in person. The lucky knew him by reputation only. Gillie was wrong about one thing, though. Drago wasn't from the Brotherhood. The Brotherhood was local. They, as well as the Circle and the *Coterie*, employed enforcers to resolve problems among the Undead. Drago was *l'enforcier*, and reported personally to the Directorate in Paris. There were fewer than a dozen vampires in the world more powerful, in both standing and ability, than the creature waiting for him in the upstairs parlor. There were fewer still more hated. It was said that Drago relished imposing harsh sanctions as though they were nothing more than spoonfuls of medicine. Dallas had never met *l'enforcier*, but was no exception in his feelings of loathing. To Dallas, who had personally suffered long and hard at the hands of so-called "Justice," Drago was but one more enemy in the world.

Dallas wasted no time in dressing. As soon as he exited his cellar sanctuary he could feel the presence of one of the Old Ones in the house, and by the time he reached the first floor, he could feel the creature's power in the air, as tangible as an ion-charged atmosphere following a thunderstorm. Ironically, Dallas could detect very little scent. Drago was so old that he carried the slight musty odor of an unused attic, nothing more. A far cry from the suffocating stink of one such as Conner Flynne.

Alek Dragovich arose like smoke from his chair upon Dallas' entrance, a move of such boneless elegance as to make the movements of young vampires like St. James and even himself look clumsy by comparison. Drago wore black silk trousers that draped with a fluidity that matched his grace, and a white, long-sleeved shirt of the finest lawn that fastened at the neck with a sapphire collar pin. The creature was tall for one so old, about Dallas' own height, and his appearance was relatively young, like that of himself—a man in his mid-thirties. But there the resemblance ended. Drago was leaner in build than Dallas and had long black hair tied at the nape of his neck. His smooth face was long and aristocratic, but the focal point of his being, as with all vampires, was his eyes. Yet Drago's were unique. Black brows tented hooded eyes of the clearest blue Dallas had ever seen on a human or vampire. Neither a pale sky blue nor a dark midnight blue, they were electric bright, like the finest London blue topaz. Color aside, they were empty, save for a pinch of boredom and a dash of arrogance.

"Alek Dragovich. You know who I am?"

Make that two dashes of arrogance. "I know. You're from the Directorate. You're *l' enforcier.*"

"Excellent. One explanation saved. Call me Drago, then. Everyone does."

"I expected an enforcer. Not *l' enforcier.*"

"Yes, of course. Normally, for a squabble such as this one, you'd be right. But I've had my eye on you for some time, Dallas Allgate."

"I've broken no laws, save human ones. I've directed no violence toward my own kind. What happened yesterday was self-defense."

"Don't have the audacity to try to explain to me what happened yesterday, *monsieur.* I know exactly what happened, and why. The reason I've been watching you is precisely because you've broken none of our laws. Good enforcers are needed all over the world. You're young yet, but promising. Some day you may be chosen. I'm here to make sure that what happens between you and St. James is not a stumbling block on that path."

"I have no desire to be part of the Brotherhood in any shape or form."

The neon eyes seemed to bore straight through Dallas. The gaze told Dallas that not showing fear of *l' enforcier* was one thing, but that showing too much disrespect was another thing altogether. "As I said, you're young." The words were drawn out as slowly and softly as a kiss...or a threat.

Dallas got the message. Now was not the time or place to debate his future with the Anti-God of the Undead. "What are you going to do about what happened yesterday? St. James has a Vampire Hunter."

"I'm not going to do anything. Yet. And I know about the Death's-head."

"It's illegal."

Nothing in Drago's piercing stare changed, but Dallas knew nonetheless that he had committed another *faux pas*. Of course Drago knew that it was illegal for a vampire to possess a Vampire Hunter.

Drago let it pass. "I will be meeting with St. James shortly. He'll be divested of the weapon, rest assured. He'll also be warned to stay away from you. I give you the same warning. If he's foolish enough to ignore my admonitions, he'll be investigated and punished accordingly. If he survives, that is."

"But if I should need help against him, I'm on my own, aren't I? You won't help."

The Ceylon sapphire at Drago's throat flashed like a third blue eye. "For one who never apprenticed, you manage to grasp the fine points. No, I won't help you. Or St. James. I am forbidden to lend aid in support of one of our kind over another. All I can do is take away the advantage he has of the Death's-head."

"And if I prevail, will I be punished?" Any satisfaction derived from killing St. James would be short-lived indeed if all Drago was going to do was finish the job St. James started.

"I'll be required to investigate. That's all I can promise right now. But this I can tell you. I may indeed be the Black Death, but, like the plague, I'm unprejudiced in those I touch. I perform my job objectively according to the laws set down by the Directorate. Nothing more."

As unprejudiced as the plague. That was supposed to be a comfort? Dallas studied Drago's features with care, expecting some small sign of self-deprecation at such arrogance, but there was no emotion in the antifreeze eyes. "I can ask no more than impartiality in the Black Death," Dallas replied with a dryness he couldn't keep from his voice.

"*C'est bien!* Then we understand each other."

Drago paused, and something finally flickered in the blue gaze. "One more thing, Allgate. You have a human female in the house. I saw her in the window when I came up the drive."

It was pointless to deny it. "Yes."

"The female involved in the scuffle in the boneyard?"

Only a cop, even a vampire cop, could reduce yesterday's life-and-death struggle to a "scuffle." *Objective?* Drago's attitude seemed to lean more towards disinterest than objectivity.

"Yes," Dallas ground out.

One of Drago's arched brows shifted its angle just a little. "'To the victor goes the spoils'?"

"I'm sure St. James would have considered her as such. I don't."

"Ah."

Drago said nothing more for a long moment, but Dallas felt the judgment of his eyes.

"You surprise me, Allgate. I'm not often surprised. I can't tell you what to do or what not to do with humans. But, a piece of advice from one who has survived the trials of a dozen lifetimes. Ours is a lonely existence. Most of our kind, in the cynicism of their years, would tell you that an *affaire de coeur* between a human and one of us can only result in a *chagrin d'amour.* Perhaps so, but don't avoid affairs of the heart. Such afflictions make Eternity bearable. Nothing else does. Certainly not revenge."

With that, Drago rose and, with a bow of his head, took his leave.

Dallas sat for a very long time before he descended to the cellar to finish his sleep. Had a five-hundred-year-old bloodsucker just advocated love with a human? Dallas didn't know what shocked him more—that, or the fact that he actually found himself almost liking the most hated brute creation on Earth.

***

Tia woke up when she heard the car come up the drive. Even though a day had passed and nothing had been on the news about a dead body showing up in the cemetery before its time, she was still afraid the cops were going to show up. And if St. James was still alive, she was just as afraid he'd come around to pick up where he left off. With everything that had happened in the past few days, nothing more could surprise her.

She was wrong. Tia blinked at the vision that exited the burgundy luxury car with the fluid grace of a gymnast. The man looked like the black sheep of the St. James family. Though not quite as outrageously dressed as St. James himself, the man's attire was more than a little over the top for Natchez on a Thursday afternoon. The man had long, jet-black hair and a face that had a world-weary, bad-boy cast to it that either spoiled or enlivened his patrician features, depending on how you looked at it. Didn't Dallas have any normal acquaintances?

The black-haired man, as if knowing she was peering through the window, looked up at her with a haughty lift of one brow, never breaking his stride. Tia decided the dispassionate look definitely corrupted any natural good looks the man had.

She wondered if Dallas was home to receive a visitor. After an excellent southern breakfast and a very thorough tour of the house, she had laid back down for a nap when the visitor's arrival had awakened her. Had Dallas come home while she had been sleeping?

She was tempted to leave her room and listen for voices when a diplomatic knock sounded at the door. She sighed. It had to be Gillie. She pulled the door open. It was.

"Mr. Allgate has a rather important visitor downstairs. He asks that you respect their, ah, privacy."

Another mystery. Great. "And what did you think I was going to do, Gillie? Listen at a keyhole?"

The brow the old man quietly lifted told her he wouldn't put it past her.

She decided to change the subject. "Do you think Dallas will be free after his meeting? I've been waiting all day to talk to him."

"Perhaps. I can't say for sure."

She frowned at Gillie. "Excuse me for asking this, but does any of this seem strange to you?"

"Strange, miss?" Gillie's face was all innocence.

"Yeah. Hiding women upstairs. Strange visitors. People who want to kill him. You know, that kind of thing."

"Hmmm. Yes, well, I have to admit this week has been more eventful than usual. Still and all, life with Mr. Allgate is never, ah, boring. And, in spite of what you may think, the man is worth it."

Tia pounced. "Gillie, would you answer some questions for me? There's so much he hasn't told me."

"I'm sorry, Miss Tia. He lives a very private life. For me to divulge any, ah, confidences, would be highly improper. Can I bring you anything while you wait?"

It was as neat a blow-off as any Tia had ever heard, or had ever come up with herself. "No, thanks, Gillie." She couldn't help smiling in appreciation.

Gillie smiled back, a small fox smile with just a hint of teeth showing.

Tia sat by the window and fidgeted for fifteen minutes, wishing she had asked Gillie for a drink to help pass the time. Finally she saw Dallas' visitor take his leave down the steps to the driveway below. Turning his head, his gaze shot up at her, and he winked. If a man could duplicate a Mona Lisa smile, this one could. And did. She wanted to throw something out the window at him.

How could he? Dallas had obviously said something to the man about last night's liaison. For a man so private with his own affairs, he was free and easy enough with her reputation. Well, one more thing to add to her list of subjects to be discussed. When Gillie came up and informed her that Dallas wouldn't be available to her until eight in the evening, her patience detonated in an explosion of pointed words at Gillie.

"Does he think the sun rises and sets with him? I've been sitting here all day waiting for him, doing absolutely nothing. Does he know that?"

"Yes, Miss Tia, he's well aware that you've been waiting

for him. It's for your safety he asked you to stay here. If you're tired of this room, you're free now to enjoy the rest of the house. Perhaps you'd like to try the library? Something there might interest you."

Gillie had already shown her the room, but she hadn't looked closely at the books. She wasn't a big reader, but maybe she could find something on Natchez, Rose Hill, or the Allgate family history. And as long as she had Gillie's blessing to be in the room, she couldn't be accused of prying. She descended to the small first-floor room at the rear of the house and studied the titles in the shelves built into the walls.

Her eyes landed on a small, leather-bound book on the end of one shelf. The book looked to be well worn as well as old. Something this worn had to be important. She carefully drew the book out and undid the ties holding the book closed. The book was in poor shape, with many of the pages torn or come loose from the binding, and she was as cautious as she could be in handling it. First she thought it might be some collector's item, worth a lot of money, but she quickly saw that it was a diary of sorts. Much of the handwriting was faded and illegible, but there were some passages she could make out.

26th January, 1788

After two days of making advances to every cove and bay on the coast, the Captain found one to his liking, a fine big cove just waiting to wrap her arms around all us lucky bastards. The lads are all as excited as green boys at a two-penny hop.

The book had her full attention now. 1788! She made herself comfortable in the massive green leather wing chair, and turned on the brass floor lamp that hooked its head, like a curious onlooker, over the back of the chair.

7th February

We are all ashore now. I reckon the Captain was waiting for the cattle and women to land, for he threw a great party today. He read a fine speech to the lads about how grand the prospect is which 'lies before a youthful nation.' The lads are just happy they can now keep the bad food down without the sea heaving it up again on them. The Captain is naming this place Sydney, after his Lordship back home.

Sydney. The only Sydney she knew was in Australia. Could it be?

10th June

Winter beats at us with yet another day of rain. The huts have flooded and a goodly number of the lads have the scurvy. The Captain is taking the fittest of us inland tomorrow to search for ground that won't kill a planting.

19th March, 1790

Wonderful news! The lads haven't been in such high spirits since the two marines were hung last year for stealing food. A grand dame of a ship, the Lady Juliana, landed today with over two hundred more convicts, all women! It'll mean more mouths to feed with nonexistent food, but I don't think that'll be on the mind of a single lad. It certainly won't be on my mind.

Tia couldn't help smiling. Men hadn't changed much in over two hundred years, had they?

5th June

The Second Fleet landed today. More convicts, as many as arrived when we did. I fear we paved the way with our blood and sweat for them, the lucky bastards. Our marines are leaving! One hundred men arrived to take their place, calling themselves the New South Wales Corps. But soldiers are soldiers. There will be a way to manipulate them.

3rd December, 1792

There's talk among the Corps that the Captain is leaving. John tries to deny it, but he smiles too much when he does. He knows something.

23rd March, 1801

Governor King finally got his wish. John is being sent back to England to face court martial. Who would have thought after all this time that John would be brought down because of something so foolish as a duel? Can it be that all my plans have come to naught? Sabra doesn't know yet. Without John's sponsorship, I fear for us. If we are separated, it will do to me what no other hardship on this land has done. I don't know how I'll go on.

She reread the passages she had been able to make out and desperately wished she could decipher the rest. It was like plugging into someone's thought stream, the people and events all happening in the present moment. She wondered who they all were—John, Sabra, but most of all, the author. She looked at the cover and inside the cover, but there was no inscription or dedication. Could the diary have belonged to one of Dallas' ancestors? It seemed likely. Why else would he have the book?

Keeping one eye on the diary and the other on the time, she returned the book to its resting place on the bookshelf prior to eight o'clock. It was a heavenly evening, and Tia would have preferred to wait on the veranda, but with nasty characters like St. James lurking about, she felt it more prudent to sit inside.

She had intended to wait in the parlor, but the furnishings in the library, though somber, were comfortable. It was a dark, masculine room, seemingly imbued with Dallas' very personality. There was a small fireplace with a black marble mantel, and the wooden shelves built into the walls were ornately hand carved with designs of leaves, vines, and grape clusters. A large brass chandelier, dark with the tarnish of age, hung over the center of the room, and radiated more gloom than light. No crystal dripped from the fixture, but rather the brass branches were like those of trees, hiding tiny predators of the forest, both animal and human. Detailed fox, hounds, horses, and hunters, all wrought in brass, twined up and down the arms of the chandelier in an endless foxhunt.

A large print framed in dark wood hung on the wall opposite the bookshelves. Tia stepped closer to take a better look at it. It depicted dispirited Native Americans—some on horseback, some in covered wagons, and some on foot—being herded by bluecoated U.S. soldiers.

As usual, Tia wasn't aware of Dallas' presence until he was standing at her shoulder, his mouth inches from her ear.

"Quite a compelling scene, isn't it?"

Hardly the sentimental greeting she might expect after a

night like they had shared, but she wasn't surprised. Even so, the timbre of his voice, as well as his very presence, made her want to jump. She forced herself to stand still when the magnetism of his body ate over her in tiny bites and chewed holes in her resolve. She tried to remember she was still mad at him for discussing her with his black-haired visitor.

She addressed the painting to fortify her will. "Yes. The 'Trail of Tears.'" She paused, studying the picture. The faces were haunting. "It's like a glimpse into the mirror of time."

Dallas moved in front of her so that she couldn't help but see his eyes. A strange light treaded the green depths. "What did you say?"

"Art. Art is a reflection of the world. So is photography. Not an exact reproduction of life, but..."

"...but the unique image burned into the artist's soul." There was surprise in his voice, and a little wonder. Wonder of her, or of the painting on the wall?

She cocked her head at the painting. "The artist, yes. But I think even more unique is the vision seen by each person who gazes upon the art itself."

"How did you know it's the 'Trail of Tears'? Did Gillie tell you?" Amazement still altered the pitch of his voice.

"No. I haven't just been a cop my whole life. I've always been interested in art."

"Yes, but this specific painting...you know it." The look he gave her made her forget the anger she had harbored all day. The light that swam in his wider-than-usual eyes could be interpreted as awe, but awe was a deceptive thing. The same look could communicate respect, reverence, or fear. She doubted he feared anything she could spring on him, but she didn't know him well enough to discern if he was merely amazed that she was more than a pushy ex-cop, or if a genuine regard for her was growing.

"Yeah, I know it," she answered softly. Her appreciation for art, especially early American art, was another thing that Bret hadn't been interested in. But this man, for all his reticence and mysterious ways, saw her in ways Bret hadn't in the nearly two years they had been together. She briefly wondered if the surprise on her face was as apparent as that in Dallas' eyes. Her gaze touched the painting again. "The, uh, policy in the 1800s of Indian removal from their homeland in the Southeast to Oklahoma, if I remember the history. Hundreds died on the journey."

"Thousands, actually. The human predicament doesn't seem to change, does it? Man's journey is customarily death. As you know too well, don't you, Tia?"

She turned back to him and nodded, soaking in his appearance as she did. He was impeccably garbed, as usual, this time in taupe silk trousers and an ivory shirt. He was clean-shaven and neatly groomed, and Tia wondered if the untamed creature that had all but consumed her last night had been a dream after all.

"You waited for me," he whispered, as if reading her mind.

"You really thought I'd leave? You don't have much faith in your abilities, do you?"

His brows crept up his forehead just a little. "Oh, I have every faith."

The look fanned anger which had cooled during the discussion of the painting. "And here I am, right? Affirmation of that faith. Well, the truth is that I'd like to get some answers before I go. We didn't get much of a chance to talk last night."

"As you wish. The night is yours. Have you eaten?"

She nodded. "Gillie said I shouldn't wait for you. Dallas, can we get out of here? Maybe go down to the river to talk? Your house is beautiful, but I've been cooped up all day. If I don't get some air I'll go crazy."

"Certainly."

"You're not afraid of St. James?"

He smiled, a genuine grin that reached his eyes and popped the long smile line into place. "With you as my bodyguard? Never."

Damn the man. It was hard to stay mad at him when he looked at her like that. She ran upstairs for her purse. By the time she returned to the back door, Dallas had sunglasses on, and Gillie had the Lincoln out of the garage.

"We'll be Under-the-Hill, Gillie. If anything happens..."

"Yes, yes, I know. I'll call you if you're needed."

Dallas drove down to Silver Street, but the parking spaces on the street were all taken. He snaked the big car past the concrete wall with "Welcome to Natchez" painted in blue letters and down the steep drive to the parking lot right on the river. They exited the car, and while Tia lamented the loss of the air-conditioning, the worst heat of the day was past.

Dallas adjusted his sunglasses and shaded his eyes with one hand. "Do you want to sit in the tavern up on the street? This is the off-season, so there shouldn't be many people in there," he asked.

"No, if you don't mind, this is fine right here by the water. It's beautiful."

The view of the sunset over the river was indeed that. The horizon over the Louisiana shore was a wash of lemon that blended in a flawless gradient to crystal blue. The color of the Mississippi was a faithful mirror image of the sky color, but the gentle movement of the water spoiled the perfect reproduction, creating instead a living marble of blue and gold. The bridge to Vidalia was scalloped lace silhouetted against the backdrop of color. They sat on the rocks at the river's edge, near each other but not touching. She had been so close to this man last night, as close as two people could possibly be. Why was she afraid to so much as touch him now?

"Dallas, who was the man who came to visit you this afternoon?"

"Just a...business associate. Why?"

"Well, he had the same sort of look about him as St. James. I just wanted to know if I should shoot him if I happen to meet him in a cemetery."

Dallas laughed, and the smile line appeared as if by magic. "His name is Alek. He's hardly what I'd call a friend, but he's no friend of St. James, either. I don't think you'll be seeing him again, but if you do, please don't shoot him. He has...connections in high places."

"You told him about me." She put as much accusation into the words as she could.

Dallas looked at her, but with the glasses he wore, she

couldn't see his eyes. "What are you talking about?"

"When he left the house I was watching. He looked up at me and gave me a wink that would have a hooker blushing. I don't mind the wink. What I mind is what you told him to evoke that wink."

Dallas laughed again, and the rich sound was so engaging she was ready to forgive him without an explanation.

"What makes you think I told him anything? He's a lecherous old bastard, and you're a beautiful woman. End of story."

He really thought she was beautiful? It was a lovely thought, but this was not the time to let flattery distract her. "He didn't look old to me." She pouted for the briefest moment. "So you didn't say anything about me?"

He took the glasses off so she could see his eyes. Like the mirror of the river, they were alive with liquid gold. "Alek is older than he looks. And no, love, I didn't tell him about you."

Love. Another distraction. Did he have any idea what he was doing to her? His eyes were innocent enough, and he didn't seem to be dodging her questions. But she had managed too many glimpses of the dark core beneath his urbane veneer to believe that his endearments were to be taken seriously. But whether his comments were artifice or all sincerity, the parts of her body he had so aroused last night responded to the distractions. She took a deep breath to try to douse the coil of heat his words lit inside her.

On to the next item on her checklist. "Tell me about St. James. Who is he? Why did he want to kill you?"

"He's just a nasty piece of work. Revenge. That's all. I ruined his family a long time ago, and now he wants me to pay for his suffering."

She rounded her eyes. "What did you do to him?"

"He lost his peerage because of me."

"His what?"

"Peerage. His title of nobility. If not for me, he'd be an earl, Lord St. James."

"You're kidding."

He looked at her. "No."

"Where is he from?"

"Great Britain. Have you ever been there?"

She shook her head.

"They take such things very seriously over there."

"Is that where you're from, too?"

"I was born in England. London, in fact. But I've lived all over the world."

"I wondered about your accent. I couldn't tell if it was British, Southern, or even Australian, dumb as that sounds."

"Not dumb. Very astute. I lived in New South Wales for a time."

New South Wales. The diary came instantly to mind. She still wanted to know more about St. James, though.

"What did you do to make him lose his title? And why?"

Dallas gazed back out over the water. Her eyes followed his to where the reflection of the dying sun replaced the molten gold with a sheen of coppery red, like a slick of blood covering the water. "It's a very long and complicated story."

"May I remind you that you said you were mine for the night? I don't plan on going anywhere. That is, except with you."

He turned toward her, and any pretense at Southern gentility fell in the look he gave her. The twilight imbued his pale skin a healthy glow, but it was the dark light in his eyes that ignited every burner inside her. This time her willpower had to work overtime to quench the thirsty flames threatening to consume her plan of questions and discovery.

"I warn you. It's rather a fantastic story."

She smiled. Would she expect anything else? "No ghosts?"

"Sorry, no ghosts. Still, I don't think you'll be bored."

"Oh, I don't think there's any danger of that."

He turned and looked again upon the river, and her gaze, as before, trailed his. Watching the swirling current was like looking back into time.

"A long time ago a man named Christian St. James put me in jail for something I didn't do. I was only twenty at the time and very naive, but the one thing I knew how to do was survive. Something I expect you know how to do as well."

He glanced at her, but she only smiled, not wanting to interrupt.

"I was accused of robbery and of trying to kill Christian. I was there, but I didn't have anything to do with what happened to St. James. But he had connections, and I didn't. Christian's father was Edward St. James, Earl of Coventry. Christian was first-born, so he was heir to the title."

Tia gave a small shrug. "Maybe his accusation was an honest mistake. It happens."

Dallas shook his head. "No. He had no real proof, but he wanted to blame someone. I was a commoner, and I was there. That's all that mattered to him. If you had seen his face in the courtroom... No, it was a mistake, but not an honest one. Christian St. James never drew an honest breath in his life."

"Is this Christian related to the St. James who tried to kill you? What did you say his name was?"

"Jermyn. Yes, Christian was Jermyn's father."

He had been right. The story was fantastic. Tia tried to study Dallas' face and body language—a habit she had acquired long ago while interrogating suspects—but Dallas gave nothing away. She caught a fleeting muscle twitch in his cheek, but his hands and body were as still as the dead. She had taken the story of Veilina and Rowan with a grain of salt. A whole shaker full, in fact. But that was just a legend. Dallas was telling this story as if it were fact. Yet he displayed none of the signs that people typically did when they lied. There was no nervous leg crossing, no picking of invisible lint from his trousers, no extraneous hand gestures.

Unless he was the best liar she had ever met, Dallas believed this story of noblemen conspiring to put him in jail. She knew Dallas was eccentric, but did it go deeper than that? Did he suffer from a kind of delusion she knew nothing about? As a cop she had always tried so hard to hang on to her sanity in the face of violence and tragedy that she had scorned those less fortunate who weren't able to grip reality as hard as she had. Had she fallen for a madman?

He glanced at her again, then continued. "I served my sentence and survived to live again, but I also survived for revenge. It's not something I'm proud of, but I don't know that I'd do anything different if I had the chance to do things over. I wanted Christian to suffer the way I had, but I didn't want to use violence. It was tempting, but it would have been too easy for both him and me. I wanted his torment to stay with him for a long, long time."

He turned to her, and this time his eyes met hers for more than a glance. "I can see those cop eyes of yours judging me already. Have I horrified you that much?"

She didn't know what to say. Afraid to say what she really thought, she looked away. "I'm not a cop anymore. Even if I was, I don't judge people."

"Yes, you do. It's all right, Tia. I confess to the same failing, and many more."

Still not knowing what to say, she threw out a question instead. "So what did you do to Christian to ruin him?"

"I bided my time, doing research into the St. James family. I examined parish records, spoke to everyone I could find who had anything to do with the family or the estate. Looking for skeletons in the closet is what I guess you'd call it. It took a long time, but I finally found what I was looking for. I ended up going back one generation, actually, to Christian's father, Edward. Edward was a widower. His young first wife, Eliza, died in childbirth. Wanting an heir, Edward married again, to a young woman named Anne. Anne did bear him a son, Christian. What I found out was that Eliza and Anne were sisters. Not a legal marriage under English law. A widower can't marry his deceased wife's sister. Anyway, it invalidated the marriage, and Christian, no longer being the legal first-born heir, lost the title he had ascended to when Edward died. And since Christian was no longer earl, that meant his son, Jermyn, also had no claim to the title."

Tia tried to digest the strange story. "So, what happened yesterday is all because Jermyn blames you for the loss of the title."

His eyes were steady on hers. "Yes."

"He's trying to do to you what you did to his father."

The eyes didn't waver, but had darkened with the setting

of the sun. "Yes."

"How can you blame him for that?"

"I don't blame him. I just don't want him to succeed."

"What was that weapon he had? I've never seen anything like it. It wasn't a knife—it didn't have a blade. More like a short lance."

"An antique. I've seen such weapons in England. The wooden shaft was probably either ash or hawthorn with a silver core."

"But why? Why a weapon like that? If he wants you dead, why not just shoot you? It's a tried-and-true procedure."

He didn't even smile at her attempt at a joke, and his eyes shifted away before he answered, the first hint Tia had that Dallas was telling less than the truth.

"I don't know. Most likely it belonged to his father, and St. James sees a kind of irony in killing me with something that Christian owned."

Tia was quiet for a moment while she debated on what to say next. It ran against her nature to willingly accept a lie, even an outwardly unimportant one like this. But cops never suffered lies, ever. The habit, even after two years, was hard to break. And if there was going to be anything lasting between them, she couldn't let this one slide.

She floated her gaze over the river, the water now as dark as his eyes. The sky had grayed, and only a soft pink glow hugging the horizon remained as evidence of the glorious sunset.

"Dallas, why are you lying to me?"

NINE

Dallas put one arm around her to draw her closer to him and focus her attention away from the view and back on his eyes. Her defenses were formidable. There was her persistent, quick mind, and her partial resistance to his power. And he couldn't forget she was an ex-cop. There had been a whole lot in his two centuries of existence that had violated the laws of man. As sanitized as his story had been, she was seeing too much of him.

He gauged her eyes, and the emotions that slid behind them. The opposition was there. He didn't want to lose her, but neither did he want to make the mistake of assuming she was no longer a danger to him. Her awareness was much too great. He had seen it earlier in the library, and he saw it now. It was the thread that bound them together, that made him want her in ways he hadn't wanted a mortal female in decades. It was the attraction, but like a lure, it was also the danger. If she saw too much of him...

Snagging her hair with one finger, he brought her face to his. But short of his kiss, she pulled back.

"You didn't answer my question. You couldn't look at me. I know when someone's not being honest with me."

"Then look at me now. Everything I told you was the truth. I know it's a bizarre story, but it happened." He tamed his every passion that threatened to spring, sealed his will behind glass eyes, and concealed his intentions behind the seductive words. He compelled her to free her own desires in the looking glass he set before her. Discovering someone else's emotions was like cracking the safe behind which they hid every strength. Discover someone's hungers and hopes, and you've unlocked the doorways to their will. He could come and go as he pleased, as often as he wanted, and he would be safe.

"Accept the truth, Tia."

She hesitated, and he kissed her, soft and deep. He released her only when the totality of his senses told him that her blood ran hot and fast, just the right temperature for that side of the vampire that deceived and seduced—the serpent. The stories were never dangerous, if told correctly. She was almost ready. The vampire continued. She would accept and believe. The serpent, after all, never lied.

She blinked and drew a long, shaky breath, taking a moment to compose herself. He let her. Finally she threw him a sideways glance that told him she was ready for him to continue.

"I think I'm safer with the stories than with you. So go on. You hadn't heard from this St. James before? He just shows up now?"

"No, I hadn't heard from him before. He found me through Marty Macklin, a private investigator."

"You know who killed Macklin, don't you."

"I have a pretty good idea."

"You should talk to the police."

"You were a cop. You really think the police would want to hear what I've told you?"

"Good point. But surely you're safe from St. James now. Even if you didn't kill him, he's probably laid up somewhere. You had to have injured him pretty badly."

"I would hate to bet my safety on that assumption. Besides, there's always Conner."

"Conner?"

"Conner Flynne. St. James' traveling companion."

"The dark, thin man who was with St. James at the inn?"

"Ah, so you were spying on me."

Tia shrugged. "I'm an ex-cop and a photographer. I guess that makes me even more nosy than your average female."

And it's going to get you dead, Tia, if you're not careful. As if she could almost feel his thoughts, she visibly shivered. He raised his head, and the stink of a very young vampire wafted on the evening breeze. *Speak of the devil.*

"Come on, let's go. Flynne doesn't have St. James' resolve, but even so, I don't want to take him for granted. We'll be safer at the inn." Dallas had no doubt that St. James was keeping a very close eye on both him and Tia through Flynne.

He was on his feet and reached down to help Tia to hers. He could see her eyes scanning the shoreline on either side of them as well as the parking lot. Had she somehow sensed Flynne as well? Perhaps her extraordinary awareness was not just for him. A prick of jealousy bit at him like a stinging insect. It was the same feeling he had experienced when he found out that Tia had gone with St. James to the cemetery. Just as quickly, though, he slapped the feeling away. Jealousy and envy were not normal afflictions of the Undead. They were human emotions, and base ones at that, suited only to fools.

The thought made him rough with Tia, and he realized he was tugging on her arm too hard. He jerked her off balance, and her foot slipped on the gravel. He didn't let her go, but instead pulled her into his arms. She didn't fight him.

"You're safe with me, Tia. Believe that," he whispered against her hair.

"I do."

"Good girl." More and more he was realizing that the key to breaching Tia's fortress was the promise of safety. He pressed a kiss against the warmth of her forehead, but instead of releasing her right away, his mouth lingered on her skin. His control interceded. "Let's get out of here."

They hurried back to the Lincoln, and Dallas tuned his senses away from Tia to the falling curtain of night around them. A scent was not always a precise sensation to gauge. The air currents played with it, tossing it about until it was nearly impossible to pinpoint. Dallas doubted that Flynne was in the small parking lot. More likely he was up above on Silver Street in one of the parked cars or buildings there.

Even inside the Lincoln, there was no relaxation for Dallas. His eyes were everywhere.

"Dallas, what is it? Did you see Flynne?"

"No, but he's nearby, I'm sure of it."

"Will we be safe at the inn? I know it's a public place, but would your townhouse be better?"

"Conner would be daft to try anything at the inn. He's a fool, but not that great a one."

They arrived at Bishop's Inn moments later, and Dallas parked in his private space behind the building. As soon as he got out of the car Dallas knew something was wrong. The faint, lingering odor of the Undead still hung in the air, but it was more than that. Dallas had no real communication with Veilina, and yet the signs of an agitated spirit were hard to miss. A second floor shutter banged incessantly, and the patio was empty of patrons in spite of the beautiful evening. They went in through the rear entrance, Dallas keeping a protective hand on Tia's arm, and stopped at the bar.

"How's it going tonight, Jaz? Everything all right?"

"Oh, Mr. Allgate, I'm glad you're here. The Lady's in a real snit tonight. I haven't seen her this stirred up in a long time. Doors have been slamming, fireplace tools knocking against each other..."

He interrupted her. "Anything else besides The Lady?"

"Well, Angie's been waiting to see you. Something came for you that..."

He broke her off again. "Get Angie and tell her I'll be right back. I'm going to escort Miss Martell upstairs."

Jaz gave Tia the once over. "I remember you. The photographer from the night of the accident. Well, Miss, I hope you have a strong constitution."

Tia smiled at the girl, but it was not a friendly smile. "I'll try not to let a slamming door upset me too much." The dryness in Tia's voice bespoke not only a disbelief but a disregard for something which all the employees of Bishop's Inn took very seriously.

Jaz's red eyebrows hitched up in a way that said that she was the expert, and Tia was the novice, but Dallas knew Jaz wouldn't dare say anything derogatory to one of his guests.

Dallas led Tia up the narrow staircase to the third floor and unlocked the door. He preceded her inside and glanced quickly around the room. Everything was in its place.

"Make yourself comfortable. I have to see Angie for a few minutes. And don't let Veilina scare you."

"Oh, she won't. She and I are old friends, remember?"

Dallas knew the absence of fear was because Tia was a nonbeliever. He briefly wondered what her reaction would be to undeniable proof of the spirit world of Midexistence. Would she still be so cocky in her fearlessness?

Angie was waiting for him at the bottom of the staircase, a large yellow envelope clutched in both hands. Her eyes still retained a glassy, bespelled look to them, as if she had just experienced something frightful and was now in shock. *Damn Flynne!* Beneath his anger at Flynne, though, was an even greater anger at himself. He should have been at the inn, attending to his business, instead of pleasuring himself with trying to decipher a mortal female.

"Angie, are you all right?"

The woman nodded, but Dallas was hardly reassured. "Come upstairs with me." Angie's pain didn't need an audience, especially Jaz's sharp little eyes. Angie faithfully followed him to the second floor banquet room, which was rarely used during the off-season summer months.

"Here. Let me take that." He gently reached out for the envelope and relieved her of it. "Sit down, Angie, and tell me who gave this to you."

She sat, but the disoriented look in her rounded eyes grew even more evident. Her gaze jerked around the room, from one object to another, as if she were in a strange place and didn't recognize anything.

"Angie, look at me." The request was more than that. It was the vampiric compelling command. Angie's gaze obediently settled on his, but her fear was still apparent in the wide-eyed appeal.

"You're safe now, Angie. No one can hurt you. You have nothing to be afraid of. Do you understand?"

Her eyes stilled a little, and she nodded.

"Tell me who delivered the envelope."

She swallowed. "One of the men who was here to see you

the other evening. The tall one with the dark hair."

Dallas nodded his understanding and encouragement. "Yes, I remember, Angie. Go on. What did he say to you?"

"Just that I was to personally give you this envelope as soon as possible. He said it was confidential and that no one but you should open it."

"Thank you, Angie. Anything else that he said or did?"

She looked confused for a moment, then shook her head. "That's all I can remember. I'm sorry, Mr. Allgate."

Dallas released the power of his stare in order to relieve some of the pressure from her mind. He considered sending her home for the rest of the evening, but thought better of it. She was safer at the inn.

"It's all right, Angie. You did well. Try to take it easy for the rest of the evening. It doesn't look too busy downstairs tonight."

A smile tried to form on Angie's mouth. "No, Veilina's in rare form tonight for some reason. A few people came in, saw the fireplace tools swinging, and left."

"Bring some sweet tea and warm muffins upstairs to Miss Martell, would you, Angie? I'll be joining her shortly."

"Right away."

Only after Angie left and closed the door did Dallas lean back in the hard wooden chair and close his eyes. The inside shutters on the second floor windows still swung open and closed, banging forcefully on the sash.

"Hush, my love. I'm here now," he whispered, his eyes still shut.

The shutters closed with a slap of wood against wood, but then were still.

"I know, I know. You hate all the Undead, myself most of all. Well, you won't have to worry about Flynne, my love. I'll make sure he never comes here again."

One shutter lazily drifted open, creaking on its ancient hinges. Dallas heard the small noise and smiled. He had learned long ago that an open shutter meant he momentarily held The Lady's favor. "Ah, my fickle love...tomorrow you'll hate me again."

With that he opened his eyes and examined the envelope closely. It was a normal business type envelope, with the name "Dallas Allgate" handwritten on the front with the word "confidential" in large letters and underlined. The flap was not only clasped shut but sealed, and the envelope itself was bulky and heavy, appearing to contain more than just papers. Dallas ripped open the top and carefully slid the contents to the tabletop in front of him.

A man's life poured out. A wristwatch, a man's ring, a driver's license, photograph, and a slip of paper spilled to the table. Dallas didn't examine the jewelry. He didn't have to. He was well acquainted with the expensive black and gold watch and the University of Mississippi class ring. The small photo on the license stared up at him, along with the words "Mississippi - The Hospitality State." The solemn face in the photo was anything but hospitable, but at least showed life. The man in the larger photograph was quite dead.

The body was propped in a sitting position against a large graveyard monument shaped like an angel. The corpse looked like it had posed for the photo—its legs crossed, and its hands in its lap as if in divine contemplation. The face was colorless, and even the eyes, open and rolled up in a silent appeal, showed no tint of life. The man's shirt was torn open to the waist, and the only color visible was a thin red pendant of blood that dripped from his collarbone like a gruesome adornment.

The note on the slip of paper was brief. "Tell Miss Martell that I won't be needing her services as a photographer after all. I believe I have the perfect cover art right here. Don't you agree? After midnight, come to the town that's as dead as your friend or your other lackeys will join him in providing me with an entertaining and satisfying evening."

Dallas swore long and loud, using profanities learned over three continents and two centuries, lowering his voice only when he heard Angie on the stairs below him.

Raemon Sovatri would do no more work for him.

"Mr. Allgate?" Angie's voice floated up the staircase.

"It's all right, Angie. Come on up." He quickly dropped the items back into the envelope and just as swiftly hid his visible anger beneath the mask of his features. It wouldn't do to upset Angie all over again.

Angie opened the door and waited at the entrance, carrying a tray. "Is everything okay?" She looked a little more herself. After all, anyone who worked on a daily basis in a building haunted by a very temperamental spirit learned to adjust to a little adversity.

"It's been a rough day for all of us, I fear. Go ahead and take the tray up. Tell Miss Martell I'll be with her in a few minutes."

She nodded and continued up the stairs.

Dallas hadn't exactly been truthful with Flynne when he told him that he cared naught for any human. It didn't do to be truthful with an adversary. But to himself Dallas admitted that while he cared little for humanity in general, he possessed a feeling of responsibility for those humans he considered his. Dallas lived a more stable life among mortals than most of the Undead, remaining in a single place for upwards of twenty years before moving on. It was never natural for him to form long-term relationships with humans, but occasionally it happened. He had known Rae for twelve years, and while the man never knew Dallas' secret, he had been a reliable, capable agent who questioned little and knew to keep his mouth shut. Raemon had been well paid for his efforts, as were all of Dallas' employees. It was like having a fellow hunter shoot your favorite hunting dog.

Dallas pulled out his cell phone and called the number for Rose Hill. Gillie was a different story. Gillie was the closest thing to a friend Dallas had. Gillie had long known what Dallas was and had accepted him from the first, without having been bespelled to embrace the situation. Any kind of vampiric power directed at a human over a length of time created a burden on the targeted mind. Unless that burden was lifted, compliance eventually disintegrated into madness. Gillie would not have lasted twenty-five years as Dallas' servant without control of his own mind.

Come on, Gillie. Answer the phone. Be there.

Worry started to join the anger that burrowed deep in

Dallas, surfacing only as an annoying muscle tic. Friendship aside, Dallas needed Gillie. Dallas didn't like to acknowledge the fact, but he was vulnerable during the day. Gillie was his eyes and ears, took care of his business and his needs. If St. James had done any harm to Gillie...

The answering machine picked up, and Gillie's recorded voice, even more staid than the live version, sounded lifeless and flat.

"Gillie, it's Dallas. Pick up. It's an emergency." He paused and was rewarded.

"I'm here, Dallas. Sorry, but I was...indisposed."

Dallas paused, for just a heartbeat. "Never mind, old man. I'm at the inn. Are you all right?"

"Yes, of course, Dallas. What's happened?"

"I'll tell you when I get there. I should be there in about fifteen minutes."

"I'll be here, of course."

Dallas disconnected the call, slipped the phone onto his belt, grabbed the envelope, and bounded up the stairs with the lightness of a cat. Angie was still in the office with Tia. Both were seated close together and chatting like old friends.

"Sorry, Angie. Something's come up. We have to get back to the townhouse." He nodded toward Tia. "We have to go. Now."

Thankfully, she didn't question him, but took one last sip of her tea and rose from her chair to follow him. He exited the building first and, holding Tia just inside the doorway, examined the night around him. There was no scent on the wind save that of the flowering trees and shrubs surrounding the patio and the woman behind him. *Good.* He pulled Tia to the car, and still she said nothing until after he started the Lincoln's engine. As if that were a signal, her questions poured forth.

"What is it? What's happened?"

"Rae's dead, and something's wrong at the townhouse."

"Rae?"

"One of my associates. St. James killed him."

"How do you know?"

Dallas inclined his head toward the envelope on the seat between them. "Look inside the envelope." He turned on the dome light so she could see the photo and read the note.

"Oh, my God. Dallas, you have to call the police on this."

"And tell them what? The body'll never be found. I guarantee that. I can't do anything for Rae, but I can for Gillie. He's at the house, but something's wrong. I called him to make sure he was all right, and he called me 'Dallas.'"

"So?"

"Gillie never calls me by my first name. Never. Always 'Sir' or 'Mr. Allgate.' It was his way of telling me he's in trouble. My guess is that Flynne's got him."

"What are you going to do?"

He turned his head slightly until she did likewise. "Kill the bastard."

She merely nodded, and he turned his attention back to the road, marveling again at the woman beside him. No foolish female theatrics, no moral indignation, not even an appeal to "let the cops take care of it." This was something she understood as well as he did, and he felt her mindset without even reaching for her mind. This was a threat. It was danger. It was one of your own in trouble.

It was survival. It was what they were both best at.

"How?" she asked.

"What?"

"How are you going to kill him?"

"Any way I can."

She shook her head. "That's not good enough. We have to have a plan."

He felt a smile threaten to surface. "Any ideas?"

"My Glock's in the trunk of the rental car in your garage."

"Your what?"

"My gun. It's a Glock 23. Just like the duty weapon I used to carry, but a little smaller. I got so used to carrying a gun on the job, I couldn't give up the habit. I always take it with me when I travel."

"What size ammo?"

"It's a .40 caliber."

He considered. It wouldn't kill Conner, but it would slow him down. "Are you any good?"

"Pretty good. I never missed a target during firearms training."

"What about real life?"

She looked straight ahead. "I've never shot at anybody."

He pulled the car over a block from the townhouse and turned to look at her. "Tia, can you do it?"

She met his gaze without a blink. "If Gillie's life is in danger, or yours, or mine...oh, yeah."

The smile tried harder to break through. "Got anything else in that trunk of yours?"

She did smile. "No bazooka, sorry. Just the gun and knife. That's all I carry."

He nodded. She was better prepared than he was. It would have been embarrassing if he felt such an emotion. *I really must see to outfitting the Lincoln for such emergencies.*

"It'll be enough. Where in the trunk is the gun?"

"The gun is put up in a case. You'll see it. Just bring me the whole thing. The knife is under the driver's seat."

"Give me your car keys."

She pulled them out and pressed them into his hand. The feel of her warm skin only added to the rush his body was already feeling. "After I get out, slide over to the driver's seat. Keep the engine running and the doors locked. If there's any danger at all, you drive off, understand? Don't worry about me."

"I've got it."

He slipped out of the car and waited, watching Tia to make sure she obeyed his instructions. She did, and he ran down the sidewalk at a pace that was slow for him until he was out of her sight. Then he accelerated to a speed that shifted into the plane of time and space unique to the Undead. A human watching him could not have registered his movement. He was at the carriage house in seconds and had the security alarm disabled and the service door unlocked just as swiftly. He found both the gun and the knife with no trouble, then spent a moment watching the house and testing the air with his senses. Nothing was visibly amiss, and he could hear no voices. But his sense of smell, as usual, aided him more than his sight or hearing did. Conner's stink permeated the yard.

He was back at the Lincoln before another moment passed. Tia gave him a worried look when he got into the car beside her.

"What happened? Was someone watching the house?"

He shook his head and handed her the case and the knife.

"Wow. That was fast. This'll only take a minute." She took out the gun, inserted a magazine, and racked the slide to chamber a round. "All set."

"All right. Keep the gun out of sight until you need it. If you need it, empty the whole clip into Flynne's heart, in as tight a group as you can."

"You don't have to tell me how to do it. That's how I was trained. Upper hydraulics." She tapped her chest.

He felt the smile he had been suppressing finally rise to the surface. "Good girl. Just remember to stay behind me. Conner is a lot faster and stronger than he looks, so don't be deceived."

"What about if you go in first and I stay out of sight?"

He shook his head. "It won't work. He'll know you're there. His senses are very acute."

"He'll be focused on you. By the time he hears or sees me it'll be too late for him."

Dallas considered her words. Under normal circumstances, a seasoned vampire should be able to sense the nearness of a female like Tia. But Conner was young, and perhaps would be too distracted by Dallas to discern her presence. It might work. "All right. Just don't shoot Gillie whatever you do. Ready? Let's go see what game Conner Flynne wants to play."

There was no point, though, in Dallas trying to take Conner by surprise. Dallas had no way to disguise the scent of the Undead any more than Flynne did. They walked through the back door.

"Gillie? Answer me." Dallas kept one arm behind him to make sure Tia stayed put.

"In here." It was Gillie's voice. The spoken words were

sparse not only in emotion but in strength, but Dallas didn't care. The man was still alive. Tia remained in the pantry while Dallas followed the voice to the parlor, feeling too much like the proverbial fly.

There, in the center of one of Dallas' prized Aubusson rugs, stood Conner Flynne. He held John Giltspur tightly against him like a shield, one arm around the man's neck in a grip very close to a choke hold. No wonder the old man's voice had sounded so thin and thready.

"Ah, Aldgate. Right on time." Conner's voice held a smugness that made Dallas want to slap him.

"Release him."

"Now don't disappoint me. Your house didn't. I didn't quite picture a commoner like you in such grand digs, but it's really quite nice. So don't you be less than I expect."

"You're no match for me, Flynne, and you know it."

Conner wagged Gillie's slim body back and forth in front of him like a dog with a toy in its mouth. "Dalys, Dalys, wake up. I don't have to be. I have your servant, don't I? You can't kill me, and no matter how fast you are, you can't save him. Pity you don't have the girl. You could trade her for this worthless old man." Conner suddenly raised his head and paused, like an animal testing the wind. "Dalys, you bad boy. You do have her, don't you? She's in this house. I can smell her. How about it? You can save one, but not both. Which will it be?"

Dallas saw no need to respond. The less he said, the better able he'd be to conceal his intentions. Only young fools like Flynne babbled on. This particular fool seemed to have no natural inclination to master or disguise his passions, and he wasn't going to live long enough to learn the art. Dallas speared Conner's eyes and penetrated his mind with the power of his years. It was not only skill that overpowered, but cunning. Not only imagination, but deception. He dazzled the younger vampire, watching the creature's eyes widen with realization.

Conner tried to fight back with his own power, but in doing so merely exposed all his thoughts to Dallas.

"You see, Flynne? It's not enough to understand. You have

to not be understood. And I can understand you all too well."

Conner's eyes appeared ready to pop from his head, but suddenly his body jerked in opposition to the restraining power. His mouth worked like a fish's, the points of his "fangs" popping in and out of view, and Dallas could feel the creature trying to combat the influence of Dallas' eyes and mind. No sounds poured from the mouth that toiled uselessly, but in a final abrupt effort of defiance, Conner twisted Gillie's body and sank his mouth to the man's neck. A strangled cry escaped the choke hold, but louder than that was the plea from the old man's eyes.

Dallas was on Conner in an instant—an instant he would have prayed was not too long, if he were one to pray. He ripped Flynne from his friend and hurled him into the fireplace. Gillie crumpled to the rug, but Dallas had no time to see to him. Conner was far from finished.

Flynne collapsed to the marble tiles, bringing all the antique mantel adornments to the floor with him. The heavy china clock shattered, and brass candlesticks landed with a dull thud to roll to the side, but a crystal vase filled with fresh cut flowers escaped damage by falling on Conner's head. The water joined with the blood on Conner's mouth and dribbled down to stain the collar of his shirt. He licked his lips, his eyes as glazed and wild as his face, while the camellias tumbled across his shoulders to plop into his lap.

Flanked by two ornate andirons topped with brass lion heads, Conner rose to his feet as if pulled, like a puppet, by invisible strings. The lions, while fierce, looked regal. Conner, mustering his most ferocious snarl, looked like a fool.

"I told you, Aldgate. Do whatever you want. You can't kill me."

"That's what you think."

Dallas was on Flynne again like a beast on wounded prey, one hand seizing the creature's throat, the other reaching behind Conner for the poker that hung next to the fireplace. Flynne's bug eyes widened ever more with the realization of Dallas' intent, but it was too late. Before the wisdom of understanding could finally be his, Flynne twitched and shuddered as Dallas drove the poker into his midsection, just below his ribcage, then bore the hooked point upward toward his heart. Dallas twisted the poker, and Conner shrieked, feebly thrashing like a fish on a spear.

Dallas sailed from the parlor, his bloody cargo tightly in tow, until he was down the back stairs and into the cellar. He yanked the poker part way out of the body, then thrust it deep into Conner's heart again, using the wide handle to rotate the poker's head. A high keening sound slid past the blood in Conner's mouth and echoed off the cellar walls, and the body became limp in Dallas' arms.

"A misbegotten creature like you should have never risen from the mud of creation, Flynne, but I'm happy to say I'm going to rectify that mistake."

With that, Dallas tugged the poker from the body. The iron stake clanged to the floor, followed by a more silent stream of blood. Dallas, with the strength of his kind, clawed his hand into the gaping wound and tore out Conner's heart. Standing over the body, Dallas cast it to the floor and spit on the death mask of the truly Dead. The glazed eyes were locked open in the horror of final understanding, and the varnish of water and blood on the lifeless face was already drying to a dull finish.

"Nothing more to say, Flynne? Silence indeed cures foolishness, does it not? That was for Gillie."

Dallas quickly rinsed his hands in the cellar's sink, then ascended to check on Gillie. Tia was with the old man, but looked up when she saw him approach. Her eyes rounded with what appeared to be more concern than aversion.

"My God, Dallas, you're covered with blood. Are you all right?"

He nodded. "It's Conner's, not mine. Is Gillie alive?"

It was her turn to dip her head. "It's a bad wound. I've been keeping pressure on, but he really should have medical attention. I would have called, but I didn't think he had the strength to keep pressure on the wound himself. I didn't want him to bleed to death while I called for an ambulance."

"You did right. No ambulance. I'll be right back. I'm going

to make some calls." He glided to the next room, close enough to keep an eye on Tia and Gillie, but far enough away for her not to hear his phone call. He called Scott MacLaren, and waited through each ring with the hope that MacLaren hadn't become another victim of St. James' games. After Sovatri, MacLaren was the man Dallas trusted most to do his bidding effectively and without questions.

"Yeah," came the answer on the other end of the line. Like Sovatri had been, MacLaren was more than a little lacking in the charm that made Natchez famous.

"Mac. This is Dallas. Can you come to the townhouse right away? Gillie's been hurt. I need someone to take care of him for me."

"I'll be right there." The line went dead. No charisma, but the man was efficient.

Dallas hadn't wanted to give out the news yet about Rae. That would come later. Right now there were more important things to worry about. He returned to Tia's side with towels and antiseptic.

"Hey, old man, are you still with us?" Dallas cradled Gillie's head in one hand while he cleaned the wound with his other.

"I'm sorry, Sir. He broke in through a window. The alarm went off, but before I could do anything..."

"No apologies, Gillie. The varmint's been dispatched."

Tia looked at him. "Conner's dead?"

Dallas met her eyes, then looked down at Gillie. "Truly dead."

The old man nodded in understanding.

"Where did the two of you go? I wanted to follow, but figured Gillie needed my help more," said Tia.

"You did the right thing. Conner's in the cellar. Gillie would have thrown a fit if I'd gotten all this blood on the Aubusson or the cypress floors." He gave her a wink, but it was for Gillie's benefit.

Weak as he was, Gillie still managed to respond with a lift of one brow. "By the looks of it, Sir, you've still left me a fine mess to clean up."

"'Fraid so, Gillie. Mac's on his way. He's going to take care of you."

"Why Mac?" A note of suspicion was lodged between the two words. Sometimes Dallas swore that Gillie had the Undead's power of the mind.

"Rae's dead. St. James killed him. What happened here tonight is just the beginning, I'm afraid."

"Does Mac know?" asked Gillie. He knew as well as Dallas did that Rae and Mac had been close friends as well as associates for years.

"No, I didn't tell him. And I won't. I need all his attention focused on taking care of you tonight."

"You're leaving?"

Dallas nodded. "As soon as I give instructions to Mac and change clothes. St. James wants a showdown. More vermin that needs killing."

"Drago..." breathed Gillie.

"To Hell with Drago."

Tia was doing an admirable job of not looking confused. "What about me? I want to go with you," she stated. There was a defiant tone to her voice that hinted she already expected to be left behind and wasn't going to accept it.

In truth, he didn't know what to do with her. If he left her behind to help take care of Gillie, he had no doubt she'd try to follow him. Short of disabling her car, he didn't know how to ensure she'd stay put. He doubted even Mac, who was as physically imposing as himself, could keep her here against her wishes. Even if she did stay with Gillie, she'd be in danger. There was the possibility that St. James' invitation was just a decoy to lure Dallas well away from Natchez, leaving all those he cared about behind, unprotected and at St. James' mercy.

On the other hand, if she went with him, and St. James was indeed waiting, he would be taking her straight into trouble. More than that, she would be a distraction to him. Every bit of worry he expended on her was energy not focused on St. James. Willingly giving an opponent an advantage was not a rule of survival.

In the end he decided to take her with him. She'd be a

distraction whether he took her or left her, and at least this way he could see to her safety. "You can go if you do two things. Clean up some of this mess before Mac gets here. Then go change into your most practical clothes."

"Where are we going?"

"To a ghost town. Hurry now."

TEN

The killer aura. She had been right. The man sitting in the Lincoln beside her certainly had it in spades. And she didn't.

With all her experience, she'd thought she understood the truth of the human predicament. She'd thought she could understand every situation she found herself thrown into—thought she understood enough about the character of others to make good decisions. *To understand and not be understood,* Dallas had said.

Well, she found herself not understanding a single thing. She hadn't been able to assume the cloak of the killer aura long enough to do the right thing.

She had seen Conner Flynne holding Gillie hostage. Saw Flynne attack him. Heard the whimper of pain exhaled from Gillie's mouth. The man had been killing Gillie, and she had stood pointing her gun, her finger on the trigger, unable to shoot. After a second, Dallas' body had blocked her shot, and in the next eyeblink Flynne had been plastered against the marble fireplace. But during that one second when she had a clear shot, she hadn't been able to do it. What if Gillie had been killed during that one second?

"Tia."

What was she doing wanting to confront St. James again? Did Dallas know he wouldn't be able to count on her in a pinch? What would he be thinking of her if Gillie had died? What was he thinking now?

"Tia." The voice was loud, right in her ear.

She flinched out of her reverie. "I'm sorry."

"What's this? No questions for me? I thought you'd have a million or so by now."

Questions? That's what he was worried about? She couldn't bring herself to admit her failure to him. Her mind shifted gears, reaching for what he seemed to expect from her.

"You can tell me where we're going."

"Rodney."

"Who?"

"It's a place, not a person. Rodney is about forty miles up the Trace. It'll take about an hour to get there, though. The highway doesn't exactly roll through where we're going."

Tia tried to get her mind to function. "I don't remember St. James' note saying anything about Rodney."

"It said to 'come to the town that's as dead as your friend.' Rodney is a ghost town, the only one near Natchez."

"God, don't tell me you have another story about spirits like Veilina and Rowan." She allowed her disdain to color her voice, but in point of fact, another one of Dallas' improbable tales just might take her mind off her brooding.

He laughed, a rare sound. "Well, I don't know any of Rodney's spirits by name."

"How does St. James know about this place?"

"I don't know. It's not exactly a tourist attraction, though the town does have a lot of stories attached to it. It used to be quite a famous place. Interested?"

She shrugged. "Sure. Why not?"

He glanced at her. "Someone with your sense of history should appreciate this. Rodney was a grand town before the Civil War. It was almost voted the capitol of the Mississippi Territory. It had an opera house and two newspapers. Anyway, this story takes place in 1863, during the War. After Vicksburg fell, the Union Navy was in charge of the Mississippi River, and the gunboat *Rattler* was specifically put in charge of keeping an eye on Rodney. Every Sunday morning the men on board would line the decks hoping for a glimpse of the southern belles as they paraded into church. But one Sunday a reverend, who was a northern sympathizer, was in town to preach that day. He invited the captain and crew to attend services. So the men disobeyed orders, put on their best uniforms, went into town, and quietly seated themselves in the church. Just as the reverend started up, a Confederate Cavalry lieutenant walked up the aisle, apologized, announced that his men had surrounded the church, and demanded that the Yankee sailors surrender."

Tia found herself smiling in spite of herself. How was it that this man, who seemed so serious and dour, could inspire so much passion? "And did they? Surrender, I mean."

"Well, one of the Yankees took a shot at the Rebel lieutenant and all Hell broke loose. Citizens dove under their pews for safety, and the skeleton crew left aboard the gunboat began firing their guns at the church when they heard the commotion. When the smoke cleared, the church and four homes had been hit, and the Rebels had seventeen prisoners, including the Yankee captain and lieutenant. The Rebel lieutenant who had started it all kept the Yankees from burning down the town by threatening to hang all his prisoners if the *Rattler* fired a single shot. The *Rattler* was infamous thereafter. It was the first time in history that a small squad of cavalry captured the crew of an ironclad."

"That's terrible. All true?"

"Tia, would I lie to you?"

She turned her head to look at him. He met her eyes briefly. "In a heartbeat. So if the town was flourishing, why did it die?"

"The river made Rodney what it was. It was the busiest riverport between St. Louis and New Orleans, but after the war a sand bar formed in the Mississippi, and the river changed course. By then cotton and slavery were gone, and Reconstruction was a hard time for the town to try to make a comeback."

Once they turned onto the Trace, there was no traffic to be seen in either direction, and no lights of any kind. Sometimes the trees receded from the road to reveal neatly mowed shoulders and fields, and other times giant limbs reached for each other across the pavement, like elderly lovers embracing. Tia could almost imagine how it was for the travelers of years long past. The countryside did have a feel of its history that was almost palpable. In such a setting, all of Dallas' strange stories seemed almost believable.

There were so many things she had wanted to ask him about earlier in the evening, but with everything that had happened, there had been no time. She still wanted to ask him about the diary, but even more she wanted to ask him about the two of them, and if he saw any future for them. Now was not the time. They had to survive the night first.

"What exactly's going to happen when we get there?" she asked.

"Simple. I'm going to kill the bastard."

"How? What if he has a gun this time?"

"I'm prepared for this round. While you were changing, I threw a few things in the trunk."

"What will you want me to do?"

She watched him carefully as he gave each answer, but this time he did more than shift his glance in her direction. He pulled the Lincoln onto the grass shoulder without a word, put the car into park, and turned the dome light on. He twisted his body toward her, lessening the space between them. He was dressed again in black jeans and a charcoal shirt. The light accented the paleness of his skin, but his eyes gleamed with a luminescence that had nothing to do with the lamplight. She suddenly felt very warm.

"This is different from what just happened at the house. I don't want you involved at all. Understand? St. James is much more dangerous than Conner was. I don't want you anywhere near him. I mean it, Tia. No heroics this time."

"But what if your life is in danger again?"

"Do what you have to do to defend yourself, but don't worry about me."

"How can you tell me to do that?"

His eyes looked glassy in their stillness. "Because this is survival. You have to do as I say. I can't afford to be distracted. If I'm thinking that you're going to be charging up into the middle of things, I'll not only lose my concentration, but St. James will know exactly where my mind is. He'll take every advantage of that."

"Then why did you bring me here?"

"Because you're safer with me than at the house."

She blinked. His eyes hadn't moved. She nodded.

He turned the light off and pulled the car back onto the road. So that was it. He was fully aware that she could have shot Conner and didn't, and he didn't trust her now. She was merely the female to be protected.

She was silent for a long time, watching the road wind languidly before them. She tried to let her mind relax, and as soon as she did, the Trace took it. The road captured her attention, like a stately white-haired lady would in a room full of young strangers. Even a Northerner like her could almost hear the whispers of time that flowed along the shoulders of the parkway. But it was more than that. There was tranquility to the empty highway that was like a presence—hushed, but as tangible as the very trees. It was something larger than she was, older and infinitely wiser. It had seen more people, more passages, and more tragedies than Tia would have seen in a hundred years as a cop. The feeling soothed her, and for a few moments, her problems shrank.

It seemed silly, but the windings of the Trace wrapped her in a mantle of safety similar to that she had felt in Dallas' presence. The road had persevered through both the destruction and healing of time, and survived still to aid the weary traveler. Despite his relative youth, there was something akin to the Trace in Dallas. It was a wisdom gained only with the passing of time spent in life, and yet it was a stillness in spirit gained only, she surmised, in death. She wondered what tragedy had happened in his life that he had attained that stillness in spirit.

She glanced at Dallas as she had so many times in the past at her partners. All the profiles before him had shown youth and masculine strength. In that regard, Dallas was no different. The straight nose and strong jaw framed by the sweep of long hair was as attractive a profile as any man Tia had ridden with.

The cops she had worked with had lived with the possibility of death and of causing death every night. But neither she nor any of them ever talked about it. She had tried not to even think about it. If she had, she couldn't have done the Job.

This man was unlike any of the cops she had known. This man had killed, and he had talked of death. Yet she hadn't been repelled or afraid, but comforted. Comforted by the killer aura. It should have been a scary thought, but it wasn't.

She had to help him. Whether he wanted her to or not, she couldn't just sit idly by while he fought St. James. Dallas may be able to see with eyesight bestowed by the aura that surrounded him, but that aura wasn't a shield against injury or pain, and it wouldn't deflect death. However, if she was going to help, she would need more information.

"How big is Rodney?" Her mind envisioned a Hollywood ghost town, with rows of deserted streets flanked by shells of abandoned buildings.

"There's three or four original buildings, plus a number of structures that have sprung up since then."

"That's all? I thought you said it was a big town."

"It was, once upon a time. Fire, time, and nature have reclaimed the land. There are a couple churches, and a Masonic lodge if I remember correctly. The rest of the buildings are hunting camps, trailers, and newer houses. Oh, and of course the cemetery. The Dead always survive when the living have fled."

Great. Another cemetery. At least she wasn't wearing white. "No one at all lives there?"

"Oh, I think there's a few hardy souls still around to keep the spirits and deer hunters company."

The Lincoln slowed, and Dallas turned sharply off the Trace onto a narrow road that challenged even shock absorbers designed for ultimate cushion and comfort. The car bounced and swayed over a patchwork of red gravel, pavement, and dirt that Tia swore was no road at all.

At last, when Tia thought they were hopelessly lost, Dallas shut off the headlights and eased the car to a stop. At first she could see nothing but darkness. After a moment her eyes adjusted to the moonlight, and she saw an alien landscape of mounds and twisted shapes, all covered by a thick blanket of vegetation, that rose on high slopes on either side of the gravel lane. She saw no lights, no buildings, no signs.

"Is this it? I don't see anything but vines."

"The infamous kudzu. Don't stand too close to it, or it'll swallow you up. The town's just up ahead. Time to get ready before St. James realizes I'm here." He popped the trunk and was out of the car like a draft, here and gone. Only seconds later she felt the car bounce as he shut the trunk, and when she turned her head to the driver's door, the butt of a shotgun angled toward her face.

"You know how to use this?" His low whisper came from outside the car, but she heard it easily. She grabbed the wooden stock and turned the weapon, automatically checking the safety. It looked like a twelve gauge pump action. This one was nicer than she was used to, but the deadly functionality was familiar.

"Yeah."

He followed the shotgun into the car, but it was only to turn the car sideways on the road. Not a small feat, considering the leanness of the lane and the bulk of the Lincoln. He put the car in park and turned to her, the glow from the car's interior lights accentuating lines in his face she hadn't noticed before. He looked older and more serious than she had ever seen him. That, too, was no small feat.

"The church is just up ahead and to the right. Stay in the car, doors locked and engine running. If you see St. James, get out of here as quickly as you can. Don't worry about me. Just go. If you have to, use the shotgun. It's loaded, but not chambered. Do you understand?"

The interior lights made his eyes gleam with an unearthly glow.

Tia nodded, but then asked, "How do you know he's at the church?"

"Just a guess, knowing St. James' flair for the flamboyant. The church is the single most famous building left in Rodney. I can't imagine he'd be anyplace else. Tia, do you understand what I said a moment ago?"

She nodded again patiently. "Yes, Dallas."

She understood all too well what she had to do.

***

He hoped for once she did see what he wanted her to see. The shotgun he had given her was loaded with shells filled with silver shot. A blast from the gun might not kill a vampire, but it would definitely slow it down. He had done all he could for Tia. Now was the time to concentrate on St. James.

Dallas ran easily but cautiously up the road, testing the draw of a Colt .45 semiautomatic pistol from his waistband. It was an oft-used armed forces handgun, and this particular specimen was nothing out of the ordinary, except for one thing. Like the silver shot in the shotgun, the Colt had a magazine full of silver bullets. Again, probably not enough to kill, just slow down.

Dallas thought about the Vampire Hunter St. James had used in the Chapel of Light graveyard. He hoped the possession of such an ancient weapon meant that St. James preferred killing an opponent in the traditional way. Dallas couldn't assume anything, though. For all he knew, St. James had an arsenal of weapons at his disposal. After all, St. James had been planning his revenge for years, and was likely to take few chances. Dallas had but two points in his favor. Conner was dead, and St. James didn't have the advantage of the sunlight he had at the cemetery. Now, at midnight, Dallas' strength was at its peak.

He reached the T-intersection and turned right along the gravel road, led by the decaying stink of the Undead. He passed a couple of buildings, currently being lived in—if the presence of a car that looked to be in running condition in the drive was any indication—and arrived at the Presbyterian Church. There, as expected, sitting behind the wrought iron fence on a tuft of long grass, was Jermyn St. James.

Like a pale avenger, St. James seemed to glow in the moonlight. His blonde hair, pallid skin, and ivory jeans and T-shirt took on a silvery sheen. For a being locked in the everlasting darkness of Midexistence, he seemed overly enamored of the one thing he could never have—the light of life.

St. James spread his arms and, like a bird taking flight, was airborne, only to land gracefully at the bottom of the shallow brick steps. "Ha, Aldgate. Right on time. I was hoping you'd find my invitation...irresistible."

"Charming, as always, though I was disappointed that you saw fit to destroy one of my men in the process. This was to have been between you and me."

St. James paced back and forth in front of the church like an anxious parishioner. "Really? Whatever gave you that idea? Drago? Did Drago warn you not to decimate the local populace in your pursuit of me?"

Dallas laughed. "Drago doesn't give a damn about the locals. You should know that."

St. James halted in front of one of the white church doors. "Drago gave me a long and not very pretty speech about what I was and was not to do. A sermon I have every intention of ignoring. I had assumed he gave you the same little lecture. Or is he taking your side in this?"

Dallas remained on the outside of the iron fence, not wanting to shrink the space between them. "Drago doesn't take sides. He told me what he wanted me to hear. Rest assured I won't be any more shackled by what he said than you are."

A sneer rotted the perfection of St. James' aristocratic features. "Really. I find that hard to believe. You toil among the mortals here like you were one of them, born and bred. You obey their laws as well as any human."

"For my own survival. The laws of man mean nothing to me otherwise, and Drago's laws mean even less. If you doubt me, ask where your friend Conner is."

Dawning realization, then anger, widened St. James' dark eyes, and his spiked hair appeared to reach even higher to the sky. "What have you done with Flynne, you miscreant?"

"He was a naughty boy. He came to my house uninvited, so now he's lying in my cellar with his heart ripped out. Fair payment for Sovatri."

"Fair? Damn you, Aldgate! Sovatri was nothing but food. I invested thirty years in Flynne. He just recently was becoming useful to me."

"Conner was a fool, and you know it. Is that why he struck your fancy? Like an ugly child, more loved because of it? "

"You were going to die tonight anyway, Aldgate, but now I'm going to make sure it's a long and painful process. Just like it was for your lackey."

Dallas couldn't see any weapons on St. James' person. The snug jeans and skintight shirt left few hiding places for guns and knives, but the tall grass surrounding the church could conceal enough weaponry for an army. Dallas had to bide his time.

"Was it you or Conner who killed Sovatri?"

"I had the pleasure. And it was. He was strong and full of rage at being divested of the mortal coil. It's always so much more satisfying to feast off strength than weakness, don't you agree? There's no kick to destroying those faint in spirit."

"I don't know about that. Conner was a fool, full of himself and empty of caution. I don't know if he was more wedded to you or his own bad judgment. Either way, he was loathe to give up the bliss of his simple-minded existence for the True Death. I was only too happy to give him a push in the right direction. And what about you, St. James? If the student is so much the fool, can the master be any different? You slather yourself with silver and gold, but they do nothing but illuminate your stupidity."

St. James leapt over the iron railing that ascended the church steps, bringing him closer to Dallas. Dallas stepped backwards toward the road, careful not to step in the shallow ditch alongside the gravel.

"And what makes you any different, Aldgate? Are you, with your fancy house and fine car, not as great a fool?"

"I think not. The poor know best how to be rich."

"Oh, spare me! You're no different from me, and you know it. Enough of this. Don't you want to know how I discovered your secret? The secret of eternal life?"

"No. Since I'm going to kill you, I don't really give a damn."

St. James jumped up onto the top of the narrow brick retaining wall at the edge of the steps. "No! This is my party!

You're here because of me, Aldgate. Me! You're not here for Sovatri or Conner or Drago, or any of your self-righteous notions. You're here because I wanted you here. And I want you to hear the whole story before *you* die." St. James paused, standing on the retaining wall with the ease of a gymnast on a balance beam. "Correction. Before *both* of you die."

Too late, Dallas sensed the same thing St. James did. The uniquely enticing scent of a human female. Miss Tia Martell.

***

Tia had waited until Dallas was out of sight, then turned off the engine and, with the shotgun in tow, followed him on foot up the road. At the intersection a sign leaning so far over as to nearly be flat on the ground commanded the Rodney traffic, such as it was, to stop.

Dallas had said the church was to the right. She sneaked a peek around the sign and saw Dallas and St. James in front of a dark building with a white cupola that she assumed was the church. She heard faint voices, but couldn't hear what they were saying. Tia looked to her left. A small dilapidated wooden building rested on the corner, its porch overhang drooping like a sleepy eyelid. She hurried to the building, the gravel scrunching softly under her shoes, to find cover while she debated on what to do next. She ran onto the porch, only to be assaulted by a red, white, and black warning sign. Like the stop sign, the lean of the sign was a badge of honor of more than its share of battles. She peered closer at the sign in the moonlight and had to stifle a laugh. It was the all too familiar "Neighborhood Watch" sign. Was it meant as a warning to the ghosts or to protect them?

She stood on the porch of the old grocery and pondered her next action. She wanted to hear what was being said, but was afraid to venture much closer to the church. Dallas had been adamant in his instructions, and his wrath was not something she looked forward to. On the other hand, if it came to a choice of suffering his anger or suffering his loss, she'd swallow the pill of his fury.

There were buildings set back from the road between her position and the church. If she moved from cover to cover, she could approach undetected. Tia drew a long breath and ran back across the intersection toward the church. The voices became louder, and she strained to decipher individual words. She had to get closer. From what she could see, Dallas stood by the road, and St. James paced the church steps. The latter was cavorting around like a playful child, not like a man who had been stabbed in the chest the day before. How could she have been so wrong about what she had seen with her own eyes?

She scurried to the back of the building to the south of the church, careful to stay out of sight of both men. The sounds were louder now, but the bass rumble of Dallas' voice was harder to understand than St. James' high-pitched voice. She caught something from St. James about discovering the secret of eternal life and heard Dallas respond that he was going to kill him. It seemed she had arrived just in time.

St. James started shouting, then all was strangely quiet.

"Correction. Before *both* of you die."

It was St. James' voice, but it was Dallas who grabbed her, yanking the gun from her grip. Where had he come from so quickly? Only a second before he had been twenty-five yards away.

"You idiot! I told you to stay put!" The growl in her ear held nothing of his slow drawl.

Before she could answer, laughter rang out, long and full of glee.

"Aldgate! And you call me the fool? I can't believe you actually brought the female with you! Destroying her along with you just may atone for Conner."

St. James bounded through the tall grass with the ease of a gazelle. Hadn't the man been injured at all?

Dallas' voice vibrated against her ear. "Take the Colt out of my waistband and stay behind me."

She obeyed this time. The growl of an angry beast was to be respected. She ran her hand along his waist until her fingers found the grip of the Colt. His voice had been as cold as the metal of the gun, but the skin under his thin shirt was as hot as the night.

"No closer, St. James, unless you want a face full of silver." Dallas' words increased in volume as he brought the shotgun to his shoulder.

St. James raised his hands in mock surrender, his pale fingers splayed upward in imitation of his spiked hair.

"Have no fear, Aldgate. I plan on entertaining myself thoroughly before the deed is done. And now that we have an additional guest..." He paused to bow deeply to Tia with a flourish. "I feel it only right she be entertained as well. Good Evening, Tia. Welcome to Rodney! Has Dallas been taking good care of you?"

He paused again, his full attention on her, not as though he expected a reply, but more like he was assessing her to discover his own answer.

"Ha, I see that he is. Your stink is all over her, Aldgate. You didn't waste any time, did you?"

The gun at Dallas' shoulder never wavered. "Give me one reason not to blow you from existence this very minute."

"Come now, Aldgate. Where's your sense of fair play?"

"You've underestimated me if you thought I ever had one. Give me a reason."

St. James wide smile shrank. "You're spoiling the party, Aldgate. You want a reason? How's this? I have two more of your lackeys. I forget their names. Richton and some other useless stripling. But rest assured I have them. They're in a place only I know about, and it's not a very healthy place."

"I don't give a damn about Richton or any of the others."

"Dallas..." she whispered, not understanding any of what was being said.

"Shut up!" He didn't turn his head as he spat the words, and she was glad she couldn't see his face.

"Don't lie to me, Aldgate. I won't suffer your lies as easily as Tia here does. Do you want to hear some truth, Tia? Then come along. The sermon at the Rodney Presbyterian Church is about to commence." With that, St. James spun around and set off like a shepherd leading his flock to the fold.

Dallas kept the barrel of the gun on St. James' back, but pulled Tia to his side so she could see his face.

"Tia, go back to the car. Now."

"No. I'm staying with you."

"Even if you don't get yourself killed, you won't like what you hear." He made it sound like a threat.

"If I hear some truth at long last, it'll be worth the risk. I'm not leaving." She imbued her words with the same chill she had heard in his.

His eyes seem to blaze in a final moment of resistance before a look of regret tamped their heat, almost as if he were saying good-bye to her. Or as if he didn't expect her, or him, to survive.

He nodded just a little.

"As you wish, Tia. Your eyes would have seen all in any case soon enough. So come along, as he says, and open yourself to the beginning of wisdom. If you can stomach the truth you want so badly, that is."

With that he turned and followed St. James back to the church. When they arrived at the wrought iron gate, St. James was leaning against the red brick next to one of the church's front doors, his arms crossed and the long grass hugging his calves like furry green boots.

"Excellent. Shall we go inside? Even though Rodney's population is one less than it was at dawn, I don't fancy being observed by the locals."

"I'm surprised you stopped at one, St. James. Why didn't you just do away with all the remaining residents and make Rodney a true ghost town? Oh, and by all means, break down the door. How long has it been since you've been in a house of God?"

Tia couldn't believe what she was hearing. Was this the same man she had made love to only last night? Having the killer aura was one thing. Advocating the death of a town, even in jest, was something else.

St. James laughed and angled against the white door to his right, butting it with his shoulder. The move looked effortless, but the wooden door splintered. "Churches don't bother me. Do they bother you? Remind you of your...deeds? And you misunderstand me. I'm here for you only. And now,

of course, Tia, too. The lifeblood of this town, such as it is..."
He snickered again, this time with obvious disdain, and pushed
in the door with a brandish of arms. "...doesn't interest me in
the least."

"After you, then," said Dallas, his smile no friendlier than
the barrel of the Remington that bobbed at St. James.

Jermyn disappeared inside, and Dallas pushed Tia behind
him again. "Wait until there's light."

Seconds later, candles flickered from the altar table, and
Dallas cautiously entered the doorway, Tia at his heels. He
came to a halt, and she moved to his side, still a little behind
him, but able to look past him. There wasn't much to see. The
candlelight sent shadows bouncing along the walls of the
sanctuary, but little of the light reached Tia. The windows were
all shuttered, and an overhang jutting out above her created a
pocket of darkness at the entranceway.

"Choir loft?" she whispered, glancing up.

"Slave gallery."

She felt stupid. Just what was she doing here with these
two madmen who were bent on killing each other?

"This is as close as we're coming, St. James. Speak your
piece and let's get on with it." Dallas' voice seemed to echo
through the church, bouncing off the walls in time with the
shadows.

"Did you see the sign on the wall outside the church?
Dedicated in 1831. Do you remember what you were doing in
1831, Aldgate? I do."

Did she hear right? What kind of gibberish was St. James
spouting now?

"It was the year I found the 'Fountain of Youth' you had
bragged about fifteen years earlier. Do you remember? You
told my father 'the Fountain of Youth isn't in Florida, it's in
Australia.' Well, after you ruined my father, I went there. I
searched ten long years to find what you had gloated about. It
wasn't easy. I had nothing to go on, and Australia is not exactly
known for legends of the Undead. But there were men in the
bush who knew. And I finally found them."

Tia's head was spinning. *Fountain of Youth? Undead?* She

wished someone would explain what St. James was talking about, but Dallas hardly looked in the mood to be answering questions.

"You want my congratulations? You've got more than you ever would have had as an earl. So why bother with me now? What will revenge gain you? Happiness? Power? Satisfaction? Justice? Will any of these brighten the darkness you live in? I know from experience they won't."

"Happiness? Is that what you aspire to? Happiness is a human affliction. Come now, Aldgate, you know what I want. It's the same thing you want—to send others on a journey. One that begins with appearance, passes through truth, and ends with destruction."

Tia eased backward to the still ajar door. St. James was indeed mad. Madmen were the most dangerous to deal with. They lived so far from reality you couldn't reason with them or invoke any kind of logic.

"Not so fast, Tia. You haven't heard the whole story, have you?" shouted St. James. She couldn't see his eyes from across the room, but felt them on her nonetheless.

"Come on, Dallas, let's get out of here. He's either seriously nuts or he's on something," she whispered.

He reached back and took her arm to prevent her from retreating any further. "No. You wanted to hear this, now hear it."

"Yes, Tia, by all means, stay and enjoy yourself. Dalys here has neglected to tell you what he really is, hasn't he?" The dancing pair of light and shadow over St. James' face in the church made him more frightening than he had ever looked in the graveyard.

"Let me guess. He's a homicidal maniac like you are," she yelled.

Laughter rang out from the chancel. "Oh, far be it for me to deny he's that. It's not quite what I was referring to, though."

"St. James, I warn you..." Though Dallas' grip on her arm was still like that of a vice, his attention was all on his opponent.

"Warn me what? You tell her, or I will." Jermyn paused,

and only silence filled the sanctuary.

She tried to tug her arm away from him. "Dallas? What's he talking about? What's all this crazy talk about eternity and the Fountain of Youth?"

He relaxed his hold on her, and she jerked her arm free. "Well?" she prodded.

"I don't inhabit the same realm of existence that you do. Neither does St. James." There was a strange quality to Dallas' voice she hadn't heard before. Not regret exactly, but sadness and perhaps resignation.

"I had kind of figured that part out. You're both out of your minds."

"No, Tia. It's not what we believe to be true. It's what *is* true. I told you that you wouldn't like it. I was born human in 1766. I haven't been human since 1802."

She bolted out the door. She ran easily down the steps and around the iron fence, but the long grass tangled around her feet and hid the shallow ditch along the gravel lane. She felt a sharp pain shoot up her leg when she placed her foot wrong, but kept going. She'd never make it to the car with a bad ankle and the speed she had seen them exhibit, but maybe she could find cover in one of the abandoned buildings across the street. She made it across the road, with feet slipping and sliding on the rough gravel, and slowed a little on the other side so as not to step in another ditch. She ventured a peek over her shoulder as she did so and saw nothing but the dark windows of the church, like shuttered eyes, and the white doors below, like a secret smile.

The large wooden building directly in front of her had all its windows boarded up. She kept running to find something not so formidable to someone trying to break in. She was soon rewarded with a small frame house with no car nearby, no lights, and high grass encroaching the building on all sides. She supposed someone might still be living there, but it didn't matter. She had to find a place to hide. She pounded on the front door, then circled the house looking for a broken or open window. She found what she was looking for at the rear of the building, but the window was too far off the ground to make entry easy.

A single shot, followed by the distinctive boom of a shotgun blast sounded from nearby, and fear gave her the impetus she needed. She was up and over the broken windowsill in seconds, and lay sprawled on the floor where she landed, trying to catch her breath. Had Dallas killed St. James? She wasn't sure what she had learned, but one thing she had discovered was not to assume anything. Could the legends she had heard possibly be true? She had laughed them all off as stories to lure tourists, but could ghosts be real? Dallas and St. James didn't seem like ghosts. They were too substantial. Ghosts didn't talk or make love. Did they? What else had she heard about? *The spirit who wanders the night, looking for revenge.* A vampire?

All the little things she had thought were strange but had shrugged off now came flooding back to her mind. *The speed. The strength. The not eating or drinking. The compelling eyes. The sense of age in one so young.* And yet there had been nothing incontrovertible. Nothing that couldn't be a trick. She hadn't seen any flying, or climbing up the sides of building, or shapeshifting into bats or wolves. And both Dallas and St. James had been in the Chapel of Light graveyard yesterday while it was still light out. No, it couldn't be. There was just no such thing as vampires.

They were just two sick men having a good time at her expense. Well, no more.

She pulled the Colt from her waistband and slid out the magazine. It was fully loaded. She popped off one of the cartridges and examined it as closely as she could in the moonlight that brightened and dimmed like a child playing hide and seek. The tip of the bullet was indeed silver in color, but she couldn't discern more than that. She reloaded the cartridge and the magazine and checked to make sure a cartridge was in the chamber, then checked her own gun, the Glock. It, too, was ready to go. The handguns didn't have the offensive power of the shotgun, but they were good defensive weapons. Whatever the men wanted from her, they wouldn't get it.

A rustle of grass and a rattle at the window snapped her out of her reverie, but she had no time to react. A very real flesh and blood body flowed through the window, scooped her up, and cradled her hard against his body, one large hand over her mouth. She tried to reach for the Colt or the Glock, but the man snatched her right arm in a tight grip, and she couldn't reach the weapons with her left hand.

"It's Dallas, so be still!" He poured the irate words directly into her ear, and she swung her head madly, as if to shake the words back out.

She was just as incensed as if it had been St. James. How dare he do this to her? She struggled against his hold, not really expecting to break it, but wanting to let him know she wasn't playing his games any longer. It did nothing but exhaust her further. His grip was tight, and the more she resisted, the more he increased the pressure.

"Listen to me, Tia, and listen well! St. James will hurt you. I won't. I'm your life. If you want to live, start doing as I say, right now!"

He ground the words into her ear, and she shivered from the combination of the nearness of his body and the power of his anger. He pulled his hand from her mouth so she could answer, but for a moment she just lay in his arms, breathing heavily while she caught her breath and thought out her next move. As if she had many choices. To struggle against him was fruitless. His strength was far too overpowering. Better to bide her time and go along with him.

"I heard the gun blast. Is St. James dead?"

"No. Unless the silver takes his head, his heart, or severs the spine, he won't die. I'm happy to say I caused him some bother, though. He got in the first shot, but I got in the best."

The meaning of his words sank in, and Tia twisted in his embrace. Blood glittered darkly against the gray of his shirt and ran down his left arm in a stark contrast to his pale skin. As she turned, she felt him draw the gun from her waistband.

"I'll take this back for now if you don't mind. I wouldn't want you to finish the job St. James started."

"Why didn't you tell me you'd been shot? Here, let me do

something with that." She didn't want to play his games, but she wasn't quite ready to see the man bleed to death.

He shook his head. "There's nothing you can do. It's a silver shot. Only Gillie will know what to do with it."

"Then for God's sake let's get out of here and go back to your house."

His head moved back and forth again, and in the light that struck his face, she saw pain compete with strength in his glittering eyes. "I can't leave. Not until I've finished St. James."

"What are you going to do? If you've already shot him and he's still alive..."

"I don't know, but we've got to get you out of here. He's nearby, and he'll want your blood."

"What?"

"There isn't time to explain. He's too close."

"But how..."

Before she could finish her question or hear his answer, she felt herself being picked off the floor like a doll and flung back out the window. She hit the ground hard and heard a crash, but the splintering noise didn't come from her hitting the grass. It came from inside the house. She got up and hobbled to a shed at the rear of the yard, the collection of broken boards providing concealment, but no real cover. She pulled her Glock, the only weapon she had left. It didn't feel familiar. It was too big. She looked at the gun. It was the Colt. Dallas had pulled the wrong gun from her.

A shout, a shot, and another shattering of wood ripped the silence, and two bodies hurled through the air to tumble to the ground. She tried to distinguish the dark of Dallas' hair and clothes from the light of St. James, but the two were a blur. It was disorienting, like trying to watch a movie played in the wrong speed. She concentrated on holding the Colt steady.

Suddenly time seemed to slow down, and the bodies disentangled. Both gleamed dark and wet with blood. She had seen gunshot victims before, lots of times, even shotgun victims, and it was never a pretty sight. She felt the heavy Colt waver in her grip.

"Aldgate is right, Tia. I do want your blood. I need it to

help repair this damage. But then so does Dalys. He showed such foresight in bringing you along tonight. You'll be the salvation for one of us, Tia, but which one?" St. James tried to laugh, but the sound was strangled and held none of the gusto it had before.

"Shoot him, Tia, now!" shouted Dallas.

"If you shoot me, Tia, be sure to shoot your lover as well. He'll kill you to save himself just as easily as I will." St. James paused for a heartbeat, but she had no answer in either action or words. She felt dizzy, almost mesmerized. The gun in her hand felt heavier by the minute.

"Go on, Aldgate, deny it. Tell her you wouldn't take her blood in an instant."

Dallas answered only with his eyes turned toward her. Not as if he were trying to compel her, but to reach out to her.

"You see, Tia? He doesn't deny it. He can't. He knows you know the truth now. And you do believe, Tia, don't you?"

The nightmarish figure grew larger and larger on the Colt's sight. She could see his wounds clearly now, the gaping dark hole in his abdomen, the peppering of dark stains on his chest and arms. A few pellets had even reached his face, spoiling the mask of beauty.

"Behold the power of the Undead, Tia. Behold, and believe."

"Don't look at his eyes, Tia."

She looked, and she saw the truth, and her vision narrowed to a pinpoint. She heard the gun go off, over and over, the shots punctuated with screams of pain and fury. Her target gone from her sight, she tried to look around, but saw neither Dallas nor St. James. She slumped against the shed, dizzy and exhausted, until a bright light hurt her eyes. She squinted and saw flames lick at the abandoned house. In a feeding frenzy, the fire grew, and the walls were consumed in a ravenous feast.

She tried to move back from the shed, but her feet tripped on a half-buried barbed wire fence, and she fell over backward into the high grass. A shadow loomed, blocking her view of the fire. Silhouetted against the light, Tia couldn't see who it was. She glanced down to check the gun still in her hands. No lock-back. She had at least one bullet left. She leveled the gun at the shadow.

"No closer."

"It's me, Tia. If I were St. James, you'd already be dead."

"And you're going to tell me you won't kill me?"

"Put the gun down, Tia. You can't kill me, and Gillie will have enough work to do on me when we get back."

The fact that he hadn't denied he'd kill her didn't escape her attention. "Maybe I should shoot you just to convince myself you're not human."

"I can convince you in any number of ways that are less painful and messy, but if that's the only you'll be convinced of what I am, go ahead. But decide quickly. We can't stay here."

"What's all this 'we'?"

"You're stalling. Shoot me or help me."

"Give me one reason I should help you."

"I can't. Only you can find the reason for that."

She couldn't do it. She put the gun up. There was a reason somewhere in her heart that wouldn't let her injure him further. She wasn't sure at the moment what it was, but she knew it was there. "Damn you, Dallas."

"You can't damn me. I was already damned two hundred years ago."

She sighed. "What do you want me to do?"

"Right now, help me get out of here."

When he extended his hand toward her, she wasn't sure if he wanted the Colt or her hand. She reached her left hand to his, and he took it, pulling her effortlessly to her feet. He didn't ask for the Colt, so she kept it. Not much was making her feel good right now, but keeping the gun, knowing it had at least one silver bullet left, was some comfort. Somewhere in the back of her mind a voice told her that he could take the gun by force any time he pleased, but right now she clung to every solace she could.

She wasn't sure that she was needed to help him to the car. More the opposite. He kept an arm on hers, and when her sore ankle would have balked at supporting her over the uneven ground, his strength kept her from falling or tripping. Once they reached the road they ran for the car. Tia didn't look back.

"You drive," he commanded when the Lincoln, still perched sideways in the road like some giant watchdog, loomed before them. "Get us back to Rose Hill as fast as you can without attracting the law."

She concentrated on negotiating the big car along the narrow lane while Dallas used his cell phone.

"Mac, pick up. It's Dallas."

When Dallas next spoke into the phone, his voice was lowered, and Tia couldn't hear anything more. When he disconnected the call, she turned her head briefly in his direction.

He answered her unspoken question. "Gillie's all right. I told him St. James is dead and that you and I were on our way back. He'll be ready for us."

"Is St. James really dead?"

Dallas nodded tiredly. "The correct term is 'truly dead.' He's experienced the True Death. What the silver didn't accomplish, the fire did."

"I still don't understand, you know. What you...and he...are. Were."

"Oh, I think you do. You just can't say the word."

"You tell me."

"The politically correct term, I suppose, is 'Undead.' However I prefer not to be lumped into the same category as revenants. A revenant is a foul, brutal creature with no sophistication and little intelligence. The word that has gained popularity with humans over the centuries is actually much more accurate."

She felt his gaze on her as she drove, but kept her sight on the road. It was hard enough negotiating the twisting lane in the dark without being distracted by his eyes. Especially while he was telling her things she didn't really want to hear. Silence was a gloomy passenger between them. She didn't want to ask, and apparently he was in no hurry to enlighten her with the word.

But the companion of stillness grew restless and

uncomfortable as the Lincoln bounced over the crude road, and Dallas finally relieved the pressure of what was unsaid.

"The word is amazingly similar wherever you go on earth. Drago would say he is *le vampire*. St. James in his quest for the theatrical would have called himself a vampyre. I suppose I am nothing more than the Vampar of Natchez."

ELEVEN

Tia hit the smooth pavement of Highway 61 almost a half hour later, but her thoughts were anything but level. A vampire was slouched next to her, bleeding all over the deluxe leather seats. As it had years ago on the Job, her mind bottled up her fear and stored it away. She had a job to do now, and this one was just as important as the job she had done then. This was survival.

She limited her immediate questions to that end. "What can Gillie do once we get to the house?"

"When I was transformed, I passed into a realm that's the reverse of everything you know. The silver that humans love is nothing but deadly poison to my kind. The bullets are still in me. Once they're removed, the wounds will heal, but only if I...feed."

She studied the pavement stretching out before her, the Lincoln swallowing the lane markers like a steady heartbeat. "You mean blood." It was not a question.

"Yes, fresh blood. And energy. Life force. For that I need human blood, not animal blood." His voice was tired and matter-of-fact, but it affected her more than if it had been strong and menacing in tone.

Her mouth felt dry, but amazingly her foot remained steady on the gas pedal. She wasn't sure what question to ask next. *Liar,* she thought. She knew the question. She just didn't want to ask it.

Once more he seemed to know her mind. Not that her question would have been hard to guess in any case. "Don't worry. I won't ask it of you. Gillie'll do it."

"Gillie's an old man! And after what he's already been

through, how can you?" The words tumbled out before she could think about what she was implying.

"Gillie has long been aware of the risks of being my servant. He accepted those risks long ago."

"But to die for you?"

"I won't kill him."

"You're so sure of that?"

Silence sat between them again, making her feel anything but close to the wounded beast she conveyed.

Finally, he answered. "No, I can't be sure." The words were hushed, so much so she barely heard them, and yet the pain they rode was all too clear.

She let the stillness settle in again, thankful for the barrier, and pushed the Lincoln well above the speed limit. Tia wished she could speed up time as well. The half hour journey south on The River Road seemed endless.

The glow of the auto's clock read half past one in the morning when Tia pulled the car into Rose Hill's driveway. She stopped adjacent to the steps leading to the back door and finally ventured a good look at Dallas. He was awake, but his skin had a strange ashen appearance, and his eyes had a dead, glassy look to them. "Can you make it inside the house?"

He nodded, but the feeble dip of his head didn't inspire much confidence.

"Damn it, Dallas," she mumbled, more to herself than him, as she got out. Rounding the car and opening his door, she put an arm around his waist to help him. Gillie met them at the back door with all the worry and censure of a father whose children had stayed out too late.

"Come upstairs. I have the red room prepared," said Gillie, dispensing the disapproval of his lowered brows equally on Tia and Dallas.

"I took two silver bullets, Gillie. One in the arm and one in my side."

"Yes, I can see that, can't I? I just hope you did St. James one better."

Dallas managed a small smile. "More than one better, Gillie."

Gillie nodded, the frown lifting a little. "I'm glad. He was a nasty piece of work. Is Miss Tia injured at all?"

"I'm fine, just a sore ankle," she answered. *Fine, right.* The man she had made love to the night before was something she thought only existed in one's imagination. She almost laughed. She had had the same thought the night before, but then he was a fantasy come true. Now he was a nightmare come true.

"She knows, Gillie. Everything."

Gillie only nodded, accepting Dallas' words as truth. She wanted to set the record straight. She didn't know nearly enough. But she said nothing as she helped Dallas up the stairs.

The bed was turned down in the red and cream-colored bedroom, and towels, bandages, and a primitive looking set of surgeon's tools sat at the ready. She sat quietly and watched Gillie perform the impromptu surgery with the care, if not quite the skill, of a doctor. If there was any doubt in her mind before that Dallas wasn't human, it was gone now. Gillie used no disinfectant and no anesthesia, yet there were no cries of pain from Dallas when Gillie probed for the bullets, only a ragged sigh of relief after the second bullet was successfully removed.

"Gillie, you know what I need now."

The old man dropped the bullet into a dish with a plink. "I'm prepared, Sir."

"No."

Both men looked at Tia, but it was Dallas who spoke. "I don't have a choice, Tia. I can heal ordinary wounds without blood, but not wounds like this."

"I mean, I'll do it. Not Gillie."

"Gillie trusts me. He knows I won't kill him or try to transform him. Do you have that kind of trust? You were going to shoot me not two hours ago."

"Exactly. I had all the reason in the world to, and I didn't, did I?"

"This isn't something you can consent to and then get cold feet halfway through. Once I start, I won't be able to stop until I've satisfied my need."

"I won't suffer any permanent damage?"

"There are...consequences. But I don't have time now to explain all of them to you. As I said, you'll have to trust me. Decide quickly. The moon is setting."

"The moon?"

"Moonlight has certain revivatory properties. It will help to do this outside, before the moon sets."

"Then let's do it."

"You're sure, Tia?"

"Don't ask me to explain something I don't understand myself. All I know is that I can't let you perish, and I can't let Gillie do this."

"As you wish."

They descended to the veranda at the rear of the house. Elegant patio furniture graced the area that was also dotted with urns of flowers and a small water fountain. An old fainting couch had a clear view of the night sky, including the small moon that was swiftly sinking to its daytime lair. Dallas stretched out on the couch and held out his hand for her, but his eyes were more of a handhold than his reaching fingers. She locked her gaze on his. His eyes had lost some of their glassy, injured-animal look, and in its place was the bright intensity of hunger. It wasn't a cold, predatory look, but one of desire and need. And of things she saw but couldn't understand.

She felt her heart start to pound, an unnecessary reminder of what she was about to do. She extended her hand and felt her fingertips brush his. His touch was warm, not at all like the cold, clammy skin she thought the Undead were supposed to have. As if she knew anything but what she saw in the movies. His fingers grasped hers, and he drew her down to the couch. Her blood seemed to thunder in her ears, yet when he spoke, his voice was all she heard.

"Put your arms around my neck."

There was no bad-boy leer, no display of teeth, only the hooded eyes that glittered at her from beneath the tangle of long hair. She obeyed, and when parts of her body came into contact with his, it was as if it was for the first time. His bulk dwarfed her, his heat washed over her, and in the background, always there, the latent power of his body and mind lingered, like an idling engine waiting to be revved. For a second she was afraid, but the sexual response she felt flare in her own foolish body swamped any sensible messages her feeble mind tried to send.

"Relax," purred the engine into her ear.

She tried to release the tension from her body, tried to block all the alarms her mind wanted to send. It would be better, after all, to surrender to the sexuality of his touch. Sex was a human function, and if she could convince herself that this was all it was, she could do this. Besides, he felt sooo good...like a fire on a raw winter evening or a shelter on a stormy night.

She felt his mouth on her forehead, pressing soft kisses against her temple. The first two were leisurely and gentle, but as his mouth trailed down her face, his kisses grew hungry, demanding. By the time his mouth reached hers, the tenderness was gone, replaced by an insistence that told her he needed her. Now.

Her journey began in breath that was gone in an instant.

Just as she felt she would suffocate, he released her mouth and dragged his own down her neck to a point just above the hardness of her collarbone. She felt a prick of her skin and gasped at the twinge of pain, but the discomfort was gone in a heartbeat. His mouth drew on her, and with each pull she felt herself transported farther and farther from any reality she had ever known.

Her mind reasserted itself, but it was not controlled by any conscious thoughts or dictates on her part. Rather, it was merely the vehicle for her journey, drawn along the conduit of lifeblood that flowed from her to him, and spurred by the physical sensations that bound her and carried her away. All her inhibitions were cut loose. All the restraints placed on her by her job, her upbringing, her family and peers vanished in an explosion of light, and she felt a freedom she'd never before experienced. There was no good and evil, no right and wrong. Temptation, seduction, intimacy and acceptance...all was human experience, to be cherished as such. And at the end of the journey Death waited, but even that seemed not an ending, but merely a point. The destination of one journey, perhaps, but the beginning of another.

Her mind slowed, exhausted from the wild ride, and she wanted nothing more than to reach her destination so she could sleep. The light faded into gray, and darkness settled around her like a comfortable throw.

"Tia...Tia..."

She vaguely heard her name. It was too loud. She wished they'd be quiet so she could sleep.

"Tia, come on, wake up! It's over. You can't sleep now."

The voices were more insistent, and someone was shaking her.

"Go 'way."

Tia heard a crack, and the stinging across her face brought her back to Rose Hill's kitchen. She put a hand to her tingling cheek and opened her eyes to see both Dallas and Gillie in front of her. She stared at Dallas, trying to remember what had happened. The ashen skin and glittering eyes were gone in the rosy kitchen light, and she wondered if any of it had been real or if it had been one long dream.

"You're going to be all right, Tia."

"I'm so tired." It was easier than explaining how she really felt. Dizzy and weak, like she had just been on the biggest roller coaster in the world.

"I know," said Dallas. But you can't go to sleep yet. I want you to have something to eat. Then both of us can rest."

The mention of food made her stomach join her head in spinning. "Not hungry. Just want to sleep."

"Soon. But first you need to build yourself back up. Gillie's got a steak sandwich here for you, so be a good girl and eat up."

Gillie pushed a plate in front of her, and when she raised her eyes from the meat still dripping juice onto the plate to Dallas' eyes, she knew she wasn't going anywhere until she forced herself to take a bite.

The simple-minded existence of the Undead. Dallas had ridiculed Conner Flynne for leading such a life, but Dallas' own life had been just as simple and uncomplicated. He had the townhouse, the inn, Gillie, and a few human associates. Other than Gillie, there had been no close human relationships, and there had certainly been no Brotherhood entanglements. There had been no apprentice and no contacts with any enforcers. Now, in the span of just four days, one of his men was dead, another two missing, he had *l'enforcier* himself knocking on his door, and he had a human female with a vampire mark living under his roof. And it wasn't over yet.

Flynne and St. James were dead, but his men were still unaccounted for. And Drago was sure to soon be darkening his door again. More than once he had announced disdain for Drago. In his show of bravado with St. James it had been easy to dismiss *l'enforcier* and his warnings, but the fact remained that two vampires had just been dispatched to the True Death. That was an action Dallas knew would not go without consequences, and even if only half the rumors he had heard about Drago were true, those consequences would not be pleasant.

But as weighing as Drago was on his mind, Dallas had more immediate concerns to deal with. He had marked Tia more heavily than he had intended, and only through the intervention and help of Gillie did she still live. She was asleep now, Gillie having banished Dallas from her room for the remainder of the night and day. Dallas smiled tiredly as he descended to his cellar chamber. Gillie had appointed himself Tia's guardian angel. What did that make Dallas? The answer came all too easily. He had played the role of the demon this night, and he had played it well.

TWELVE

Tia's sense of smell brought her back to the realm of everyday, if not normal, existence. The strength of hot, black coffee vied with the delight of hot cinnamon bread and bacon to tempt her nose. She gingerly pushed herself to a sitting position on the grand bed, rubbing her eyes and willing her body to function. If the meal tasted half as good as it smelled, she wanted to be able to enjoy it to its fullest.

She blinked her eyes and was greeted by Gillie carrying the biggest bed tray she had ever seen.

"How are you feeling tonight, Miss Tia?"

"Better. And I'm famished. I've never smelled anything so good. But what time is it?"

"Six o'clock. You slept all day, but I'm glad to see the long sleep has revived you." He carefully set the tray on the bed before her. Besides the coffee, bacon, and bread there was orange juice, a slab of ham, and fried potatoes. A breakfast fit for a king at six o'clock at night. A subtle reminder that her life had indeed taken a sharp left turn from the road of normalcy.

Tia didn't want to think about that yet. She took a sip of the coffee and indulged in an entire pat of butter on the slice of warm bread, eventually doing justice to the coffee, juice, bread, and bacon before slowing down to ask Gillie the inevitable question.

"Is it all true, Gillie? Last night? Or did I just have the dream to end all dreams?"

"A lot happened last night, I'm afraid, and I wasn't witness to all of it. To what exactly are you referring, Miss?"

She had to smile at that. Did anything faze Gillie? "Well, let's start with the big one. That Dallas is a...God, I can't even say it."

"A preternatural being commonly referred to by us humble humans as a vampire? Yes, quite true."

"And Conner Flynne and St. James?"

Gillie nodded.

"I don't understand. How can such...things...really exist without the world knowing about them?"

"Without knowing? There isn't a country on earth that doesn't have some sort of legend of the Undead. Where do you think such stories come from?"

"Stories, yes. But in all this time no one has realized that there's truth to the stories?"

"Flynne and St. James aside, vampires are very cautious creatures. You see how easily Mr. Allgate has been able to live in this community undetected. But that's not all. The vampire community takes care of its own. Humans who learn the truth are swiftly dealt with."

"But you've known what he is for a long time."

A wistful smile preceded Gillie's answer. "Yes, twenty-five years. But I'm his seneschal. As such, I could never betray him."

"You're his what?"

"Seneschal. It's a very old word, but one I prefer to 'servant' or 'steward'."

"And now I know the truth. So what happens to me?" She looked down at the remains on the bed tray. "Is this my final meal?" She asked the question half as a joke, but the food she had just eaten sat hard in the pit of her stomach, and she had no appetite for anything more.

"Mr. Allgate will not allow harm to come to you. If he had wanted you dead, he would have killed you last night."

A dubious reassurance. "How is he so sure I won't try to harm him?"

"You'll have to ask him that yourself. Take you time bathing and dressing. He won't be up for another hour and a half." Gillie took the bed tray in hand. "If you need anything, use the intercom on the wall."

"Thank you, Gillie." The thank-you was definitely for the

meal. She didn't know how grateful she was for the confirmation that the man she had made love to was a "preternatural being." She wasn't even sure what the word meant. Alien? Supernatural? Well, she'd be enlightened thoroughly tonight. She wasn't sure if she looked forward to it or not.

***

She waited in the gardens, enjoying the colors of the flowers before the darkening sky leeched the reds and pinks from the blooms. She hadn't wanted to wait in the parlor. Even though Gillie and Scott MacLaren had cleaned up the mess as though it had never happened, the memory of the fight with Conner was too fresh in her mind. She also hadn't wanted to wait on the veranda. The memory of sharing blood with Dallas was even fresher. The garden, on the other hand, had an undefiled solitude and pristine beauty to it. She wished she knew the names for all the various flowering trees and shrubs, but gardening had never been one of her hobbies. She knew well what roses looked like, though, and was puzzled by the lack of roses on the estate. The name of the place was Rose Hill, after all.

He was standing behind her before she realized he had come up the path. She told herself she should be accustomed to his stealth by now, but his sudden appearances always managed to surprise her.

"No, no roses. It's a widely held theory among occultists that the petals and fragrance are a bane to all evil. As much as I'd like to dismiss such rubbish, I'm afraid that evil does include me, for I do find the aroma of roses most repellent."

How did he know what she was thinking? She turned to face him. His disquieting stealth was one thing. The magnetism of his blatant sexuality and latent strength was something that not only struck her anew every time she saw him, but truly shook her. Her body seemed to have a will completely independent of her mind. "Why the name, then? Why 'Rose Hill'?"

He stood for a moment, his gaze on her face, but somehow looking through and beyond her as well. She waited patiently for his answer, knowing full well he had heard her.

**

The question was an easy one—as easy as it had been to find her in the gardens. He was attuned to her scent and her presence even more than he had been before last night. It was the mark. The part of her that was his now, this day and forever more. Even her thoughts, nothing more than general impressions before, were as clear to him as words on a page. And yet her question, as simple and innocent as it was, caught him off guard. He had expected her first question to be something about bats, fangs, or some other such nonsense. Instead, she was asking about roses. Her question did more than take him unawares, though. It stirred a memory long sleeping.

Sydney, 1788. Dalys lay awake in his tent outside the place the Captain had christened Rose Hill and listened to the steady patter and drip of rain against fabric. A pretty name, he thought, for this piece of sodden earth. Tomorrow he and his fellow convicts were to begin building a settlement at Rose Hill. A smile fended off the chill in the air. He already knew how it would go. The marines and lads alike would look to him. His skills and endurance had made him indispensable in only a few months. Another smile, this one with a twist, came at his next thought. The very skills that ensured his survival in this hell had landed him here in the first place. But St. James would yet pay. Revenge would keep Dalys Aldgate alive. He would make his way somehow back to England. And he would live again.

Dallas sighed. The memory, created when he was still human, was bittersweet when recalled by his non-human mind. St. James, both father and son, had paid. Revenge had indeed kept Dalys alive. He had made his way back to England. But Life? Could his existence now, so far from the boundaries of human experience, be called Life?

He was aware that she was waiting for him to answer.

"I was a convict in New South Wales. Slave labor. It was my job to help build the first settlement there. The captain called the place Rose Hill. When I built this townhouse in

1828, the name seemed a natural."

She frowned in thought. He waited for the inevitable next question.

"New South Wales? Then you *are* the author of the diary?"

That, too, was a surprise. He hadn't realized she had found and read the diary. He nodded.

"It was fascinating, but I couldn't tell who all the people you referred to were. And, of course I didn't know you had written it."

"Are you ready to hear the whole story?"

Her eyes sought his, and even in the lowering darkness he could see the blue of her eyes and the hunger that shone in their depths. For the story, of course, but also for him. In spite of knowing what he was, her desire was apparent.

It was the mark again. The vampiric mirror was a powerful device. A product of the power of the vampire's eyes, it was an indispensable tool for manipulation, destruction, and the resulting pleasure such actions brought. As forceful as the mirror was, though, the mark was stronger. It was a blood tie, and nothing on earth was more elemental, more binding in its pure essence, than that.

He offered his hand to her as a test. She hesitated, and he saw evidence of the conflict behind her eyes in the lines on her forehead. Finally, however, her fingertips stretched out to graze his, tentatively at first, then she interlocked her slender fingers with his large ones. She stood waiting, as if to be led on a journey, but when he didn't move, she reached for his other hand. The small move set waves of desire surging through him, and still holding both her hands, he pulled her forward until the heat from her body rode his, spurring him to explore the mark further. He canted his head, his mouth inches from hers, and paused, waiting for her. The mark didn't disappoint. She leaned forward, and when her lips brushed his, her passion was apparent even in the light touch. The warm scent of her blood and the ardor of her body nearly undid him, and he pulled back from her before deepening the kiss. The test had been conclusive enough.

A moment of sadness held him still. If the mirror hadn't

taken her will, the mark had. He frowned. Such a prospect had never bothered him before. He had always enjoyed his dominance, as all vampires did. Why then, did it disturb him to know that the only reason she wanted him was the influence of the mark?

"I think we'd better get to it," she breathed.

"What?"

"The story."

He exhaled a long breath. "Of course. The story. Where shall we sit?"

She nodded toward the lawn that sloped gently from the garden up to the trees ringing the yard. "How about there?"

"The grass?"

"What's wrong with that?"

He smiled. "As you wish."

They settled on the lush green of the lawn, and he began where all good stories should begin.

"I was born in London in 1766. As St. James was so fond of saying, I was born and bred a commoner. I was luckier than most, though. Maybe it was because of my size, or maybe my mind was quicker than most, but I was apprenticed to a farrier at a young age. His wife was something of a saint. She saw that I was well fed and taught me to read and write. Many apprentices weren't so fortunate. A good many were considered nothing more than cheap labor and treated as such. By the time I was twenty, I was managing the Knights Chaise Company out of Knightsbridge. We hired out chaises, mostly for the young and wealthy."

"What's a 'chaise'?"

"A carriage. It was a good life. Viscount St. James took it all away from me."

"Not this one. Not Jermyn."

"No, his father, Christian. I was coachman the day Christian hired our finest post-chaise. Two hours out on the common we were stopped by two highwaymen. I didn't suffer such leeches easily, so I had words with them. Christian assumed I was in league with the buggers and foolishly pulled a weapon. The highwaymen shot and robbed him, and when I was left unscathed, St. James took it as further proof that I was guilty. Party-to-a-crime is what you call it now, I believe."

She nodded.

"St. James prosecuted me. The law then was very different from what it is today. There were no police and no district attorneys. Prosecution was private, usually done by the victim himself, and there was no such thing as intermediate punishment. You were either let go or hanged. My supposed offense was a capital felony, so I was sentenced to hang, but my employer petitioned the crown on my behalf, and I was pardoned. Pardon didn't always mean release, though. In my case it was conditional on agreeing to transportation."

"I don't understand."

"I was goods, convict labor, to be shipped wherever I was needed. Before the war, Britain's trash was shipped to the colonies, but by the time I was sentenced, America was no longer an option. So, in my case, that wherever was Australia."

Dallas' eyelids grew heavy with the memories, and he let his lids slide shut. It had been a long time since he had recalled this story, yet none of the details had faded with time. His vampiric mind, unbound by human limitations, preserved every memory intact, even those generated while he has still human. Some would have called it a blessing, but as was the way of Midexistence, what was godsend to humans was curse to the Undead. It meant his battles with Christian and Jermyn both would always be fresh. It meant he could never forget the years wasted in the pursuit of revenge. It meant that every horrific deed he ever committed would haunt him. And it meant he would never forget the mixed feelings he had had in that courtroom in 1786.

***

The rumble of the magistrate's throat. The verdict. "The sentence of death is hereby pardoned on condition of transportation, said transportation to take place when and where practicable..."

Life.

The smattering of conversation, accompanied by sporadic coughing, broke the singular eye contact Dalys had created with his accuser. He caught one last image of Viscount St. James' face before being turned away by a bailiff. The young lord's brows had risen from a state of boredom to one of surprise, and the furtive smile had dropped completely from sight.

Many would say that transportation was the same as hanging, and less humane, but to Dalys, who had been prepared for certain death, it was life itself. Like the hearty meals he had once enjoyed, he savored the moment. He closed his eyes, breathed slow and deep, and swallowed, banishing the dryness in his throat. He had already survived six months of the fevers and foul conditions that haunted Newgate while awaiting the assizes. He would survive the prison again, no matter how long it took. He was young, quick, and strong, the years of apprentice blacksmithing only adding to a build that was already sturdy.

Life. He would embrace it like a lover. A smile curved his mouth at the thought.

***

"Dallas? You're smiling. Was Australia that nice?"

His smile widened, but it was a sad smile. "No. Australia wasn't nice. It was a godforsaken pit of depression, drink, and disease. It was especially hard for those transported when I was. We were part of The First Fleet. There were no settlements, and the weather was demoralizing. Blistering in the summer, and cold and rainy in the winter. It was a wonder any of us survived."

"But you did."

He nodded. "That first New South Wales winter did more to whet my will to survive than even the eight months at sea had. I didn't go so far as to make friends with the marines at the garrison, but they were quick to notice me. They made sure my rum wasn't watered and my ration of pork generous."

"Why?"

"The better I could work. But I didn't mind the hard work. And it wasn't all bad. The ship Lady Juliana soon arrived with two hundred women convicts."

"Women convicts?"

"Don't sound so shocked. You sure you want to hear all this? It might offend your twentieth century morals."

"Oh, there isn't a whole lot that can offend me. I was a cop, remember? I just didn't think that many women back then committed such serious crimes."

"They weren't serious by today's standard. Their crime, like mine, was being a commoner. Most of the women convicts were domestics caught in theft. The reason they were given transportation, though, was to service us."

"Excuse me?"

He smiled, and this time it held a bit of mirth. "Those in charge felt that unless we were properly serviced, we'd develop all kinds of...gross disorders."

Tia laughed, and it was a good sound to hear. "So I take it that being the hard-working, dedicated convict you were, you got a woman?"

He nodded. "Umm. I even got my pick."

"Ooohh. And what was she like?"

***

Sabra. The smile dropped from his face as the memories, stagnant for so long, stirred and swam to the surface.

Life could indeed be sweet.

Dalys kissed Sabra on the mouth one more time before she laughed and pushed him away.

"Go on, now. Sun's up. Your children'll be wantin' your attentions as much as I do."

"Hmmm. But a nicker and nudge of a muzzle are no match for you, my love."

"Well, I certainly hope not." Sabra rolled off the bed and threw her pillow at him, hitting him square in the face.

"I've heard that Captain Phillip is leaving for England. Is it true?" she asked, her tone surprisingly innocent for one so knowledgeable in so many areas.

"I think so. His health hasn't improved."

"Who'll take over, do you think?"

Dalys smiled. "Talk is that it'll be Grose."

"Really? That would be good for us, wouldn't it?"

He stepped up behind her, swept the dark tumble of curls

*from her neck, and mouthed his answer against her skin. "Very
good for us."*

Yes, life could be sweet.

***

"Dallas?" Tia's voice broke through the fog of memories.
"I understand if you don't want to talk about it."

"No, it's all right. It was...a long time ago. Her name was
Sabra. She was the first woman I ever really loved. We both
worked for a man named John MacArthur. He was the
unofficial leader of the Rum Corps."

"Rum Corps?"

Dallas smiled. "The New South Wales Corps, but
everybody called it the Rum Corps because they paid us off
with rum. MacArthur was an amoral bastard, but he had a
strength and tenacity I admired. As soon as he found out about
my skill and experience with horses he appropriated me for
his stable. Sabra helped run his household. The work was
relatively easy, and for me nothing was better than working
with horses. And of course it didn't hurt to show loyalty to the
most influential man in the community."

"Of course."

Dallas picked up the lights of a car coming up the drive
and sighed. Any visitor this time of the evening couldn't be
good news. Especially if it was who he thought it was.

"Tia, stay here. I'll see who it is."

A few seconds later his fear was confirmed. Dallas strolled
back across the lawn to Tia in normal time. He was in no
particular hurry now that he knew who his guest was.

"It's Drago."

"Who?"

"Alek Dragovich. The man who stopped by the other day.
The one who leered at you. Remember?"

"Of course. As if I could forget one of your charming
friends."

"He's no friend. Come along. He may want to talk with
you as well."

"Why? Who is he, anyway?"

No flattering labels came to mind. "Go upstairs. If you're

required, you'll be sent for."

"Dallas..." She fairly sputtered his name. Tia Martell did not like being told what to do. Even with the mark, that hadn't changed. But she did as he bade her.

Dallas entered the parlor to find Drago, his dark brows wedged together, inspecting the mantel of the fireplace like a disapproving housekeeper about to chastise a remiss parlor maid.

"You find something in my furnishings not to your liking, Drago?"

L' enforcier tilted hooded eyes toward Dallas, and this time more than boredom emanated from their blue depths. "As a matter of fact, I do. I can smell blood all over this room, and it's not human blood. Do you care to explain how it is that our previous chat seems to have had so little impact on your actions?"

Dallas was not going to let himself be intimidated. "They killed my man, Sovatri. Conner Flynne broke into the house and was going to kill my servant. I was only protecting what was mine."

"Ah. Then I can assume that the delightful Mr. Flynne has met *la Belle Mort?*"

Dallas cocked his head and pursed his lips. "I guess you can assume that. I ripped the bastard's heart out."

Drago lifted a brow. "Resourceful. Messy, but resourceful. The body has been properly disposed of?"

"Shipped straight to Hell."

Drago actually let a small smile slip. "You don't lie to me, Dallas. I like that. The Flynne case is closed." He fingered the drapes at the window, but when he turned again to face Dallas, the smile was gone. "However, what happened last night in Rodney is quite another matter."

"No difference."

"*Aucune différence?* Let's see. Three of your men are dead. Rodney is now a true ghost town in every respect, two buildings are burnt to the ground, and a historic landmark is lucky to still be standing. Where do you want to begin?"

"You don't give a damn about the humans, Drago. The

buildings that burned were abandoned shacks, and the church, I'm sure, has survived worse over time than a damaged door and a few bullet holes. You forgot to mention the only thing you do care about."

Drago spread his arms. "Enlighten me."

"St. James."

"Ah, yes, St. James, *l' enfant terrible.* He ignored my warnings as well. I was forced to impose quite a few sanctions on our bad boy."

The silence in the parlor was absolute. There was no longer even the antique mantel clock to relieve the stillness with its tick-tock.

Dallas had a bad feeling. "St. James is dead."

Before the word "dead" was out of Dallas' mouth, he felt his body being slammed against the wall. Pinned by Drago's hand around his neck, all Dallas could see was the neon of Drago's eyes, burning like a blue flame. Drago's hand tightened, and he banged Dallas' head against the wall. "No! St. James is not dead! *Cela a ete mal fait, mon ami, mal fait.* Badly done! You start a job like that, you make damn certain you finish it! *Comprendez-vous?*" Drago cracked Dallas' head again for emphasis.

Dallas could neither break the hold nor speak to answer, so made do with the limited movement he did have control over, a small dip forward of his head. It was enough. Drago flung him across the room like a toy that disappointed, and Dallas tumbled over the Aubusson carpet to crash into one of his mahogany Chippendale armchairs. The chair toppled over, and Dallas, uninjured but smarting, was slow to rise to his feet.

"I shot him full of silver, then he burned in the fire. I heard his screams. No vampire can survive that." As if by saying it, Dallas could confirm it did happen.

"But you didn't stay to make sure, did you? You didn't clean up after your mess. You took the girl and ran."

"I was shot with silver as well."

"You had the girl. You could have fed on her then and there."

Dallas didn't know what to say to make Drago understand. "If I would have taken her straight away I would have killed her. I didn't want to do that." It was the last thing Drago would understand, but he had no other truth, and Drago would smell a lie.

Drago made a slow circuit of the parlor, like an inspector searching a scene for clues. "Well, while the two of you fled the scene, our bad boy managed to crawl from the fire. The town's remaining residents flocked to the evening's entertainment, so St. James didn't have far to go to find blood to heal himself. He'll be permanently scarred wherever the fire scorched flesh already damaged by the silver, but he lives."

"He'll just come for me again. You know he will. He'll want revenge more than ever now."

Drago stopped at the fireplace, and trailed the fingers of one hand down the smooth marble. "I think not. He's under strict orders to return to whatever circus in Florida he came from. If he has the impertinence to disobey, he'll answer directly to me. And rest assured *I* won't leave the job half done."

Dallas righted the overturned chair and sank into it. "What about my men? They're dead?"

Drago nodded. "I persuaded St. James to tell me where they were. An abandoned hunting camp near Rodney. They were dead when I arrived. Here." He pulled an envelope from a trousers pocket and flipped it to Dallas.

Dallas ripped open the envelope. Two drivers licenses slid out. Richton and Keller. His two missing men.

"What else?" asked Dallas, suddenly very tired.

Drago finally ceased pacing and poured himself into the companion armchair. "Ah, yes, there is the matter of what am I to do with you and your human female."

"She had nothing to do with any of this."

Drago rolled his eyes to the ceiling, as if he could discern everything he needed to know about Tia from a floor and several rooms away. Dallas had no doubt that Drago could do just that. "Interesting that you plead her case before your own. Well, well." The lazy eyes focused on Dallas again. "As for you, Allgate, I impose no sanctions against you but one. You did nothing to provoke St. James in any of this. What you did to his father was years ago, and not directed at Jermyn. However, I do need to impress on you the importance of not leaving a half completed mess behind as you did in Rodney." The bored, empty cast to the blue eyes settled in, and Drago dropped his gaze to flick a piece of lint from his trousers. "How am I to do that?"

"I get the message."

"I'm afraid that's not enough."

Dallas wasn't sure what words Drago wanted to hear. "As long as St. James stays away, this won't happen again."

Drago seemed to consider for a moment, still occupied with the appearance of his fine clothes. "A better answer. Very well. Suffice it to say I'll be keeping a very close eye on you, Allgate. Very close."

"Do what you need to do." It was probably not the right response, but Dallas was getting very tired of all of this.

A draft of cold air abruptly swept through the room, swaying even the heavy drapes, and the lights flickered, plunging the room into darkness. Dallas was out of his chair instantly, but Drago was quicker, ensnaring Dallas' mind and body as surely as if dozens of knives pinned him to the wall. It was a power Dallas had never before felt, and his helpless gaze could do nothing more than submit to the mastery of the antifreeze eyes. Drago hovered in the air before him like an apparition of evil, his arms extended and his long black hair swirling around his face. Dallas felt the ancient power crawl over his skin like tiny knives, slicing and stabbing their way from his arms across his shoulders to his neck and face.

Dallas wanted to scream, but he couldn't. The knives, with their invisible blades, carved at his mind, and Dallas felt as if every memory, every belief, was being dissected and laid before him, bloody and unrecognizable. He tried to form thoughts, but they were shredded quicker than they could form. Finally, even his sight was stripped away, and Dallas saw nothing but a red light before him, strobing faster and faster until the red was gone and everything turned black.

Dallas came to, finding himself face down on the Aubusson carpet. He had no idea if he'd been out for seconds or hours. He tried moving his arms, and this time his muscles obeyed the commands of his mind. The lights were on, and the first thing Dallas saw was the blood on his arms and on the carpet beneath him. The second thing he saw was Drago slouched in the Chippendale, his legs crossed and boredom draped once more over his features.

Dallas had never known a vampire to be able to cause physical injury solely with his mind. "Damn you, Drago."

"It irritates me when I'm not taken seriously. Don't make that mistake again, Allgate. Do we understand each other?" The sharpness in his voice belied the indifference in his look.

Dallas rose to his feet and felt his face. His fingers came away covered with blood. He looked at Drago. "I understand."

"Good. Now we can move on to this human female you are so concerned with. Since she was with you in Rodney, I assume she knows what we are."

"She knows."

"Then you know she's a danger to us," said Drago, his voice once more as smooth and cultured as ever.

"She carries my mark."

"You didn't answer my question."

Did Drago enjoy pretending to be obtuse? "She carries my mark. She's no threat."

"Yes, Allgate, I heard you the first time. Mark or no mark, you know the options. Kill her or bring her over."

Dallas tried to draw a deep breath. There seemed to be no air in the room. Ever since Drago had arrived, it was as though his power had sucked all the oxygen from the room. "This from someone who just yesterday was advocating an *affaire de coeur* with a human?"

"I suggested a liaison, not for you to give her a personal tour of Midexistence."

"I won't kill her."

Drago raked a hand casually through his hair. "Then make her one of us."

"And if I do neither?"

A sigh bordering on the theatrical wafted across the space between them. "Just two minutes ago you were privileged to witness a demonstration the likes of which few have ever seen, and fewer still have survived, and yet here you are already questioning my orders. Did I not make myself clear?"

"You made yourself very clear. But I've never let go of my intentions just because someone demanded it of me, and I'm not going to start now."

"Admirable. However, you have no choice in the matter. I'll be generous. I'll give you a week to make your decision. If you don't make it, I will personally take care of the problem. This is your only sanction, *mon ami.* Don't make me impose more."

"I understand you."

Drago was on his feet. "Good. Then our business is concluded." He paused at the front door long enough to glance back and lazily arch a brow. "Sorry about the carpet. *Bonsoir, monsieur.*"

Dallas held the door open long after Drago had gone, drawing in deep gulps of the fresh night air. The parlor had felt like a cold, airless vault, suffocating and lifeless.

"Gillie!" Somehow Dallas knew the man would be within easy earshot. He was not disappointed. Before Dallas could savor three more breaths, Gillie was at his side.

"Yes, Sir?"

"Another mess, Gillie. There's fresh blood on the Aubusson."

The man sighed, almost as dramatically as Drago had. "This is becoming an unpleasant habit." With that, he turned on his heels and headed back to the kitchen.

Dallas accompanied him, running his fingers over his face again. "Indeed. One I hope will be done with soon. Gillie, tell me how bad my face is."

Gillie gave him a critical look, one brow raised. "Your face will heal. I'm more worried about my carpet."

The man could be exasperating. "The cuts, Gillie, the cuts. How bad are they?"

Gillie turned away and gave a hrrumph. "If Miss Tia hasn't

been scared away by what you are, she won't be put off by a few cuts."

With a growl, Dallas retired to the library and slammed the door. He sank into the leather wing chair, forgoing any light. He needed some time to himself before he confronted Tia again. It wasn't the cuts, already forgotten, but what he was going to do with her. One week. He hated being told what to do. Even by his elders.

A soft knock on the door interrupted his contemplation.

"It's just me, Sir."

"Come in, Gillie."

The man stepped inside, flipped on the light and shut the door behind him. "Sorry to bother you, but I thought it best to know what transpired between you and Mr. Drago."

"You mean you didn't hear every word at your listening post, Gillie? Shame on you. You're slipping in your old age."

Gillie cleared his throat. "I'm afraid some of Mr. Drago's words were loud enough for the dead to hear."

"Yes, he entertained himself at my expense, as you could see. Did you hear the rest? St. James is still alive, and Richton and Keller are dead."

Gillie nodded solemnly.

"Keep security on the house as tight as possible, but I don't want any more of the boys involved unless it's absolutely necessary. If it is, call Mac and no one else, understand?"

Gillie nodded again. "I'll see to it." He turned, as if to leave, but then stopped. "So Mr. Drago impressed you for one so old, heh?"

Dallas smiled. "His power is more potent than I'd guessed, that's true, but nothing on this earth survives time without eroding, not even the Undead. No vampire lives forever. Not even Drago. So no hero worship, all right?"

"Don't start digging his grave yet, Sir. And don't ever underestimate him. Leave that mistake for St. James to make."

As the recipient of the countless cuts and wall slams, Dallas was not about to underestimate Drago, but he balked at thanking Gillie for the unsolicited advice. Sometimes Dallas did need to hear the obvious. He just didn't like it.

THIRTEEN

Tia crossed from the bed to the window for the countless time. Mr. Dragovich had left over a half hour ago, but Dallas had still not come upstairs or sent for her. She was sure that this "Drago" was another vampire. He had too much of the same look about him that Dallas and St. James had. The killer aura, the world-weary eyes in the young faces, and the fluidity and grace of every move they made were part of all three men. She was glad not to have had to speak with Drago. She was sure she wouldn't like him.

Wouldn't like him. She had to fight a wide smile. What kind of reaction was that to a bloodsucking monster with Hannibal Lechter eyes? For that matter, was her reaction to Dallas any better? Any more reasonable? This time she couldn't stop the smile from bursting into a quick belly laugh. None of it made any sense, including her reactions. She should be shocked by everything that had happened. Perhaps she was, and it just hadn't truly hit her yet. During her years as a cop, she had been dispatched to numerous "dead on entry" complaints—people who had died of natural causes. Every time the surviving family member on the scene had been calm, answering her questions and even offering her coffee. No doubt the reality of the situation set in long after she was gone. Perhaps she was in such a stage.

She also should be frightened. In Rodney, there had been no time for fear. Everything had transpired so quickly she had barely had time to think. All her movements had been dictated by her long-ago training and her instinct to survive. Now that it was over, the fear should have set in. But strangely it hadn't. What was there to be afraid of? That she would be killed? She had lived with that fear every day of her life as a street cop. But somehow in Dallas' presence that fear was always allayed. Besides, he could have killed her on a number of occasions and hadn't.

Dallas had said something about the life of a vampire being the reversal of everything human. She supposed she should be worried that her life would never again be normal, but that was the most ludicrous worry of all. Her life had been far from normal for many years. A cop's life was about the most abnormal life she could envision. What other profession was not only privy to the range of human drama that cops were, but to the private slices of life that no one else was allowed to see? Who else could knock on your door in the middle of the night and ask to have your home and life laid bare for inspection? Even the past two years as a photographer had been anything but normal with the constant traveling.

She looked at her watch again and, worried now, decided to make sure for herself that Dallas was all right. She almost laughed again. *Making sure a vampire was all right.* Oh well, it made as much sense as anything else she had experienced the past few days.

She found Gillie, and he directed her to the library. She rapped at the closed door.

"Come in, Tia."

She peered around the door. "How did you know it was me and not Gillie?"

He gazed at her with haggard eyes. "Your scent is different."

"Sorry I asked," she mumbled under her breath. "Are you okay?" she asked in a measurably louder voice.

"No."

She stood still a moment, caught off guard by the utterance of the simple word. This was a being who had never exuded anything but confidence and power. For him to admit to a need was something she thought she'd never hear. Without thinking, she slid onto his lap and put her arms around his neck. He held her, and when she tucked her feet up beneath her, he cradled her and stroked her hair. The strength of his body wrapped around her, his heat sealed her in, and she was content to huddle against his chest and listen to the beat of his heart. That he was anything less, or more, than human was the last thing on her mind.

***

It had been a long, long time since Dallas had held a woman like this. A strong woman, with hair like a raven's wing. He gathered a handful of black waves and brought it to his face. He buried his senses in the rich silkiness, smelling even the lingering fragrance of the shampoo she had used, and the weight of two hundred years fell away in a second.

Sabra, Sabra...what happened to you, love?

Sabra awakened with such a jolt that Dalys knew something was wrong. "What is it, love? A nightmare?"

She was slow to answer, as if still locked in another world. Moonlight sifted through the window, reflecting a strange light in her dark eyes. Her skin glowed pale and translucent, like a polished moonstone.

"Sabra, wake up, love. It's all right. You're all right now." He stroked her face with the back of his hand, and softened his voice to the sultry bass tones he knew could soothe the most high-strung of horseflesh.

Her too-bright eyes finally focused on him, and she wound her arms around his neck.

"Oh, Dal. I had the strangest dream. I was lost in the bush."

He raised his brows, like a father would to a child telling a fantastic story. "You, lost in the bush? What were you doing there?"

"I don't know. I was wandering and I came upon some bushmen. They were holding a ceremony. A death ceremony."

Dalys shivered, colder now that he held her in his arms than before.

"They all sat around a dead man, and each of them had a small knife. They all cut the dead man, and he bled all over the ground."

He rocked her in his arms, his hands brushing the tangled

hair from her face. "The dead don't bleed, silly."

Her soft voice floated up from the safety of his embrace. *"This one did. Then they saw me and came to me. They spoke to me, and I understood them."*

"What did they say, love?"

"'The blood is the life. It is so for both the living and the dead. We help our brother on his journey by providing a road of blood.'"

He felt chills scratch their way down his spine, and he tried to hold her closer, one hand encircling her neck.

She jerked her head away. *"Dalys, you're hurting me."*

He frowned, releasing her. He lifted the curtain of her hair and saw the black marks on her neck. *"Did you hurt yourself today?"* He gently touched the wound, but she pulled back again.

"Don't. I don't know. I don't remember anything."

He held her closely, and she had no more nightmares that night.

Dalys kept a worried vigilance over her for the next week. Sabra seemed listless, uninterested in the concerns of the household, but more to the point, his attentions. Her thin face took on a gaunt look, and she had no appetite at all. When he suggested she see MacArthur's physician, she laughed. *"I'm not one of your bloody brood mares, Dalys. I'm just tired, nothing more. And Adeline can see to the Master's table. She does little enough around here as 'tis."*

He ignored the barb about treating her like one of his animals. She had always been a lusty bed partner, as eager as he. *"Adeline has her hands full helping Elizabeth. You know that."*

"Oh, Dal, just let me sleep. I'll be better tomorrow, and then you'll have your arms full." A poke to his ribs and a sly wink accompanied her plea, and he let her sleep.

The following night, she was true to her word. He had obligingly left her alone, his late night partner a tankard of ale instead. He dozed, and was surprised and pleased to awaken to the feel of her body pressed against his, her mouth searching for his.

"Sabra..."

"Shhh, love. Just relax. I'm going to take you with me. You'll have everything you ever wanted."

He fell back against the bed and accepted the depth of her kiss with a strange yearning. Her legs straddled him, and her hands stole possessively over his face, as though they couldn't get enough of the feel of him. Like rays of sunlight, they warmed him wherever they touched, but her mouth burned hot on him, like a brand searing flesh. Yet the more her touch demanded of him, the colder he felt, until a paralysis gripped him. Her tongue painted a line of fire to a spot below one ear, and one hand raked his neck and chest to rest over his heart. He tried to press himself up to her, but she pushed him back down.

"Don't be scared, love. Your life has always been about journeys. Isn't that what you told me? This is but one more journey..." she whispered in his ear, and a sadness crept into her voice.

Scared? He had never been afraid of anything in his life. Had never feared any man, nor the future, not even death itself. Images of his past flashed behind his eyelids like a lightning storm. Newgate Prison. The courtroom. And eyes. Dozens of eyes, from the bored blue orbs of the magistrate to the haughty gray gaze of Christian St. James, they were all fixed on him. And yet the eyes weren't what scared him. What was in his heart did. He felt his chest would burst with the longing he now felt. But longing for...what?

"I've never been so scared...like my heart will stop beating." He heard the words float above him, and realized he had given them voice, but her melancholy laugh absorbed the words quickly. She bent her head to his chest, and he felt her tears and her reply soft and wet against his heart.

"No, don't let it stop. Not yet, love, not yet..."

He felt the quick sting of her teeth tearing his flesh, then a slow rapture that drained him of strength as she suckled the lifeblood from him. He closed his eyes and surrendered to the fear and longing he had never realized he carried. Like old friends, they walked with him, supporting him until he came to stand before a wall of mirrors. He saw his reflection like he had never seen it before. A damned man stood before him, naked and vulnerable. Damned by his country and his fellow man, still his soul fought for life.

"That's it, love, step through now to the other side. Life awaits you." Her words resounded around him, and he embraced the mirror, feeling not hard glass, but his mouth pressed against hot skin. He drew on her neck with a hunger, and as he filled his mouth with her sweet blood, he felt the dread and yearning fall aside. He became one with the reflection, and all he had known changed in an instant. Matter became shadow, night became day, and death became life. He fed as an infant would, not understanding, not caring, just needing and taking, until he was sated. At last, the roaring in his ears eased, and he fell back, exhausted.

"Welcome, my love. You've crossed the threshold."

Her words were as incomprehensible to him as soothing sounds to a baby, and he slept, knowing nothing, feeling nothing. When at last he awoke, the boundaries of time and dimension had sloughed off like an old skin, and a new perception governed all he saw and felt. Everything was possible, life was eternal, and power yet unknown and unexplored was his for the taking. Only one thing was out of reach for evermore.

Like the vestiges of his humanity, his soul had not passed through the mirror.

Sabra, Sabra...where did you go, my love?

Tia twisted in his arms, and the movement stirred him. Could he do it? Could he lose Tia to Midexistence the way he had lost Sabra? Sabra had left him and MacArthur's employ soon after his transformation. She had other needs then, ones he couldn't fill. He had remained, foolishly thinking he still needed MacArthur, but nothing was ever the same. Given his pick of women convicts, he had tried to find another like Sabra, but most had been slovenly and too easy. The things they saw reflected in his eyes frightened a few, but most were only too happy to be invited into his bed at night. Their misfortune and his pleasure, but too short-lived.

"Ummm. Dallas?"

"Yes, love?"

She squirmed in his embrace and pulled away so that she could see his face. "Why did you call me that?"

He couldn't lie. He couldn't tell her he loved her. As much as he didn't want to lose her, love was a human emotion. She would know the lie. "An old habit. A very old habit."

"Sabra." It was no question. The truth swam in her liquid blue eyes.

It was all he could do to nod.

"You never told me about her."

"Are you sure it's something you want to hear?"

"No, but..." All her conflicting emotions warred in her eyes, and her thoughts laid themselves bare to him at the surface of her mind. Her reason fought the reality of what he was, yet the rest of her itched to be led deeper into the mystery of what he had been. She was almost ready. It was the point in the relationship that vampires savored most, the point at which the victim has completed the journey from appearance to reality. All outward attitudes have been peeled away, all facades knocked down, and all masks ripped off. The victim, stripped to the core, revealed only their most basic desires. Tia was almost there. The time was approaching. The time the vampire's destruction of its victim was most satisfying.

His vampiric lust stirred, awakened by her nearness and the distress of her eyes. And her blood. Always the blood.

Maybe he shouldn't wait. Maybe he should just put an end to the dilemma right now. He couldn't let her go back north. Drago would follow and kill her. And yet he didn't want to lose her the way he had lost Sabra. That had been a lingering agony that had never had an ending. This was the only path left. A quick end to her pain, and a resolution to his problem.

"Dallas..."

Plea or protest, it didn't matter. He pulled her higher on his lap and took her face in his hands, his eyes lowered to the white column framed by his forearms. Better he do this than Drago. He couldn't bear the thought of that ancient creature holding her like this. He leaned his head forward, and his lips sampled hers, reveling in the sweetness that greeted him.

She managed to whisper his name again in between kisses, but he neither stopped nor answered her.

He could already taste her energy, her life force, in the warmth and passion of her mouth. Soon he'd taste her blood again, and that, combined with her energy, comprised her very essence. Last night when he was injured was need. This final time would be the perfect harmony of need and desire.

A sound broke through the roaring of his own blood in his ears and her blood under his hands and mouth, so close. In the next instant Tia was pushing away from him and slithering off his lap. Someone was knocking insistently on the door.

"Sir?"

Damn Gillie. He gave Tia another few seconds to adjust her clothes and smooth her hair before he told the man to enter.

Gillie swung open the door and stepped inside. If the old man wondered just what he and Tia had been doing in the library with the door closed, Gillie gave no indication, not even his customary eyebrow quirk.

"Sorry to bother you, Sir. I suppose it could have waited, but Miss Angie's on the phone and wants to know if you'll be coming to the inn tonight. She says the paperwork is starting to pile up."

Dallas laughed. Even for the Undead, the dictates of daily living never ceased. "I'll take it in the kitchen, Gillie. Tia, I'll be right back."

But as soon as he was out of the library, all mirth slid from his face. *Did Tia have any idea how close he had just come to killing her?* No, of course not. The mirror, now more than ever, would show her only what she wanted to see. And what did he want? He didn't have the excuse of a false image to explain his own behavior. The monster that he was had demanded her death, but even as his lust had called for it, something in him was glad that Angie and Gillie had intervened. He wanted her with him, alive, not cold in the ground or wandering the earth like the damned creature he was. The preservation of life. It was a strange concept for him to grasp.

***

Tia exhaled a long sigh after Dallas left the library. One thing she couldn't debate in her mind was the undeniable attraction his body held for hers, and that attraction hadn't lessened one little bit with the knowledge he wasn't human. Perhaps if he had displayed the cold skin, red eyes, and fangs she had seen on the movie screen she wouldn't want him so much, but aside from the centuries that played in his eyes and the grace of one who didn't have to worry about tired muscles or arthritis, he looked human. In spite of her body's disappointment, though, she had been glad for Gillie's interruption. Her emotions were too unstable to risk getting too close to Dallas again.

Her eyes were caught by the "Trail of Tears" print. *Evil.* Now that had been evil. Soldiers dragging women and children from their homes and driving them halfway across the country in the dead of winter. Thousands had died, Dallas had told her. And that had been human against human. Was one being who wanted nothing more than to survive truly evil, when this was the kind of thing that man did to man, and continued to do all around the world, even today?

She thought about St. James. Had even he been evil? He had wanted nothing but revenge. How many shootings had she been dispatched to that had been perpetrated for that reason or something even less? St. James had killed innocent people. So did humans every day in the city. Innocent people shot in drive-bys or in armed robberies happened all the time. Were those suspects evil? Not according to the defense attorneys and social workers. People were just "misunderstood" or had been exposed to "bad influences."

It was all so confusing. But Dallas and St. James weren't "people." Society would dictate she should think of them as evil, regardless of their actions, but could she? Were their motives any different from human motives?

Tia looked again at the "Trail of Tears." It seemed a strange picture for a vampire to have hanging in his house. She would have expected some dark and gloomy landscape, or an animal print depicting a pack of wolves at a kill, or even some lurid portrait of a nude, but soldiers herding Indians? It was strange indeed.

When Tia turned, Dallas was standing in the doorway, his arms crossed and his head tilted to one side, as if he were studying her as closely as she was studying the painting on the wall. As usual, she hadn't heard him approach.

"I have some work to do at the inn. I think it best you come along."

Something in that didn't sound quite right to her. "Umm, you *want* me to come, or it's a good idea if I come?"

The hooded eyes blinked but once. "St. James isn't dead."

"What?"

"Drago was kind enough to inform me that St. James was able to pull himself from the fire before it consumed him."

Dallas' low voice had a dry edge Tia couldn't miss. Dislike for Drago or self-directed irritation? "I don't understand. I thought you said..."

He cut her off. "I underestimated the bastard. It won't happen again. If the cur has any brains he'll heed Drago's warning and slink back to wherever he came from with his tail between his legs. But just in case...I'm not taking any chances."

"But what about Gillie and your other men? Aren't they in danger if St. James comes back? "

Dallas lifted his brows. "I think I'll suggest to Mac he go on an impromptu all-expenses paid vacation, but Gillie won't leave. He's a stubborn old man." He jerked his head. "Come on, you can have a drink and a late supper while I get some work done."

Ten minutes later she sat at the small bar at the rear of Bishop's Inn nursing a drink while Angie brought Dallas up to date on news.

"How's The Lady been?" asked Dallas.

"She's bad off over something. All week she's been cryin' and throwin' tantrums. Ever since that accident happened outside and that poor man was killed. Rachel up and quit last night. Said she could take the windows rattlin' but not the cryin' from upstairs. Can't say I blame her. I've never seen The Lady so worked up."

Dallas nodded. "That accident bothered all of us. All right, put an ad in the paper for a new waitress. I'll be upstairs with Miss Martell."

He extended a hand toward Tia, and she took it, following him up the narrow stairs to the third floor. Tia could feel the eyes of Angie and Jaz glued to her back. Tia supposed she couldn't blame the women for wondering just who she was to be trailing after Dallas like she owned him. She wondered if they were jealous, then had to stifle a laugh. If they only knew. Once on the third floor, however, a thump from behind a wall shifted her thoughts from the living and breathing women to the one who wasn't.

"Then it's true? Veilina is real?" Real didn't seem the right word. "I mean, her ghost really exists?"

"Of course. You doubted it?"

"Silly me. I didn't think that ghosts were any more real than...well, you know. Is Veilina upset because of me?"

Dallas sank into the chair behind the desk with an ease and familiarity Tia wished she felt. "No, I don't think so. I think it's more likely she's bothered by Flynne and St. James having been here."

"Oh." Tia pulled up one of the empty chairs and settled in, squirming to get comfortable on the hard seat. "So, do your superhuman abilities extend to talking and working at the same time?"

He smiled, a rare beam of pleasure, not sadness, and the deep smile line that ran almost the entire length of his face popped into view. "Naturally. What would you like to hear?"

"You didn't finish telling me about Sabra."

The smile line vanished as if it had never been there at all, and Dallas' eyes studied the papers in front of him. "Sabra was my woman. I was very much in love with her." He shuffled a few papers. "She made those years of being a convict bearable. But in 1801 I lost her."

"Lost her? She died?"

She saw a muscle twitch in his face, but he didn't look up. "She went into the bush. I'm not sure why. Apparently she came across some sort of death ceremony. I was never able to find out what she stumbled on. Secrets in the bush are guarded more closely than those anywhere else on earth. She died, yes, and was reborn into the realm of Midexistence."

"She became a vampire?" Tia whispered the question, immediately feeling silly. Who did she think was going to overhear?

Dallas nodded. "I was her first conquest and creation. I'm not sure why she did it. Maybe she thought we could remain together in eternity, but it doesn't work that way. More likely it was just vampiric aggressiveness or envy that she was no longer among the living and I still was." He shook his head. "I don't know."

"How does it work? Vampirism, I mean."

He finally looked up at her. "I couldn't explain it any more than you could explain to me what it is that gives you life. All I can tell you is that the human body dies, and a kind of anti-life, a negative energy, reanimates the body."

"I thought it was the blood."

"The blood is the catalyst," he said softly.

"What you did to me..."

"Was not enough for you to become one of the Undead, don't worry. For that to happen, you'd have to take a substantial amount of my blood."

Tia fidgeted with the hem of her shirt, her eyes glued to the errant button thread that needed trimming. "Did you ever mean to do that to me?" She raised her eyes only when she heard him answer.

"No. I didn't want you to become like Sabra."

His eyes were steady on hers, and he displayed none of the obvious signs of a liar, but how could she know for sure? She couldn't. It hit her that she was trusting an inhuman creature with her life. For the first time it really hit her, and she was scared. After Rodney, on the drive back to Natchez and on the veranda, there hadn't been time to think. Later, when she had thought about it, she had tried to hold her emotions at bay by logically addressing the issue, putting him and her and everything that had happened into neat, color-coded little boxes. In the library, her body's messages had drowned out anything her mind could try to voice.

But now, at the inn, she felt trapped. With St. James still out there, she knew Dallas wouldn't let her leave even if she wanted to. There was a chain around her, and the being that held the other end was a thing she didn't think she'd ever be able to truly understand. No matter how many questions she asked, how would she know he'd answer them with the truth?

"Last night you said there'd be consequences to...what I did. What did you mean?"

Dallas didn't answer right away, and his attention, for all appearances, was on his work, but Tia knew he had heard her.

"It's a blood tie."

That wasn't much of an answer. "Meaning?"

He sighed. "Meaning I can sense your presence and feelings even more than I could before. As for you, it should inspire a measure of the same kind of trust in me that Gillie feels. And it should provide a kind of protection against other vampires. My scent is on you now. That should make you...unattractive to others."

She nodded, but suspected at the very best he was embellishing the truth, and at the worse, lying. She strongly doubted that a vampire mark was beneficial to the human half in any shape or form, but she kept her skepticism to herself.

He coaxed her into ordering a prime rib and salad from the kitchen, but she could only finish half of it, still full from her early evening "breakfast." Still, the food made her drowsy, and she curled on the couch for a nap while Dallas worked. She couldn't get comfortable, though, no matter how she twisted and squirmed. She felt cold in the evening summer heat, and every time she opened her eyes, shadows teased her peripheral vision. Finally, though, her uneasiness sank into a restless sleep.

A long hallway stretched before her, not a narrow corridor, but the wide hall of the grandest mansion she had ever been in. She journeyed down the hallway, passing elaborately

*carved tables, monstrously large chairs, and cabinets that
nearly reached to the high ceiling. She pressed on, coming
upon no doors or entranceways, until the hall ended in a dead
end wall. Mounted upon the end wall was the largest oval
mirror she had ever seen, the gilt frame wider than her hand.
She saw her reflection in the mirror, but where there should
have been one face staring back, there were two. Not quite
superimposed, it was a double image, the nose of one face
about six inches from that of the other. One face was healthy
and tanned from the exposure of the Mississippi sun, but the
other was pale and faded, an imitation of life.*

An abrupt noise awakened Tia, and sealed the dream fresh
in her memory. She blinked her eyes, and saw Dallas staring
at her. The room was quiet. "What was that?"

Dallas' eyes flicked to the ceiling. "My Lady, I suppose,
reminding me that it's time I got back home."

Tia sat up and ran her hands through her hair. "Your Lady?"
Her gaze lapped the room and came to rest again on Dallas.
"My God. 'The Vampar of Natchez.' When you said it on the
way back from Rodney it didn't hit me. You're Veilina's Devon,
the rich planter. The jilted fiancé who conspired to kill her
lover."

"Devon Alexander. One of my aliases over the years."

"I don't care what your name was! How could you do that
to her? She once loved you, and you destroyed her!"

His vampire eyes were cool and glassy in the dim light. "I
have no explanation you'd either understand or find
satisfaction in," he replied, his voice as low as the lamplight.
"Come. It's time to go."

Tia remained seated, gripping the leather cushion. "No. I
want to hear it."

"Without your judgmental interruptions?"

This was one story she badly wanted to hear. She exhaled
a sigh that was more a huff, but nodded.

He leaned back in his chair, and his eyes seemed focused
on a point somewhere above and beyond her. "I was still a
very young vampire then. I hadn't yet found a way to control
my thirst for revenge or my aggression against humans. Veilina

was the first human female I played at being in love with. It was a difficult relationship for a novice like myself to master."

She conceded him that. If her situation was any indication, the vampire-human relationship seemed no easier to manage even now.

She let him continue. "At first I thought Veilina was playing games with me, trying to make me jealous by feigning love for the stable boy. One night we had a terrible fight, and she told me she had never really loved me—that it was only my wealth she was interested in. The betrayal was something the vampire wasn't prepared to deal with. I conspired with Veilina's father to kill Rowan. I thought…I thought with the stable boy out of the way that I could make Veilina mine."

Tia curled on the sofa and wrapped her arms around her, suddenly chilled. She forced herself to wait for the rest.

"After Veilina died I found a letter she had left for me. In the letter she said she had really loved me once—that her denial of that love during our fight was made in anger. She said she felt partially responsible for Rowan's death. She felt I might never have carried out my plan to kill him had she not infuriated me so much with her lie."

Tia glanced around the room. "So how does The Lady feel about you now? I would think she would hate you, but…"

"Deciphering The Lady's motives isn't always easy, not even for me after all this time. Sometimes it's hate. She seems to relish torturing me with her very presence, reminding me of what I did. On the other hand, she's very protective of me, almost as though she still loved me. As though I am hers alone to torment. Come. It's late."

This time she obediently went with him, having no choice, but was glad for the silence of the ride back to the townhouse. She tried to digest what he had told her. They were just excuses for violence, just like all the excuses she had heard so many times on the Job. Youth…misunderstanding…anger. None of them justified killing. She hadn't bought into the excuses as a cop, and she couldn't now.

This time not even the nearness of his body a foot from hers distracted her from her feelings of disgust. She had done her best to convince herself that the creature next to her wasn't evil, but the fact remained that destruction and revenge were a part of his life he neither turned away from nor lamented. When they arrived at the townhouse, Tia was equally glad that he didn't suggest she sleep with him. Instead, he pointed out the intercom button in her bedroom that connected directly to the cellar, and gave her back the Colt, fully reloaded with silver bullets.

"I don't think St. James will try anything in my own backyard, and he's probably not yet recuperated from his injuries, but I won't assume anything this time around. If you need me, call. I can function well enough inside the house during daylight hours."

She nodded, having no intention of calling him. Gillie knocked on her door soon after Dallas took his leave, and she invited him in.

"Gillie, have you ever had a dream that was more like a vision?"

His expression was as solemn as ever. "A presentment? I have. Why? Did you have one?"

"Earlier this evening." She described the strange dream of the double vision to him. "It was so strong, I can't help thinking it means something. I'm just not sure what. That I'm going to die? Or that I'm going to live a second life as one of the Undead? What else could it mean, do you think? Did you ever have a dream like that?"

Gillie's brows knitted together in thought. "I don't recall a vision exactly like that one. It might mean those things, of course, but not necessarily. It could mean simply that your life has arrived at a fork, and that two futures stand before you. You must decide which to make reality." He turned sad eyes to her and took her hand. "I can't help you make your decision, Tia."

"No. I understand. But thanks, Gillie." Somehow, looking at the old man's face, she knew he'd support her in whatever decision she made.

Blood wasn't the only bond there was.

FOURTEEN

Tia woke before noon, her sleep broken as much from her unsettled mind as from her nap at the inn. She tugged the bedroom drapes open, and the late morning sun filled her with a kind of energy and urgency.

She thought again about everything she had learned the night before, and the fear and anger that had blossomed in the darkness hadn't been dispelled one bit by the daylight. And Sabra and Veilina were just as real to her now as they had been in the dim light of the inn.

Dallas had loved Sabra, but that had been as a human. Had every woman he had met since then been an attempt to relive that experience? Veilina had apparently been 'loved' well enough by Dallas-Devon until she made the mistake of turning from him. Then his true self had emerged from the cocoon of gentility with a vengeance. If she stayed, would she, too, be 'loved' until he decided she no longer fit the role to be played? What then?

She couldn't love a man—any kind of man—who wanted nothing more than to use her. The dream of the double image had been a warning from Veilina. She was sure of it.

There was another life out there for her, one that embraced the light of day. If she left now, she could put a lot of distance between herself and Dallas. She doubted she meant enough to him for him to follow her north. And St. James...well, St. James wanted Dallas, not her. She would go home, resume her relatively normal life, and forget her trip to Natchez had ever happened.

She showered and dressed quickly. When Gillie tapped softly on the door to see if she wanted any breakfast, she asked him if she could just have coffee and fruit. She finished packing, took a last look at the room, then descended to the kitchen.

She met Gillie's eyes and felt guilty. "I have to go, Gillie. There's too much here I can't handle."

"I understand, Miss."

"He'll be angry with you for letting me go, won't he?"

"I'll blame my incompetence on my advancing years and feeble mind. He won't buy it, but it'll dilute any wrath he feels inclined to direct my way. Here, have a biscuit. It'll give you energy."

She smiled. She would miss Gillie. A small voice somewhere in the back of her mind told her she'd miss Dallas, too, but she ignored it. "You know his secret is safe with me, don't you, Gillie?" she asked in between mouthfuls of warm bakery.

The old man nodded. "I believe that. I think Mr. Allgate will, too, once the lava cools."

She winced. "Come on, Gillie. I can't possibly matter that much to someone who's lived, for…how long? Two hundred years?"

"Two hundred and thirty-five years. I think you underestimate yourself."

"It's not me he wants." Tia popped the final crumbling bit of biscuit into her mouth and washed it down with the last of her coffee. "Thanks for everything, Gillie. Everything. Especially your help with this."

"Oh, I haven't begun helping yet. Run back upstairs and prepare a second outfit. One you can either wear over your first outfit or can carry in a small bag. Make sure the second set is something that disguises your looks as much as possible. Oh, and put up your hair."

She cocked her head in question.

"The house is most likely still being watched," he said, his voice patient.

"But I'm sure my car is known. What good does it do to change clothes?"

"I've taken care of that. Hurry now." He clapped his hands

together as if to encourage a lazy child.

Tia gave him a broad smile and obeyed. Fifteen minutes later, wearing a sleeveless blouse with a long skirt and carrying a large bag, Tia left with Gillie in the Rose Hill truck. He drove, and at the first stoplight they halted at he handed her a set of car keys.

"I had Mac rent a car for you first thing this morning. It's parked in the lot of the store we're going to. We'll both go in, as if to shop, then once inside, you'll find the ladies' room and change clothes. You let your hair down, put on sunglasses, dump the extra outfit and the bag, then you leave alone and head for the rental car. Anyone watching will, hopefully, be put off by the switch long enough for you to get away."

Tia was dumbfounded into momentary silence. "You planned all this before I even woke up? How did you know I'd want to leave?"

"I had a sense of it last night. As I said, I get presentments, too."

"But why? Why do all this for me when it goes against your orders?"

Gillie's short gray hair seemed to bristle on end. "I don't take orders. I follow suggestions. Most of the time. Let's just say that while I have no regrets in my own life, I'm a big proponent of choice. If it's your wish to leave, you should be able to leave."

She wanted to hug the old man. Moments later, inside the city's largest superstore, she did just that. Shortly after, wearing capri pants, a long-sleeved shirt tied at the waist, and sunglasses, she strode with confidence out of the store. Carrying a plastic shopping bag, she headed for the red Mustang parked six aisles down from where Gillie had parked the truck.

The next few minutes seemed the longest of all, but by the time they had elapsed, she was on Highway 61 North out of town, away from a haunted inn, a restless ghostly spirit, and three vampires that were three too many for comfort.

She had had to leave her photography equipment and most of her clothes and belongings behind, but Gillie had promised to ship everything to her. Nothing, after all, was as important as getting away from all this madness. The one thing that Gillie had insisted she take was the Colt, fully loaded with silver ammunition. Tia hadn't argued.

With every mile that rolled under the wheels, Tia relaxed more. By the time she had traveled fifty miles up the Trace, she stopped looking in her rearview mirror every ten seconds. She kept her mind blank, trying to replace her slowly diminishing anxiety with nothing more than appreciation for the beauty of the Trace Parkway.

Dallas was the last thing she wanted to think about, and she shoved him out of her mind each time he tried to intrude. If she thought about him, she'd go crazy. But more than that, if she allowed the memory of his green amber eyes and mesmerizing low voice into her head she was afraid she'd turn the car around without a moment's hesitation.

Fifteen minutes later Tia saw a sign for a wayside with a restroom. Stopping the car was the last thing she wanted to do, but she had consumed too much coffee to keep going much further. She checked her mirror again. No car had come up behind her or passed her for at least ten miles. She pulled into the wayside and hurried into the building. Less than five minutes had elapsed when she came out again, but the sight that greeted her sent her heart plummeting so low that she wondered how its beating could still be thundering in her ears.

A familiar, striking figure leaned against the hood of a burgundy Riviera with both his arms folded across his chest and his booted feet crossed at the ankles. Black hair hung to below the man's shoulders, and high arched brows gave blue eyes that might otherwise be beautiful a spoiled, bored air.

"*Bonjour, mademoiselle.* I don't believe I've had the pleasure." His soft voice lingered on the last word, giving his eyes a chance to travel the length of her body.

It was a look similar to the one he had given her when she first saw him at the townhouse, and it made her skin crawl wherever his gaze touched her. Her feet felt as dead as the thing lounging by the car, and the Colt, so near in the shoulder bag that hung at her side, felt just as useless. If his speed was anything like Dallas', he'd be on her before she could dig the gun out. Better to wait.

"You know who I am. What do you want with me?" Her mind wanted to throw the words out, but they barely rolled out past the tightness in her throat.

"And you know who I am as well, don't you, *mademoiselle* Martell? But let's do this properly." He pushed off of the car and gave her a bow as smooth as a fold of silk. "Alek Dragovich, *a votre service.*"

She told herself she wasn't impressed, but neither her mind nor body bought it. "I don't speak French."

"I think you understand my meaning well enough."

She was afraid she did. "I know who you are and what you are. What do you want?" She was also afraid he knew she didn't feel as brave as her words.

"Oh, many things, *mademoiselle*. But for now a little chat with do." He swung open the passenger door of the Riviera. "Sit."

Getting into his car was the last thing Tia wanted to do, but the blue eyes were as powerful an incentive as if he held two guns on her. She plopped down on the leather seat, her legs having no strength to support her, and clutched her bag on her lap, the Colt a small but needed reassurance. The creature flowed through the driver's door onto the seat next to her, and when he slammed his door, she couldn't breathe. He was no taller than Dallas, yet his presence seemed to expand until he completely filled the interior of the big car, leaving no room even for oxygen. But, as if he knew her distress, he turned the engine on and the air conditioner began circulating cool air around her. It helped a little.

He turned toward her, and though she didn't want to look at him, she couldn't do anything else but. She had always seen him at a distance, and if his appearance had then been imposing, it was stunning close up. His hair was as blue-black and shiny as fresh tar, and it was swept back from a slight widow's peak to flow across his shoulders in dark swells. His chiseled mouth, framed on either side by twin smile lines, was anchored by a shallow cleft in his chin. But by far the feature that held her attention was his eyes. They were as devoid of life as they were full of color.

"What has Allgate told you about me?"

The softness of the cultured voice frightened her as much as his eyes did. "Nothing. All I know is that you're...like him."

"Certainement, but not exactly like him. Allgate and St. James are but children, and I am their father, here to do a father's job. It is my duty to...inspire obedience and to correct improper behavior. *Comprendez-vous?"*

She shook her head. "I don't know what you're talking about."

His eyes violated her like the unwanted touch of a stranger's hands, and even when she squeezed her lids shut she felt him invade her. Never in her life had she felt as helpless against anyone or anything.

He breathed a long sigh, almost into her ear, and she shivered.

"Ah, I see. You have no children. Let me try something else. I am like *la police.* I enforce laws and punish those who do not obey. This I think you understand, yes?"

She understood, and hated him more for it. The hostility gave her strength. "I get it. You police your own kind. Like Internal Affairs. No wonder Dallas said you were no friend."

Drago laughed, and it was like the ashes of a long-dead fire being poured over her. Her head shook with an involuntary cleansing shudder, but nothing was accomplished except the dislodging of long strands of hair into her eyes.

His laughter abruptly ceased. He reached his hand to her face, and with one finger skimmed the errant locks back to their home at her temple. He then gathered a handful of hair at her neck and held it aside. The feel of his skin against hers made her shudder again, but his touch was surprisingly gentle. He let the hair fall back into place.

"Tell me. How is it that with Allgate's mark you are able to run from him? That is what you are doing, *mademoiselle,* isn't it? Running away? You almost eluded even me with your switch of clothes and car."

She wanted to tell him that what she was doing was none

of his business, but his blue gaze was a pressure she couldn't fight. "I don't understand any of what's happened, least of all, this 'mark.'"

"Allgate didn't explain it to you?"

"He tried. I didn't want to listen."

"Ah. Curious. Still, your lack of understanding should have no effect on the mark's influence. Yet here you are...with me." He raised his hand once more to finger her long hair. "And what am I to do with you?"

She wanted to shrink from his touch, but there was no place to go. Besides, pride kept her from flinching. He might know she was afraid of him, but she wasn't going to show it. "Let me go."

"That is the one thing, I'm afraid, I cannot do." He lifted a thick strand of her hair and let it slide down through his fingertips, as if he could taste and absorb its texture through his skin. "Tell me something else, *mademoiselle,* and the truth only, *s'il vous plait.* You have no feelings for Allgate?"

"What does it matter? He has no feelings for me."

"You are so sure of this?"

She managed a small laugh. "He's not human. He doesn't have feelings any more than you do." All she could think about was Dallas' revenge against Christian St. James and his betrayal of Veilina.

His hand moved from her hair to grasp her chin and force her gaze to his, but there was no roughness in his touch. She felt the warmth from his fingers penetrate her skin. It was a strange sensation from one so cold.

"I hope you are right, *mademoiselle,* I hope you are right."

***

As soon as Dallas woke that evening and ascended from the cellar, he knew something was wrong. Tia's scent was faint, like that of a perfume that lingers after a woman leaves a room, and he couldn't feel her presence at all through the mark. He flew to her room and encountered nothing but her suitcase and camera bag, carefully packed and waiting patiently on the bed.

He found Gillie seated on a stone bench in the garden,

watering the flowers. "Where is she?"

"Gone."

Dallas knew Gillie would never lie to him, but the small word of truth angered him as much as a fabrication would have. "Where, Gillie?"

The old man shrugged. "Home. Back north. She wanted to go. I wouldn't have been able to stop her. She's a very stubborn woman, you know."

Dallas sank to the bench, back to back with Gillie, and shook his head. "Stubborn? She carries my mark."

"Pardon me for saying so, Sir, but your 'mark' isn't the most powerful force on earth. She was scared. Who among us mortals would not have been after what she survived in the cemetery and at Rodney?"

"She knew I wasn't going to allow her to be harmed."

Gillie laughed, a dry sound like the rustle of fallen leaves. "She was more afraid of you than of anything else."

"Then St. James has her, and she's dead. Or Drago, and she's as good as dead."

"Perhaps not, Sir. I helped her leave in disguise and in a new rental car."

Dallas shook his head again. "I should have known you'd do no less. Such a trick might work with St. James, but it won't fool Drago. You yourself warned me not to underestimate him."

"It's been almost eight hours, and there's been nothing."

"There will be, Gillie. There will be."

Dallas rose and left Gillie to the flowers, returning to his upstairs master bedroom, one of the few rooms at Rose Hill that held no recent memories of Tia, Drago, Conner or St. James. He needed to think, and he wanted no distractions from such memories. Dallas had no doubt that either Drago or St. James would soon make an encore appearance, and he needed to be prepared.

Why was he so upset over losing Tia? Perhaps it was simple. Perhaps, as with Raemon, he was piqued by the loss of a valued possession. No. There was no such simple answer. Was it wounded pride over her defeating his mark so easily?

Was it the loss of his pleasure? Surely it was both, yet there was no satisfaction in embracing either as an explanation. Yet to delve deeper was to examine feelings that were too human, and that was something he had not done for a long, long time. He doubted he even had the capacity for such self-evaluation.

He turned his thoughts instead to St. James and Drago. The Undead were easier to understand. At least St. James was. If Jermyn made a reappearance, there was only one thing to do. Finish the job he had "done badly," as Drago had so eloquently phrased it. Dallas knew he was stronger than St. James, even with the disadvantage of not being a day vampire. Nothing would have to be sacrificed.

Drago was another matter altogether. *L'enforcier* would not be defeated in a battle of strength. Will was the only weapon Dallas had against the more powerful vampire. If he relinquished that weapon and gave in to Drago, Tia would be lost. Yet if he asserted his will, there was still no guarantee he'd be able to save Tia. *The preservation of life.* Could he fight to save Tia, knowing she wanted nothing to do with him? Such a selfless act was foreign to him.

Dallas went downstairs and followed the whistling of a teapot to the kitchen. Gillie was preparing for his evening cup.

"I need your help, Gillie."

"I thought you might. Tell me, is it the young lady who has you baffled, or yourself?"

Dallas joined his friend at the table. "Both, I fear. I can't understand a human who behaves the way she does, and even less can I understand why I care that I can't."

Gillie sighed. "Oh, dear. I'm not sure the wisest man on earth can help you there, Sir."

Dallas gave the man a look that could crack stone, and Gillie raised both brows in resignation.

"Very well, Sir. I'll try. Let's start by clarifying the muddle..."

***

An hour later, Gillie retired for the night, in truth doing nothing for Dallas except to further muddy the waters. In frustration, Dallas wandered the rooms of the townhouse in darkness, as silent as a cat.

The old man was right about one thing. Dallas needed to clear his vision. He needed to stop trying to see through the human eyes he no longer possessed. Clarity of vision was one of the true vampiric gifts, and Dallas needed to remember that. It was the unique talent of the vampire to be able to strip away all appearances from a person or thing, and to see it in its true reality.

With a purpose now, Dallas turned his steps toward the small library and pulled the diary from the bookshelf, the old diary Tia had been so taken with. He hadn't looked at it in decades and wasn't sure why he had even kept it all these years. It contained nothing his memory couldn't pull, undiminished, from the past, yet he'd never been able to part with the book. Written both before and after his transformation, perhaps it was a link to his human past he was reluctant to sever.

He carefully separated fragile pages, looking for one entry in particular.

23rd March, 1801

Governor King finally got his wish. John is being sent back to England to face court martial. Who would have thought after all this time that John would be brought down because of something so foolish as a duel? Can it be that all my plans have come to naught? Sabra doesn't know yet. Without John's sponsorship, I fear for us. If we are separated, it will do to me what no other hardship on this land has done. I don't know how I'll go on.

Written before his transformation, Dalys had lamented the loss of his sponsor, John MacArthur. Dalys had seen the man then as determined and strong, to be sure, but also as intuitive and just plain lucky. Dalys had seen it as only prudent to champion such a man, convict though he was.

Dallas remembered well the day MacArthur left, even without the help of the diary.

John extended his hand to Dalys. It was an honor rarely afforded a convict.

"You've done well for me, Aldgate."

"I fear I'd have been more use to you if I'd known sheep rather than horses."

MacArthur smiled, a sentimentality Dalys had seldom seen. "You're not a shepherd, laddie. There's no shame in that." He paused, and the smile faded. "I can't protect you once I've gone, but I promise you two things. One. I won't forget your loyalty. You've stood by me for ten years, and no freeman has done better. Second. Do not fear. This is not the end of it. I will return. And when I do, I promise I'll do right by you."

"I'll wait, Sir. Waiting is what convicts are best at."

"You won't always be a convict, Aldgate. This I know."

"As do I," said Dalys.

"Well said, lad. Kiss that pretty woman of yours for me, won't you?"

Dalys would keep that promise. He hoped against hope that MacArthur would keep his.

MacArthur did keep his word, but by then the whole world had changed. How differently Dalys saw John with vampiric eyes. Stripped of his "luck" and braggadocio, Dalys saw the heart of the man—cunning and ruthless.

Dallas scanned the pages in the diary, and found the next entry he sought.

7th April, 1805

MacArthur was true to his word, the pompous ass. He has returned in triumph! I see him now for what he is, a serpent that chokes the life out of this community. I am a great fan of irony. It amuses me that we are now so much alike. Our first meeting since his return was uncomfortable, yet he suspects nothing. He spouts concern for my health and wags his head over my intolerance for the sunlight, yet I know all he feels is disappointment that I can no longer work my miracles with his horses. His grant of 5000 additional acres for sheep breeding gave me the perfect excuse to request to be overseer of the 30 convicts he was given. Sheep and convicts are stupid beasts. The qualities in my touch and voice that now trigger fear and disquiet in the horses make the sheep quite malleable, and the convicts even more so.

5th August, 1806

It is time to leave. Sabra is lost to me, the horses are lost to me, and I grow bored with the posturing of MacArthur and Bligh. Elizabeth calls Bligh "violent, rash, and tyrannical," but her husband is no better. I smell another mutiny coming. This is John's war. Mine still awaits me in England.

Dallas couldn't help remembering his departure from Australia. In a way, it had been as much a turning point in his life as the shedding of his humanity.

Dalys stood at the rail on the forecastle of the Parramatta *and watched the horizon swallow the remains of the day. A tiny coral bead hovered, winked, then slipped out of sight, and all that still spoke of daylight were the dusky clouds that stretched, rosy and warm, above the horizon for a few moments more. Soon, they too darkened, and the dawn of night was complete. He drew a deep breath of the balmy sea air, and tried to feel a measure of hope. He had been glad to be done with Australia. It had been all too easy to leave. Even without his new-found power, he was confident he could have convinced MacArthur to free him, but it had been truly child's play to gain compliance with nothing more than a glance.*

He had grown tired of sheep, and had become bored with the convicts and Corps alike. Nothing was a challenge, except the one constant in his life. Survival. And that, with practice, was becoming easier and easier. He needed a new life and new challenges, and England would provide those, and more. Revenge. He hadn't forgotten Christian St. James. He only hoped the miscreant was still alive.

And when he was done draining England of challenges, the world itself would be his to take.

They had been moments in time that Dallas had not and would not ever forget. He closed the diary and slid it mindfully back to its home on the shelf. He sensed that this new day, too, would be a turning point in his life. The clarity of his vampiric sight would reduce all his problems—Tia, Drago, and St. James—to the only decision to be made. Life or death.

It would be simple, after all.

FIFTEEN

When Drago put the big Buick in gear and headed back south on the Trace, Tia's remaining hopes sank to somewhere around her ankles, where her heart already weighed her down. It was obvious Drago wanted more from her than a "little chat."

"You never answered me. What are you going to do with me? Take me back to Dallas?"

Drago's right brow arched, as if he didn't know the answer and didn't really care. "Oh, eventually. First, though, I see that another *tete-a-tete* with Allgate is in order regarding his carelessness in letting you slip away so easily."

"I wasn't his prisoner. He didn't have me locked up."

"No, more's the pity. I would have much preferred my morning repose to this little rabbit hunt."

"You enjoy making light of people's lives, don't you? Playing all these little games?"

She stared at his profile and saw all his features, from the high forehead down to the strong jaw, but when he turned his head to answer her, all she could see were the pools of his eyes, so deep you could drown in them, if you didn't freeze first.

"Do not mistake my manner for my intent, *mademoiselle*. Many people, both human and Undead, do. It's a mistake they don't make twice."

If that was intended to frighten her, it did, but it didn't shut her up. "Why do you do this? Meddle in the affairs of others?"

"You were with *la police*, yes? Then you understand orders."

"Who gives you orders?"

He smiled, but there was a twist to the sensuous mouth that indicated more bitterness than fondness. "Those who have more power than I, of course. Was that not how it was with you?"

She squirmed at the discomforting thought of a creature more powerful than Drago. "But within those orders you have discretion, don't you?"

This time he laughed, but it was a soft, self-deprecating sound. "Ah, *discretion*, of course. Self-restraint and sound judgment—the very essence of *l'enforcier.*"

Tia didn't ask any more questions.

An hour later they were heading for the river and the bridge to Vidalia. Drago had passed the road leading to Rose Hill.

"Where are we going?" she asked.

"I need to make sure you're safe. And, of course, comfortable. It's not an antebellum mansion, I'm sorry to say, but it's all I can offer you."

The "all" turned out to be nothing less than the presidential suite of Natchez's largest hotel, high on a small bluff overlooking the Mississippi River. One thing she had to say for the Undead. They all lived well. "Compact" and "economy" were words obviously not in their vocabularies.

Drago escorted her into the suite, and though it was barely mid-afternoon, all the heavy drapes were closed, and only one small table lamp was on. Tia almost didn't see the woman lounging on the burgundy and green sofa.

"Who's the little chookie, Drago?" asked the woman in a strange accent.

"The object of Allgate's *grande passion*," answered Drago in his finest theatrical voice.

"Really. She doesn't look like much," said the woman, standing to get a better look at Tia.

That was enough for Tia to take an immediate dislike to the woman. Tia took a step forward, put one hand on her hip and sized her opponent up. The woman was at least two inches shorter, but her thin build and high-heeled boots gave her the appearance of height. She had long brunette hair, smoky eyes, and wore a white sleeveless turtleneck and tight rust-colored leather pants. She appeared to be in her twenties, yet there was a hard, worn look to the young face. Tia had seen it over and over in women barely out of their teens who had abused themselves with drugs and unhealthy lifestyles.

"She defeated Allgate's mark," said Drago, a fox smile telling Tia he was immensely enjoying the standoff between the two women.

The brunette glanced sideways at him. Her painted mouth turned downward as one dark brow lifted. "That doesn't necessarily mean anything. Perhaps it's a failing on Allgate's part."

Drago's smile widened. "Do you think Allgate is weak, *ma cherie?*"

"No." There was no hesitation or doubt in her voice.

"Neither do I. It's a puzzle."

"I'm sure you'll figure it out," said the woman, her voice dry. She cocked her head at Tia. "What's the chook's name, Drago?"

Tia cut Drago off. "I can speak for myself. I'm Syntia Martell. And you are?"

"Well, I can see that if she's going to be staying here we're going to have to teach the chook some manners. I'm Juliana Sage. I'll answer to 'Juliana.'"

"Or '*ma cherie*'?" added Tia.

Drago's grin displayed very white teeth. It was the first real smile Tia had seen on the creature's face. However, no such affectation transformed Juliana's features. If anything, her hard face took on a more brittle cast, and her eyes, as opaque as Drago's were clear, glittered with dark lights.

"You will show me respect, Miss Martell. If you don't, I can promise that the short time spent here will seem very long indeed," said Juliana.

Drago sighed. "Would you excuse us for a few moments, *cherie*...Juliana? I'll give *mademoiselle* her first lesson in proper deportment."

Juliana glared at both Drago and Tia, then, with a forced curve to her copper-red mouth, glided out of the room into the adjoining bedroom, shutting the door.

"Sit, *mademoiselle*." The voice was not gentle, and the word "please" was as noticeably absent from the request as his smile of a moment ago.

Tia sat in a large armchair across a cherrywood cocktail table from the sofa, deliberately avoiding the possibility that she and Drago would end up seated next to each other. She was just as angry as the two vampires seemed to be, and the strength of the emotion gave her fuel against Drago. "I am not going to take etiquette lessons from *you*. Just tell me, why am I here with that...thing?"

Drago stretched out on the sofa, his feet up and crossed at the ankles. "You know what she is?"

"Of course. It's obvious. She's a witch."

Drago's smile flared anew. For a second he looked almost human, but he tamped it before he answered. "She's a vampire, and quite a powerful one. She's here to keep an eye on you while I'm gone. And it wouldn't do to overly antagonize Juliana. She has a good measure of control, but like her patience, it has limits. Don't test them. You will lose, *mademoiselle*."

"You're not leaving yet, are you? Dallas won't be awake for hours." She didn't know why, but if it came down to a choice between staying with Drago or Juliana, Drago somehow seemed the lesser of the two evils. At least there was a small part of his arrogant, irritating manner that could pass for charm. Juliana was just plain nasty.

"No, *mademoiselle*, I'm not leaving yet. Juliana and I have business to discuss. In the meantime you're free to amuse yourself with whatever the suite has to offer. If you're hungry, let me know and I will order room service for you. All I require is that you behave yourself. Do I make myself clear?"

Tia sighed. What choice did she have? "Yes, very clear."

"And you will show Juliana respect."

She hesitated. Kowtowing to the disagreeable creature in the next room was the last thing Tia felt like doing.

Drago's antifreeze gaze caught hers and held it. Though the table separated them, Tia felt like he was right next to her. The air conditioner was on high, and the room was comfortably cool, but it was hard to breathe nonetheless.

"Think carefully, Tia. This is not a game. There is nothing in her job description, or in mine, for that matter, about the protection of human life." His voice was so soft as to barely be heard, but there was more warning in the blue eyes than in either his words or tone.

That he had used her first name instead of "mademoiselle" was not lost on Tia. She leaned back in the chair, fighting the familiarity he seemed intent on fostering, but it didn't help. His presence filled the entire room. "I understand. I'll be civil. Just keep her away from me."

"Does that mean you prefer my company instead?" he asked, both brows raised.

"No!"

He laughed softly, an acknowledgment of the lie.

Still wearing his fox smile, Drago rose and rapped at the bedroom door, and Tia and Juliana traded places. Before Tia could pull the door shut, though, Juliana braced it open with her body.

"Wait a minute. Drago, did you check her purse? She might have a mobile phone."

"No, come to think of it, I didn't."

Juliana stripped the bag from Tia's shoulder before Tia could react. "Wouldn't do to have her calling Allgate now, would it?" Juliana rummaged through the bag and immediately pulled the Colt out, pointing its barrel at the ceiling for Drago to see. "Well. Bit of a worry, this."

Drago's gaze appraised the gun, then slid to Tia. The smile was gone from his face. Juliana tossed him the gun, and he caught it with one hand while still watching her. With a dexterity she had never seen, he locked back the slide, ejected the round in the chamber, and caught the cartridge in his hand before it fell to the floor. His gaze still fastened on hers, he rolled the cartridge between his thumb and forefinger, his fingers touching only the casing. Very deliberately he lifted the round and ran the tip of the bullet down the side of his face, almost like a caress. Tia saw a wince twist his features before he blanked his face again, and she knew the caress had been painful.

"Silver." There was no charm at all in the quiet voice. "Who gave you the gun, *mademoiselle?*"

The room was so still she could hear her heart beat. There was no point in lying, even if his eyes had allowed her to. "Dallas gave it to me in Rodney to use in self defense against St. James."

"You're no longer in Rodney, and our bad boy is far away, licking his wounds. Why do you still have it?"

She felt like a prisoner being interviewed, then realized that was exactly what she was. "Gillie gave it to me when I left this morning. For self defense."

"Against...?"

"You or St. James."

"Allgate's servant gave you this today. Not Allgate himself?"

"No."

He released the pressure of his gaze, and Tia drew a long breath. He removed the magazine from the Colt, reinserted the loose cartridge into the clip, then flipped both the weapon and clip back to Juliana. "Dispose of these."

She snatched them easily. "You disappoint me, Drago. I would never have expected such carelessness in *l'enforcier.*"

"How fortunate I am to have you here, *ma cherie*, to correct my errors."

The soft voice made Tia shiver, and she was glad this last had not been directed at her. Juliana looked about to say something in reply, then obviously thought better of it. Instead, she threw the purse back at Tia. Tia caught it and closed the bedroom door, thankful for the respite from the two sets of vampire eyes. She was about to sit on the bed when she heard the voices resume in the next room. She moved back to the door to listen.

Juliana's voice, aroused in anger, was easy to hear. "At first I was honored to have been asked to assist the great *enforcier* Alek Dragovich, but I've really landed in it this time, haven't I?"

Tia couldn't hear Drago's reply, but it must have been

short, because Juliana's voice went on. "Nikolena's not going to like this one bit."

"All to the good, *cherie*." If Drago said more, Tia couldn't hear.

The volume of Juliana's voice rose even more. "How can you say that? Your authority is only through her good graces. You've got one dead, one good and knackered, and now this. You think the Directress isn't going to be a little put out over this?"

"*Ca ne fait rien.* Nikolena's been put out for almost two hundred years. She's not happy unless I displease her. But you, *ma cherie*, I brought you here for a very specific purpose. But if you're not happy, you're free to return to the outback any time you want."

"Sydney is *not* the outback," Juliana retorted, but her voice had noticeably lowered.

Tia heard no more of the conversation after that.

Frustrated, she threw herself down onto the king size bed. She still didn't know what she was doing here. She had asked Drago more than once, and he had neatly dodged her questions, admitting only that he was going to take her to Dallas "eventually." She had no idea what he meant to do with her in the meantime.

Alek Dragovich. She silently rolled the name around her tongue with distaste. A Russian-sounding name and a French accent. Nothing about Drago made any sense. She knew he was a vampire, and one of considerable power in the vampire community. By his own admission, he did some kind of internal policing, but that was about all she knew. She tried to recall everything Dallas had told her about Drago. It hadn't been much. All Dallas had said was that he was a "lecherous old bastard" and that he had connections in high places. She wished now that she had asked Dallas more questions about him, but it had been apparent that Dallas cared little for Drago and even less about discussing him.

Lecherous old bastard. Aside from the wink at the house and the bold appraisal he had made of her on the Trace, Drago had expressed little interest in her as a woman. He had touched her in the car and had fingered her hair. She hadn't enjoyed his handling, but the movements had seemed almost detached and dispassionate, done more out of habit than desire.

St. James, on the other hand, had fondled her and kissed her in the Chapel of Light cemetery. If Dallas hadn't prevailed there and at Rodney, Tia had no doubt St. James would have either taken her against her will or destroyed her will to the point she didn't object to his advances. Strangely, Tia had no such fear of Drago. He seemed to have no real interest in her other than as some kind of game piece involving Dallas. And now that Juliana was with Drago, Tia's fear of being an object of vampiric desire lessened even more. That was not to say that Tia didn't fear Drago. Quite the contrary. She just wasn't afraid that Drago lusted after her.

Tia's thoughts turned to Juliana. Why was she here? To assist *l'enforcier*, she had said, but assist in what? Tia couldn't believe that Juliana was merely some sort of baby-sitter or watchdog, here simply to keep an eye on her. Just moments ago Tia had overheard Drago say he had brought Juliana from Australia for a very specific purpose. What purpose? *Australia.* Was it just coincidence that Juliana was from Sydney and Dallas had lived there as a convict? Perhaps Dallas had also lived there during his two hundred years as a vampire. Tia knew Dallas had been in England and Mississippi during the early 1800's, but that still left the post Civil War years unaccounted for. An unreasonable jealousy started to grip Tia, and she curled into a ball on top of the bedspread.

Could vampires love each other? Tia had no way to know. Even if she had been familiar with vampire lore, she was fast learning that the truth had little to do with the legend. The jealousy hurt, and Tia tried to fight it with logic. What did she care if Dallas knew Juliana from years past? Tia had been trying to leave Dallas, hadn't she? What did she care about him, or what he did now? What did she care what he had done decades ago? But she did care, and the hurt was not so easily dismissed.

The questions and emotion drained her, and Tia took off her shirt, pants, and shoes and crawled under the bedclothes.

The comfort of the bed and the quiet of the room soothed her, and she realized how tired she really was. She had not slept well the night before. Her final waking thought was of Dallas and how badly she wanted to see him again.

She was alone in the dark, and the only thing separating her from the other creatures of the night was the box of windows surrounding her. More visible to her enemies than they were to her, she drove and drove, but her fear only increased with the distance. Suddenly she was running, and the shots sounded all around her. There was no safe direction to flee, no target to fight back against.

She awoke with a start, the thin blanket twisted around her. For a moment she didn't know where she was, then saw the glowing numbers of the bedside clock and remembered. The hotel. She had napped for three hours. She rubbed her face and fell back on the bed. At least she hadn't had any strange "presentments." The cop dream, while disturbing, was familiar. It made her long for Dallas even more. Somehow, in his presence, her fear of death disappeared.

She rose and stepped to the door but heard no sounds from the other side. She had no doubt, though, that at least one vampire infested the next room. There was no strange odor to either Drago or Juliana, but Tia nevertheless felt dirty. She took a shower, wishing she had fresh clothes to change into, but she made do with what she had. Her last morning at Rose Hill seemed a long time ago. Her growling stomach confirmed the feeling.

Dressed, she tried the bedroom door. It was unlocked. She pushed it slowly open. No lamps were on, but enough light seeped into the room from the edges of the drapes for her to see that the hideaway bed was open and supporting Juliana's body.

At first she didn't see Drago, then he was directly in front of her. Dallas had done the same thing, but with Drago the inhuman movement truly annoyed her. "I wish you wouldn't do that."

"My apologizes, *mademoiselle*. Did you rest well?"

As though he cared, she thought. She was in no mood for

meaningless pleasantries and didn't bother answering. What would Drago care about dreams of fear? "You said if I was hungry I could eat."

He blinked, but the hooded eyes revealed little. "But of course. Choose whatever you like from the menu, and I'll order for you."

He turned a light on for her, and she scanned the room service menu, deciding at last on a salad, filet mignon, and cheesecake. She didn't feel one bit guilty. It was going on a vampire's expense account.

The delivery of the meal woke Juliana. Tia ate with exaggerated relish, hoping that at least one of the vampires missed the human pleasure of satisfying hunger through food. But they ignored her even more than she pretended to ignore them, and they continued conversing with each other in tones too low for Tia to hear. Juliana had closed the hideaway bed and sat sideways on the sofa, her slender legs draped over the cushions. Drago stood just feet away at the window, lifting the edge of the drapes just enough to peer out.

Only when Tia had her fill did she decide to question Drago again. "So, Drago, tell me again why I'm here."

"You're our guest, *mademoiselle*. We are here but to serve you." His voice sounded like that of a host greeting a very unwelcome visitor. He didn't bother turning towards her.

Tia wanted to laugh. "Right. Well, if I'm going to remain your guest much longer, I'm going to need some clean clothes."

Drago finally let the fabric fall into place, and he faced her, inclining his head, but his voice sounded no less bored. "Of course. Juliana will go out tonight and get some for you."

The look Juliana gave Drago told everyone she begged to differ. She dropped her feet to the floor and leaned forward. "You didn't bring me all the way here so I could toodle around town running errands for the chookie, did you? Let's do this thing tonight and get it over with."

He turned toward Juliana, a benevolent smile at odds with the dispassion of his eyes. "*Cherie, cherie.* You must learn patience. If you're going to suffer eternity, you must learn to make time your friend, not your enemy."

Juliana ignored the smile. "Don't preach to me, Drago. I'm not a novice begging for your wisdom. I know all about waiting and being patient."

The smile vanished. "Really, *cherie*. Then you will do it now and not complain. When it is dark enough, you will go out and purchase appropriate clothing for our guest."

"I'm not your bloody servant, Drago."

"You will do as I say, *cherie*." The words were very soft.

His eyes held Juliana's until a look of fear washed over her face. She flinched, and Tia saw a drop of red well up on the woman's cheek, as bright as her lipstick. Juliana wiped the blood from her face before it could run down her cheek, and she stared at the smudge on her fingertip, disbelief joining fear in widening her eyes.

"There. Now you are my 'bloody' servant, *cherie*. You will do as I say, *c'est compris?*"

Juliana answered only with a glare at Drago. A second later she was in the bedroom, moving so fast that Tia wouldn't have known where she had gone but for the slam of the adjoining door.

Drago drew a deep breath, and Tia sat very still. She wasn't sure what had just happened, but it didn't take a genius to know that it was not a good idea to challenge Drago's authority past a certain point. She would have to remember that.

He looked at her. She swallowed down the rest of her questions. He smiled and bowed. "Not to worry, *mademoiselle*. A new wardrobe is as good as yours."

Tia gave him a wan smile in return and turned on the television. Watching the evening news gave her a good excuse to avoid interaction with Drago. Had she really thought, just hours before, that this psycho vampire cop was charming?

***

The following evening, Dallas retired to the scented breezes of the veranda. He sat slouched on the chaise lounge and let the fresh air and moonlight wash over him. The gardeners had come earlier and mowed the lawn, and the sweet smell of freshly cut grass combined with the bouquet of azaleas, camellias, and dogwood to tease his senses. Dallas relaxed and pondered his future. It was something he didn't often do, but it had been a hellish week.

Perhaps the week's turmoil was a sign that it was time for Dallas to move on. He was forced to make a change every twenty years or so. One couldn't stay in a place forever, not age, and have it go unnoticed. He would hate to leave Rose Hill and Natchez. The place had both a natural and man-made beauty to it and an Old South grace that gave him peace. More than that, though, was the timelessness of the place. In a world so full of changing technology and changing faces it was comforting to be around buildings that were as old as he was; around legends and stories that didn't die out with time. He was as rooted here as an unnatural creature like himself could be. But he had been here twenty-five years now, and it was getting harder and harder to pass for fifty when he looked thirty-five. Perhaps it was time to move back to England again.

Tia. Nothing this past week had shaken him to his core as had his reaction to Syntia Martell. He was already missing her more than he would miss Rose Hill, Bishop's Inn, or Natchez itself. He could always return to the city again in another fifty years, but Tia was gone from his life forever. She had indeed been special, and, as with Veilina, he hadn't realized how special until she was gone.

He heard a car in the drive and somehow knew it would be Drago. Fencing with Alek Dragovich was the last thing Dallas felt like doing, but perhaps it was best to get it over with tonight. Come tomorrow Drago would be winging his way back to Paris or wherever, and Dallas could get on with his life.

Dallas opened the front door, not at all surprised to find Drago lounging on the front steps, impeccably dressed, as usual, in black and white. Dallas held the door wide in mute invitation. Once in the parlor, Drago began circling the room slowly, like a restless animal in a cage.

Dallas was in no mood for Drago's melodramatics. "What is it this time, Drago?"

"Nothing more than a follow up to my last visit. Ah, I see you were able to clean the carpet. I'm glad. Have you heard anything more from St. James?"

It was all Dallas could do to keep his composure. "If I had, I'm sure you would know about it."

Drago shifted his eyes from the floor to Dallas, and Dallas felt their weight.

"I'll take that as a 'no,'" said Drago, his voice low with warning. "And what of the *mademoiselle?*" he asked in a considerably higher voice.

"What about her?"

"Her scent is faded from the house. Have you already taken care of her as I asked?"

It would be fruitless to lie to Drago. "No."

Drago's brows arched. "No? Yet she is not here, is she?"

"No."

"*Monsieur*, these monosyllabic answers tire me. Tell me where she is."

Dallas sighed. "I don't know where she is. She left earlier in the day. I assume she's headed back home."

Drago ran a hand over the carved backrest of one of the Chippendale chairs. "That was rather careless of you, don't you think?"

"I thought the mark would hold her."

"Hmm. It would appear you either overestimated yourself or underestimated her. Which do you think is the case, *mon ami?*"

Dallas felt like a fish on the end of a line, but there was nothing to do except let Drago play him. "I don't know. She has an usually high resistance to us."

"'Us?' Or just you?"

"I don't know, Drago."

Drago tipped the chair backwards to balance on two legs, then slammed the chair forward to thump the floor. "You don't know. Well, *mon ami*, your sanction still stands. So what are you going to do now, I wonder?

Dallas' patience was at an end. "You enjoy asking me questions I don't have answers for, don't you? There's nothing I can do, as you damn well know."

Lines appeared at the corner of Drago's mouth, and his

teeth clenched, just visible through the unsmiling mouth. "You can find her and bring her back!"

"Listen, Drago. I'm tired of your theatrics, I'm tired of your tactics, and I'm tired of you. You're not going to bully me into something I either cannot do or will not do. As I told you before, do what you will to me, or leave me in peace."

To Dallas' surprise, Drago laughed. "*Bravo, mon ami!* I've always liked you, Allgate. Never more than now, when you've got your back against the wall. You may yet make a fine enforcer."

L'enforcier looked to be in no hurry to leave, exiting the parlor only to loiter on the veranda. He suddenly seemed content to sprawl on one of the lounge chairs and forgo his usual pacing. Drago didn't say so, but perhaps even the Anti-God himself delighted in the languor that hung in the warm night air. He spoke with his eyes closed, as if savoring the very night with his remaining senses. "So, *mon ami.* What now?"

Dallas' limited patience was at an end. He said nothing in reply.

Drago appeared to digest the silence, then sighed and pulled a small cell phone from his belt and slowly tapped in a number, as if he had all night. The message, though, was brief. "Rose Hill, now. Both of you."

It was an unusually succinct conversation for Drago, one he didn't seem inclined to want to explain to Dallas. "I have people I want you to meet," was all Drago would say.

Dallas was too tired to run all the possibilities through his mind. Enforcer business? Perhaps Drago intended on issuing more sanctions against him and needed witnesses. Whatever kind of business it was, Dallas had no doubt it would neither be to his benefit nor liking.

Dallas and Drago moved from the veranda back to the parlor to await their mysterious guests. The waiting was as brief as Drago's phone conversation had been. A scant ten minutes later the front door chime sounded. Dallas rose to answer it, aware that Drago was right on his heel. Dallas swung the door open, and there, framed by the two white columns flanking either side of the entranceway, were two women he knew only too well.

"My God," he breathed, stepping backward with an uncharacteristic stumble right into Drago. Dallas didn't feel Drago's hands steady him or see his mouth curve in a sly smile. His full attention was on the dark-haired women facing him, neither of whom looked too happy to see him.

"Sabra..."

Juliana strode into the hallway, pulling Tia with her. "What? No greeting for your...what did Drago call her? ...your *grande passion?"* With that Juliana shoved Tia in front of her, but Tia halted, her eyes wide in shock, advancing no farther towards Dallas.

"Sabra?" parroted Tia, her eyes shifting between Dallas and Juliana.

Seeing Sabra was the last thing Dallas had expected. That Drago had Tia could have been predicted, but Dallas hadn't seen Sabra since she'd left him two hundred years ago. He honestly thought she had died the True Death. In all his travels around the world, he had neither run across her nor heard anything of her. And now she stood before him, looking exactly as he remembered her, her thin frame belying the strength behind her dark eyes. The only thing that was different was the brittle quality that hardened her features.

She spoke up, obviously not as surprised to see him as he was to see her. "Drago, since our host has apparently been rendered speechless, introductions, please?"

Drago stepped to Juliana's side. "*Bien sur.* I have the pleasure of introducing Juliana Sage, my associate on this assignment. She's a member of the Australian Council based in Sydney. I asked her here for several reasons, one of which, of course, is that she is acquainted with Dallas Allgate. He knew her long ago as Sabra Sage. However she prefers now to be addressed as Juliana. She is also here to help me make recommendations. And, I believe, everyone here knows *mademoiselle* Syntia Martell. She is the reason we are all gathered here tonight."

Drago dipped his head, pulled on the cuffs of his sleeves

and straightened again. "Well, *mon ami*, here she is. I ask you again. What are you going to do?" The tail of one heavy eyebrow wagged.

Dallas studied Juliana. Her dark eyes, once so full of warm desire, glittered now with a cold lust, but it wasn't for him or for any part of the life they had once shared. If he had doubted she was lost to him forever, he doubted it no more. His gaze slipped to Tia. *She* wasn't lost to him. Not yet.

Dallas saw Tia glance sideways at Drago, and he saw fear vie with the confusion in her eyes. It was she who first replied, not Dallas. "What do you mean, I'm the reason you're all here?"

Dallas could feel his heart pounding deep inside him, and he realized with surprise that he was afraid—more afraid than he had been since the night Sabra brought him across to the Other Side. That night he had lost his soul. Tonight he wasn't afraid of Drago. It was loss, again, that he feared.

"Tia, come here." Dallas loosed no compelling power on her nor any other vampire trick. It was just a simple entreaty, spoken softly. He kept his attention on Tia, aware that neither Drago nor anyone else had answered her question. It came down now to trust. Was anything left of the night they had shared in his bedroom only scant days ago? His heart pounded harder, a painful pressure in his chest.

Her eyes met his, and a thousand questions swam in their blue depths. She didn't move. She wouldn't come to him. Not Tia. She was too cynical, too suspicious. The ex-cop's mind would want too many of her questions answered first. She turned her head, and her gaze touched Drago and Juliana. Dallas thought Tia was going to repeat her unanswered question when suddenly she stepped quietly to his side, still keeping her eyes on the two enforcers.

"Dallas, what are these unpleasant creatures doing here?"

Dallas let out a long breath he hadn't realized he had been holding. "You trust me to tell you the truth?"

"More than I trust them."

That wasn't saying a lot, but it was a start. He took a deep breath. "Drago gave me some very specific instructions regarding you. He and...Juliana...are here to make sure I follow those instructions."

"I don't understand. What instructions?"

"He feels you've witnessed too much. That with all you've learned you're a danger to us."

Her mouth opened, as if to ask another question, but she didn't. He could see comprehension flood her eyes. Finally the words she didn't want to voice were spoken. "What are you supposed to do with me?"

Dallas turned her so that she faced him. "Transform you to one of us. Or kill you outright. It was my choice."

Tia twisted her arm back to dislodge the grip he still had on her shoulder, but it was to Drago she whirled in anger. "You son of a bitch! Why didn't you just do it when you had the chance? Or don't you like doing your own dirty work?"

Drago's smile disappeared. "It would have been my pleasure, *mademoiselle*, not 'dirty work.' However, you are Allgate's problem to solve, not mine."

Tia confronted Dallas again, but took a step back at the same time. "And just which option did you decide on?"

He looked at her. "Neither." He moved between Tia and the enforcers and faced Drago. "I won't do it, Drago. I won't kill her. And if you try to take her from me, I'll fight you. Both of you. I know I'm no match for you. You've impressed that on me more than enough times, but I'll fight you anyway."

All semblance of life seemed to shrink from behind Drago's features. His skin hung slack on the underlying facial bones, and the hooded blue eyes showed no movement. When at last he spoke, it was as if his lips didn't move to mouth the words. "She'll die either way, *monsieur*. And do you really want her to witness your going to *la Belle Mort*? It's not a pretty sight."

Dallas saw Juliana, just behind Drago. In contrast to Drago's, Juliana's eyes were everywhere, and the hardness in her face seemed to take on a fragility, as if it would crack.

He looked at Drago. "You would really kill me, Drago?"

Drago's blue eyes showed a sharp focus, but no emotion. The only telltale sign on the lax face was the vertical furrow between his eyebrows. "I should not relish killing you, but if you oppose me so strongly you leave me no other option, I would do it, *certainement.* Do not make the mistake of thinking I wouldn't, *mon ami."*

Dallas believed him. Strangely, though, he didn't feel any fear. All his anxiety and exhaustion had lifted the moment Tia had stepped to his side. "I don't seek the True Death, but I'm not afraid of it. And Tia has seen death before."

The crease in Drago's brow deepened. "And it frightens her, does it not? She hides it well, but I can see the fear in her as plain as day. Or as night. And what about you, *monsieur?* Are you truly prepared to die? I don't think so. You're a survivor, Allgate. She's just a human, after all. Think about it, and you won't let it come to this."

"I respect your power, Drago, and I trust your word when you say you have no compunction against killing me. But also know that my word is given no more lightly than yours is. I mean what I say."

"Do not throw down the gauntlet at me, *monsieur.* You will regret it."

Before Dallas could answer, Juliana strode forward. "You're wrong, Drago. Dallas is a survivor, true. He always has been. But I know him better than you ever will. He's strong, but his strength comes from his convictions, not brutality. If he says he won't kill the chook, he won't, and nothing you can say or do will make him change his mind."

All eyes turned on Juliana. Enough life flowed back into Drago's face for him to lock his brows together in disapproval. "May I remind you, *ma cherie,* that you are here as my representative?"

Her dark eyes flashed. "I'm not here to be your rubber stamp, Drago. I'm here because I know Dallas. And I'm telling you he won't back down."

Drago's upper lip nearly vanished, baring his teeth. "You forget yourself, *cherie.* Don't make me remind you again."

Juliana shook her head, the flounce of her mane of dark hair seeming to give her slight frame more height and bulk. "I'm stating my opinion, Drago, nothing more. Isn't that one of the reasons I'm here?"

"Opinion, *cherie*, or opposition? Your voice seems to be imbued more with the latter than the former."

Juliana took two more steps away from Drago and widened her stance. "You don't like opposition, do you? What are you so afraid of? Are we such a threat to you, Drago?"

One of Drago's brows slowly arched "'We?'"

She walked up to Dallas, looked him square in the eye, then turned to stand at his side. "Fight him if you must, Drago, but you'll have to fight me, too."

Drago stared. "I can have you banned from the Council for all eternity for this little display of insubordination. Is it worth it?"

Dallas stared at her as well.

Juliana's eyes looked up at him and widened, and some of their hardness melted away. For the first time since she arrived, she looked like the woman he remembered in his memories. A small smile softened her hard mouth as well, and she turned back to Drago. "Neither of us wants to oppose you, Drago. Conviction isn't the same thing as opposition."

Drago's expression remained hard. "You didn't answer my question, *cherie*."

Her smile faded. "It's worth it," she said without hesitation.

One brow canted. "And if such a fight means death?" asked Drago.

"I've already been dead for two hundred years. I once loved this man more than anything on earth. If standing by his side means the True Death, I can think of no better way to end this agony of existence."

Drago's second brow cocked. A muscle in his cheek twitched. Then, as if by magic, life seemed to pump again through his veins, animating his features. The long smile lines popped in and out, and the hard, chiseled mouth twisted into a wry smile. "Much as I love to plague Nikolena, I don't think it would be prudent, even for me, to submit a report detailing the deaths of three vampires. She will throw enough of a fit as it is." He faced Tia and gave her a small bow. "Very well, *mademoiselle*. I once again use my *discretion*. You may live.

With conditions, of course."

Dallas felt each of the women at his side let out a slow breath in response to the ease in tension, but immediately had a new dilemma. He wasn't sure which female to next give his attention to. Drago solved the problem for him.

"Come outside with me, Tia. Let Allgate have a word with Juliana. He hasn't seen her in two hundred years."

Tia didn't budge from Dallas' side. "If you think I'm going anywhere with you, Drago, you're crazy."

It was Juliana who now came to Drago's defense. "You'll be safe with Drago. He's as honorable in his own way as Dallas is. He's given you life. He won't ever take that away from you."

Dallas could still see the doubt in Tia's eyes. He put his hands on her shoulders. "She's right. He won't hurt you now. Give us just a few moments, will you?"

Tia nodded, clearly still not liking it, but trusting him. *Trusting him.* Those two words still sounded so foreign to him. Still, she did as he asked, and slowly followed Drago to the veranda, looking back at Dallas only once.

Dallas waited until Drago and Tia were outside before he turned to Juliana. "Thank you for what you did. I've both felt and witnessed Drago's wrath. You put yourself at great risk."

Juliana tilted her head to the side. "It was a calculated risk. Drago admires straight-up fortitude."

He led Juliana into the parlor. "As long as it's not laced with too much disrespect."

"Yes, exactly."

They sat on a sofa upholstered in a brocade of sky blue and white. "You won't suffer later for your 'insubordination,' will you?"

She smiled, the first one Dallas had seen on her face since she arrived on his stoop. "I'll get one of Drago's patented tongue-lashings, perhaps. I don't think he'll do more. In any case, it'll have been worth it. That was the truth. I did it for you, Dal, not for the chook. I want you to know that."

"I know. Tell me, are you happy being an enforcer?"

The smile faded, but she nodded. "I was a convict for

over ten years. Yes, even after all this time, it feels good to be one of those who wields the power."

"We were happy, you and I."

"We were convicts, Dal. No better than slaves. We did nothing but work day after day in servitude to make MacArthur richer than he already was. I released myself from that, and I wanted to release you, too. You always talked about life, about surviving..."

"Life, yes. And tell me, did you find 'life' in your release?"

"*A* life. As did Drago, as did you, as do all the Undead. I've tried to make the best of it."

He reached out and touched a wavy tendril of her hair. "I loved you. I always wondered if you knew how much."

She pushed his hand down, but gently. "I did know, but don't do this, Dal. Just don't. It's pointless to talk about such things now."

He shook his head. "Why, Sabra? Why did you bring me across? And why did you leave? I was using MacArthur as much as he was using me. I would have found a way for him to free us—I know I would have."

She tried to harden her expression, but her eyes betrayed her pain. "When I was transformed, I had no idea what was happening. It was something I stumbled across in the bush by mistake. Once I realized what I had done, I knew there was no future for us. Everything I had wanted vanished overnight, replaced by desires I knew you wouldn't understand. The only thing I had left to give you was the gift. I thought it would help you. You had struggled so hard to survive, and you wanted so much to live. I foolishly thought I was doing you a favor. The 'gift of eternal life.'"

Life. The mockery of life that was Midexistence burned in his throat as he tried to talk. "But why did you leave? We could have still worked together, helped each other. I was lost for a long time, Sabra, not knowing any others of our kind."

She averted her eyes from him. "I told you. My desires changed. I no longer had any interest in MacArthur's ranch, his sheep, any of it. And you...you were lost to me, Dal. Lost forever. Let's stop this. There's no point in reliving the past or in wishing for what might have been. What happened, happened. There's no changing it and no turning back."

He considered her words for a heartbeat, then nodded his agreement. *It was pointless, yes, with Sabra.* He reached for her and gently pulled her to him. There was no joy in her response, but she didn't resist the embrace. "No, love, there's no turning back," he whispered into her hair.

***

Tia trailed Drago to the patio, but once there, he remained standing while he bade her sit.

"Would you care for something cool to drink, *mademoiselle?*"

"Ah, I don't think Gillie's still up."

He inclined his head to her. "It would be my pleasure to bring you something. Providing you don't take the opportunity to try to run away again."

"Don't worry. Being waited on by the chief honcho of all vampires...this I have to see."

"I'm hardly the 'chief honcho,'" he commented dryly before bowing and disappearing. She was glad for the few minutes alone. She tried to relax in the lounge chair, but found herself shaking as if she'd just gotten off the wildest roller coaster ride of her life. She hadn't felt her heart pounding at the time, but now that it was over, she realized how much of a shock tonight had been. Seeing Dallas after she'd resigned herself to never looking into those green eyes again had been traumatic enough, but to learn that Juliana was Sabra was just as shocking. That her life had nearly been forfeit almost seemed overshadowed by the feelings that now threatened to swamp her. Dallas had just risked his very life for her. But was it really for her, or just for his convictions? And now he was with Sabra, the first woman he had ever loved. Tia had almost felt like the runner up in a pageant when Dallas had first seen the women at the front door. His green eyes had been all on Sabra, not her.

Drago appeared in the doorway, framed by the French doors and backlit by the lamplight from the room beyond. He looked the archetype of eighteenth century elegance with his long locks tied at the nape of his neck, not a hair out of place, and the white poet's shirt that streamed from his shoulders like a living work of art.

"Mademoiselle?"

He held out a tall glass of lemonade to her, and she took it, careful not to brush his fingers with hers. In spite of his benevolent demeanor, she still didn't trust him. In fact, the more gracious he was to her, the more suspicious she became.

"Thank you. What do you want with me now, Drago?"

He draped himself on the fainting couch, and the inner tips of his brows lifted in a show of hurt feelings. "Why, Tia! What makes you think I still want something from you?"

She took a sip of the lemonade and almost choked on it. "Because you're being far too nice to me, and the one thing you are definitely not, is nice."

He put a hand over his heart, drawing her eyes to the expanse of bare chest visible at the open neckline. "You wound me, *mademoiselle*. All I wish is a little chat."

She remembered the last time he said he wanted nothing more than "a little chat," and she shivered. She longed to be with Dallas. "Can we just get on with this?"

He smiled. "As you wish. I need to know what your true feelings are for *monsieur* Allgate, and what it is you intend to do now."

She set the drink down on a small table. "I don't think that's any of your business."

Drago locked his hands behind his head, and the hooded eyes reminded Tia of a cat that gives the appearance of being half asleep. "Ah, but it is my business. I gave you life, and Juliana was correct when she said I'll never take that away from you. But I still have a responsibility to my own kind to protect them from the harm of discovery. The extent of your feelings for Allgate will determine how comfortable I am with the knowledge you possess."

"I'm not going to tell anyone what I know, if that's what you mean. As far as what I intend to do now, I don't know yet."

He just looked at her through shuttered eyes, appraising

her, and she wished he'd go away again. She couldn't relax with him lounging next to her, and she couldn't think about Dallas with him so close. If she tried to, she was afraid Drago would snatch the thoughts right out of her head.

Finally, he lowered his arms and crossed them over his chest. "Very well, *mademoiselle.* I believe you. Just remember that it is a very heavy responsibility you carry with you from now on. Treat it as such."

"Oh, I don't take any of this lightly."

"Good." He rose with the lightness of a child. "I'll leave you to your own devices for a while. The three of us have more business to discuss. Besides, it takes no great intellect to see that you don't particularly enjoy my companionship."

"Don't take it personally. I just tend to have an aversion to people...or things...who want to see me dead."

Drago smiled. "Believe it or not, *mademoiselle,* I like you. I don't say that to too many people, human or otherwise. Here." A business card appeared in his hand as if by magic. "If ever you or Dallas need help, call upon me."

Tia couldn't imagine any situation that would prompt her to call Drago for help, but she took the card and smiled in return. "Thank you."

He bowed in acknowledgment. *"De rien, mademoiselle. Au revoir."*

She glanced down at the card, and when she looked up, he was gone. She stared at the card again, holding it up so that the light spilling from the French doors illuminated it. All it contained was "Alek Dragovich" and a phone number.

Now that Drago was gone, Tia could think about Dallas, but the thoughts still didn't come easily. The facts were hard to dismiss. She had left Dallas, and the only reason she was back now was because Drago had dragged her back. But now that she was back, did she want to stay? She had seen Dallas as vengeful, manipulative, and dangerous. Tonight she had seen a side displaying honor, courage, and loyalty. How could she know which side portrayed the true man? And if both sides were a part of him, as she suspected they were, how could she reconcile the one with the other?

Her heart laughed, ignoring the logic of her mind. In her heart she yearned for Dallas with a desire she had never had before—a blind desire that didn't care what he was or what he had done in the past. She had always felt safe with him. More than that, though, was the understanding he had of all the dark and tormented places in her soul. No other man she had ever met had come close to having that kind of understanding.

She laughed again, but this time the sound was bitter. What she wanted might not matter at all. She really had no idea what kind of feelings Dallas had for her, if any. And now there was Sabra. Dallas could very well decide he wanted to be part of her existence again. None of Tia's questions could be answered until she spoke with him alone. She curled up on the lounge chair to wait. It had been a very long night, and it promised not to end anytime soon.

***

Drago loomed in the arched doorway leading into the parlor, coming no further into the room, yet making his presence felt solely through his appearance. He leaned against the archway, his left arm stroking his chin and his right arm crossed over his chest.

Dallas didn't really mind the subtle interruption. Juliana had refused to discuss their days spent together in New South Wales as Sabra and Dalys. The conversation had turned to her life following her transformation, and while Dallas was interested to know what Juliana had been doing during their time apart, it was nothing that Drago couldn't hear as well.

"You may as well come in, Drago," said Dallas. There was no point in delaying the inevitable. Drago's lost-in-thought pose could mean only one thing—that Drago wasn't done with him yet. "What about Tia?"

Drago joined them in the parlor, making himself comfortable in a Chippendale armchair. "*Mademoiselle* awaits you on the patio. It seems she does not care overly much for my company."

Dallas couldn't help grinning, and he saw that Juliana, too, could not stop a small smile at Drago's expense. "But first I take it you have more business with me," said Dallas.

"Ah, yes. To business. I've been keeping an eye on you from afar for quite a while, but felt the time was near at hand to personally observe your actions. The arrival in Mississippi of St. James and Flynne merely expedited matters. They needed to be watched, and you needed to be evaluated. It worked out perfectly. Of course, I would have preferred that a vampire not meet *la Belle Mort* in the process, but *c'est la vie.* Sometimes these things are unavoidable."

Dallas stared at Drago, all traces of humor gone. "You mean this was all...some kind of test?"

Drago rubbed the curved mahogany of an armrest with one hand, the ruffles on his cuff nearly reaching the tips of his fingers. "If you like. It gave me the perfect opportunity to observe your skills in dealing with others of our kind and to judge your abilities in resolving conflict. And, of course, to see how you handle pressure."

"You bastard!" Dallas turned toward Juliana. "And you were in on all this?"

"I arrived here a couple days after Drago did. He needed help in both watching all the parties involved and in assessing your skills. We need good enforcers, Dal."

"I have no desire to be an enforcer."

Drago interrupted in a soft voice. "Don't unleash your anger on Juliana. She's only here because I asked her to come. Vent your hostility on me if you must, but know that I haven't lied to you, Allgate. And I didn't engineer St. James coming here. That was entirely his idea. I merely took advantage of the opportunity."

"I told you before, Drago. I have no wish to travel endlessly or to pry into the affairs of others."

Drago sighed. "*Cherie,* haven't you been selling him on the benefits of being a council member?"

Dallas answered for Juliana. "We had other things to talk about."

"Ah, *bien sur,* of course. I cannot force you into being an enforcer, Allgate. I just want you to consider it as an option for the future. Your travel, unlike mine, would not be endless. Since you are not a day vampire, like Juliana, you would be a local enforcer. She does not normally travel overseas. I had to make special arrangements to bring her here. And it is not 'prying' that we do. We settle disputes and try to avert conflict. It is to the preservation of our kind that we direct our efforts. It is something that can give purpose to an existence that, with time, becomes too unresponsive to the world around it."

"I am hardly 'unresponsive' to the world around me."

"No, you aren't. But you can't continue your life here in Natchez much longer. You've been here...what? Twenty-five years already. All I ask is that you think about it. We will talk again in the future."

A future visit from Drago. Now that was something to look forward to. "I'll think about it."

"Good. In spite of the unhappy outcome with Flynne and St. James, you handled yourself well this week, *mon ami.* You exhibited a cool head and great strength, resorting to violence only in self-defense of yourself or your people. But most of all you showed a moral strength in defending your beliefs even under extreme pressure. Your only mistake was in not seeing the job done thoroughly in Rodney. That carelessness can be overlooked in one as young as yourself. Do think about it."

"I make no promises, Drago."

Drago sighed and rose from the chair. "No, I feared you wouldn't. Juliana and I will bid you farewell. Oh, and regarding *mademoiselle* Martell, I leave it to you to make sure she is no danger to us. How you do that is up to you. Just don't disappoint me, Allgate." He held out a hand toward Juliana. "Come, *cherie.* Our business is concluded."

Dallas stood. "One minute, Drago. I'd like to say good bye to her first, if you don't mind."

Drago smiled and bowed. *"Au revoir, mon ami.* Until we meet again." With that, he was gone.

Dallas turned to Juliana and held out a hand to her. She took it, her slender hand small in his, and he pulled her to her feet. There were so many things he wanted to say to her, but her dark eyes warned that she didn't want to hear most of it. "Thank you for what you did for me. I won't forget it."

"No. It is not our way to forget...anything...is it? Our memories are always as fresh as the day we live them, aren't they?"

Dallas supposed it was as close to acknowledging what they had shared in the past as she would ever come. "Yes, they are. I wish you well." He pulled her forward and embraced her gently, stroking the hair that was little more tamed than she was. He pressed a light kiss to her temple and released her.

She answered with a touch of her hand to his face. "I can't change what happened two hundred years ago. I don't ask forgiveness for what I did, but maybe what I did tonight can atone a little for what I did to you."

"I don't blame you for this existence, Sabra. I never did. I still hold on to what I have with everything I've got."

She smiled. "Yes, you do. And you have a second chance, Dal. Make the most of it," she whispered, then, like Drago, was gone.

SIXTEEN

Tia floated in and out of sleep until something woke her. Her eyes fluttered open, and a shadow fell across her. A man stood silhouetted in the doorway, and for an instant she thought Drago had returned, but the man's build was different, and she quickly realized it was Dallas.

She wanted nothing more than to have him hold her and reassure her that everything was all right, but there was still too much of the unknown between them, and she waited on the chair. He said nothing, his face a black mask of shadow.

"Are they gone?" was all she could think to ask.

Dallas didn't move. "They're gone."

"For good?"

There was a brief pause. "I don't know if I'll see Juliana again. I fear Drago will be another story."

"Will Drago keep checking on me?"

He shook his head. "I don't think so." He paused again, then stepped onto the veranda. "The house stinks. It needs a good airing. No better time to leave. Come. Gillie has all your things packed." He held out his hand to her.

She ignored his outstretched hand and remained on the chaise, the realization that her fears were all too true paralyzing her. "Leave?"

"You have nothing more to worry about. St. James is gone, and Drago is done with you. It's me he wants now—for the Brotherhood. If he comes back, it'll be to argue his case until I capitulate. But Juliana was right. To you he's given life. He won't go back on that."

Was he reading her fear and misinterpreting its cause? "I wasn't afraid of leaving."

"Good. I'll drive you to a hotel. Tomorrow I'll have Mac take you to Jackson. You can catch your flight from there."

She somehow found her feet. If they were going to argue, she wanted to be able to face him. "That's not what I meant. I wasn't afraid of St. James. Or Drago, for that matter."

He dropped his hand. "Then you should be afraid of me." The low voice was very soft.

What was he talking about? He had just saved her life. "Dallas..."

"Gillie's not here to be your guardian angel, Juliana's not here to be a chaperone, and Drago's not here to keep me on a leash. The farther away from me you are, the better off you'll be. Wasn't that the conclusion you yourself came to just two days ago?"

So that was it. How could she argue? She had been the one to leave him. He hadn't left her. Would he listen to anything she had to say now? "Dallas, we have so much to talk about. I haven't even thanked you for what you did for me tonight." She wanted nothing more than to have him hold her, but the rift between them was suddenly wider than it had been five minutes ago.

"So all you want is to talk? I'll make a deal with you. Come with me to a hotel, and you can talk all you want."

Much as she wanted to talk, she balked at the idea of being coerced out of the house. She had had enough of being forced to go where she didn't want to go the past couple of days. "No. No more hotels. I've spent the last two days in a hotel, and it wasn't very pleasant. Can't we just sit in the garden?"

He sighed and nodded. "I'm sure it was the company and not the hotel itself you found so disagreeable. But I can't blame you for not enjoying two days in Drago's presence. I can barely stand him for ten minutes." He held out his hand to her again. This time she took it, and the warmth and strength of his grip only tormented her further, teasing her with promises she feared would never be kept.

They walked to the stone bench at the edge of the flower garden and sat down. She let go of his hand and took a deep breath of the sultry night air. "Thank you for what you did for me tonight. You gambled with your own life to save mine. I wanted to thank Juliana, too. I'm sure she didn't do it for me, but I still would have liked to thank her."

"Juliana did what she had to do. As did I."

"And why did you do it, Dallas?"

"Did you believe I wouldn't? Did you really think I'd take your life?" he asked softly.

She looked down at her hands. She wanted to say "no," but she couldn't deny the fear that had sent her running from Natchez. Though the fear seemed in abeyance now, if she was going to be honest, she should at least admit her doubts. "I don't know. You'd saved my life earlier, and yet..."

"Yet you feared me. You ran, and you only came back because Drago brought you back."

It was the precise truth, and she couldn't say otherwise. "I was afraid. When I learned what you did to Veilina...and then, later that night, I had a strange dream. What Gillie calls a 'presentment.' I was afraid it was a premonition that I was either going to die, or become like you."

He leaned forward, his forearms resting on his thighs, his long hair sliding forward to curtain his face. "My point exactly. I know only too well what I am. Listen to me, Tia. There's a beast within me. A beast that can rage out of control. With both Christian and Veilina that beast took over. Revenge and betrayal. And the reason the beast took over was because I let myself get too emotionally involved with humans. That's why you're leaving as soon as possible."

She looked at him, but he continued to stare at the ground. "Leave? I told you—I don't want to leave now." Did he truly not want her? Perhaps he was looking forward to being an enforcer to spend more time with Juliana.

He sat up and turned to her, sweeping the hair from his eyes, but his features were unreadable in the darkness. "Didn't you hear anything I just said? What do you want, Tia?"

She wanted him. Didn't everyone have a dark side? But she had seen his humanity as well, and there was more of that in this man than in many people she had met in her life. Yes, she wanted him, but she couldn't tell him so. Not yet. Not until she found out what he wanted. "Dallas, I'm trying to be truthful with you. Please be the same with me. Why do you want me to leave? Is it Juliana? You still love her, don't you." It was no question in Tia's mind.

A frown creased his brow. "Juliana?" He shifted his glance to the flowers. "No. I loved her when I was human and she was Sabra Sage. We can no longer have that. She knows it as well as I do. Two vampires cannot share that kind of love, Tia. The energy of life has to be present in at least one of the parties for the kind of desire you're talking about to exist. All Juliana and I can have now are respect, understanding, and perhaps, someday, friendship. And, of course, the memories. Those never fade. But love? No."

The sorrow in Dallas' soft voice tore at Tia's already shredded emotions. "Then why do you want me to leave?"

"Because it's too dangerous for you to stay. St. James reminded me that I'm no different from him. I'm a creature whose brutal nature would only end up hurting you, one way or another."

"You're not the same as St. James. He wanted to hurt me. You don't."

"But I would, nevertheless. He wanted me to admit to him that he and I were no different. I wouldn't. But he was right. It's my nature to take and use, just as it is his."

"Dallas, look at me, please." She waited until he turned and gazed at her with eyes that gleamed. "He isn't right. I know he iasn't."

"You see only what you want to see. If you had vampiric senses, you would see what I truly am—what I truly look like, feel like—and believe me, you would not like the scent of the Undead."

"There's nothing wrong with my senses. I know exactly what I'm looking at." She wanted to hit him. "Damn you, Dallas. All right. I'll make a counter-offer to your deal. Let me stay here tonight. Make love to me. Tomorrow, if you still want me to leave, I'll leave."

His eyes flashed at her in the moonlight. "No. It's too dangerous."

"You made love to me before."

"And I almost killed you. You had no idea how close I came to taking your blood."

"But you didn't. I'm willing to risk it."

He threw his head back, almost as if he were appealing to the night. "You are the stubbornest, most bullheaded female I've ever met." He dropped his head and brought his face very close to hers. He stared directly into her eyes, and if the dancing sparkles of light she saw reflected were any indication, his pupils were vibrating with an inhuman speed. "I could just compel you, you know."

She stared back. "You can try."

For a long moment, neither of them moved nor spoke. She didn't drop her eyes or look away, but met his gaze with as much faith and fervor as she could muster. Surprisingly, though, he unleashed no menacing, compelling stare, just the look of glittering beauty that failed to mask his desire.

After a moment he leaned back and cocked his head to one side. "Very well, Tia. One night. With one condition. You spend it in my lair. You will understand, at last, what I am, if you understand nothing else this night."

"Your lair? Don't tell me you're going to make love to me in a coffin." She laughed, but the sound quickly died.

For the first time since he had stepped onto the veranda, a smile of wicked delight lit Dallas Allgate's solemn face.

SEVENTEEN

He didn't think of it as conceding.

Dallas had no real desire to lose her, so her begging to stay was nothing short of victory. Still, the conversation had bothered him. The danger he had spoken of was all too real.

He first led her through the French doors to the kitchen. "If you wish anything to eat or drink, help yourself. Grab what you like and bring it with you. There's no room service where we're going."

She opened the refrigerator and took out some bottled water. "This is fine."

He raised a brow at her choice. "Tia, Tia. Here. Allow me." He circuited the room, gathering a bottle of wine, a crystal goblet, and a bowl of diced fresh fruit that Gillie had prepared the day before.

It was her turn to cock a brow at him. "I was seduced the very first time you laid eyes on me, Dallas. The wine and fruit..." Her voice dropped to a whisper. "They're not necessary."

He smiled. "Indulge a creature to whom image is everything, will you? Besides, I think you need some glamour in your life. As you have said, it has been too imbued with the harsh realities."

When she didn't argue further, he ushered her to his first floor bedroom adjacent to the library. He handed her the fruit so he could flip on the light, then turned to her. "No one has ever been inside the room I am about to show you except Gillie, and even he doesn't have a key. There are several staircases to the general cellar. This one leads directly to my sleeping quarters. I had this house built in 1828 to my specific design. Fortunately during that era, secret staircases, hidden rooms, and listening posts were common enough additions to large houses. This is your last chance to leave, Tia."

He gave her credit for not looking overly nervous. "No. I'm staying."

"As you wish." Could it be that she really did want him, even knowing full well what he was? He thought the mark of blood to be the most powerful bond between vampire and mortal, but she had overcome that in leaving him. Could the bond that kept her here now really be more solid than that of the mark?

He turned to a paneled wall, and with a speed so swift he knew she wouldn't be able to see or duplicate his actions, he pressed the release for the hidden door. A section of the wall smoothly and silently skated to the side along an invisible track, revealing a narrow staircase. "Follow me, then."

He descended the stairs, pausing at the bottom to rapidly unlock the next door. It swung inward noiselessly. He stood in the doorway and beckoned her. "Come, Tia."

She alighted from the final step and paused beside him. "No lights?"

"Ah. Forgive me," he said with a smile. He hit a switch, and light from a stained glass wall sconce above the headboard of his bed bathed the room in a soft glow. He hit a second switch, and picture lights on the walls illuminated various paintings and tapestries. He took the fruit from her, set it and the wine down, then watched her face as she stepped past him into the room. He was rewarded by a widening of her eyes and a sensual parting of her lips, as if a comment on his lair was almost, but not quite, ready to fall.

"Well? Are you disappointed...or relieved?" he asked.

"Disappointed?" she parroted, turning slowly to take in the whole room, stopping when her eyes fell on the king size sleigh bed.

"That the infamous three 'C's are missing."

She shook her head vaguely, obviously not understanding him.

He smiled again. "Cobwebs, coffins, and candles."

"Umm, I can understand no cobwebs or coffins. I'm sure Hollywood probably invented those, but what's wrong with candles?"

He stepped into the room and stood beside her. "Actually, you can thank Mr. Stoker for the popularization of the coffin image, as well as most other images presently associated with the Undead. As for candlelight...well, it, like the rose, is a bane to evil. The light isn't painful to me as such, but I can do without the symbolism."

She turned to him with a questioning brow. "Symbolism?"

"The rays of the sun. And the spiritual symbolism."

"Oh." Her gaze returned to the room, and he saw her take in the bed again with its sage green linen; the stained glass sconce done in a peacock feather design of green, blue, and gold; and the paintings on the wall that ranged from a reproduction Monet to pastoral scenes of English countryside to a portrait of Rumer, his prized stallion from his days of managing MacArthur's stables.

Finally she shook her head again and faced him. "I don't know what to say. It's beautiful. Masculine, but beautiful. I guess I expected black and gloom, not greens and browns and lots of horses."

He looked at the Monet and smiled. *The Seine at Giverny* was a soothing blur of color. "Strangely, I find the colors of nature more restful than black. I spend enough time as it is in the black of night. As for the horses, I've always had a passion for them. I can't go near them, now. There's something in what I am that spooks them. When I was alive, however, there was no creature on earth I loved better than the noble horse. The gray stallion there is Rumer. That's English for 'gypsy.' He was my favorite."

She took a step closer to him and put her hands against his chest. He felt the heat of her palms as acutely as if he had been naked. He drew a shuddering breath, and her scent embraced him, stirring the desire that was always present when she was. He hadn't wanted her to leave. Could Juliana be right? Was this his second chance at something he thought to have lost forever?

He placed his hands on her shoulders and pulled her closer. The beat of life, so enticing and sweet, thundered in his ears, pulsed under his fingers, and filled his nostrils. It was the vampiric lust, but it was also something more than that. It was the feeling about her that had eluded his understanding since the day he had met her.

She looked up into his eyes. "For a creature who claims to have so little in common with humans, you lead a surprisingly human existence."

"Superficially, perhaps, but..."

She laid a finger against his lips. "Shhh." Swift hands ran up his chest to his neck, and she pulled his head down to hers, pressing her lips to his as soon as they were within reach. The taste of her, as always, almost undid him. He held her in a brief kiss, then released her to gather the reins of his control.

"What is it you want, Tia?" he whispered in her ear.

"For you to take me on a ride on that magnificent bed of yours."

The reins just collected dropped again.

***

She had longed for the intimacy of his kiss, but this one had been too meteoric, flaring with desire, but coming to an end just as she had parted her lips to welcome him. He let her go and, like a shadow, glided to the door to close it.

"There. Locked underground with no windows. Much like a coffin after all, isn't it?" he asked softly.

"I'm not afraid, Dallas." *But was he?* He had pulled away from her kiss as though he feared where it would lead. Was he truly afraid of hurting her?

He merely turned and stared at her, forgoing the reply of "you should be" that she expected to hear. Instead, never taking his eyes from her, he slowly undid his linen shirt. Her eyes followed his hands, marveling at the way his fingers unerringly performed the delicate task of each small button. When the shirt hung open, he stepped to the table and poured a little of the wine into the goblet. She sat on the edge of the bed and waited for him.

He sat next to her and offered her the wine without a word.

She took a sip, then set the goblet down, much more interested in the sight and taste of what was before her. She dipped her hands into the shadow that played between the open edges of the white shirt and felt the heat of the hard muscles underneath. He closed his eyes and waited as she slipped the shirt back off his shoulders and down his arms. She had to lean forward to finish the sweet labor, and when the fabric dropped behind him, her arms, already around him, tightened to an embrace.

"A sleigh bed in Mississippi. I love it," she whispered in his ear.

His arms responded in a matching embrace. "Actually, I acquired it a long time ago in Alaska. Someone once told me that my life was about journeys."

"Alaska?"

"The gold rush was a good opportunity to obtain wealth, and the long nights...well, they had a certain appeal."

She burrowed her mouth beneath his thick hair to his ear. "I'll bet they did."

She slid her hands back to his chest and gently pushed him just far enough away so that she could reach the buttons of her own blouse, but he quickly took over, deftly unpopping each tiny pearl button of the sheer blouse she wore.

It was one of the outfits that Juliana had purchased for her. Tia had cattily thought that Juliana would buy her something either unflattering or outrageous, and was genuinely surprised to see the sheer blouse delicately embroidered with a floral design, and the long, fluid black skirt with a matching gray floral pattern. When she had donned the outfit earlier today, Drago had appraised her not with the expected leer, but with a regard that had brought a rare spark of admiration to his world-weary blue eyes. Drago's assessment of her did nothing more than amuse her, but the look in Dallas' eyes now made her shiver. She was aware that her breathing, heavier now than a moment before, was causing her breasts to rise and fall enticingly. His downcast eyes, traveling every inch of her, hardly failed to notice either their movement or the lace camisole holding them. The blouse and camisole soon joined the linen shirt in a pool of white on the lush carpet of golden-brown, but all the colors around her were soon forgotten when he kissed her again. She was barely aware of their remaining clothing flying to the floor.

This time when his mouth joined hers it wasn't just the warmth and softness she felt, but the restrained power and desire that ran through him like an electric current. The soft kiss deepened, and he drew on her with a hunger she hadn't felt in him before. It thrilled and excited her, and she in turn tried to convey to him with her lips all the things she had so inadequately communicated with her words.

She wasn't sure if he understood or not, knew only that his need was as great as hers. She knotted her fingers in his long hair and felt his hands warm her skin, and when their bodies fell back onto the bed, their legs entwined as well.

It was like a dream, but like no dream she had ever had. Her dark dreams had always been nightmares filled with the accusatory stares of victims and suspects alike. And always, presiding over all, Death had sat and waited.

This dream, just as dark and far from daylight, didn't eclipse those that came before, but expanded them, adding whole new dimensions and perspectives. His touch said that her fears were accepted, and his kiss told her that there was more to the night than what she had known. His hands, with a dexterity even greater than when he had divested her of her delicate garments, paved the way for his mouth with caresses that burned, flicks that teased, and strokes that drew feelings of longing and desire from places so deep within her she hadn't known they existed. Streaming down her throat, across her shoulders, and over and around her breasts his hands coursed, not only arousing her, but urging her. *It's all right,* they told her. *Accept what is, and explore what could be.*

His mouth was still on hers, ending each kiss like a farewell full of promises, only to kiss her anew, fulfilling each promise. She untangled her fingers from his hair, and, as he did to her with his hands, she did to him. His was a body not sculpted in a gym, but by hard labor. She felt the contours of his shoulders, back, arms, and chest, and wanted to cry for each pain and hardship that had forged the hard muscles.

When his mouth finally began its journey down the path his hands had traced, she paused in her exploration to revel in his. His tongue set flames of liquid fire to skin already warmed and sensitized by his hands. He traveled her neck only to linger at her throat, his tongue licking at her, his lips marking each spot with a slow kiss.

Suddenly she felt the muscles under her palms tense, and, his breaths coming hard and heavy, he hesitated, at last nestling his forehead at the base of her throat. She waited until his breathing steadied and his muscles relaxed, her hands feather-light on his back.

With a deep inhalation he renewed his voyage, lowering his mouth to the well between her breasts. She first felt his breath against her skin, so hot the rest of her body shivered in relative cold. She lowered her hands to the small of his back and urged him with the gentle kneading of the muscles there. He kissed the hard line along her sternum, then lifted his lips to reach the top of one breast. She arched into him, and her hands dug into his muscles, no longer gentle. He dipped his mouth to her nipple, and teased it with his tongue and lips until it hardened under his onslaught. She released the grip of her fingers, and her hands raked up his back, seeking both to respond to the pleasure he wrought and to find a refuge from the ache of his tormenting touch.

Her legs found the solution instead, hooking his. She rolled to the side, flipping him on his back. He was heavy, but the move on her part was easily done, learned long ago as part of her training in defense and arrest tactics. He sprawled on the huge bed, his breathing labored, his lips drawn back, and his eyes dark and glazed, as if his passion was a drug that transported his body to a whole new realm. His hair framed his face, as wild as his eyes, and his skin glowed in the lamplight with a pale, golden sheen. The drawn-back lips revealed the sharp eyeteeth she had noticed before, but by far the greatest evidence of his desire was his manhood, undiminished by his journey to the Other Side. She straddled him, facing the foot of the bed, and took him in her hands. She wasn't necessarily trying to pay him back for his sweet torment of her, but, in a release of her fears and constraints, to fully explore the magnificent creature beneath her. His moan, more animalistic than human, only served to spur her to love him with an abandon she had never before experienced. She stroked the velvet skin, awed that something so soft could sheath such hardness. She kissed him as he had kissed her, a combination of tongue and lips that elicited a low sound that was half-groan, half-growl, proof that she both pleased and plagued him with sensations that tested the boundaries of his control.

She felt his hands on her hips, drawing her up to him. His hands circled her buttocks and ran down her thighs, and the ache deep within her that hadn't diminished since he had stepped onto the veranda mounted again. She laid her face low on his abdomen, still caressing him. She felt the muscles under her cheek suddenly contract as he lifted his head, and she felt his hands move to a position low on her hips. The brief warning did nothing to prepare her for the assault of sensation that followed when his tongue touched her most sensitive spot. Her body jerked in sweet shock, but his hands held her securely, allowing him to continue. His tongue stroked her until she thought she would explode.

She pulled away when she could stand no more and turned around so that she faced him once more, but was startled by his appearance. His disheveled hair glimmered like spun glass, and his eyes were opaque, but his skin, drawn tightly against the bones of his face, was just the opposite—so translucent he looked to be made out of ivory wax. She supposed it was the result of being deep in the throes of vampiric lust, but the sight was not pretty. More than that, it was disturbing. Was this the physical manifestation of the beast he had spoken of?

No sound came from her mouth, but she knew her features, caught in the emotional turbulence of the moment, would not be able to mask her shock.

Dallas' animal eyes narrowed. "Take a good look, Tia," he growled. "This is what I am. Is this what you wanted to see?"

No. She closed her eyes and concentrated on the gravely

voice that carried the pain and suffering of two hundred years. It was the same voice that had touched something deep within her that first evening at the inn.

"Is this the creature you wanted to make love to you?"

Was it? It was still Dallas—still the same man. If the beast was indeed a part of him, she would have to accept it if she wanted to stay with him. What kind of lover would she be if she could love only the handsome image he had shown her, and not all of him? She was determined that he know she could survive in his world.

Her throat constricted with her emotions, and it was all she could do to nod. She gave him her complete answer in the language of her body, laying on top of him and rubbing herself slowly against him, willing him to return her embrace. His body was rigid with a tension she suspected was close to unbearable, and she despaired that they would be unable to continue, but just as a tear slipped from her eye to his chest, his arms wrapped around her, one encircling her waist, the other cradling her head.

"Take me, then, love," he whispered, his voice sounding almost human again.

He loosened his hold so she could sit up, then helped her as she positioned herself above him. He held her hips, and as she lowered her weight onto him, he pulled her down until she encased all of him. Their joining was a sweet end to the tension that throbbed through her, but the journey had only begun. She started a slow rhythm, lifting herself up and sinking back down, stroking every inch of him with every cycle. She glanced down at his face and saw that his mouth was open and his eyes closed. She closed hers as well, and let the sensation of his body filling hers transport her back to the dream.

It was still night, but now there were no cages and no boundaries. All was accepted, all was allowed, and all was possible. There was no right or wrong, good or evil, no shame, and no limits. Surrender, always a bad thing unless someone else was doing it, was now a thing to be embraced. Appearance and reality melted together, and fantasy and fact became indistinguishable.

The ache built in her again with every stroke they completed, but it was hard for her to increase their pace. He saw the need, and rolled her onto her back. He took over, and his speed and power brought both of them to the culmination of the journey. He brought her to the brink, and when her release came, his swiftly followed. He stayed with her and held her, and when his trembling body told her he struggled to deny his vampiric release, she eased his burden and slid out of his grasp.

She walked on weak legs to where the bowl of fruit sat and savored the sweetness of several chunks of strawberry and melon before turning back to the bed, not sure what she would see. She was more afraid now that it was over than she had been before. Could her rational self accept the vampire as easily as her passionate self had?

Wobbly steps brought her back to the bed. Though his hair was still untamed and his body gleamed with the sweat of lovemaking, the beast was gone, replaced by the vision of the man she still knew so little about. Except how he made her feel. If Drago was the Anti-God, then this surely was the Anti-Lover, unfettered by the decorum and restraints of the daylight world, able to create for her any fantasy she could ever imagine. Except the one she truly wanted—a man who would love her for always, unconditionally.

She took a long sip of wine and sat down on the edge of the bed.

He held out a hand to her. "Did I hurt you?"

She shook her head. She took his hand, and he pulled her to the center of the huge bed. "What about you? Your need was not filled."

He smiled. "I wouldn't exactly say that. The vampire's release was denied, yes, but, like any hunger, it can be controlled. Most of the time, that is. But the human release...I still feel it, in all its glory, have no fear."

She reached a tentative hand to stroke his face and stared into the eyes that had paled to the clarity of green amber. His human eyes. The eyes she loved so much. It wasn't just their beauty, but what she saw in them. The strength and pain of so many years…and the ability to see so deeply into her soul. They closed at the feel of her fingers tracing the line of his jaw to his mouth. She touched his lips with her fingertips, and when he opened his lids again, it was the vampire's dark eyes that gleamed at her. She tried to snatch her hand away, but his large hand smothered hers. He raised her hand to his mouth, pressed a kiss to her palm, and lowered her hand to her lap. "It is best, love, not to stir the bloodlust too much."

She nodded. "So what happens now?"

"What do you want to happen?"

So that was it. That's all that was on his mind—creating fantasies for her. Correction. One last fantasy. He had made no indication that he had changed his mind about tomorrow. She took a deep breath. She didn't want to think about tomorrow, but already worries about his "deal" were intruding into her thoughts.

"I'd like to spend what time I can with you. Is that possible?"

She held her breath, her whole life hanging on his reply, but all he did was nod.

When he did speak, it wasn't what she really wanted to hear. "Are you hungry or thirsty? We can go back upstairs if you are. And there's a bathroom to the right."

She let out her breath and pasted on a brave smile, trying not to show the disappointment that suddenly burned the back of her lids with bitter tears. After what they had just experienced, how could he still consider asking her to leave him forever? Had he in fact already made the decision and was just too cowardly to tell her? Perhaps it was something he didn't want to face yet at all.

She would not cry in front of the vampire. She had never cried in front of any man, not even Bret when he left her. She would not cry now, though the pain was far greater than any loss or sorrow she felt at Bret's final good-bye. She hid her feelings in a quick reply.

"I could use something more to eat, I think. I'll just clean up a little first, if you don't mind." She grabbed her clothes from the floor and headed for the bathroom.

"Be my guest."

But she was already around the corner and out of sight before she heard his words.

***

The door closed behind her, and he leaned his head back against the formidable curved headboard. He felt the unforgiving hardness of the wood not in the least.

She had done it. She had seen the vampire as he really looked. The sight had shocked her, but she had still wanted him. She had given herself to the demon creature with the unholy black eyes, the abnormal canine teeth, and the death-pale skin just as easily as she had to her fantasy lover Dallas Allgate scant days ago.

Such a destruction of the fantasy would have sent any other woman screaming in terror. But not Tia. It would seem that whatever she felt for him was truly stronger than the mark of blood.

Harder to understand was what he felt for her. The ritual of human lovemaking had indeed been sweet. A pleasure long forsworn, he had immersed himself as thoroughly as he could in the light and warmth of her body. He had reveled in her sweetness and life, but to deny satisfying the bloodlust had been hard. This was but one night. Could he take her night after night and not take her blood? The need would only grow stronger with time. And if he should take her once, with consent, stopping well short of doing her permanent harm, what was to prevent him from taking her a second, third, and fourth time? Eventually he would kill her. He couldn't bear the thought.

Tomorrow, as hard as it would be, he would have to order her to leave.

EIGHTEEN

The persistent buzz of the cellar intercom finally broke through Dallas' sleep of the dead. He cracked his eyelids open. Tia was nowhere to be seen. Turning his head, he looked at the time display glowing at him from the nearby clock, its cold luminescence as dispassionate as the droning of the intercom. Just past five o'clock in the afternoon. A low sound like a growl rumbled from deep within his chest. Far too early for him to be up.

Drago's last visit had been less than twenty-four hours ago. If Drago was back again so soon to ask more of his idiot questions, Dallas was going to be upset. Or had Tia left and gotten herself into more trouble? Only if by some miracle it was good news would this interruption of his sleep be worth it.

He hit the intercom button. "Yes, Gillie?"

Gillie's usual calm voice was almost stuttering. "You'd better take this call, Sir. It's the inn. There's a...hostage situation."

"Is it Tia?"

There was a short pause. "No, Sir. It's the inn. It's Angie."

Where was Tia? "All right, Gillie." He picked up the extension. "Angie? Stay calm and tell me what's happened."

"There's a man here. He's got us in the banquet room, and he...he threatened to do terrible things to us unless I called you."

Dallas could feel her fear through the phone line. "Who's 'us'? You and who else?"

"Me, Jaz, and your friend, Miss Martell."

Dallas could taste an unfamiliar sensation in the back of

his throat, sour and caustic. The welling of raw fear. "Is it a man with blonde hair?"

"Yes..." It sounded like she wanted to add more, but she didn't.

"It'll be okay, Angie. I'll be right there. Just do as he says until I arrive, okay? And make sure Jaz and Tia don't provoke him. Do you understand, Angie?"

"Yes. He said to tell you one more thing. Not to bring any weapons or he'd kill us."

"All right. Tell him I got the message. I'll be there in ten minutes."

Dallas hung up the phone and sighed. Damn Drago and his useless sanctions! Dallas had known St. James would be back, and with a renewed vengeance. He ran up the stairs and set to dressing quickly. Gillie appeared in the doorway.

"It's St. James again, Gillie. He's got the girls at the inn, including Tia." Dallas couldn't keep the accusation out of his voice.

"I'm sorry, Sir. She said she wanted to go out for a walk. I thought it would be safe."

"Damn it all! Gillie..." In his frustration, Dallas was at a loss for words.

Gille wasn't. "You can't go, Sir. It's only five."

"I know what time it is. It ends today. One way or another."

Gillie sighed, but it was one of sadness, not disapproval. "Instructions, Sir?"

"You know what to do should I...not return. If anything happens to the girls, make sure they're properly taken care of, understand? No expense is to be spared."

"Sir..."

Dallas saw the old man's eyes gleam with an uncharacteristic moisture, but there was no time now for sentimentality. "Bring the car around, Gillie." The softness in Dallas' voice was the only concession to his feelings for his friend.

The man nodded, turned, and left without a word.

There were several hours of daylight left, but if Dallas could confront St. James within the dim interior of the inn, that was much more preferable to confronting him outdoors. Dallas' strength and abilities would be diminished indoors, but as long as he avoided direct sunlight, he would be able to maintain a measure of control over his power.

Dressed again all in black, he donned dark sunglasses and his long coat and hurried to the shelter of the Lincoln with its tinted windows. During the quick sprint to the car Dallas felt a wave of dizziness wash over him, and he sat with the engine idling for a full minute before he put the car in gear.

Badly done, mon ami, badly done! Drago's admonishments filled his mind and, like a back seat driver, scolded him anew. It was easy to damn Drago, but Dallas knew the reprimand was deserved. Dallas should have made sure the job was done properly in Rodney. He hadn't then. This time he would.

Five minutes later he was at the inn. He parked the car as close to the rear door as he could, swiftly unlocked the door and entered. The inn should have been animated with the good cheer and efficient operation of the early dinner crowd, but the rooms were strangely quiet. There were no patrons in the dining room, and half-eaten dinners sat neglected on several tables. Drinks on the bar waited to be consumed. The kitchen was void of cooks, and a pot of soup warmed on a still-hot burner. Dallas turned off the stove and oven and returned to the dining area. He shrugged out of his coat, draped it over a chair at one of the empty tables, and flipped the sunglasses onto the place mat.

One thing did fill the room. The stink of the Undead. Dallas had no trouble recognizing the unmistakable odor of Jermyn St. James. Dallas followed the trail of scent up the narrow staircase to the second floor banquet room. The door was closed.

Dallas pushed the door open, at the same time trying to avoid being framed in the fatal funnel of the doorway. If St. James had a weapon with silver shot, Dallas had no wish to make himself an easy target.

"Come in, Aldgate, and join the party."

Dallas, taking a peek into the room, saw St. James seated at the largest table, like an honored guest waiting to be served.

St. James spread his arms wide in invitation. "I'm afraid you missed the first course. My compliments to your staff. Delicious fare. Especially the redhead. She fought like a wildcat. Life force brimming with unbridled energy and blood as sweet as any I've ever tasted. Pity you didn't have three or four more like her working for you."

Dallas flowed into the room like raging water but stopped cold when he saw the tangled bodies of the three women on the floor. Those of Angie and Jaz were still, but Tia, though bound and gagged, was conscious and breathing. His eyes briefly met hers—round eyes brimming with fear and a supplication so heartfelt he had to look away. He couldn't afford the distraction.

Dallas' swept the rest of the room quickly. He wanted to make sure no other surprises awaited him. "What have you done with the rest of my staff? And the patrons? If there's a panic and the law shows up on my curb..."

St. James' manic laugh cut him off. "Really, Aldgate. The law worries me even less than you do. If they do show up, it's of no consequence. But do you really think I planned this little outing so carelessly? The customers were told the restaurant was closing early because of a power outage. Everyone left calmly. Your minions are in the cellar. A victory feast for when I'm done with you."

Dallas thought about his remaining staff. All young and hard working. At least Sovatri, Richton, and Keller had had some expectation of danger in the work they had done for him, but the employees at the inn were simply cooks and waiters. Innocents. Just like the citizens at Rodney St. James had killed. Survival was one thing, but what St. James was doing was just needless slaughter, bad not only for the human population, but the Undead community as well.

Dallas turned his furious gaze on St. James with all the power he could muster, but could do no more than stare at the man's hideous face. Circular red and black wounds, two on the left side of his face, one on the right, and one on his neck, gaped angry and raw. The combination of silver shot and fire had not killed, but they had caused damage that would never heal. St. James leered, a mockery of the charming smile that once graced his handsome face.

"Behold your work, Aldgate. Are you pleased with it?"

Renewed anger surged through Dallas, giving him the strength the light stole. There was rage in abundance at the monstrosity before him, but even greater was the self-vehemence Dallas felt. If he had not botched the job in Rodney, the women would still be alive. "Nothing about you will ever please me except to see you sent to the True Death."

St. James rose, the splatters of blood on his ruffled white shirt now clearly visible in the late afternoon rays angling through the windows. "Oh, but you've tried twice and failed, haven't you? You're the one who will die tonight, and the sweetness of that memory will help me endure eternity with these wounds that no amount of blood will ever heal."

Dallas stood well out of the shafts of light, but even so, when St. James opened his dark eyes wide, Dallas felt caught by their power. Anger alone was no match for St. James and his weapon of the light.

"That's right, Aldgate, look at me. Look at the pain and suffering you've caused one of your own kind. Look at the abomination you've created with your vengeance. And when you can stand no more of the hideous creature before you, turn your vision to all the rest of the horror you've wrought in two hundred years. See it and re-live it all before you perish."

Dallas fought to resist, but his will, no more substantial than a shadow, disappeared before the inescapable daylight. Silver and gold dazzled his eyes, blinding him to all but his own reflection. To humans, the mirror showed fantasies. To an inhabitant of Midexistence, the reverse, as always, prevailed. The mirror showed truth.

He saw Devon Alexander standing in this very room in 1829, shaking hands with Liam Bishop to seal a pact that would change his life for decades to come. Wealthy and cunning, Bishop was a survivor. Not unlike MacArthur. Only the strong survived. Bishop had raised a glass in toast to the bargain, and though Devon had declined to drink, he had shared all too heartily in the joyous prospect of seeing the mute stable boy, Rowan Kiley, dispatched to a better life.

Dallas tried to fight the memories, but they flashed before his mind's eye with a vengeance, bringing with them all the sensations of that faraway time.

Lust. What did Devon care for the life of one human? Veilina was his prize, and he meant to reclaim her. Beautiful and filled with a wicked spirit, she had been the epitome of vampiric conquest, promising countless hours of pleasure spent in the pursuit of unwrapping layer after layer of vanity and pride.

Betrayal. Rowan, the mute, had been weak. But the stable boy had taken it all away from him in the one unselfish act of saving her life. And his love, Veilina, had not been true. When she needed help the most, it was not him she turned to, but Rowan. All his attentions and all his flattery were forgotten in the single touch of the mute's hand.

Revenge. Killing the stable boy had been easy. Too easy. There had been no satisfaction in the deed, any more than there had been in the destruction of Christian St. James only a few years before. It had left him feeling empty, still hungry for something that could never bring satisfaction in a thousand years.

Damnation. Killing had been easy. Reclaiming his prize had not. Rowan's love had revealed Veilina's true spirit in a way that all Devon's seductions had failed to do, and the woman thus exposed was true and pure, imbued with an innate goodness he had never seen. But her heart could not do one thing. Forgive Devon for his treachery. For he had not asked it.

He heard her voice from across time—from a time when Mississippi was a new state, Rose Hill was a new jewel adorning Natchez, and he himself, newly come from England, was starting a fresh life in a land full of promise.

"How could you, Devon? How could you do such a thing? What kind of cold-blooded monster are you to kill a boy who never did anything to harm anyone?" Veilina's blind eyes could not look upon him with accusation, but he felt her words touch even his cold heart. "I thought you loved me, Devon. I trusted that love, even after the accident. How could you do that to me?"

Her words had moved him; still, he had been unable to ask for her forgiveness. He had no explanation for her, nothing that she would understand, but neither would he repent to her. He was what he was, and he never apologized for that.

Was he any different from St. James? Had he ever been any different? He had perceived a "need" in all his killings, but had they, in fact, been any less wanton than those of St. James? The memories of the passing years curled away like pages of a burning book, only to reveal the dark side of every new life he had begun. When the promise of war between brothers threatened the South, he had fled Mississippi altogether for California, trying to put as much distance as he could from his past. But it was the same wherever he went. Dalton Allgate in Sacramento and San Francisco after gold was discovered, Dalys Alexander in Australia, and Devon Aldgate in Alaska in the early 1900s—all had done whatever they needed to in order to survive. Poverty had given him the tools for survival when he was young, his tutelage under MacArthur had developed a wealth of skills using those tools, and the demands of life as one of the Undead had honed them to perfection.

But to what end? He had survived, but countless others had not. Images of those faces flashed in his mind, one after another, and while not all were as hideous as that of St. James, each triggered its own horror.

Dallas suddenly felt old. Weary and weak, he sagged to the floor next to a hutch full of glassware, his remaining strength drained by the emotion spent in reliving the memories. The room was stifling, yet he felt a cold touch at his shoulder. Mistress Death was standing in the wings, waiting patiently for St. James and the sunlight to make their final moves.

Not yet. Not yet. He wasn't ready. If he couldn't kill St. James, there was still one thing he should have done and hadn't. It was what would set him apart, once and for all, from St. James. It had unknowingly haunted him for one hundred and seventy-two years.

It was simple. It was the one thing the young stable boy had done so easily. It was the one thing that Dallas, with all his strength and power, had never been able to do. It was the selfless act.

Dallas struggled to clear his vision, concentrating all his remaining strength on breaking free from the grasp of St. James' terrible gaze. With a final shake of his head, the reflections shattered. The years of memories were bound together and put away, and his mind was freed. Dallas opened his eyes and saw no horror but St. James. Weakened as well by the ordeal, St. James stood before Dallas, braced against a table, his arms outstretched, his wounds oozing fresh blood.

Dallas pushed himself to his feet. He would not do this final thing from a position of defeat, but from one of strength and control. He stood and gathered all his remaining resources.

"Veilina! Forgive me! I should have never made that pact with your father. Forgive me, please..."

Dallas heard a slam. An inside shutter of one window had banged shut.

St. James' desperate laughter filled the sudden silence. "You fool! What are you doing? There's no one here but me, and I'll never forgive you for what you've done."

"Veilina, I was wrong! I was wrong to kill Rowan. His love for you was truer than mine. Forgive me!"

Another slam sounded. The inside shutter of the second window. The room was thrown into a comfortable gloom. St. James glanced around the room in confusion. "Are you daft, Aldgate? No one's going to forgive you for anything. You're damned, and you're going to die the True Death a damned man."

A measure of strength returned with the darkness, but it wasn't enough. "Veilina, please hear me."

The windows banged again as both outside shutters rattled shut, effectively banishing all light from the room.

Dallas felt cold air wash over him like a shadow, but this time it wasn't Mistress Death. The table behind St. James started shaking, its legs banging against the floor, and the utensils at the place settings vibrated in an angry patter. Dallas steadied himself against the wall. "No, St. James, I don't think I'll die a damned man. But you will."

The door to the stairs swung open and a new presence made itself felt, but before Dallas could react, St. James lunged toward him. Just as quickly, a fork flew at St. James, narrowly missing his head.

"If that's the best you can do, Aldgate..." He never finished the sentence, for in the next instant a steak knife bounced from the table and hurled itself at St. James, piercing his flesh above his heart. He cried out, his momentum carrying him straight into Dallas' arms.

"I didn't do it, but I'll happily take credit for this." Dallas grabbed the handle of the knife and thrust the blade in deeper. St. James screamed in agony and struggled to pull the knife out, but he succeeded only in slamming himself and Dallas into the wooden cupboard. The heavy piece of furniture held its ground, but tumblers and wine goblets were thrown to the floor in a crescendo of shattering glass. St. James fell on the broken shards, pulling Dallas down on top of him, and the two writhed in a mass of thrashing limbs.

"Ah, *excellent.* I see I am not too late," came an all-too-familiar voice from above.

Dallas rolled over and tore St. James from him. With a burst of renewed strength, Dallas hurled the body across the room. St. James landed on a tabletop and skidded across it, sending everything in his path flying. Utensils, place mats, and salt shakers were still soaring to the floor when St. James' body bullseyed the center of an adjoining table. The sound of splintering wood erupted as the force proved too much for the old furnishing. Dallas stood, ready to defend himself, but his attention was now split between Drago and St. James.

"If you're here to watch, Drago, stay out of my way," growled Dallas.

"Watch, *mon ami?* You misunderstand my intentions. I am here to do more than observe this time. I am here to enforce my sanction on *monsieur* St. James."

Dallas took a step forward. "This is my fight to finish. Stay out of it."

"Yes, Drago, stay out of it." St. James got up and, with a twisted smile born more of pain than pleasure, pulled the knife from his chest. "Your 'sanctions' don't govern my life. You're a useless vestige of the past. Your kind is no longer needed in our world any more than the old superstitions that hold us back. We could rule the world if it weren't for meddling dinosaurs like you."

Drago crossed his arms. "I can forgive the impetuousness of youth on both your parts, *monsieurs*, but not your disrespect."

With one swipe of his arm, St. James sent the broken table tumbling across the room. "You can't touch me and you know it. It's forbidden for an enforcer to interfere in a conflict."

"Is it? A very amusing person reminded me just recently that I have something called '*discretion.*' A very good word in either French or English. 'Freedom to judge and act on one's own.' Yes, I like that. A good word. Do you agree, St. James?"

St. James licked his lips, but if the gesture was intended to mimic a hungry beast, it failed. The fear surfacing in his dark eyes made Jermyn appear more like a man whose mouth has gone dry with dread.

His words, though, were as full of bravado as ever. "You're old, Drago. You're a laughingstock. The Brotherhood has never frightened me, and you least of all. You're nothing but Nikolena's dog, and all the Undead know it. When you get too far out of line, she yanks your chain, and you slink back to her, eager to please. You wouldn't dare kill me."

Dallas stepped to Drago's side. "Let me finish him, Drago. This is between him and me."

Drago shook his head. "No, *mon ami*. He has just made this very personal. This one will go against my record, not yours."

Dallas put a restraining arm in front of Drago. He knew that even on his best day he lacked the power to prevail over *l'enforcier*, but this was something Dallas had to do. He did something he never did. He prayed that Drago would reach into his mind and understand. "Drago, please. Allow me the chance to correct my mistake." Dallas gazed square into the eyes of ice that burned with a cold fury evident even in the gloom of the dark room.

To Dallas' surprise, Drago didn't try to exert his authority or punish Dallas' impudence, but simply nodded. "Very well, *mon ami.* You have earned that chance."

Some of the fear visibly lifted from St. James, and a smile almost stretched between the gaping shotgun wounds on either side of his face. "Ah, so we do agree on something after all, Aldgate. The less interference by the Brotherhood and the Directorate, the better."

Dallas forced his gaze from the ugly lesions on St. James' face to his dark eyes. "You're wrong. We don't agree on anything. It's simple. I'm just selfish. I want the pleasure of sending you to the True Death all to myself." In point of fact Dallas did agree with much of Jermyn's assessment of the Directorate and its branches, but he wasn't about to let either St. James or Drago be privy to that opinion.

St. James pointed his finger at Drago. "Then at least make this a fair contest, Drago. Promise me you won't side with Aldgate against me."

The intensity of Drago's eyes was matched by that of his voice, and St. James' arm suddenly jerked downward, as if hit by an invisible force. *"Espece d'idiot!* You fool! Did I not warn you to stay away from here? You have the audacity to disobey me and then beg for favors? I should kill you right now for defying me. I promise you nothing."

St. James rubbed his arm. "At least guarantee that the survivor, whether it be me or Aldgate, be free from any new sanctions. I don't fancy my victory being rewarded with my death."

A laugh that was half snarl burst from Drago. "You want to fight, *monsieur?* Very well, then fight. But accept the consequences. I make no promises or guarantees to either one of you."

Dallas took an aggressive step forward. "Enough whining, St. James. You invited me to this party, so get on with it. I promise you all the entertainment you want."

Drago stepped back into the blackness of the doorway, and St. James turned at last to Dallas with a lopsided leer.

"Oh, you will entertain me, I have no doubt. As will the delectable Miss Martell. I was surprised to learn she was still with you. I would have thought the experience in Rodney would have been too much for her. At the very least I figured the discovery that her new lover was a blood sucking monster would send her fleeing in terror."

Dallas had heard enough. He loosed all the power of his vampiric mind on St. James, willing his opponent to submit to the mirror, much as St. James had done to him earlier. St. James' eyes took on a glassy, unfocused stare, and Dallas fought to maintain the compelling force. "Miss Martell will be safe, now and forever, from the abomination *you* embody, St. James. That's all that you need to know. Now take a good look at yourself, and see if you can live with your own horror."

St. James made small choking sounds, and his unseeing, glazed eyes blinked rapidly, as if to clear his vision.

Dallas felt a surge of satisfaction. "Truth is a monster, isn't it? Do you now see all your grandiose fantasies for what they really are?"

Dallas knew St. James was vulnerable, but he felt his own strength start to flag. Though the room was dark, it was still daylight outside. Dallas' powers would not be at their peak until sunset, and he had not fed. St. James, on the other hand, had feasted well just moments ago. The fresh blood would give him a boost in strength and energy that Dallas feared would be more than he could overcome.

Dallas needed to make his move now, before his advantage was lost. He flew at St. James, seizing him by the neck and propelling him into the wall. The impact broke the grip of the compelling stare, however, and St. James focused his eyes once more on his enemy.

Dallas tightened his grip over the wound on St. James' neck, and pain contorted the hideous face. "Did you see the truth? Did you see your fountain of youth as the false kingdom it really is? It's a prison, St. James, isn't it? Full of all the same sufferings as life—hunger, pain, deceit, and persecution."

St. James croaked out his reply. "You're wrong on all counts. I never sought the fountain of youth to find a kingdom. I sought it to be able to avenge myself on you. And it may be a prison for you, but it's not for me. I enjoy it, and I plan to keep on enjoying it. You'll never kill me like this, Aldgate." He twisted free of Dallas' grasp and spun away, leaving Dallas with nothing but blood covering his hands.

Dallas, never taking his eyes from St. James, knelt down to wipe his hands on a napkin that was part of the litter on the floor. As he stood, a steak knife levitated off the floor and hung in the air before him. He grabbed it and lunged at St. James. "No? Guess again."

St. James reached for a similar knife still part of an undisturbed place setting, but the knife slid quickly out of his reach. He grabbed for another, but it, too, jerked away from him. "Stop it, Drago! You said you'd stay out of it."

Drago smiled from the doorway, his white teeth visible even in the shadows. "I have nothing to do with it, *monsieur*, I assure you."

St. James had time to utter an oath, but not to search further for a weapon. Dallas was on him, knocking him to the floor among the scattered flatware and place mats. Dallas fell on top of him.

"Where exactly did you take the brunt of that shotgun blast? Here?" Dallas plunged the knife into St. James' side. A squeal of pain filled the room. "It burns, doesn't it? Silver burns like fire. Some say worse than fire. What do you say, St. James?"

Nothing erupted from St. James' mouth but another shriek of pain. Echoing the scream was the blood that started to well from the fresh wound. Dallas tried to draw out the knife to drive it home into Jermyn's heart, but at that instant St. James managed to pull his feet to his chest and push them against Dallas' abdomen. The handle of the knife, wet with blood, slipped out of Dallas' grasp as he was thrust backward, off balance, to land halfway across the room in a pile of broken glassware and splintered wood.

St. James pulled the knife from his side and lurched toward

the windows. With a burst of inhuman strength, he ripped the inside shutter from one window, grabbed a nearby wooden chair, and flung the chair through the window. The glass panes shattered, and the impact tore the outside shutter from one of its hinges. A soft glow flooded the room, and a square of pale light fell right on Dallas.

Dallas moaned, not so much in pain, but at the dizziness that washed over him as his strength ebbed. He had neither the power nor time for the speed necessary to get off the floor before St. James pounced on him. The most he could do was to try to roll to the side. Dallas felt the knife pierce his flesh. If he hadn't twisted, the knife would have run through his heart. As it was, the blade entered between ribs and punctured his lung. For a long second a numbness prevailed, but in the next instant the pain of an unbearable heat tore a scream from his throat.

St. James thrust the blade in up to the handle. "Answer your own damn question now, Aldgate! What does it feel like? Does it burn like fire or more like the flames of perdition? We're more alike than you want to admit, you and I. What pleases me pleases you, and what hurts me hurts you, and all the self-righteous speeches in the world can't change that."

The agony from the silver burn and the enervation caused by the light consumed Dallas. He could neither respond nor fight back. In desperation, his hand felt along the floorboards for a piece of cutlery. He felt broken glass slice at his skin, but the pain was nothing compared to the knife wound. Suddenly he felt the handle of a knife slide against his palm, and he curled his fingers around the heavy haft. He tightened his grip, then waited several seconds longer to marshal his remaining physical and mental strength.

"What's the matter, Aldgate? No energy left for one of your ready repartees?" A sound almost like a sob broke St. James' voice. "Come on! Admit it! All I want is for you to admit that you're no different from me. We're both demons of vengeance. Tell me that in my place you wouldn't have done exactly as I did!"

A soundless denial roared through Dallas' mind, and he

swung his arm with all the force he could, stabbing the wounded side that already streamed blood. St. James cried out, but refused to let loose of his own deadly grip. The two bodies rolled across the floor until they crashed into the sturdy legs of a dining table. St. James ended up on top again, and the impact loosened Dallas' grip on the handle of the knife imbedded in his opponent's side. Unable to do more, Dallas' head fell back to the floor and his arms dropped to his sides.

With one hand on each knife handle, St. James pulled both out and held them high in the air, points down, over Dallas' heart. "Tell me! Tell me I'm justified! You would have done the same thing to avenge a father you loved!"

Dallas had no answer. The bloody blades continued to hover above him, and once again he felt the cold touch at his shoulder. He closed his eyes and could only reflect on his own life, not that of St. James. He had survived life to endure the hell of Midexistence the best way he could. He had few regrets. Those he did have had haunted him a long time. The loss of Sabra...his betrayal of Veilina...and now the possible loss of Tia. Strangely, that last hurt the most—not because of what he had actually had with Tia, but for what could have been.

"I want an answer! Tell me I'm justified, Drago! He destroyed an old man who had done nothing! Tell me that in the centuries of your existence you haven't done the same thing a hundred times over."

Dallas heard Drago's soft voice float above him, almost in his ear.

"Ah, but I'm not the one being judged on this day, *monsieur.*"

"Damn you, Drago, and all enforcers! What gives you the right to judge others of your own kind? You're not a god— just a bigger monster with a more inflated ego." St. James' hands started to tremble, and the knife points wavered as he raised the weapons for a final strike.

Dallas looked up and saw Drago above him. *L'enforcier's* voice filled the room. "No, we have no God, you and I, but you have the Anti-God, and I am He. And I have decided that you will kill no more."

With a final howl that was half scream of victory, half cry of defeat, St. James thrust the blades toward Dallas' heart. The blades never reached him, though. St. James' body was torn from Dallas and flung across the room. A crash and a thump sounded as yet another dining table met its demise.

In a movement so swift even Dallas had trouble following it, Drago pulled a rapier from its wall display above the fireplace with his right hand. "This wouldn't happen to be silver, Allgate, would it?"

Dallas raised himself on one elbow. "Steel. But the cutlery is all sterling. Be my guest."

L'enforcier snagged a knife from the floor with his left hand. *"Merci, mon ami.* These will do."

St. James scuttled backward until he hit the wall. "No! It's forbidden! It's against the law!"

Drago was on him like a beast on prey. "You put a lot of faith into a system you say you don't believe in, *monsieur.* Your sanction is imposed."

"No! You said you'd let us finish it!"

"I made no promises. All I promise you now is a quick death."

The rapier staked St. James to the wall, and the knife made swift work of his jugular, ensuring that any more words of protest died before falling from his lips. An oil painting from the wall above twitched and fell on St. James' body, bouncing off one shoulder to land at his feet. It was the portrait of a young woman with long, red hair, hazel eyes, and the barest wisp of a smile. *Veilina Bishop.*

His labor done, Drago flipped the knife to Dallas with a high arch of his brows.

"I dislike being called 'old.'"

Dallas picked the knife from the air. "I'll try to remember that," he said dryly.

Drago plucked a fallen napkin from the floor, wiped his hands, and nodded toward the women in the corner. "If you're able, you'd better see to your humans."

Dallas, knowing that Tia was not badly, if at all, injured,

saw to Angie and Jaz first. He found a faint pulse on Angie, but Jaz was beyond help. He then quickly undid the ropes and gag binding Tia.

"Oh, God, Dallas..." she whispered.

He could see her eyes alternating between his own knife wounds and the bodies of the two other women. "Are you hurt?" he asked, brushing her hair away from her face with his fingers.

She shook her head. "No, but..."

He cut her off. There was still too much to do. "Then I need you to help. Run upstairs and get a blanket from the cedar chest next to the sofa. Keep Angie warm and stay with her. I have to make some calls."

Tia nodded and hurried up to the third floor. He called Gillie and instructed the man to come to the inn right away. Dallas also called a doctor he knew who could be counted on to be discreet.

Drago helped remove the dead vampire's body, as well as that of Jaz, from the inn, then helped Dallas release the employees locked in the cellar. Dallas told them that the blond man had taken Jaz as a hostage and had fled the inn with her after a confrontation with Dallas in the banquet room. The story was accompanied by compelling gazes from both Dallas and Drago, assurance that the humans would all relate the same story, with conviction, to the police. It should be a safe story. The police would search without success for two bodies that would never be found.

When all had been taken care of, Drago prepared to take his leave. He paused before getting into the Riviera. "I will see you at your town house later tonight, *mon ami*. It appears we still have business to conclude."

"Drago..."

"*Oui?*"

"Thank you."

Drago nodded. "*Je vous en prie*. My pleasure. However, after tonight, I fear you'll regret such sentiment." He slammed the door of his Riviera and drove off before Dallas could reply.

NINETEEN

It was well after midnight. Jaz was gone. Angie was alive, but in critical condition under private care. The inn was closed down for an indefinite period. The police had been unavoidable, but through the influence of his and Drago's compelling eyes, questions had been kept to a minimum. For the time being.

This time Gillie had provided the blood required to heal Dallas' silver wound. Dallas had hated to do it, but there was no other choice. The old man was now resting, and Dallas expected and hoped he would recover completely from the ordeal. Tia, too, was resting. She hadn't wanted to witness Dallas' healing process.

Dallas was exhausted.

It had been a debilitating week, no doubt about it. He couldn't remember ever having sustained two silver wounds in such a short period of time. The only good thing that had happened had been the death of an ugly vampire. A small smile touched Dallas' mouth. *No,* he corrected, *two good things had happened.* He had asked for Veilina's forgiveness, and she had given it. Or so it pleased him to think. St. James had been sent to the True Death through the combined efforts of himself, a tortured spirit, and an enforcer with issues. Somehow, it had seemed appropriate at the time.

Veilina and Drago had saved Dallas' life in the process. He didn't mind owing his life to Veilina. He owed her for much more than that. He did, however, very much mind owing Drago. Already Dallas was regretting his 'thank you' to *l' enforcier*. What would Drago demand in return? It was a sobering question.

And Tia... Juliana had said that this was his "second chance." Drago had said that nothing makes eternity bearable except for affairs of the heart. Could everyone else be right, after all? He still had no answer. Giving advice was easy, but he was the one who would have to live with the consequences. What if he allowed Tia to stay and he ended up destroying her in a rage of bloodlust?

Drago arrived soon after. Dallas, for a change, was not annoyed at *l'enforcier's* arrival. Like it or not, he would need more of Drago's help with the St. James incident. They discussed what had happened earlier that evening at the inn and debated contingencies for whatever consequences may arise. There were bound to be more questions asked about Jaz's disappearance. Angie would be a problem too, but vampiric control of her memories of this day should take care of her.

Finally, at two o'clock, Drago lifted his eyes to the ceiling.

"The *mademoiselle* grows restless. She will not come downstairs while I am here. Very well. I think we have done all there is to do for tonight. I will leave you to your *affaire de coeur. Au revoir, mon ami.*"

Drago let himself out, pulling the door closed behind him with a soft snick. Five minutes later Tia came downstairs.

"Is he gone?" she asked.

She looked breathtaking in a form-fitting black flock mini-dress with a tiny purple floral design. "I think you know he is, else you wouldn't have come down. You look very nice." A sad smile accompanied his appraisal of her.

"Thanks. Juliana went shopping for me. She bought me this outfit." She cocked a brow. "All of you seem to have a rather highly developed sense of style. Yourself included."

He opened his eyes wide in a declaration of innocence. "Me? I just like to dress tastefully, that's all."

She smiled. "Hmm. In silk and linen that costs a pretty penny."

He lifted his arms to his waist in mock surrender to her argument. "Guilty as charged. I like to live well."

Her smile faded. "We have to talk, Dallas."

He sat on the sofa in the parlor, and she joined him, but he noticed she was careful to leave a good two feet between them. He let loose the first salvo, hoping to bring the conversation to a quick close. "I know you can't want to stay now. Not with what happened at the inn tonight."

She took a deep breath. "I've been involved in lots of horrible incidents before. None, I'll admit, that I've been so personally involved in, but I survived. Thanks to you."

"You didn't answer the question."

"I did a lot of thinking while you were talking to Drago. I still want to be with you."

He shook his head in disbelief. "How can you? You were a cop. 'Protect and Serve.' How can you reconcile that with all the violence you just witnessed?"

She gave a snort of disdain. "'Protect and Serve.' I think some public relations genius probably thought that one up to make what we do more palatable to the public. I never thought of myself in that light. Oh sure, once in a while I did good for some innocent victim, but mostly my job was a very selfish one. Staying alive. Looking out for my partner and my own comfort. Keeping warm, dry, and fed. I've had nightmares almost every night for eight years now. Not nightmares about some innocent person being hurt, but about me. About my being hurt. You're the first person I've ever met who has made me feel safe—who has been able to counteract all the power of those nightmares."

He shook his head. "The man who comforted you wasn't real, Tia. How can I make you understand?" He paused, searching for the words. In the end, he simply told her the truth. "Tia, listen. I am nothing more than a mirror for humans to gaze upon. What reflects back to each individual is what they long to see. It is the vampire's cunning to show each human his or her fantasy, his heaven, and it is the vampire's sustenance to turn that heaven into hell."

She sat quietly, but the intensity of her gaze grew. He could see she was trying to understand. "You tried to do that with me?"

"In the beginning, yes. You wanted a protector. I gave

you a protector. I don't want it to be that way with you now. I don't. But I am what I am, and I can't change that. I have a need, but it's not a need to nurture. It's a need to destroy."

"I can't believe you want to destroy me, not after all you've done to save me. You're not this mirror you talk about. A mirror is an inanimate object. You're not. You have a mind, an intelligence."

He tilted his head back and gazed up at the ceiling. "But no soul. And that's what makes me more akin to an inanimate object than a human."

"The very fact that we're having this conversation proves otherwise to me."

He turned to her, and his voice had no reply. He reached one arm to the back of her head, and she leaned into his embrace, wrapping her arms around him. He buried his face alongside her neck and wove his hands into her hair. "I wish your words could change me. I really wish they could. I do want you, Tia. But it's not a human want."

He breathed against her skin. "You're afraid of me, even now, this close to you, when you can feel my hunger."

"No. I'm not afraid. What you feel is nothing but my own hunger."

He pulled away from her so that she could see his eyes. "If you knew the horror I've wrought in only a decade of my life, you wouldn't want to touch me. And if you knew everything I've done in two centuries, you most surely wouldn't want me to touch you."

Her eyes stayed intently on his, as if she were trying not only to ferret out his feelings, but relay hers to him. "Everything that's happened to you...everything you've ever done...all these things are a part of you, yes. But I won't believe that that's all you are." She looked down. "In fact, one of the things that keeps me from wanting to leave is your knowledge and understanding of all the horrible things that happen in the world." She lifted her eyes to his again. "I know that sounds crazy, but it's true. I've experienced a lot of terrible things in my life, too. Oh, not what you have, by any means. But I've witnessed violence, brutality, pain, and death, too, and no one

I've ever met has been able to help me understand the feelings of fear the way you have."

He laughed, a melancholy sound. "I should inspire fear, yet you're telling me I allay yours?"

She nodded. "I don't really know how to explain it. Maybe it's because you've been around so long—because you have experienced so much. You put things in perspective for me. There's a stillness in you. A kind of peace. It's the same feeling I got when I drove on the Trace. I know that sounds silly, but it, like you, has endured over time and survives still, in spite of everything that's happened. It makes me believe I'll survive, too."

He shook his head. "From the first moment I tried to bespell you I could tell you were seeing things that no other woman ever had. Others saw their fantasies, but never beyond. You did. I couldn't understand it. It vexed me, but it also made me want you all the more."

"Then let me stay with you. You asked me what I wanted. I want you. I want to stay with you."

"Tia, the fact that you feel no fear of me makes me no less dangerous. In fact, it makes you all the more vulnerable. Fear is what keeps us alive. Without it, you will be hurt, believe me."

"I can't believe you'll hurt me. Not after everything you've done for me."

"My world is a reversal of everything normal. Everything I am is a gross distortion of human nature. What do I have to do to make you understand that?"

She reached her hand up and smoothed the long hair from his face. "I think I do understand. There are two sides. But what's wrong with that? It's not as though one side is all good and the other all evil. Isn't the 'Trail of Tears' a reminder of that? Man can be just as cruel to his fellow man as any so-called beast or monster can be."

He made no move to pull her hand away. "You're not going to listen to any argument I put forth, are you?"

She smiled. "No."

He closed his eyes and let out a long, soft sigh. Of pleasure at her touch? Encouraged, she touched the side of his face, running her palm down his cheek to his neck. His lips parted, and he opened his eyes to stare into hers.

"Do you mind?" she asked.

"Do I mind what?"

"My touching you."

He shuttered his eyes again. "Your touch is like rays of sunlight. Not the way it is now—burning and debilitating— but the way it used to be. Warm and light." He reached a hand up and laced his large fingers with hers, then brought the back of her hand to his lips. He pressed his mouth against her hand in a lingering kiss.

"If you stayed, Tia, I would take all that warmth and light and pay you back with nothing but pain." He mouthed the words against the back of her hand.

She pulled away from him. "Then why did you save me? First with Drago, and then tonight?"

"I saved you for the same reason I want you to leave. I don't want to see you destroyed."

She let out a sigh of frustration. "Yes, but why? I must mean something to you for you to risk your life."

"You ask me to examine feelings that are foreign to me, Tia."

"I don't believe that. You understand loyalty and friendship. I see it in your interaction with Gillie and the people who work for you."

It was Dallas' turn to let out a deep breath. "A game I play to survive in the human world."

***

There were only a few hours left until dawn. They were at a stalemate. Tia hadn't pressed him for his final decision, and he hadn't given it to her. It seemed that both of them desired nothing more than to delay the inevitable. Tia insisted on sleeping with him. It was vastly more pleasurable than arguing with him, she said, and he couldn't disagree. If indeed it was to be their final night together, he couldn't deny her, or himself. Her touch, not just willingly bestowed but gladly so, was bittersweet, but perhaps more pleasurable for being so. The bite of pain behind the ecstasy reminded him that she was his for a brief time only and not something to be taken for granted. He couldn't say no.

They descended once more to his cellar lair. He, in his sweatpants, and she, in her satin nightdress, curled in the middle of the giant sleigh bed, safe, at least for the moment, in each other's arms.

"Dallas, talk to me." Her voice was as soft as the rest of her.

"About what?"

"I don't care. Anything. I just like to hear the sound of your voice. It does things to me."

He smiled. He had long been aware of the effect of his low voice on others, especially on members of the opposite sex. It was one of his human-born traits, not one of his vampiric acquisitions. Sabra had often commented on it, teasing him that his voice was the reason he had been so good with the horses. Perhaps she had been right.

He thought about which story to tell her. He decided on Sacramento. He had changed his name from Devon Alexander to Dalton Allgate when he left Mississippi for California, the promise of gold much more alluring than the threat of Civil War. It had been an exciting era, and profitable, too, but he was barely past the discovery of gold at Sutter's mill when he felt her breathing settle into the rhythm of sleep. He continued to hold her close, her warmth and the scent of her blood too arousing to his senses to allow him to more than doze.

She stirred before dawn, and he felt her sigh when she turned in his embrace to look at the bedside clock. "Dallas?" His name was a hushed whisper.

"Yes, love."

She was silent for a moment, and he almost thought she had fallen asleep again, when her voice floated to him.

"You call me that, but I know it doesn't mean anything. You've most likely made your decision about me, and I think I can guess what it is. I just want you to know something before I leave. You may scorn 'love' as just another useless human emotion, something you don't think is part of the

Undead existence, and maybe it isn't. But I love you." She paused, and he felt her chest expand with a deeply drawn breath. He didn't know how to answer, but she didn't seem to expect one.

She continued before the silence grew heavy. "You've lived a dozen different lifetimes under as many different names, and I don't know any of those men. I don't even know your real name, and I'm not sure I understand even a tiny part of the man called 'Dallas Allgate,' but I do know that under all those personas is a being whose strength and passion for life makes me feel like no one else ever has. Maybe all these roles the vampire plays are supposed to display the intentions of others, but it seems to me that all they've done is to display yourself."

He had even less of an answer. Women had declared their love for him over the years, but no mortal woman had ever dared to claim to conceive the vampire's reality. Such arrogance should have angered him, but it didn't. It shook him.

She slept again, but he couldn't. He wasn't used to sleeping at night, and her admission had done nothing to lull him. Quite the opposite. He carefully eased his body away from hers, covering her with the velvet spread to replace the lost warmth of his presence. He sat on the edge of the bed and ran a hand through his hair. The picture lights were still on, and he gazed at one piece of artwork after another, as if one of them could give him an answer to his dilemma. He thought he had made up his mind, just as she had guessed, but now...

He balanced his elbows on his knees and dropped his head to his hands, staring at the floor in frustration. A small white rectangle caught his eye. He stared at the thing, and his brow lowered. *What was this?*

He picked up the card, and had no trouble reading the name on it, even in the low light. "Alek Dragovich." He tossed the card onto the bedside table in disgust. Where had that damn thing come from? He had no recollection of Drago giving him a business card.

But a recollection, unbidden, did come to mind, and Dallas'

vampiric memory remembered the moment word for word. *Most of our kind, in the cynicism of their years, would tell you that an affaire de coeur between a human and one of us can only result in a chagrin d'amour. Perhaps so, but don't avoid affairs of the heart. Such afflictions make Eternity bearable.*

Drago's strange words. An idea came to Dallas, but he quickly dismissed it. He would not beg *l'enforcier* for advice. Especially on something like this. Another idea surfaced. *Juliana.* She had hinted that Tia was his "second chance." He had once loved Sabra more than anything on earth. If anyone understood his predicament, Juliana would.

He picked up the business card again and stared at it. Juliana would still be in Drago's company, and she would still be up. He took the card and ascended to the first floor, leaving Tia nestled in the center of the sleigh bed.

In his first floor bedroom, he picked up the cordless phone and punched in the number on the business card.

"Dragovich."

Dallas drew a deep breath. "Drago, it's Allgate."

"Ah, *mon ami.* Don't tell me you've made a decision already to join us."

"Hardly. Let me speak to Juliana."

"She's not here. I gave her the night off, and she went out to amuse herself. Is it some question I can help you with?"

"No. Sorry to have bothered you."

"Allgate, wait. It must be something important for you to have called. I can contact her and have her call you back, or I can relay a message."

"It's personal."

"But of course, *mon ami.* What else would it be?" Drago paused, but went on before Dallas could reply. "Ah, but no. It's not Juliana, is it? It's *mademoiselle* Martell."

Damn the creature. Drago's insight was uncanny, even without the benefit of eye contact. "Forget it, Drago."

"Dallas."

The use of his given name gave him pause. "I'm still here."

"Don't tell me she again wishes to run from the vampire... No, I think not. It is you who wishes to run, *mon ami.* Am I right?"

"I don't want to kill her, Drago." It was as close as Dallas could force himself to come to telling Drago the truth.

"And you won't. The answer is an easy one, Allgate. Live as one being, not two. *Bonne chance, mon ami.*"

The line went dead. *Good luck?* Did Drago actually believe in such rubbish? What did luck have to do with anything? Damn Drago and his riddles! He wished Gillie was here. Gillie would understand such nonsense. Dallas looked at the window. The sky was beginning to lighten. It would be dawn soon. It was time.

He descended to the cellar and gazed at Tia. She was still sleeping, the faintest of smiles on her mouth. He stood before *The Seine at Giverny* and stared at the painting. It depicted the river, with the trees on the shore above, and the upside down reflection in the water below. There was no difference in the reality and the reflection. All was a haze of green, blue, and white. He heard her stir behind him.

"Well?" she asked without preamble.

His inability to come up with a solution left him no choice. He answered her still facing the painting. "I'll call Mac. He'll give you a ride. He's a good man. You'll be perfectly safe with him."

Even turned away from her he could feel the hope drop from her features. "I've already voiced every argument I can think of. I said I'd abide by your decision, and I will." Her voice was hushed, almost as though she were being strangled.

He closed his eyes, as if that could help keep the sound of her pain from his ears.

"I would like just one favor from you before I go, which was all I wanted in the first place. To photograph you."

He kept his eyes shut. "I told you. I don't photograph. The camera sees only the reality of what I am, not the image the rest of the world sees. If you're lucky, you'll get a face of shadows. If not, you'll get a mask of death. Is that how you want to remember me, Tia?"

"Well, the first shots I took weren't great, but they weren't that bad, either."

He opened his eyes. "What first shots?"

He heard her slide from the bed and stand behind him. "You know. At the Chapel of Light cemetery when you were fighting St. James. When I tried to distract St. James with the flash."

He turned slowly to face her.

"When I ran away I left my equipment, but I took that film with me. When Juliana went shopping for me yesterday I gave her the film to get it developed at the one-hour photo. The photos are upstairs now in the suitcase of things from the hotel."

He unlocked the door for her. "Get them. Now."

She stared at him, wide-eyed, then fled up the stairs. Two minutes later she was back, breathing heavily, the suitcase in hand.

"Show me," he ordered.

She swung the suitcase onto the bed and unzipped it. She took out the packets of photos and handed them to him. "You'll need a better light. Some of them are pretty dark."

He turned on the table lamp next to the bed and pulled out the photos from their sleeve.

"The first ones are all of St. James, when he was posing for me. They didn't come out. All shadows, like you said. I thought it was my fault at first. My inexperience in shooting outdoors at that time of day. The light was very tricky."

He stared at the photos under the lamplight. He couldn't distinguish St. James' features in a single one, not even in shots that were close-ups. His face was an out-of-focus blur, a collage of shadows. In one shot, Dallas thought he saw lurid eyes and the hint of a leer from behind the shadow. "See? The vampire doesn't photograph."

She handed him another set. "Look at these. The last ones are those I took when St. James had that weapon and was about to kill you. I tried to aim the flash at his eyes to divert his attention, but I caught you in the shots as well."

He took the photos from her and shuffled through them, his fingers feeling clumsy for the first time in his life. He came to the photos she referred to and let the rest slide to the floor.

In the first he saw nothing but the back of his own head and the blur that was St. James. In the next shot, though, Tia had caught his profile. His face showed pain, but it was there. His eyes, closed against the light and the dirt St. James had flung at his face. His nose, flared in anger. His mouth, showing teeth clenched in the life and death struggle. It wasn't a pretty picture, but there he was. He studied the rest of them. They all depicted his features clearly.

He set the photos down on the table carefully and turned to her. "I don't understand."

She reached out to touch his face, and the warmth of her fingers seared him. "I think I do. This is your reality, Dallas. As much as you keep trying to deny it. Accept it. And forgive yourself. That's all." She let her hand drop to her side.

"But the beast…you saw what the beast did last night at the inn. *That's* my reality."

"No, Dallas. Last night wasn't the beast. Last night was the human. You asked for Veilina's forgiveness. Maybe St. James didn't know what you were doing, but I did. Asking forgiveness is a very human thing to do. There isn't only one image and one reality, Dallas. The human and the beast are both your reality. Accept your human side, Dallas. It's your strength, not your weakness. Veilina forgave you. Now forgive yourself."

Live life as one being. Drago had said it was easy. Could it really be as simple as that? Forgiveness? Veilina had forgiven him. Could he forgive himself two centuries of vengeance and horror? And acceptance. Tia accepted him. If he could accept himself as well, was that enough?

Fate. Destiny. Luck. Love. All the things he no longer believed in stared at him in the form of Miss Syntia Marie Martell. Her blue eyes, so reminiscent of the daytime sky, were once painful to gaze upon, but no more. They no longer teased him with what could never again be his, but held the promise of what could be his. If he could only believe.

The last photo still in his hand fluttered to the floor. "No."

Pain welled behind the blue eyes, and this time it was her suffering he felt, not his own. "I mean no more photos. You won't have any need for them. You'll be seeing my face often enough from now on."

Her liquid eyes rounded in surprise. "What?"

"But we won't be able to stay here any longer. How do you feel about California? I have a rather nice estate near San Francisco."

Joy lit her face until worry darkened it once more. "What about the danger you spoke of?"

"There will always be a risk, I can't deny it. But if you're willing..." He held out a hand to her. "Accept, Tia, and be loved." The words were voiced to her, but they cast back to his own mind and heart. *Accept, and be loved.*

She took his hand, and this time, when his mouth met hers, the only image that burned in his mind's eye was the reality of her love for him, and his for her.

Life could indeed be sweet.

EPILOGUE

Bishop's Inn eventually re-opened, with Angie Cole as the new owner. The inn's resident spirit seemed more animated than ever, and a new legend was born. Some claimed that the ghost was still that of Veilina Bishop, but others insisted that it was now that of Jaz, the young waitress who was abducted and never heard from again. The second floor banquet room was permanently closed. The manifestations that were seen and heard in that room were too much even for the most intrepid and undaunted of employees and patrons.

Area residents and caretakers never saw the mysterious Mr. Allgate at Rose Hill again, and neighborhood gossip had it that a young man named MacLaren had moved into the townhouse.

Only a few like John Giltspur knew the truth of the reclusive Dallas Allgate's whereabouts. Those few would tell you that he and a young woman named Syntia Martell traveled the country with the leisurely ease of a couple with nothing but time on their hands, spending part of the year in California and part in Alaska. When eyebrows were raised at the choice of Alaska, John Giltspur would only smile, lift a brow, and reply with three short words.

"It's the nights."

As for *l'enforcier*, he was never successful in recruiting Dallas Allgate into the Brotherhood. Alek Dragovich gave up on Dallas at long last, but the one thing he never gave up on was the belief of his own counsel. The elusive *affaire de coeur.*

After all, it was the one thing that made Eternity bearable.

Don't Miss Jaye Roycraft's

AFTERIMAGE
ISBN 1-893896-74-9

Alek Dragovich, *l'enforcier,* is feeling the weight of his years and has yet to find the elusive *affaire d'amour* that would lighten his burden. Nothing, but nothing, is going well.

His position in the Directorate is in jeopardy, and even his mentor Nikolena is threatening to remove her support if Drago doesn't stop employing his unorthodox methods of resolving his cases. Nikolena gives Drago one last chance to redeem himself when she learns that a high-ranking member of the Brotherhood is using forbidden methods to ascend the hierarchy. Drago's job is to locate and eliminate Nikolena's suspect. Still, Drago has little interest in Nikolena's schemes until this one becomes personal. When someone tries to kill him…that's personal.

That "someone" is raven-haired Gypsy Marya Jaks, daughter of a *dhampir,* offspring of a vampire and his mortal wife. *Dhampirs* are famous among the Roma for their ability to detect vampires, thereby making them perfect vampire killers. When Marya learns that Drago has deemed her a threat to the vampire community and ordered her termination, she strikes back.

Drago, the hunter, has become the hunted, but is it Marya who truly wants him dead or Nikolena's mysterious power-hungry vampire? Drago resolves to keep Marya alive until he can learn the truth, and he must summon the strength of will to elevate himself from pawn to player in the deadliest of games.

As for Marya, the afterimage of Drago's neon blue eyes has haunted her from the first moment she encountered him in her bedroom, but will the image signify her destruction, or a bond so powerful it can overcome a legacy of hatred?

COMING IN FEBRUARY 2002